Someone's Watching

Also by Sharon Potts

In Their Blood

Someone's Watching

A Novel

Sharon Potts

Oceanview Publishing

LONGBOAT KEY, FLORIDA

ISBN: 978-1-60809-013-6

Published in the United States of America by Oceanview Publishing, Longboat Key, Florida
www.oceanviewpub.com

10 9 8 7 6 5 4 3 2 1

PRINTED IN THE UNITED STATES OF AMERICA

This is dedicated to my glorious mom,
for whom life was all about joy, laughter, and learning.

ANNA HECHT, 1916–2010

Acknowledgments

Wow. My second published novel! It seems I was only just writing my acknowledgments for *In Their Blood*, trying to remember the dozens of people who had been involved during the five or so years leading to its publication. And now, a year later, I'm doing it again. Of course, I never would have gotten to "Book Two" without the support of everyone who helped make *In Their Blood* a reality—so my deepest gratitude continues to all of you who gave me flight. Special mention to:

Delia Foley, sister-in-law, critiquer, and friend extraordinaire.

Patricia Gussin, editor-in-chief and flight commander at Oceanview Publishing.

Elizabeth Trupin-Pulli, literary agent and cheering squad.

Maryglenn McCombs, Garcia's mom, and perhaps the greatest publicist in the universe.

There's tremendous pressure to create a second novel that's at least as good as the first in a fraction of the time. Luckily, I had a secret weapon, an amazing critique group, who redirected me when I was going off track and saved me from rewriting hundreds of pages. Thank you Christine Kling, Neil Plakcy, Mike Jastrzebski, Miriam Auerbach, and Victoria Landis.

Then there are the folks who helped me get the details right.

Nathaniel Sandler, Miami Beach enthusiast and lover of the written word, Lieutenant Felix Ortega of the Miami Beach Police

Criminal Investigations/Homicide Unit, and Jack Turken, M.D., friend and medical consultant. Please excuse any liberties I've taken with your favorite city, Nate, and in my fictional investigation, Lieutenant. And Jack—if I didn't get the dosages right, that's entirely my fault, not yours.

Someone's Watching never would have been written if I hadn't had the opportunity to peer into the world of twenty-somethings through the eyes of my amazing kids—Ben and Sarah. I'll tell you again, kids, even if I've already said it a million times, I marvel at the adults you've become. You two, more than anything in my life, are my most satisfying reward, my greatest joy.

And finally, my gratitude to my best friend, personal support system, first and most important editor. I started writing ten years ago and probably would have given up in frustration many times if not for the faith and encouragement of my husband, Joe. Thank you, Darling.

Someone's Watching

Chapter 1

He was staring at her cleavage and she tried to be cool, like she did this kind of thing all the time. The spaghetti strap on her white sundress slipped off. Kate adjusted it back over her sunburned shoulder, then sipped the pink fruity drink he had bought her. The steel band in a tiki hut was playing reggae, and the night air smelled like fish and brine.

"So," he said, "you girls down on spring break?" His tongue darted over the thin white line that split his upper lip into two uneven halves. His name was Carl and the other guy was Luis. They were med students—at least that's what Carl said when they sat down at the outdoor bar next to Kate and Joanne.

"Yeah," Kate said. "We're staying in South Beach with some friends, but we decided to check out the Keys."

Kate gave Joanne a warning look. Her best friend was clutching an oversized handbag against her chest, ignoring the drink in front of her. The last thing Kate wanted was for the two guys to know they were still in high school.

"That's cool," Carl said. He had dark hair and thick eyebrows and the scarred upper lip made him look a little like Elvis. But his friend Luis was the really sexy one with his shaved head and tattoos all over his muscled arms. Kate didn't think they looked like med students, but hey, what would she know, having been holed up in Small-Town-Nowhere her whole life?

"The club scene can get old real quick," Carl said. "It's much more laid back here. We're at a house on the bay. Pretty nice place. It even has an indoor pool."

Luis seemed less than impressed with Kate and Joanne and was checking out the other girls as they came into the bar area from the parking lot or the beach. He wore a tank top, and every time he moved, his biceps rippled through his tattoos.

Kate sucked on the straw in her drink and caught Luis's eye. She knew she was cute with her blue eyes, dimples, and long, black hair. And even though she had a few extra pounds on her, the boys back home in Deland didn't seem to mind her in jeans.

Luis smiled at her with even white teeth against his tanned face. God, he was hot. If she was going to lose it, he was definitely the one. Maybe they'd invite the girls back to their house with its indoor pool.

She held her shoulders back and tossed her hair. She couldn't believe she was doing this—her dad would kill her if he knew—but for the first time in her life she felt special. Let her dad find out. She really didn't care. He might actually notice she existed.

The music was getting louder, the beat throbbing against the swish of metal. She crossed her legs, swinging her foot back and forth. She was wearing new white sandals with these cool clear plastic heels.

"Wanna dance?" Luis asked. His voice was low and rough, like sandpaper.

"Sure." Kate slid off the bar stool. She was a little wobbly, not used to drinking. "Come dance with us," she said to Joanne, feeling badly about leaving her friend alone with Carl.

Joanne shook her head. She was small and blonde and looked about twelve, even under all the makeup Kate had put on for her. Joanne hadn't wanted to drive down to Key Largo, but Kate had begged her. Promised that the rest of the week they'd hang out by their hotel on South Beach if Kate could just have this one night.

One night out of her father's radar, so she could lose her virginity and not have to show up for her freshman year in college like some over-protected weirdo.

Luis tugged on Kate's hand and glanced back at Carl. "Why don't you get the girls a couple of fresh drinks?"

The dance floor was wooden planks set in the sand. Kate rolled her head back as she got into the beat. Palm trees shifted in the warm breeze and stars glittered against the dark sky. Bodies spun around her. The light from hanging lanterns bounced off Luis's bald, sweaty head. He slipped his tattooed arm around her waist and pulled her closer. Her sunburn made her hot all over. Luis brushed her lips with his. Her heart was beating like a maraca. What was she doing? Was she crazy?

"I, I have to sit down." She was trembling. What she really needed was to get the hell out of here before she did something insane. What had she been thinking?

She returned to her stool at the bar. Two fresh pink drinks were in front of her and Joanne. "We need to be getting back to Miami," Kate said.

"Right." Carl said. "You high school kids probably have a curfew."

Kate's cheeks heated up.

"Hey man," Luis said to Carl, "no reason to be a dick. If the girls gotta go, they gotta go." He rested his hand on Kate's shoulder. "No sweat, baby. But the least you can do is finish your drinks. My friend was nice enough to buy them for you."

Joanne reached into her bag and pulled a twenty out of her wallet. "Here," she said, waving the bill at Carl. "This is for our drinks. We're leaving."

"And now you insult me?" Carl said.

Luis's breath was in Kate's ear. It gave her goose bumps. "Please don't go."

"Let's just stay a little longer, Joanne," Kate said. "We don't want to hurt anyone's feelings. Okay?"

Mascara was smeared under Joanne's eyes, and her nose, too big for her narrow face, was red-tipped like she was about to cry. "If that's what you want." Joanne gulped down the pink liquid.

Luis was so close, Kate could smell his sweat mingling with his cologne. The muscles beneath the tattoos were smooth as boulders. "Damn, you're sexy," he whispered.

Kate sipped her drink, afraid to leave, afraid to stay. The music got louder, softer. The breeze off the ocean warmed her, chilled her. The stars got larger, larger, like giant asteroids ready to explode.

Luis's arm was around her. She could feel the heat off his body. They were walking, but she could hardly stand. He held her up. Her words came out like someone else's voice. "Where are we going?"

"It's okay, baby," he said. "Everything's all right."

She was tired, so tired. Her eyes kept closing. Smell of leather, gasoline. Engine noise. Cool air. Warm breath against her cheek. The car stopped.

Kate opened her eyes. Trees all around. A jumping red dragon. Big white house, like a giant box on legs.

She was flying, or being carried. Her sandals scraped against something smooth and bumpy. Pebbles. Millions, billions, trillions of pebbles. A sandal fell off. She tried to say something, but it felt like there was glue in her mouth.

A baby was crying. "Let me go," the baby sobbed. "Please let me go."

Someone was holding Joanne. The one called Carl. He carried her like a baby. "Please let me go," Joanne cried.

Kate got scared. "Joanne," she tried to say, but nothing came out.

"Here you go," someone said, and put something in Kate's mouth.

Kate was dreaming. Such a lovely dream. Talcum powder and rainbows. Splashing water. Something silky beneath her. Silky, dark, blurry. A tongue in her mouth. Butterfly kisses up and down her skin. Everything nice. So nice.

A stab of pain.

Wet, falling. Help, I'm falling.

Help.

Squeezing, squeezing. Tighter, tighter. Stop.

Stop.

Breathe. Can't breathe.

Drowning. I'm drowning.

Stop. Stop.

STOP.

Time went in and out. Black all around.

She got up and walked toward lightness. White walls covered with dragons. Red, blue, green. Rooms with no people. Windows like mirrors everywhere. She saw herself. Hair wild, long legs, full breasts. No clothes. Where were her clothes? Where was Joanne?

In front of her was a big, glowing blue square. A pool. A swimming pool. Lights from beneath. Someone floating. Long blonde hair spreading like a halo. Joanne swimming. Naked. Not swimming. Floating. Joanne naked? Not possible.

"Joanne," Kate called. "Joanne, come out."

Joanne floating. Face down. Face down in the water.

"Joanne?" she whispered.

Heat behind her, touching her shoulder. Sweat and cologne.

Joanne floating.

"Fuck," a rough, sandpapery voice said. "Look what you've done."

Chapter 2

The plastic grocery bags swung from the handlebars as Robbie Ivy walked her bicycle onto the wrought iron stand in front of her apartment complex. The Sunday afternoon sun was strong, despite the shade of the palm trees, and she was perspiring in her T-shirt and worn jeans.

Robbie pushed a bar lock through her second-hand bicycle's frame and front wheel and locked it in place on the rack. Then she wove the extra-thick metal chain around the wheels, frame, and rack, clicked the lock closed, and pocketed the keys. With all the hardware, she felt a bit like a warden in a penitentiary. But this was the third bicycle she'd bought in the three months since she'd moved here after she and Jeremy had decided to take a break from each other. She was determined not to lose this one, even as she noted the bare, bent frame of what was once a bicycle attached to the stand. The vultures had stripped down the bike taking both wheels, the seat, handlebars, and the wire basket.

Remind me again why I decided to live on South Beach?

Robbie ran her fingers through her sweaty chin-length black hair, then slipped her arms through her canvas satchel and grocery bags. Truth was, she liked it here. Liked the vividness of the colors, the crumbling old buildings, the salty smell of the ocean. But mostly she was here because of the warmth. After Boston, she'd decided she had no use for cold or the changing seasons. Year-round summer worked just fine for her.

She carried her bundles past hibiscus bushes and flowering bougainvillea. The neighborhood still had the feel of old Miami Beach. The two-story U-shaped apartment complex had been built in the 1930's Art Deco style with rounded corners and glass block walls. Rusty air-conditioning units sprouted from the faded seafoam green concrete block walls that surrounded a small swimming pool and cracked, pebbled Chattahoochee deck.

Robbie ran up the outside stairs to her second floor corner apartment. Just down the catwalk, her neighbor Gabriele was fumbling with his house keys, still in his evening clothes. His Dutch-boy platinum blonde wig and white lacy dress made a striking contrast with his long, black, muscular arms. A bit different from the jeans and button-downs he wore when he headed off to teach English at the local college.

"Need some help?" she called to him.

"Robbie. Thank God. Yes, please. Come save my life again. I must have the wrong key."

Robbie left her groceries in front of her apartment and went to join Gabriele. She examined the keys on his key ring, matching up the brand names with the locks on his door. The top bolt clicked open.

"You're a miracle worker," Gabriele said, leaning over to touch one of her beaded, feather earrings. "Are these new? They're exquisite, just like you."

"Thank you. I'll make you a pair."

"You're too good to me." He fluttered his tapered, black fingers in front of his lacy bodice. "First you do my taxes, which, by the way, I promise I'll keep my records better organized in the future."

She unlocked the bottom and pushed the door open. "Sure you will."

He tossed his head, the straight edge of the platinum wig swinging over his shoulder. "You know me too well, girlfriend." He blew her a kiss. "But if there's anything you need, just ask. I'm your Galatea—putty in your hands."

"I thought Pygmalion carved his beloved Galatea out of ivory."

He grinned. "Someone's been reading her Ovid."

"Have a nice beauty sleep, professor."

Robbie returned to her own door, unbolted the two locks, and went inside with her groceries. It was a great little apartment. Cozy. And cheap. One side overlooked the pool, the other a wide street with a view of other low-rise pastel buildings. Palm trees were everywhere. Very different from the brick high-rise in Boston where Robbie had grown up, a place she could only remember as chilly, dark, and sad.

Matilda purred and rubbed against her ankles.

"Just a sec, kitten." Robbie put the bundles on the small kitchen table, then scooped up the cat. She buried her face in Matilda's soft white fur to take in her sunshine smell. "Any calls or visitors?"

Matilda meowed.

She let the cat spring from her arms onto the hardwood floor. Against the living room walls, mismatched bookcases that Robbie had picked up at estate sales overflowed with books, and her white sofa was covered with a thin layer of cat hair. In the center of the room were tables with half-finished necklaces and earrings, trays of colored beads, spools of wires, and plastic bags of feathers.

Jewelry making was the latest in a series of projects Robbie had taken up since she and Jeremy had separated. She was just trying to keep it simple for now—no car, no mortgage, no real job. And definitely no relationships that smelled of a future. Robbie was a little worn out from throwing her heart into something, then having it stabbed and gutted. Some people looked at her funny on hearing she'd once been a CPA on a fast track to corporate success. "And now you're a bartender?" they'd say, like she was serving vomit, not alcohol.

But they didn't understand that the tragic death of Robbie's mentor had been another deposit of scar tissue on top of old layers that had never healed. And even though Robbie and Jeremy had taken some time to get away from everything, Robbie still occasionally felt a cumulative ache. So for now, jewelry making and bartending were fine. Well, at least they didn't make her hurt.

Robbie went back into the kitchen alcove and unpacked her groceries—a bag of salad, two boxes of pasta, a jar of spaghetti sauce, coffee, and bananas.

For dinner tonight, she'd have pasta. Just like last night. Maybe Gabriele would want to come over. No. He'd probably be sleeping.

Robbie sat down at the small oak table and picked up the painted ceramic salt and pepper shakers. They were in the shape of a mother and daughter wearing bonnets and dresses with aprons. Robbie used to play with them for hours when she was a child while she waited for her mom to come home from work.

She considered making dinner for Brett. But did she even want to see him tonight? They'd been dating for about a month, and while Brett was a lot of fun, she had to be in the right mood for his frenetic energy.

Should she call Jeremy? They'd told each other they would still be friends, but neither one had gotten in touch with the other in the months they'd been apart. She took out her cell phone and opened it. Just for dinner.

But what if Jeremy misconstrued the call, thinking she wanted to get back together?

She closed the phone. The mother and daughter shakers looked up at her stoically, as they had when she was a child.

A knock on the door startled her. She sat up, alert.

Through the sheer curtains in front of the kitchen window, she could see a hunched, gray-haired man. No one she knew. He wore a well-cut navy blazer, but hadn't shaved in a day or so.

She went to the front door. "Can I help you?" she asked through the door.

"Roberta Brooks?" the man asked.

Something crashed inside her. *Roberta Brooks*, a child's voice in her head repeated. *My name is Roberta Brooks and I live at—*

The walls shifted. Robbie leaned against the door, trying to catch her breath.

"Are you there?" the man asked. "Roberta?"

She knew the voice. She hadn't heard it in eighteen years. Not since she was seven and he had kissed her goodbye.

"Please let me in. I need to speak with you, Roberta."

"That's not my name."

There was silence for almost a minute. An eternity as she remembered her tears and how she had clung to him.

"I keep forgetting," he said. "You're Robbie now. Robbie Ivy. Please let me talk to you, just for a minute."

Why had he come here? Why after all these years?

She took a deep breath, trying to compose herself, then opened the door.

Blue eyes—so much like her own. They watered at the sight of her.

He's nothing to you, she told herself.

The black hair had gone gray, and he was shorter than she remembered, only five eight or nine. How he used to tower over her and lift her high into the air. But this man seemed too unsteady to carry much of anything. And his face was wrong—deep wrinkles around his eyes and in his forehead, sagging cheeks that blurred his once-square jaw. A few wild white hairs protruded from his black eyebrows.

"Roberta," he said, "you're all grown up."

Daddy, she wanted to say. Instead, she held herself straight. "What do you want?"

"May I come in?" He seemed to be trying to peer around her. "Just for a minute?"

She glanced behind her at her home, her sanctuary. "I'd rather we talk by the pool."

"I understand."

His voice touched a place deep inside her, but she wasn't going to be taken in by him. Not after how he had treated her and her mother.

They went down to the courtyard and sat on stone benches on opposite sides of a table with an umbrella sticking up through its center. He turned his wedding ring around and around on his finger. His fingers were long and slender and the nails covered the nail bed with almost no white. Just like Robbie's.

"You have your mother's voice," he said, "and the same Boston accent, but you look just like—"

"Would you please tell me why you're here?"

"It's just . . . You're right." He ran his fingers through his hair. The gesture so familiar. "I'm here because I need your help."

"My help? How dare you—"

"Please. Let me finish. It's about your sister."

"Sister? What are you talking about?"

"Damn." He looked down at the mildewed mosaic tabletop. "I guess your mother didn't tell you."

Robbie's heart hiccupped. "Tell me what? What are you talking about? I don't have a sister."

"But you do. A half sister."

Not possible. Robbie was an only child. An only child with no mother, an absent father. No family at all.

"Her name is Kaitlin. She just turned eighteen."

Half sister. Eighteen. Her father had left them eighteen years ago.

Robbie got up and went to the edge of the pool. A palm frond had fallen into the deep end and shifted ever so slightly as the water burbled.

He came over and stood beside her. "I thought you knew."

The sting of his words reminded her of when her mom put antiseptic on a cut. Just as then, she forced herself to hold back tears until the pain subsided. All these years she'd had a sister. A little sister named Kaitlin. And no one had told her.

"Kaitlin's a senior in high school. She came to Miami Beach with some friends a few days ago on her spring break."

Her sister was here? In Miami?

"But she's disappeared," he said.

"Disappeared? What are you talking about?"

"She wasn't answering her cell phone. Neither was her best friend, Joanne, so I drove here from home this morning. I spoke with the other girls they'd come down with. None of them have seen Kaitlin or Joanne since early Friday."

A bright green iguana emerged cautiously into the sunlight, then darted back into the bushes.

"I'm sorry to lay this on you," he said, "but I'm desperate. Kaitlin and her friend are good girls. They're both going off to college in the fall. Maybe they got in with a bad crowd. I was hoping you'd know where I might begin to look for her."

"Me?" She turned to him suddenly. "How did you even know where I live?"

He cocked his head, as though surprised by her question. "I've always kept an eye on you. I watched you going off to college, then when you took a job down here. I know about what you've been through."

"You know? You know all about me? How can you say you've

been watching me my entire life and never tried to contact me?"

"I never wanted to lose you. It wasn't my choice."

"No. Stop it. It was your choice. And you can't come here and act like the last eighteen years didn't happen. You're not my father anymore. You lost that right."

"Dear God, Roberta. I never meant to hurt you."

"Please, go away. I'm sorry your daughter's missing, but I can't help you. Go to the police if you're worried about her."

He looked down at the cracked pebbled deck beneath his feet. "I've been to the police. They were not encouraging."

This was not her problem. He was a stranger to her. Both he and his daughter.

"I'm going inside now," she said. "I hope you find her, but please don't come to see me again." She started walking through the hibiscus bushes and palm trees toward the stairs.

"Roberta." He took a few steps after her. "Please, take this." He reached into his jacket pocket and held out a small manila envelope.

She grabbed the envelope, then ran up the stairs to her apartment slamming the door behind her. She sank to the floor and began to cry. She cried and cried into Matilda's soft warm fur until she was spent.

The manila envelope lay beside her. Robbie picked it up. Inside was a piece of paper with typed information—names, addresses, date of birth, height, weight—but it was the picture that caused the breath to snag in her chest.

It was a yearbook photo of a smiling girl with a heart-shaped face, long black hair, prominent dimples, and vivid blue eyes. Kaitlin Brooks, it said on the back.

But Robbie could just as well have been staring at her own high school photo.

Chapter 3

This time she didn't think twice as she punched Jeremy's number into her cell phone.

He answered on the first ring. "Robbie."

"I need to talk to you," she said.

"Where are you?"

"Can you meet me by the old fishing pier?"

"I'm leaving now."

"Thank you," Robbie said.

She ran down the stairs and unlocked her bicycle from the stand, afraid to look around. Afraid he may have lingered. That he'd try to talk to her again. But there was no sign of anyone.

She biked through side streets of sun-bleached buildings, then around a crowd of teens in cutoffs and bikini tops crossing Ocean Drive, until she reached the very end of South Beach. It was late afternoon and the sun cast shadows from the low deco hotels over hot pavement the color of dirty bubblegum. People carrying beach chairs and towels were heading back toward their cars. A breeze came off the surf. Robbie stood next to her bike, momentarily disoriented. The smell of coconut oil and ocean air settled her. Jeremy would help her make sense of her feelings. Just like he used to. She locked her bike to a post and went down to South Pointe Park.

This had been Jeremy's and her favorite place when they'd first returned to Miami after spending last summer traveling cross-country. For the months they'd been away, it had just been the two of them and they hadn't needed anyone else. But when they got back to reality in September, Jeremy was restless for a life of people and friends and having fun. It was as though he was trying to cram his entire youth into each day. And she'd remembered what her mother had always told her. *There's no such thing as forever.* So Robbie had suggested they take a break. Jeremy had protested, but she knew deep inside it was what he needed, maybe even what he wanted. And perhaps on some level, it was what she wanted, too.

Robbie walked down the narrow strip of riprap that jutted into the ocean like a road to nowhere. The packed-sand path ended and she balanced herself as she stepped from boulder to boulder. Several people were fishing from the rocks closest to the water. A short distance away, waves lapped at the barnacle-covered pilings of the old fishing pier, which was no longer accessible. It had been blocked off and looked like a strong wind could take it down.

Robbie reached the end of the boulders. A gigantic cruise ship was gliding out through the blue-green waters of Government Cut. Passengers stood at the ship's railings, waving.

Waving goodbye.

Her father was back. Why couldn't he have just left things the way they'd been?

She turned carefully, watching the shoreline until she spotted him. Jeremy, tall and lean, was running down the beach and onto the ledge of boulders. He was wearing gym shorts and a T-shirt that said Personal Trainer, so he must have come straight from a session with a client. He reached the end of the path and sprang from rock to rock with the grace of a deer.

His brown hair was long again, like when she'd first seen him at his parents' funeral, and a short beard covered his prominent cleft chin and hollow cheeks. He slowed when he saw her. He was breathing hard and sweat glistened on his arms and forehead.

Jeremy Stroeb. Why couldn't it have been forever?

"Hey." He stepped onto a boulder next to hers and leaned toward her as though uncertain what to do.

She stood on her toes and kissed him on the cheek, wanting more. Knowing it wasn't possible.

Sweat was dripping down his broad forehead into his dark brown eyes. He wiped it off. His nose was flat and slightly off center. He'd once joked about using it to catch a hardball when he was a kid.

"You okay?" he asked.

"I guess." She sat down on the flat rock surface and folded her arms around her knees, ignoring the spray from the crashing waves. Jeremy sank down beside her and stretched out his legs. They were tan and muscular and covered with golden hair.

"So what happened?" he asked.

The cruise ship was now on the horizon. In the distance, it looked like a toy boat.

"My father came to see me."

"Your father? I thought he was out of your life."

"So did I."

"What did he want?" Jeremy asked.

"To ask me to help him find my sister."

"Shit! You have a sister?"

She nodded.

Jeremy reached out—she thought to touch her—but he took something out of her hair. A turquoise feather had come loose from one of her earrings. He twirled it between his fingers.

"Maybe you'd better start at the beginning," he said.

"Which beginning? When he left or when he came back?"

"I remember you told me he divorced your mom to marry someone else when you were a kid. That's when you moved to Boston."

"That's right."

"I thought you never saw him or heard from him again."

"I didn't."

"How did he know where you were?"

"He said he's been following my life."

"Following your life? You mean stalking you?"

"No. I don't think it was like that."

An old man with weathered brown skin and a ratty straw hat wedged a bucket of flopping fish into the nearby rocks.

"So why didn't he ever try to talk to you before today?"

"He didn't say. He just acted like the last eighteen years never happened."

"That's screwed up."

"Tell me about it." Robbie turned her emerald ring around her finger, then stopped. It was the same nervous mannerism her father had.

"Do you know where he's been all these years?"

"I guess he stayed in central Florida—in Deland. That's the address on the contact info he gave me. It looks like he still has his medical practice."

"He's a doctor?"

"That's right."

"Don't tell me—the woman he married when he left your mom was his nurse?"

"You know the funny thing about stereotypes is they don't feel like stereotypes when they're happening to you."

"Sorry."

The old man baited his fishing hook and cast into the churning waves.

"He left me some information about my sister," Robbie said. "From her date of birth, he would have known that he had another kid on the way when he ditched my mother."

"Ouch."

"Yeah. My poor mom. I guess I sensed how hurt she was because I never asked about my dad, about what happened. And it was probably better that way. If I'd known he'd chosen his new kid over me, it would have been even tougher."

The old man hooked something. Several people gathered on the nearby rocks to watch him pull the gyrating fish out of the water, remove the hook, then drop the fish in his bucket.

"I haven't thought about my dad in years," Robbie said. "At the beginning, I cried myself to sleep every night. But eventually, he started fading away and I could hardly remember what he looked like. Then, when I was older and thought about how he treated my mom, I told myself I'd spit in his face if he ever came back."

"And did you?"

Robbie looked at the water creeping in between the rocks and shook her head.

"Come here." Jeremy slipped his arm around her and pulled her close. She buried her face in the familiar scent of his sweat.

A seagull perched on the railing of the abandoned fishing pier. It was just like it used to be—the two of them, no words necessary. She wanted to ask how he was doing, to make sure he was okay without her.

"Tell me about your sister," he said.

"Her name's Kaitlin. She's eighteen and she's a senior in high school."

"Just like Elise."

"That's right. It seems we both have kid sisters. Anyway, my father said she came to South Beach with some friends, but Kaitlin and another girl have been missing since Friday."

"Two days. Not so long." Jeremy ran his finger across the smooth surface of the rock he was sitting on. "Maybe they wanted to disappear."

"Maybe. I told my father I couldn't help him and to go to the police. And I really didn't want to help him. I was so mad at him. And also at this daughter of his who took him from me. Who had him her whole life. And I'm thinking, this girl's nothing to me. I feel no connection or responsibility for her."

Jeremy frowned.

"Then, I looked at her photo. And Jeremy, it was so strange. Instead of her being some random person, it was like looking at myself at her age. And I thought, dear God, I have a sister that I don't even know. I have to find her."

"Then you should."

She watched the waves break against the pier pilings. "I know this sounds stupid, but I'm afraid."

"Of?"

"What if she doesn't want to know me? She's eighteen. She's grown up without me. She's had a father and a mother and her own life. Maybe she's not interested in complicating it with a half sister."

He touched her chin with the tip of his finger and turned her face toward his. "You know, Robbie, you can't keep avoiding relationships because you're afraid the people you care about will push you away."

There was something in his eyes that made her wonder who he was talking about.

He shifted toward her, so close she could see the short brown and gold hairs of his moustache touching the edge of his lips.

So close. So close. The sound of crashing waves and screeching seagulls surrounded them. At first, she didn't realize her phone was ringing inside her satchel.

Jeremy pulled away. "Answer it."

"No, that's okay."

"Go ahead."

The moment was lost. She reached inside her bag and pulled out the cell. Brett's name flashed on the screen.

"Take your call," Jeremy said.

Before she could object, Jeremy strode across the boulders and stood a few feet away. Robbie flipped open her phone. "Hi."

"Hey baby. It's been a bitch of a day." Brett sounded cheerful. "Can't believe I had to work on a Sunday, but in the PR world, there's no rest for the weary."

She studied Jeremy in profile against the backdrop of waves spilling against the coastline, towering condos and hotels fading into purple.

"Robbie?" Brett was saying. "Are you there?"

"Yeah. Sorry."

"How about meeting me at Segafredo? We can get a drink. Maybe have some dinner."

"Dinner?" Hadn't she been thinking about calling him for dinner?

"Sure. I've got all night."

"Actually, something's come up," she said, watching Jeremy massage his hand.

"And maybe we can see a movie later."

It was as though Brett hadn't heard her. "I'm sorry," she said, "But—"

"Hang on a sec, would you?"

She could hear someone talking to Brett in the background.

"Shit, Robbie. Mike needs me. Turns out tonight's not going to work after all. Maybe tomorrow?"

"Sure," Robbie said.

"Later," he said.

She turned her phone to vibrate, put it back in her satchel, then stood up on the rocks and crossed over to Jeremy.

He was balanced on a boulder, the wind whipping his hair around his face, arms crossed in front of him. The scar on the back of his hand was a year old, but still looked raw. Fortunately, the bullet hadn't caused any permanent damage. "Brett Chandler?" he said.

"Yeah."

"I'd heard you were dating him."

"He's a nice guy," Robbie said, feeling the schism widening.

A couple of large-breasted teenage girls in bikinis were hopping from rock to rock, giggling. "Hey, Jeremy," one of them called out. "What's good tonight?"

"Townhouse."

"Cool," she said. "See you there."

"Still partying?" Robbie said.

"Sure. Why not?" Jeremy glanced at his watch. "Sorry to cut out on you, but I've got a client in twenty minutes."

"Oh. No problem. You should go."

He rubbed the back of his neck. "You could talk to Judy Lieber, you know. Maybe she can find out something about your sister."

"Right," Robbie said. "That's a good idea."

He started across the rocks back toward the beach. When he got to the path, his pace quickened to a jog, to a run. She watched him. Watched as he crossed onto the sand and raced along the surf, getting smaller and smaller and smaller.

Chapter 4

It was back. That feeling in the pit of her stomach like a clump of dried mud. When she was a kid, Robbie sometimes imagined it would sprout weeds that would grow out of her mouth and ears. Then everyone would know her secret. About how lonely and empty she was—with nothing inside her but hardened sludge. She remembered once standing alone in the brick courtyard in front of her apartment building throwing a rubber ball against the wall—ninety-seven, ninety-eight, ninety-nine.

Robbie left the pier and returned to her apartment feeling sorry for herself. Matilda was lying across Robbie's laptop computer on the kitchen table, the photo of Kaitlin beneath her soft white fur. Robbie eased the picture out.

Yes—Kaitlin looked a lot like Robbie had, but there were also differences in Kaitlin—a wider nose, longer chin. There was an openness in the blue eyes, a playfulness. One side of Kaitlin's mouth was turned down ever so slightly and she looked like she was getting ready to wink at the photographer. Had she been flirting with him?

The malaise evaporated. What the heck was Robbie doing? She wasn't the needy type. She'd always taken care of herself, just like her mother had taught her to do. So why was she acting like a drama queen?

This girl was her sister. Robbie needed to try to find her and make sure she was okay. It no longer matter what her father had and had not done, or whether Jeremy, or Brett, or anyone was going to help her.

She lifted Matilda off the table. "Down you go, little girl."

The cat meowed as she landed on the floor.

Robbie blew off the cat hair from her laptop, opened it, then logged onto Facebook. She searched for Kaitlin Brooks, but found no one who matched a high school senior living in Deland, Florida. The closest she came was a girl named Kate Brooks. Unfortunately, Kate didn't allow people who weren't her friends to view her profile and in lieu of a photo of herself had posted what looked like a tattoo of an arrowhead. Maybe it was Kaitlin, maybe not. Robbie thought about what message she should send her that wouldn't be too alarming, but might still get a response.

Are you Kaitlin Brooks from Deland? I think we have some friends in common. Please get back to me.

Then she looked again at the photo of the smiling girl. "I'm going to find you, little sister. And when I do, I'm not letting you go."

When Robbie woke up the next morning, the first thing she did was check for a reply from Kate Brooks. Nothing. She got dressed, skipped coffee, and biked over to the police station on Washington Avenue. It was a modern, white building with a wide plaza out front, just down the street from the old City Hall. Robbie locked her bike to the stand, using just the bar, figuring with all the cops walking around, it wasn't likely that someone would steal her bike.

The morning light poured into the open lobby area of the station through large windows. Two teenage girls in very short dresses appeared to be sleeping, one sprawled out on a concrete bench, the other on the floor, her head resting on a backpack, bare feet black-soled. Platform heels lay in a pile beside her. Robbie doubled back. The girl on the bench had long black hair.

Robbie got closer, examining the sleeping girl's features for something familiar. How young she looked, even under smudged makeup. The girl's eyes opened—brown and red-rimmed. She sat up and gave Robbie a tentative smile.

"I'm sorry," Robbie said. "I thought you were someone else."

The girl put her head back down on the bench and closed her eyes.

Robbie went to the check-in window, glancing back at the two girls, wondering what kind of mess they'd gotten themselves into. Thinking about Kaitlin.

"Can I help you?" asked a heavyset police officer. He looked down at Robbie over a counter covered with paperwork.

"I'd like to see Detective Judy Lieber. My name's Robbie Ivy."

"Is she expecting you?"

"No, but she knows me." Robbie wondered what the detective would make of her reappearance. It had been a year since they'd seen each other. A year since the double murder of a couple of ordinary people on a quiet residential island in Miami Beach. One of the victims had been Robbie's mentor. The mentor who had been Jeremy's mother. But Jeremy had also lost his father that night.

Robbie often wondered, would the killer have been caught as quickly if Jeremy hadn't pursued his parents' murderer? She didn't think so. And much like Jeremy, it wasn't in Robbie's nature to leave things to other people.

The officer was talking to someone on the phone. It occurred to Robbie that Lieber might not be in. But no matter. If she wasn't, Robbie would speak to someone else. She had made up her mind. She wasn't leaving here until she was sure something was being done to find her sister.

A balding uniformed cop carrying a clipboard crossed the lobby to the two sleeping girls. The girls sat up and stretched. Robbie heard the cop say something about safe space and calling their parents.

The door to the elevator opened and Detective Lieber emerged. Robbie felt a mixture of pleasure and sadness as she took in the slim middle-aged woman with graying shoulder-length brown hair, deep-set brown eyes, and a furrow in her brow. Lieber wore a poorly fitting pantsuit and black sneaker-like shoes, not very different from how she dressed a year ago.

"Robbie," Lieber said, clasping Robbie's hand in her own. "It's so good to see you. I've often thought about you and Jeremy. How are you? How's Jeremy doing?"

"Everything's good," Robbie said, hearing a quiver in her voice. She hadn't considered that the detective was bound up with memories Robbie would have preferred keeping buried. "Mostly good."

"I don't think I would have recognized you on the street." Lieber took a step back. "You've let your hair grow. It suits you, but you look younger—especially with the feathered earrings and jeans. Quite a change from the serious businesswoman."

"I've changed on the inside, too."

"I imagine you have." Lieber's own face and demeanor were much the same as Robbie remembered—light wrinkles around her eyes, sun-spotted skin, a tautness in her movements that suggested she could spring into action at the least provocation.

"Are you in a hurry?" Lieber asked. "Or do you have time for breakfast?"

"Actually, I wanted to talk to you about something."

"Sure, but I'm starving. Let's run across the street to the diner. I want to hear what you've been up to."

As they waited for the light at the corner of heavily trafficked Washington Avenue, Robbie told Lieber about her job as a bartender at The Garage and her jewelry-making hobby. They crossed the street and detoured around construction, passing a tattoo parlor, a tanning salon, a souvenir store selling T-shirts. The air smelled like decaying garbage. A large crowd of tourists pushed past them, separating

Robbie from Lieber. And for an instant, Robbie was back in Boston's Faneuil Hall, her mother's hand slipping out of hers, the crowd swallowing her up.

"Mommy," Robbie almost called out, but the moment passed and Lieber was again beside her.

"So," Lieber said, "the last I heard, you and Jeremy drove off to see America. Took his dad's old red Corvair. I kept worrying about the car breaking down and you two being stranded."

"It broke down once or twice. Jeremy fixed it."

"Did he now?" Lieber grinned. Robbie always sensed Lieber had a soft spot for Jeremy.

They climbed the four steps up to the entrance of the 11th Street Diner, a railroad car converted into a restaurant. Lieber held open the door and they stepped inside. With its red leatherette booths, counter service, and covered platters of cakes and pies, it reminded Robbie of a diner not far from the building where Robbie and her mom had lived. Sometimes when her mom was too tired from the chemo treatments to cook, they'd go there for dinner. Her mom would order soup, but hardly touch it.

"There's a booth." Lieber waved to a waitress and grabbed a couple of menus.

The table was near a window. Outside, a homeless woman with a shopping cart was going through last night's trash. Someone with long dark hair walked by. Robbie strained to see her.

"Three egg whites scrambled with Swiss cheese," Lieber said to the waitress. "Wheat toast and coffee. What are you having, Robbie?"

The dark-haired person stopped to give the homeless woman something. Robbie could see her face—a grown woman. Not Kaitlin. Was Robbie going to imagine her sister everywhere?

"Robbie?" Lieber said.

"I'm sorry." Robbie relaxed against the benchseat. "I'll have coffee and a toasted multigrain bagel, please."

The waitress left with the menus.

"So bartending for now," Lieber said. "Quite a change from being a CPA."

"I don't miss it."

"I had the impression you were very good at it."

"Oh, I liked the numbers and puzzles, but I'm glad to be away from the obsession with power and money."

The waitress put two mugs of coffee and a small pitcher of cream on the table.

"Tell me about Jeremy," Lieber said, bringing the mug to her lips and blowing on the black coffee. "What's he up to?"

"He's doing fine. He has an apartment at the SOBE Grande."

"Nice place."

Robbie added cream and sugar to her coffee. "Well, his parents left him and his sister a little money."

"That's right."

"Not that he's goofing off or anything like that," Robbie said, wondering why she felt the need to justify. "Jeremy works hard. He's a personal trainer at a couple of gyms."

"No corporate world for him, either."

"Anything but. He's enjoying South Beach."

"Well, that's good. He had to grow up too quickly when his parents died. I'm glad he's taking some time for himself."

The waitress put their orders down on paper placemats, covering the map of Florida and picture of an alligator.

"Thanks so much." Lieber tasted her eggs, then reached for the salt and pepper and sprinkled them freely.

"May I ask you something on a professional level?" Robbie asked.

Lieber looked up from her food.

"Do you handle the missing person cases?"

"Some of them."

"I wanted to ask you about one in particular."

Lieber's brown eyes were alert.

"My father came to see me yesterday." Robbie glanced away from Lieber's gaze. She didn't like withholding things from the detective, but now wasn't the time to get into the family history. "He told me my younger sister and her friend were in Miami Beach on spring break. They're missing."

"I know," Lieber said.

"You know?"

"I happened to be on duty yesterday morning and I spoke with your father. He told me about Kaitlin and her friend, Joanne. He also said he had an older daughter here in town who went by the name Robbie Ivy. I figured that's why you came to see me."

Why had Lieber waited until now to mention this? "So you told him you knew me?"

"I didn't feel that would be appropriate, not knowing your relationship with him. I did ask if it was possible that Kaitlin was staying with you and he was very definite that she wasn't. I thought his certainty a bit odd."

Robbie looked down at her untouched bagel. It was burned at the edge.

"Had you seen your sister before she and her friend disappeared?" Lieber asked.

"No. I had no idea she was in Miami."

"Did she call you?"

"No."

Lieber opened her mouth as though she wanted to ask something else, but instead picked up her coffee and took a sip.

How peculiar this must all seem to Lieber. Robbie had come to ask the detective about her sister, and yet this sister hadn't bothered to call or let Robbie know she was in town.

"Your father's very worried, naturally," Lieber said. "He doesn't believe the two girls would go off by themselves."

"But you think they may have?"

"I spoke with the other girls who came to South Beach with Kaitlin and Joanne. They said your sister and her friend had been acting strangely."

"Strangely how?"

"Keeping to themselves. Like they had some secret. In fact, Kaitlin had hinted to the others that she and Joanne might disappear for a day or two and to please not worry or call their parents."

"A day or two," Robbie said. "When was the last time anyone saw them?"

"Friday morning."

"Today's Monday. That's three days."

"True. But we've looked for the car they drove down in from Deland and we haven't been able to find it. Which isn't to say it's not here on Miami Beach. There are lots of places it can be, but it does reinforce the possibility they drove somewhere else for a few days."

"So you think they took off for their own private vacation and turned off their cell phones?"

"That's the most likely explanation. I imagine your sister and her friend will reappear any time now, completely oblivious to the anguish they've caused their parents."

"But what if they're still here?"

Lieber took out two sheets of paper from her shoulder bag and handed them to Robbie. "Missing" bulletins. *Kaitlin (Kate) Brooks*, the top one read.

Kate. So the Kate Brooks that Robbie had left a message for on Facebook was very likely her sister.

The photo of Kate was the same graduation picture Robbie's father had given her, and there was a description—five foot four, a hundred twenty pounds, and the circumstances of her disappearance.

"She resembles you," Lieber said.

"Yes."

The other flyer had a picture of Joanne Sparks. She was five feet, ninety-five pounds, had light hair and a young face with a nose that she hadn't quite grown into.

"I'm not optimistic the flyers will do anything," Lieber said. "Like I told your father, my best guess is Kaitlin and Joanne went off by themselves for a few days. But who knows?" She sipped her coffee. "If they're runaways, I doubt anyone would recognize them from the flyers. They'll blend in, dressing and acting like the girls who frequent the clubs. They'd bear almost no resemblance to the photos their parents have given us."

"You're assuming if they're still in South Beach they're runaways?"

"I'm just saying it's a possibility."

"Have you checked their hotel room? Did they take all their stuff with them?"

Lieber's lips tugged upward like she was containing a smile. "Still the investigator, are you?"

"I just want to find her."

"I understand." Lieber put her coffee down. "I got to the girls' hotel before your father and the other parents had a chance to pack up and check out."

"The friends are gone?"

"Yeah. Your father apparently called all the parents and they drove down and herded their own daughters out of here. But I spoke with the kids before they left town, and I checked the room Kate and Joanne were sharing. Their makeup and toothbrushes were missing, and according to their friends, some of their clothes, as well."

"So they were planning on coming back."

"Probably. Which is why I'm not alarmed." Lieber looked at Robbie with a slight frown. "Is there something you know about your sister that you're not telling me?"

"Not a thing." Robbie pushed her plate away. "I don't know a thing about her."

"I don't understand."

There was a picture of Cinderella's castle next to the alligator on the placemat. Robbie and her mom and dad once went to Disney World when Robbie was little.

"My father left me and my mom when I was seven. I hadn't heard from him since, until yesterday. I didn't even know I had a sister."

"Ah, I see." Lieber nodded.

"I must find her."

"But unless Kaitlin and her friend want to be found, there's very little the police can do."

"Then this is it? You're done?"

The detective gave Robbie a reproving look.

"I'm sorry. I didn't mean to sound off like that. It's just—this has affected me an awful lot." Robbie leaned back in the booth. How terribly alone she felt without her mom, without a close friend, without Jeremy.

"I can only imagine how difficult this is for you," Lieber said. "But until there's some tangible reason to believe the girls' disappearance wasn't intentional, there's not much more we can do."

"So what you're saying is without a dead body or a ransom note, the police investigation is over."

"You're being awfully hard on the police."

"I always believed you were determined to get the bad guy."

"If you're talking about Jeremy's parents, that was a murder investigation."

"I understand. This isn't."

The waitress came by. "Can I get you something else?"

"That's right, Robbie. This isn't."

"I'll bring the check," the waitress said and left.

Robbie folded her hands over the "Missing" flyers. "With or without the police, I'm going to find Kaitlin."

"Ah, Robbie." Lieber shook her head ever so slightly, then reached into her wallet for money. "I only hope when you do you're not disappointed."

Chapter 5

Kate hurt. It felt like hundreds of little people with heavy boots were stomping around inside her. Especially in her head. She rolled over. Sheets warm and damp. A feather sticking out of the pillow jabbed her in the cheek. She pulled it out. Where was she? A room. A bed. Curtains pulled all around. A dragon on the wall.

She licked her lips. Wrong somehow. Like she had a bad fever. Did she? She tried to think, to remember, but everything was foggy. And everything hurt.

Voices outside the room. Low. Blurry. Angry.

One stood out—higher, almost hysterical. "You've got to get them the fuck out of here."

Then the other voice—deep, sandpapery.

It was coming back to her. Tattoos, shaved head. *It's okay, baby. Everything's all right.*

Joanne. Where was Joanne? Kate sat up too quickly, the room spinning all around her. And then, her abdomen convulsed as she remembered. Joanne was dead.

"That's your problem," said the hysterical voice. "You figure it out. Just make sure it doesn't connect back to me."

Kate sank back against the pillow. She could feel hot tears turn cold as they soaked her hair. "Joanne," she whispered.

The door opened, letting in brightness. People with shadowed faces.

"Well, look who's awake," said the sandpaper voice.

Someone leaned into the room. "I don't care what you have to do. Just get them the fuck out of here."

Chapter 6

After Robbie left Detective Lieber, she biked to Kinko's with the flyers of Kate and Joanne. Kate, not Kaitlin. Robbie sensed this was how her sister thought of herself, despite what their father called her.

She wrote "Call Robbie" and her cell phone number on the flyers and ran off three hundred copies of each. She hoped the detective was right—that Kate and her friend were simply being a couple of irresponsible teenagers. But Robbie also knew they were more likely to find Kate quickly if Robbie did her part.

Robbie walked up and down Ocean Drive, Collins Avenue, Lincoln Road, and Washington Avenue, posting the flyers in every restaurant, every store, outside every club, that was willing to take them. Most of the people she spoke to said no when she asked if they recognized Kate or Joanne, but they let her leave the flyers behind.

By late Monday afternoon, Robbie was tired, hot, discouraged. But she had to get to work. She went home, showered, changed into a fresh T-shirt and jeans, then pedaled across town for her bartending shift at The Garage.

The traffic swelled with housewives running errands and grocery shopping. The west side of Miami Beach was mostly a residential neighborhood, with few tourists. It was unlikely that her sister would have come here, but Robbie still looked closely at each young woman with long dark hair.

The Garage was located just off West Avenue in an industrial neighborhood of one- and two-story concrete block auto repair and car painting shops.

Just outside the lounge, Robbie chained and bar-locked her bike to a post and took her satchel filled with flyers of Kate and Joanne out of the basket. She propped open the front door of the lounge to let some of last night's carcinogens clear out. The main bar area was dim and thick with the lingering smell of smoke, perfume, and spilled alcohol. Although the trash and cigarette butts had been cleared away, the room had the sad feel of a basement rec room after a party. The sofas and chairs were actually bench and bucket seats from cars modified to stand firmly on the unfinished concrete floor. They were arranged in groupings or pushed against the walls beneath blown-up photos of junkyards, crashed cars, and auto repair bays. In the center of the room was a worn billiard table, chalk dust suspended above it in the diffused sunlight that leaked in from the windows and open door.

Robbie arranged small stacks of "Missing" flyers on scratched tables and on the bar. On good nights, the lounge attracted several hundred people. Maybe someone would recognize Kate or Joanne.

She went into the office and turned on the music—hip-hop and indie rock—then grabbed some lemons and limes from the kitchen. She settled herself on a stool behind the curved bar with its varnished dark wood, glasses sparkling above it, and began cutting the limes.

"How's it goin'?" Robbie's boss asked, coming in from the back with a case of beer. He put the case down and gave Robbie a kiss on the cheek. Leonard was a cranky, fifty-something man who liked muscle tees that showed off his thick arms, and unfortunately, his beer belly. He wore his white hair short and a single diamond stud in his left ear.

"Why are you carrying that?" she asked.

"The new barback called in sick and I sure as shit don't want you lugging a thirty-six pound weight."

"I can handle it."

"Maybe, but weren't you the one who told me to try to avoid potential worker's comp claims?"

"Well, good. I like it when you're cost conscious. And by the way, I was looking into the lounge's health insurance coverage and I found a couple of options for you that are cheaper with better coverage."

Leonard grinned.

"What's so funny?"

"Last week you were telling me how to control beverage costs. The week before that how to manage inventory. Are you sure you don't want to take over a manager shift?"

"I like bartending."

"Right. You can still tend bar, but you'd be so great managing."

"Thanks, but I don't need the title. I'm happy to do it this way."

"I get it. No commitments."

"I didn't say that."

"No you didn't say it."

Robbie didn't like the sarcastic edge to his remark, but let it pass.

Leonard picked up one of the flyers on the bar. "What's this?"

"They're a couple of girls from back home. They're missing."

"It says Deland," Leonard said. "I thought you were from Boston."

"Deland before Boston."

The door to the bar opened. It was Ben, one of Jeremy's friends. Robbie checked behind him, but no one else came in.

"A celebratory rum and coke, Robbie," Ben said, approaching

the bar with a big smile. He held up his fist, punching it against hers. He'd shaved his head since the last time she saw him. "You're looking at a free man."

"Free from what?"

"The chains of oppression," Ben said. "I quit my job."

"Really?" she said, turning to fix his drink. "So what are you going to do?"

"I don't know." He grinned at Leonard. "Become a bartender maybe?"

"Right," Leonard said. "From investment banker to bartender. That's moving up in the world."

Robbie put the rum and coke down in front of Ben. "Congratulations. This one's on me."

"Hell no," said Ben. "Tonight, I'm buying you guys a drink."

Leonard went to pour himself a Scotch.

"Thank you, Ben," Robbie said, "but I'm sticking to water tonight."

"Cute little Robbie," he said. "We've missed you."

Her throat tightened up. She wondered who "we" referred to. She used to hang out with Jeremy and his friends all the time and it had meant a lot to her.

When Robbie was growing up, her mom was often sick and Robbie had chosen to be with her when she could, rather than go out with school friends. Robbie hadn't known how nice it was to be part of a group.

"So, what's up?" Ben said, taking a sip of his drink. "Still dating that asshole?"

"Brett's not an asshole," Robbie said.

"Come on, Robbie. I don't get what you see in Mr. Trendsetter with his designer wardrobe."

Leonard brought his Scotch over and touched his glass against Ben's as an unfamiliar customer came into the bar. The man stood just inside the doorway, blinking his eyes to adjust from the outside light to dimness. He looked like a boater in a loose sweatshirt, khakis, Docksiders, and a billed cap that read Bud N' Mary's, a marina down in the Keys.

"So what do you think?" Ben asked Leonard as the man approached the bar. "Can you use someone else with an advanced degree? Robbie looks pretty happy and she was once a hard-ass, miserable CPA."

"I was never a hard-ass," Robbie said.

Mr. Bud N' Mary hesitated as though deciding where to sit.

"Fine," Ben said. "Then former tight-ass, boring CPA."

"I was never boring."

"But tight-assed, am I right?"

"Maybe a little."

"And now look at her," Ben said. "Tending bar at one of the hottest bars in the world. That's what I aspire to."

"Unfortunately, Ben," Leonard said, "you don't have her looks. Or charm."

Mr. Bud N' Mary sat down at the far end of the bar away from Leonard and Ben.

"Thanks for the compliments, guys, but you'll have to excuse me. I have a real customer."

Robbie put a napkin down on the polished wood in front of the man. "What can I get you?"

"A Heineken."

Robbie returned with the beer and set it in front of him. "Five dollars, please, or you can give me a credit card and I'll run a tab."

He put a twenty down. He was probably in his mid- to late-thirties, average build, average everything. Brown eyes, tired face. He had a five o'clock shadow and a pink nose and forehead, as though from too much recent sun, and wore black, industrial-framed glasses. The lenses were dirty with what looked like sea spray.

She lingered to see if he wanted to chat. "Are you from around here?" she asked, leaving his change on the bar.

"Not exactly. I've got my boat docked at the Miami Beach Marina." He turned to point south, then pulled his arm back, as though embarrassed. His shyness reminded her of someone. Her father.

"Long walk from there to here," she said.

"Not so bad. I like walking."

He sipped his beer, glancing over at her from time to time, trying not to be obvious. Lots of guys tried to pick her up and Robbie had learned the art of being friendly without giving off the "available" vibes. She put a dish of salty snacks in front of him.

"So you live on the boat?" she asked.

"I wish." He reached into the snack dish. No wedding ring, black hairs on the back of his fingers, and something odd. His fingernails were perfect, as though they'd been manicured. "I try to get down to South Beach as often as I can. It's never as often as I'd like."

She sensed he was lonely. Her father had seemed lonely, too. She wondered that he hadn't called her or come by since yesterday.

Leonard was still talking to Ben at the other end of the bar. She checked Ben's drink—half full.

"What kind of boat?" she asked.

"A little guy. Twenty-six foot Chris-Craft cabin cruiser. Perfect for fishing and small enough for me to handle alone. I've named her *Aimless*." He grinned and his face was transformed. No longer nondescript, but almost handsome and something else. She'd have to say charismatic.

"I just took her down to the Keys for a few days. I was supposed to head back home, but I decided there's plenty of time to get back into the rat race. Let me enjoy myself for a change."

"I know what you mean," Robbie said.

He sucked in his lower lip like a nervous kid. "What's your name, by the way?"

"Robbie. And you are?"

He hesitated. "Puck."

"Puck? Like Shakespeare's?"

"I don't look much like a clever, mischievous elf, do I?"

"Not quite."

"Got the nickname in high school. I had the role in the play." He folded his hands and looked down at them. "If you're interested, I could take you out sometime. On the boat, I mean."

"Yo, Robbie," Ben called. He tapped on his glass.

She went to make him another.

"He's a little old for you," Ben said. "But a definite improvement over Brett Bragger."

"Here's your drink," Robbie said. "And thanks for the unsolicited advice." She wiped down the bar.

"That doesn't look so tough," Ben said to Leonard. "I'd be a great bartender."

Robbie half listened to Ben and Leonard. She was reluctant to return to Puck with the invitation to go out on his boat open, but maybe he didn't mean anything by it. She glanced over. He had finished his beer and was twisting a paper napkin into tiny white worms.

"Another?" she said, returning to Puck and picking up his empty.

He pushed his heavy glasses up on his nose. "I made things awkward for you."

"No. Of course not."

"I didn't mean to come across like I was trying to pick you up."

"Not a problem. Can I get you another Heineken?"

"Sure."

She flicked off the cap and set the bottle on the bar in front of him. His elbow was resting on the flyer of Robbie's sister.

Puck took a pull of his beer. "So you're a CPA?"

"Excuse me?"

"I overheard you talking when I came in."

"Was," she said. "I used to work in public accounting."

"What made you decide to get out?"

She didn't really want to get into the whole story. "It bothers me that it's no longer possible for the average person to know who he can trust and who he can't. And while there are plenty of honest CPAs out there, I prefer being my own person and not part of some group that occasionally has questionable practices."

"It's not just CPAs who lie and cheat. Lawyers, businessmen, financial advisors. No one's immune to greed or corruption."

She was surprised by the conviction in his voice. "What do you do for a living, Puck?"

He cradled his beer bottle and stared at it.

"Sorry. I didn't mean to pry."

The bill of his cap shadowed his eyes. "I guess I try to make the world a little better in my own way."

The door opened and a small crowd pushed into the bar.

"Excuse me," Robbie said, and went to her new customers.

By midnight, Robbie was working nonstop, fixing drinks, ringing up the charges. Occasionally Puck would order another beer, but she didn't have time to talk to him.

At two in the morning, the lounge was in full swing, but Robbie's shift was over. She said goodnight to the other bartender who'd come in to relieve her, and headed outside to her bicycle.

Zelda, a skinny, homeless woman who slept on a bench outside the bar, shuffled up to Robbie. "There's a creep watching the bar," she said. Zelda was wearing torn black leggings and what appeared to be a cut-down graduation gown. On her hands were fingerless black gloves. Her nails were long and painted a glittery scarlet. "Keeps going to the window and checking inside. Been here all night."

"Oh yeah?" Robbie said, not really paying attention. Zelda was always giving Robbie a report, hoping for food or money.

"Then he goes and sits in his car. Black. Tinted windows." Zelda looked up and down the street. "Don't know where he went to."

"Well, thanks for keeping a lookout."

"I made sure no one stole your bike," Zelda said.

"I appreciate it." Robbie reached into her satchel.

"Is she bothering you?" Puck called out as he approached from the doorway of the bar.

"Not at all. She watches my bike." Robbie handed Zelda a couple of energy bars.

"It's been six hundred and forty-three days," Zelda said. "Not one little sip."

"Good for you, Zelda."

"Damn right, good for me." She took the bars, tore the packaging off one of them, and went back to her bench.

"Is it safe for you to go home on that?" Puck asked.

"On my bike? Sure. I do it all the time." Robbie smiled. "What about you? Is it safe for you to walk these mean South Beach streets all the way back to your boat?"

He tipped his cap and gave her a half smile.

"Well, goodnight then," she said, and pedaled away.

There was very little traffic, but she kept to the side streets so she wouldn't get hit by some speeding drunken driver. She had a heightened awareness of her surroundings. The streets were dark. No people out. But there wouldn't be. Most people were asleep at two a.m.

A car was behind her. Robbie pulled closer to the sidewalk. The car sped up, passing her. She picked up her pace the rest of the way home. She took this route every night after work, so why was she spooked? Puck's remark questioning whether it was safe?

When she got to her apartment building, she got off her bike and walked it to the bike stand, checking over her shoulder. Shadows shifted. Palm trees.

A car drove past. Black, with tinted windows. Robbie waited for it to turn at the corner. She locked up her bike, brushing off the thought that she may have been followed.

Chapter 7

Marylou Madison sat on a bench watching the surf break in the distance. Families wearing bathing suits and sandals crossed in front of her carrying folding chairs and coolers of food. In the nearby grass, a black man with long hair like twisted twine stood by a blanket covered with fake jewelry and watches. He had a sickly parrot on his shoulder. The bird had plucked out most of its feathers. Marylou looked away, disturbed by the sight.

She took a few deep breaths. The sound of the waves settled her. She remembered when she was a little girl, her mother once held a conch shell to Marylou's ear and told her to listen to the ocean. "Someday," her mother had said, "I'll get back there."

Marylou had stolen the conch shell when her mother wasn't around and hidden it behind the old furnace in the cellar. Marylou could find it, even in the pitch black, even when she was in so much pain from the beatings that she had to crawl across the cold, damp cellar floor. Then she'd wrap herself in a moldy blanket, listen to the ocean, and try not to think about the darkness and how much she hurt.

Marylou crossed her arms. She was chilled, despite the towel she'd wrapped around her shoulders.

She didn't like it here in this strange town, but here was where she needed to be. This was the best way she knew to help him, to take care of him. The only way she would finally fulfill her mother's dreams.

A beach patrol vehicle thundered by. The black man swept up the blanket with the contents intact in one quick motion, then walked away without missing a beat, the sick parrot firmly perched on his shoulder.

Marylou's little boy was alone in the room. She needed to get back to him.

Chapter 8

Robbie had Kate on her mind when she woke up Tuesday morning. After checking Facebook and finding no messages from her sister, she decided to jog down to the Fifth Street beach, popular with the young crowd. Robbie took off her sneakers, tied the laces together, then hung them around her neck. She spent the next few hours trudging through the sand looking at girls who resembled Kate's photo. Occasionally she'd see someone who could have been Kate, but when Robbie got closer or talked to the girl, she realized it wasn't her sister.

Robbie knew this was probably a futile exercise, but she needed to do something to channel her frustration. Like when her mom had been in surgery. Robbie couldn't just stay in the waiting room. So she'd gone to the medical library and researched and photocopied the latest experimental treatments for breast cancer. Robbie didn't understand most of the technical medical terminology, and she knew the doctors would most likely dismiss her efforts, but she really believed that she might find something that everyone else had overlooked.

The surf was receding, widening the beach area, and as it got later, more and more people sprawled out on towels in the sand. Robbie looked around her at the expanse of beach, the increasing number of people. A hunched, gray-haired man was walking in the distance. Her father? Was he also out here looking for Kate? She hadn't heard from him since he'd come by on Sunday.

Robbie could feel the sun burning her skin, even with sunscreen slathered on her arms, legs, and face.

What was she doing? She'd never find her sister this way.

She noticed a child running toward her, zigzagging wildly in the sand. She tried to get out of his way, but he crashed into her, almost upsetting her balance.

"Eric," a woman's high-pitched voice shouted from behind her. "Watch where you're going."

Robbie looked down at the little boy. Maybe six or seven years old. Straight brown hair, angry eyes, and his mouth puckered like he'd just tasted a lemon.

"I'm so sorry," the woman said, breathless from running down the street. Her long, tangled blonde hair obscured her face as she pulled Eric against her and he struggled to get free. She was wearing a skimpy tank top, which exposed a lot of cleavage, and there was a tattoo of a mermaid on her arm. "Sometimes he gets too excited." She released the little boy from her embrace, then swatted the sand off his back and legs with a beach towel.

Robbie recognized her. What was her name? Maddy—that was it. Maddy had started recently as a bartender at The Garage, though she and Robbie worked different shifts. Robbie remembered something about Maddy being a single mom.

"You're Maddy, right?" Robbie asked.

Maddy looked back in surprise. Her hazel eyes were small and naked without her customary makeup, and the way she bit down on her full lower lip made Robbie realize how young she probably was—maybe mid-twenties. "Oh, I know you," Maddy said. "Don't you work at the lounge?"

Robbie nodded.

"Yeah, that's right. I was surprised when I first saw you. You don't look like you belong."

"Well—"

Maddy covered a laugh with her free hand. Her fingernails were bitten down. "I mean that in a good way. You look like you own the place, not like a working girl."

"We all have to make a living."

"Shit, don't I know that." Maddy ruffled Eric's hair, but he pushed her hand away. "And it's so expensive here," Maddy said. "Not like back home."

"You just moved here, right?"

"Yeah. From up north." Maddy didn't seem like she wanted to be more specific.

"You have family in Miami?" Robbie asked.

Maddy shook her head. "Eric and I are all the family we need. Right, honey?" The little boy was squirming, looking everywhere but at his mother. "We can manage just fine on our own."

That's what Robbie's mother used to say to her. Looking at Maddy and her child made Robbie wonder whether that had been the best thing for Robbie. And what about this little boy? Who watched Eric when Maddy was tending bar?

"There's the boyfriend, of course." Maddy giggled. "But I'm sure you know about boyfriends. They're not exactly family."

Eric was pulling hard trying to break his mother's grasp on his hand.

"Eric, be good."

Eric tugged. "Ma, come on."

"Sorry," Maddy said to Robbie. "Gotta go. Boyfriend's waiting."

"Sure. See you around."

"Yeah. I'm trying to pick up a couple of extra shifts at the lounge."

The mother and son crossed the street toward an old hotel with a flashing pink and blue marquee. Was that where they lived? A skanky guy with sunglasses and broad shoulders stood in front of the hotel and flailed his arms as Maddy approached. He sounded angry. Maddy pushed past him, holding Eric in front of her. The guy followed her into the hotel.

Boyfriends. Not exactly family.

What exactly was family?

Robbie thought about the stooped, gray-haired man she'd seen walking on the beach earlier. It probably had been her father, doing exactly what Robbie had been doing all morning: looking for Kate.

His other daughter.

His family.

Chapter 9

Robbie returned home from the beach and was actually relieved when Brett called in the early afternoon and asked her to go with him to an event for one of his public relations clients. Ordinarily, she begged off when Brett invited her to the social scene.

She showered and got dressed in white shorts and a fringed vest that she'd made herself during her sewing phase, which had preceded the jewelry making. Then she French-braided a section of her hair with beads and feathers, tucked it behind her ear, and checked herself in the mirror. Her skin had a pinkish glow from the sun, her blue eyes were large, and her lashes so thick that she never wore mascara. Like her sister's eyes in the photo.

She stuffed a few flyers in her satchel, just in case she found an opportunity to pass them out.

There was a rat-a-tat on her front door. Brett's knock. She opened the door and had a hard time controlling her smile.

Brett Chandler had a lopsided grin, big ears, small nose, and blond hair spiking like a grown-up Dennis the Menace. It didn't matter if Ben and Jeremy's other friends didn't like him, there was something about Brett that made Robbie feel good. This afternoon, he was wearing a narrow red tie and an untucked checkered shirt with its sleeves rolled to his elbows.

"Ms. Robbie Ivy," he said, grabbing her and swinging her

around, causing her braid to go flying. He was much taller than she and wiry but strong.

Matilda meowed and weaved around his cuffed jeans and black hightops as he put Robbie down. They had met a month ago at The Garage, while Robbie was tending bar. Brett seemed to know every-one of importance or with money, having grown up on the Beach and gone to private school since kindergarten.

He took Robbie in. "Somebody got some sun."

"Yeah. I was at the beach."

"Well, you look like really hot. Fieldstone's either going to adopt you or have you killed."

"Fieldstone?"

"Yeah. Gina Tyler Fieldstone. She's promoting her new book at the event tonight. Her husband's Stanford Fieldstone. You know, from the tire family?"

"Isn't that Firestone?"

"Firestone, Fieldstone, whatever. I just know he's got family money and he's on some fast political track. He's probably using Gina and her book to build his people base. Anyway, should be a lot of good contacts there."

Robbie pushed her braid back behind her ear. "I could use a pos-itive distraction."

"Oh yeah? Something wrong?" Brett's face became serious.

"Some unexpected surprises in my life since yesterday. It seems that—"

His cell phone rang. He glanced at it. "Sorry. I need to take this." He turned toward the front door and lowered his voice. "Hey. What's up?"

Robbie went into the kitchen, took her satchel from the table, then checked to make sure Matilda had food and water.

Brett was done with his call when she returned to the foyer.

"Man," he said, "I honestly don't know what those guys would do without me. Ready to go?"

He had probably forgotten that she'd been in the middle of telling him something. But Brett was often like that. She suspected that he had attention deficit disorder and wasn't on meds for it. She'd tell him about her father and sister later, when he wasn't so distracted.

Brett leaned against the front door and ushered Robbie outside. Matilda meowed, trying to follow.

"Not you, kitten," Robbie said, gently coaxing the cat back into the apartment. "You keep the mice away."

Brett's shiny black BMW was parked in the loading zone in front of Robbie's building with its flashers blinking. Its windows were tinted too dark, which made it difficult to see inside. She didn't quite get why guys thought looking "hood" was cool.

He held open the passenger door for her and she slid in. A year ago, she never would have imagined herself with someone like Brett. But there was something so undemanding about him. And for now, that worked just fine. No pressure to think about commitments. But wasn't that what Leonard had been criticizing her about?

"I'm sorry I've been in a dead zone," Brett said, pulling into the street. "I never thought public relations was going to be twenty-four seven."

"Anything particular happening?"

"Just some screwups with a couple of guys who work for us at the clubs. Such idiots. But we've got it under control now."

He joined the bumper-to-bumper traffic on Collins. They could have just as well walked to the hotel from Robbie's apartment and made it in less time, but Brett was like a lost boy without his car nearby. She thought about bringing up her sister again, but decided it was a bad time. She reached into her bag and made sure the ringtone on her phone was turned to high in case someone was trying to reach her about Kate.

Two blocks down, Brett turned into an alleyway with a valet sign. The valet handed him a ticket. Robbie got out on her side without waiting for Brett to come around.

They walked up the steps of The Pulse Hotel past gurgling fountains, then through the lobby and into the cool, dark lounge area. Ceiling fans with blades shaped like giant lily pads spun above them. The floors were gray stone and there was a narrow, rectangular pool with flowing water.

"There he is." Brett grinned and strode toward the long, ebony bar with his hand outstretched.

Robbie followed, curious who Brett was so excited to see.

"Mister M." Brett shook hands with a skinny, freckled, older man whose thin orange hair was combed back in a ponytail.

Robbie recognized Brett's boss, Mike, or Mister M, as he was known around Miami Beach. The skin around his watery gray eyes was pulled too tight, which gave him an almost Asian look and made it difficult for him to blink.

"Here's our girl," Mike said in a tinny voice as he air kissed Robbie's cheeks. Mike was wearing his usual—a short-sleeved white embroidered guayabera shirt—the traditional Cuban dress shirt. It hung loosely on his emaciated frame. He had a dazzling smile with too-perfect white teeth.

Mike signaled the bartender, who put a couple of drinks on the bar. "Tonight's specialty. Mojitos. Unless you'd prefer a rum punch," Mike said to Robbie.

"A mojito's fine, thanks," she said.

Brett handed one to Robbie, then clinked his own glass against hers.

"Well, drink up, you two," Mike said, "and enjoy." He walked off, waving over his shoulder without turning around.

Brett thrummed his fingers against the bar, watching the groups of people as they came into the lounge.

"Go ahead, Brett," Robbie said. "Mingle. You don't have to babysit me. I'm fine."

"You sure?"

"Absolutely."

"I'll be back soon," he said, reminding her of a schoolboy who just heard the recess bell. And once again she was struck by how different he was from Jeremy.

She pulled out the stack of "Missing" flyers from her satchel and put several down on each corner of the bar. Maybe she'd get lucky and one of the guests would recognize her sister.

She sensed that someone was watching her and turned. Her eyes connected with Mister M's watery ones. Maybe he didn't like her putting flyers around at one of his events. Brett's boss's tight, unnatural face showed no emotion as he walked toward her.

He picked up one of the flyers and studied the photo. "Call Robbie?" He glanced up at her. "Robbie you?"

"Yup. Hope you don't mind me leaving them out here."

"She looks like you. A relative?"

"Kind of."

He twirled his thin orange ponytail around his fingers as he waited for her to say more. She didn't. She didn't want Brett hearing about Kate from Mike.

"I'll keep an eye out." Mike folded the flyer and put it in his pocket. "By the way—it's probably not a good idea for you to give out your phone number like that. Creeps can call you and bother you."

"Thanks, but that's the advantage of having a boy's name."

He walked away without saying anything else.

Talk about creeps. Robbie wondered why Brett was so enthusiastic about working for someone like Mike.

She left the bar and wandered over to an indoor atrium filled with exotic plants. There was a noticeable change in the affluence and sophistication of the crowd as it got later. The arriving women became taller, skinnier, younger; the men, by contrast, got shorter, stockier, and older.

The room was filled almost to capacity, the noise level deafening. Gorgeous young women in short skirts and hot guys flexing their biceps beneath tight T-shirts moved through the crowd with trays of drinks and hors d'oeuvres. One of the waitresses had long black hair and blue eyes. There was something familiar in the way she moved. Robbie got closer.

The girl held out a platter of what looked like biscotti. She said something to Robbie.

"What?" Robbie shouted.

"It's Indian Fry bread," the girl repeated, louder this time. She was skinny, pale. Her eyes were wrong for Kate—too close together, no sparkle. Robbie took a piece of bread and a napkin. "Thank you."

There was no sign of Brett in the sea of black. Robbie sipped her drink. It was too sweet and a mint leaf had sunk to the bottom of the glass. She wiped the grease from her fingers on her napkin, left the half-eaten bread and her drink on a tray, then made her way outside.

She stood on the hotel steps blinking against the strong sunlight. The heat made her sunburn hurt. It was after six p.m. but felt like midday. Tourists walked by in wrinkled shorts, snapping pictures of the hotels and South Beach scene. A black sedan with tinted windows pulled up in front of the hotel and a slender, graceful woman got of the car. There was something odd about the woman that made Robbie do a double take. Although neatly dressed in a black sheath with a white cardigan over her shoulders, the look was wrong for South Beach. In fact, the outmoded style was completely inconsistent with the woman, who was quite attractive. Her dress was too long and her hair—ash brown and streaked with blonde—was in an upswept hairdo that was popular back in the '60s.

The woman's driver was a young guy with a blond buzz cut, bloated face, and small eyes. He wore a dark suit that pulled under his arms, white shirt, and a tie that was loosened, probably to accommodate his thick neck.

The guy took a ticket from the valet, then escorted the woman up the steps, passing close to Robbie on their way to the hotel lobby. The woman looked distracted as she adjusted a gold clasp holding the front of her cardigan sweater together.

Strange pair, Robbie thought.

She took her cell phone out of her bag and checked it. No missed calls. It would be another hour before Brett was free to leave. She took a deep breath of humid air and returned through the lobby into the dark, bustling ant pile.

After pushing through the crowd, she found Brett in front of a podium, holding a microphone up to his mouth. An adjacent table was stacked with books—*In Search of Self* by Gina Tyler Fieldstone.

"Good evening," Brett said to the crowded room. "And welcome."

None of the ants paid any attention to him.

A shrill whistle came from the bar. People stopped what they were doing and looked. Mike—Mister M—had two fingers in front of his big, white grin. He winked at Brett.

"Hello, everyone," Brett said, this time with the crowd's attention. "I'd like to introduce our remarkable guest, who has a lot to say about how women can learn to take control of their lives. She's the author of *In Search of Self*. And yeah, sure, maybe her husband's always mentioned in the editorial columns as the great crusader who will clean up America, but our guest is the real force to be reckoned with. Please join me in welcoming Ms. Gina Tyler Fieldstone."

The applause was tepid as the attractive woman in the white cardigan came through a door behind the podium. She surveyed the room, a muscle in her neck twitching. And then she smiled. A lovely, radiant smile. "Thank you, Brett. And thank you all for joining me this evening."

Robbie stepped closer in order to see her better. She had never heard of Gina Fieldstone or her husband before Brett mentioned them earlier. But if Mrs. Fieldstone was using her book to help her husband's political career, she had definitely misjudged this hip audience.

She was probably in her late thirties, the age Robbie's mother had been when she was last healthy and vibrant. And for a moment, Robbie was back with her mother, holding her hand, her mother smiling at her.

Robbie snapped back to the present and tried to focus on Gina. She was talking about taking control of your future. She had a crisp, low voice with a flat accent that Robbie couldn't quite place. Midwest? Northwest? The crowd listened for a few minutes and then people started chatting and wandering away. This group believed they had already figured their futures out, thank you very much. They certainly didn't need some lady dressed for a church supper to be telling them what to do.

The din rose. Gina spoke louder into the microphone, reminding Robbie of a missionary, so focused on her message she didn't seem to care that no one was listening. "My own experiences," Gina said. "I was only fifteen. What did I know? My mother told me I couldn't keep my baby. And although I cried and argued with her, I suppose on some level I knew she was right. I was barely able to take care of myself; how could I take on the responsibility of raising a child?"

Robbie stepped closer to the podium. Gina was clutching the mike with a sense of urgency. She had the bone structure of a model—high cheekbones, straight nose, broad forehead. Her eyes were large and an unusual color, almost like amethysts.

Gina told about giving up her daughter, then years later searching to find her and never succeeding. It was a heartbreaking story, and one that struck Robbie hard. Especially after the visit from her own father. Here this woman had spent years looking for the child she had been forced to give up, while her father had willingly let Robbie go and made not the least effort to get in touch with her.

Gina took a deep breath. "Thank you again." She stepped down from the podium to lukewarm applause, but kept her head high.

Many attendees had wandered over to the bar. Brett was back up at the podium announcing that Gina's books were for sale and Gina would be happy to personally sign them, but only two people went to purchase a book.

Robbie reached into her satchel for money to buy a book herself. No one came behind her on line.

The heavyset escort stood beside Gina as she sat at a small table signing the books. He kept glancing at Robbie, but maybe that was his job. He leaned over and said something in Gina's ear, then backed away, hands in his pants pockets, scowl on his face.

Robbie stepped up to the table with her book.

Gina smiled. Her front teeth overlapped slightly and a strand of streaked brown hair had fallen loose from her otherwise perfect coiffeur. She pushed it away from her eyes and behind her ear. She wore small pearl earrings. "Phew," she said. "Glad that's over with."

The fervor and intensity were gone, but Robbie felt a powerful connection. Gina had lost her daughter. Robbie had lost her mother.

"I enjoyed your talk very much," Robbie said.

"Thank you. I appreciate your saying that." Gina held up a thin silver pen. Her fingers were long and delicate and she wore a plain gold wedding band. "How would you like me to inscribe the book?"

"To Robbie, would be fine. R-O-B-B-I-E."

"Robbie," Gina repeated and wrote.

Robbie took the book back and held it against her chest, reluctant to leave without saying what was on her mind. But the bulky escort had taken a step closer to Gina. His eyes were the color of dirty lavender.

Gina looked at Robbie expectantly, then glanced over her shoulder at her escort. She let out a short laugh. It was melodious and lingering like the low notes on a xylophone. "Aidan," she said, "I'm parched. Would you mind bringing me a glass of water with a slice of lemon?"

Her escort grunted and headed toward the bar.

"Aidan's pretty scary," Gina said. "My husband's idea. Stanford's with the U.S. Department of Justice, and he seems to think I need protection from his political enemies. But I worry that Aidan's frightening off my book audience because he looks like such a thug."

"He is a little intense," Robbie said.

Gina threw her head back and laughed her beautiful laugh. "I can tell you're big on understatement." She folded her hands and rested them on the table beside the pen. "But you looked like you wanted to say something to me."

Robbie nodded. "Your talk really touched me. I understand your need to find your child. To make sure she's okay." Why was she telling a stranger this? But Gina seemed like anything but a stranger. The resemblance to Robbie's mother and to Rachel, Robbie's mentor, was profound. "I just found out that I have a sister I never knew about. But she's missing."

Gina's hand went to her throat. "Missing?"

"She and a friend disappeared a few days ago on South Beach. They were on spring break." Robbie reached into her satchel and took out the flyers of Kate and Joanne.

Gina studied the photos. "May I keep these? I come in contact with a lot of people during my tour. Maybe I'll recognize your sister."

"Please," Robbie said. "I'd be very grateful."

Aidan returned with the glass of water and put it down on the table, but Robbie noticed that Gina didn't even take a sip.

Robbie felt someone's hand on her shoulder. Brett's.

"Hope everything worked out to your satisfaction," Brett said to Gina.

"Yes. Thank you very much." Gina stood up and pulled her cardigan tighter around her.

"If there's anything else I can do for you, feel free to call me anytime. Me or Mike. We're always at your service."

"Thank you. I will." Gina nodded at Robbie, then went toward the door with Aidan. She walked without any wasted movement as though she'd been trained as a model or in cotillion classes. Aidan trailed after her like a lumbering gorilla.

Brett pulled off his red tie and shoved it into the pocket of his jeans.

"I'm sorry the event didn't go very well," Robbie said.

"Are you kidding? It went great."

"It did? It didn't look like Gina sold many books."

"Right. But that wasn't the point. She got great exposure. Over two hundred people showed up."

"What good is exposure if no one bought the book?"

"Because that's two hundred people who now know the name Fieldstone."

"I must be dense. Why does that matter?"

"You know," Brett said, as though she was supposed to. "For her husband." He surveyed the emptying room. "I'll just check with Mike, then we're out of here. There's a new restaurant I want to take you to."

Robbie sat down on a sofa near the atrium to wait for him and opened the book. A lot of work had gone into it. She doubted that Gina had gone to all this trouble just to advance her husband's career.

She flipped through the pages. The book contained stories about women who had also been forced to give their children up for adoption. In many cases, there were photos of the mother happily reunited with her child after many years. But the photo of Gina at the end of the book was of herself alone. She had never found her own daughter.

Robbie noticed the skinny server with long black hair and blue eyes standing behind an areca palm, stuffing hors d'oeuvres into her mouth.

She closed the book. She wondered what Kate was doing at this moment. She checked her cell phone for messages.

There were none.

Chapter 10

After the Fieldstone event, it turned out Brett couldn't go for dinner after all. Something unexpected had come up, Brett explained to
Robbie, and Mike needed him. He offered to drive Robbie home,
but she preferred walking alone, relieved to be away from the South
Beach tumult.

She went to bed early, but her mind was caught up in memories.
Her childhood house on the St. Johns River, Spanish moss hanging
from towering oak trees, frogs croaking in the stillness. Her dad returning home from the hospital after a late night emergency call.
How he stood on the flagstone patio that smelled like magnolias,
staring at nothing.

What's wrong, Daddy?

A smile that she knew he'd faked for her. *I didn't know you were
there, princess. Come give your old man a hug.*

And she had. She'd hugged him as tight as she could, but she
knew it wasn't enough to make his sadness go away. Then later that
night, she overheard him talking to her mother. *There's nothing I can
do,* he told her. *Absolutely nothing.*

Robbie finally got out of bed around eight in the morning and
changed into her running shorts and tank top. Her route took her
across the north end of Lummus Park and up the stamped-concrete
path that ran alongside the ocean. Seagulls squawked above her and
the sound of waves breaking helped clear her head. She passed the

condo that housed the health club where Jeremy sometimes worked, and glanced over at the beach hoping to see his lean, tanned body doing pushups or running a client in the sand. But there were only a couple of sunbathers stretched out on towels.

Running had always been an outlet for her. There were days in Boston when she'd run for miles, even in the cold of winter. She wasn't sure whether it was because she didn't have friends or because it gave her an excuse not to make any.

The path continued up wooden steps to the boardwalk, the planks absorbing her pounding footfalls. She heard a growing chuffing noise overhead. A helicopter crossing above her.

At 41st Street, she ran down the boardwalk steps and cut over to Indian Creek, where she turned back south. She was perplexed by what she saw. Cars were backed up along Indian Creek Drive and a cop was redirecting traffic. There was rarely a buildup here, especially on a weekday morning. Robbie slowed her jog, noticing flashing lights, police cars, vans from the TV news stations. A collision? Or had a car gone into the creek?

She slowed down, curious, but she couldn't see much. A crowd had gathered—a mix of tourists and locals from the low-rise buildings and old hotels along Indian Creek. The helicopter was hovering directly overhead like a vulture; it had the logo of a local news station.

Robbie stood next to a heavyset guy in shorts and flip-flops holding a plastic bag from Walgreens. Sweat had beaded on his forehead. "What happened?" she asked over the roaring of the helicopter.

"Don't know," he shouted. "Just got here. But there are divers."

Robbie pushed through the crowd. Divers, she thought. Could be a car. Or a body. Whose body? But her mind didn't want to go there.

The water reeked of decaying vegetation, and sprouted mangrove bushes with large, tangled roots. She could see better now.

There were people standing on the footbridge that crossed a narrow expanse of the creek. Yellow crime-scene tape marked large areas on both sides of the waterway, which appeared to have been closed to boat traffic. A tent had been set up just beyond the creek bed on a flat grassy area. What was that about? People loitered up to the edge of the tape, many filming the activity with their cell phones or cameras. They were smiling, having a good time. South Beach—fun and games any time, day or night.

And then she saw him in the crowd. Her father. Amongst the tank tops, T-shirts, and shorts, her dad stood out in his white oxford shirt and navy slacks. He stared at the water, his face expressionless. And she remembered him looking out at the river that night so many years ago. *There's nothing I can do. Absolutely nothing.*

What had they found in the water? Kate? Dear God—let it not be Kate. But it couldn't be her half sister, she reasoned. Her father wouldn't be here if Kate had been found. Then what was going on in the tent?

Robbie got closer to the crime-scene tape. Marked and unmarked police cars were parked helter-skelter in the street and on the grass. She saw uniformed cops, crime-scene technicians. A diver was talking to a woman wearing denim Capri pants and a light blue short-sleeved shirt. Lieber, out of her customary detective clothes, as though called here from off duty.

Robbie stared at the detective, willing Lieber to look in Robbie's direction. She was desperate to know what had happened. The diver adjusted his gear and headed back toward the water. "Detective Lieber," Robbie called out, not sure she could be heard over the helicopter noise.

But Lieber turned to Robbie's voice, held up her hand to indicate she'd be right with her, then went over to a couple of uniformed cops.

Robbie waited, trying to calm her breathing. Her father was

still looking into the water, as though he could see down to its murky bottom. *There's nothing I can do.*

"Robbie," Lieber called. "Can you step over here? I just have a minute."

Robbie joined Lieber under a shady ficus tree a short distance from the crime scene area. The helicopter cast a shadow over the water. It was difficult to hear anything with its noise all around them.

"What's happened?" Robbie said. "My father's here. Did something happen to Kate?"

Lieber shook her head. "No. Not Kate." Her hair was clipped back, a strand of grayish brown escaping over her eye. She pushed it back. She looked haggard.

"Tell me. Please." Sweat was dripping beneath Robbie's T-shirt and shorts.

"We got a call early this morning," Lieber said. "The body of a teenage girl was found in the creek, tangled in some mangrove roots."

Robbie let out a gasp.

"It's Joanne Sparks."

"Oh, no." Robbie covered her mouth with her hands. She remembered the photo of the girl on the "Missing" flyer—the narrow face and large nose that now would never mature into adulthood.

"Her parents came down from Deland a couple of days ago to search for her. They've identified Joanne's body." Lieber glanced back at the tent.

"Oh God. Joanne's in the tent?"

"The ME is still examining the body."

"And Joanne's parents? They're in there?"

Lieber shook her head. "They went back to their hotel. Joanne's mother needed to be sedated."

Joanne's parents. Imagine identifying your eighteen-year-old dead daughter's body. Eighteen. Her mom and dad should have been preparing for their daughter's high school graduation, filled with anxiety about her going away to college next year. Not this.

The muscles in Lieber's face were tight. She opened her shoulder bag and fumbled inside. Then she closed the bag and flipped it behind her, apparently not finding what she'd been looking for.

"What condition——" Robbie said. "Her parents must have been——"

Lieber nodded, as though she understood what Robbie was trying to say. "Joanne hadn't been in the water for very long."

"Can you tell how she died?" Robbie asked.

"We won't know for certain until we have the medical examiner's report, but right now, it appears she drowned."

"In Indian Creek? No one goes swimming in Indian Creek."

"She could have fallen out of a boat, or been drunk. It's best not to speculate until the medical examiner gives her report." Lieber glanced at the cops and investigators huddling near the side of the creek. "I'm sorry, but I need to go."

Robbie saw one of the divers climb up the bank. If Joanne had been found, what were they looking for? "Oh my God," Robbie said. "Kate." Robbie felt a tightening in her chest. "You think she may have drowned, too?"

"It's possible. The last time they were seen, the girls were together. And, well, unfortunately, no one's heard from Kate."

Robbie glanced over to where her father had been standing earlier. He was gone. "Have you spoken to my father?"

"He came here with Joanne's parents. He was very supportive, but then he became quite agitated."

"Well, of course he was agitated," Robbie said. "His daughter's friend is dead and no one knows where Kate is."

Lieber took in a short breath. "Like I told your father, we're trying to understand what happened so we can take the appropriate action. And now, I really need to get back to my team."

"But that could take hours or days. You can't just assume Kate also drowned. What if she's in some kind of trouble? Shouldn't you be looking for her?"

"Look where?" Then her expression softened. "I know you're concerned about Kate, but honestly, without the ME's report on Joanne, we don't have much to go on. All we have are questions. Had the two girls been together? Does Kate know what happened to Joanne? Was she involved?"

"Wait a minute. What do you mean involved?"

"I'm just saying there's the question of why Kate hasn't come to the police."

"Maybe she can't. What if this wasn't an accident? And what if whoever did this to Joanne has done something to Kate?"

Lieber rested her hand on Robbie's shoulder. "Go home, Robbie. You know I'll do everything I can to find her."

"I know." Robbie was unable to meet Lieber's eyes.

"And if you talk to your father," Lieber said as she walked away, "tell him that we're not a bunch of fat, lazy bureaucrats who are sitting on our asses while South Beach burns."

Robbie watched Lieber join the group by the creek.

The helicopter swooped lower, scattering leaves and debris. Then it rose and drifted away into the sharp blue sky. The sound of droning became softer and softer and softer.

Chapter 11

Robbie jogged back to her apartment. Breathing was difficult. Her sister's friend was dead. It was tragic, but it only heightened Robbie's sense of urgency to find Kate. But where could she be? And how was all this affecting their father?

Robbie ran upstairs. It was after nine, too late for the local news. She wondered if the TV cameras had captured footage for the early morning broadcasts. Would any of Kate or Joanne's friends have seen it? And what about Kate? Could she have been watching from somewhere? Robbie logged onto her computer and went straight to Facebook. First she looked for a message from Kate Brooks. Nothing.

Then Robbie searched for Joanne Sparks. She was annoyed with herself for not having thought of this earlier. And there she was. Although the photo was different from the one on the police flyer, Robbie recognized the young, narrow face. Joanne was smiling, hugging a horse. Happy. Alive. Unlike Kate Brooks, Joanne had not blocked her profile. Just what Robbie had been hoping for.

She looked for messages on Joanne's Facebook wall. Somehow, Joanne's friends had already gotten the news of her death and set up a group to share their grief.

> *Oh no. This can't be real... I love you Joanne...*
> *You can't really be gone... you'll always be in my heart...*

Robbie scrolled down the recent comments, hoping but not really expecting one from Kate Brooks, and finding none.

She went to Joanne's photo albums, feeling a deep ache as she clicked through them. Joanne with the cheerleading squad. Joanne riding a tall dappled horse bareback, Joanne with her friends. And there was what Robbie had been looking for—a pretty blue-eyed girl with long dark hair—laughing with Joanne in photo after photo. Robbie held the cursor over one of the images. "Kate Brooks," it said.

Robbie began going through the comments and photos more slowly, scrutinizing them for something that might provide a clue as to where Joanne and Kate had gone when they'd separated from the rest of their group last Friday. She scanned the comments written over a week ago on Joanne's wall. There was the familiar arrowhead picture, the one Kate Brooks used for her own profile.

South Beach here we come. Woo-woo! Kate had written. Then something more cryptic. *We'll return broken, but fixed.*

There was a knock on the door. Not Brett's knock, but the same tentative tap Robbie had heard three days ago. Her stomach twisted. So he'd come to see her after all.

She looked out the kitchen window. Her father was pacing. Then he perched on the catwalk railing and tapped his foot impatiently. He wore cordovan penny loafers, just like she remembered from her childhood. He used to let her put the pennies in when he got a new pair.

Robbie opened the door.

His gray hair was disheveled and there were large perspiration stains on his white shirt. He moistened his lips with his tongue before he spoke. "Hello, Roberta. Can we talk for just a minute?"

"Sure." She leaned against the open door so he could pass.

He seemed surprised that she was offering her apartment. "Thank you."

She gestured toward the small oak table in the kitchen.

He sat down on one of the two chairs and took in the mother and daughter salt and pepper shakers on the table, the undersized stove and sink, and the toaster oven, butcher block with assorted knives, and coffee maker that sat on the white countertop.

"Would you like coffee or some water?" Robbie asked.

"Water would be great."

She handed him a bottle from the refrigerator.

"Thanks." He took a long swallow.

"I saw you at the creek," Robbie said.

"I figured. I saw you talking to that detective."

"Judy Lieber."

"That's right. Lieber." He picked up the mother and daughter shakers and tapped their ceramic heads together lightly.

"She told me you'd gone to the creek with Joanne's parents. That you were a big comfort to them."

"I've known Joanne all her life," he said, putting the shakers down on the table. "She and Kaitlin were best friends."

"I'm sorry." Robbie pulled out the other chair and sat down across from him.

"I wish I knew what to do," he said. "Where to look for her. I've checked all the local hospitals and she's not at any of them. If only I could be sure she's all right." He took another gulp of water. His face was pale. "I'm very angry with the police. I said some insulting things to that detective. I hope she doesn't hold that against Kaitlin."

"I'm sure she won't. Detective Lieber understands you're upset."

"But why aren't they doing more to find her?" He put his head in his hands.

She thought about the night so many years ago at the river. How sad he was. *Come give your old man a hug,* he'd said. She wanted to touch his shoulder now, but held back. "I think when they get the medical examiner's report, they'll at least have something to go on."

He lifted his head. "You're right, of course. I'm just so damn worried."

"Of course you are."

He twisted his wedding ring around his finger.

It occurred to Robbie for the first time that maybe he hadn't come down to Miami by himself. That Kate's mother was probably here with him. And the idea left her cold.

"You have to understand," he said. "Kaitlin was my second chance."

"Second chance for what?" she asked, tensing.

"Being a father. And now, what if I've lost her, too?"

But you haven't lost me, Robbie wanted to scream. I'm right here. Instead, she said, "I've been trying to figure out what the girls were planning. Why they left the rest of their group."

"You've been talking to Kaitlin's friends?"

"No. I went on Facebook." She touched the laptop screen. "I was able to get on Joanne's page."

"You can do that? Kaitlin's always on her computer, but I never made much sense out of what she was doing."

"She goes by Kate, doesn't she?"

His blue eyes widened.

"It said 'Kate' on the Missing flyer."

He nodded. "That's right. Her friends call her Kate, but she'll always be my little Kaitlin to me."

Robbie felt another stab.

"Have you found anything?" he asked. "Anything helpful about Kaitlin?"

"I'm not sure. Kids are usually a little cryptic in their messages to each other."

"I suppose. But Kaitlin's always been very direct with me. I'd know if she had been planning something. That's why I'm so worried.

I tried to explain that to the police. She must be in trouble, or she would have called me."

"You're sure?"

"Of course. I'm her father."

She couldn't express the anger she felt at his words. His certainty about this daughter of his; that she would go to him if she was in trouble. "Kate wrote to Joanne last week on Facebook," Robbie said. "I think it had something to do with what they were planning while they were down here. She turned the laptop back toward him and pointed.

He read, "We'll return broken, but fixed." He shook his head. "I don't know what that means."

"I guess you don't know her as well as you thought."

He folded his fingers and looked down at them. "I suppose not."

She wanted to stop the meanness, but things were still mixed up in her head. "What about her mother?" Robbie said. "How's their relationship?"

"Kaitlin's mother died six years ago when Kaitlin was twelve." Robbie stared at him.

"You wouldn't have known that. She was killed in a car accident. Her fault. She'd been drinking. She had…she had a problem with alcohol."

Poor Kate. Robbie thought about the five years of sickness her own mother went through after she was diagnosed with breast cancer. She had died when Robbie was eighteen, but at least Robbie had had her mother as she entered womanhood. But Kate would have had no one but her father to help her through those difficult years. "I'm sorry," Robbie said.

"Both my girls have had a tough time," he said. "Both lost their mothers."

But one had a father, at least.

He seemed to read the unspoken words in her eyes. He slowly pushed the chair back and stood. "This is difficult for me, Robbie. All of it. Losing Kaitlin, finding you. I'm sorry I keep coming back here and burdening you."

He stepped out of the kitchen, but paused at the sight of the living room tables covered with beads and feathers. "You make jewelry," he said.

He went over to one of the tables and picked up a beaded necklace. "Pocahontas," he said, then put the necklace down. "You're my little Pocahontas."

The words echoed in her mind. She watched him go to the door. He glanced back, and his bloodshot eyes were begging her for something. But she couldn't speak.

So he turned away, closing the door behind him.

Robbie picked up the necklace. *You're my little Pocahontas*, he'd said. Just like he used to when he tucked her into bed.

Chapter 12

Jeremy leaned against the railing at the edge of the bay. Behind him loomed the SOBE Grande, three magnificent, mostly glass buildings with balconies and amazing views. He and Robbie had moved into the north tower when they returned from the trip he'd honestly believed would crystallize everything for him. So why was he feeling even more uncertain about his future than ever?

A few boats were moored at the dock reserved for residents. The boats bobbed in the choppy water. This was where he came when he was hurting. It had been over a year since his parents had been killed, but some days the sense of loss was so strong he found it hard to breathe. So he'd come out here to feel the breeze against his face and try to remember the good times. His mom, dad, sister—the four of them out fishing, then barbequing on one of the nameless islands in the bay. His mom reading a book under the umbrella his dad set up in the sand. Jeremy, Elise, and their dad diving for pennies beside the anchored boat.

The memories. That was the main reason he had pressured Robbie to rent an apartment here. The studio was expensive and too small for them, but it was on the bay, and that was all Jeremy needed. Robbie had hated living at the SOBE Grande with its two swimming pools, volleyball court, and boat marina. It was too big, too plastic, too full of people they had nothing in common with. She called it Spoiled-Obnoxious-Brat Eden. And Jeremy had loved the acronym.

Laughed about it with her, because he agreed. That was exactly what the SOBE Grande was.

But it wasn't long after they moved here that Robbie began acting weird. Said that maybe he wasn't ready for a commitment. And while it was true that after years of being in loner mode, he was practically mainlining the social scene, Jeremy didn't understand why he and Robbie couldn't have both—friends and each other.

Now he was beginning to wonder if she'd ended their relationship because she was worried that he was going to leave her. Just like her father had done.

He wanted to see her, talk to her. He'd heard the news about that girl—her half sister's friend being found dead yesterday—but he hadn't called her. He figured if Robbie wanted to lean on him, she would call. And she hadn't. Maybe his theory about the reason for their breakup was bullshit and the truth was she'd grown tired of Jeremy. Or maybe she was leaning on Brett Chandler now. Whatever. The fact was Jeremy was here and Robbie was somewhere else. And that's the way it was going to be.

Jeremy rested his elbows on the railing. The downtown Miami skyline was directly across the water. The early afternoon sun glinted off the towering office buildings, condos, and cranes perched on the rooftops of construction-in-progress.

His phone buzzed, surprising him. Lately he'd gotten into the habit of deliberately "forgetting" his phone at home, tired of the endless calls and messages about things he didn't care about. But he had his phone with him now, just in case Robbie was trying to reach him.

But it wasn't Robbie. He read the text message from Ben. *Pregame at my place, then BURN.*

OK, Jeremy wrote back, wondering why he no longer felt excited by the prospect of the club scene and partying with his friends.

Behind him, near the pool, came the sound of metal scraping

against concrete. Someone moving a lounge chair to maximize exposure to the sun. Twittering laughter. Cigarette smoke. Coconut oil. The girls were down. The SOBE Grande attracted all types. The rich girls, living on allowances from daddy. The working girls, who crammed three or four to an apartment to stretch their earnings as waitresses and salesgirls, while they waited for a break in modeling. And the club girls, who partied all night and slept much of the day. They clustered around the pool with their own kind, stretched out on lounge chairs. He could usually pick out the club girls. They were the ones who sunbathed topless.

A butterfly, Robbie had called him. "You're still a butterfly," she'd said, "picking up the dew from all the pretty flowers. Not ready to settle for one." And she was right. Or was she?

A blonde girl in a white bikini was standing near the railing a short distance from him. She hugged herself like she was cold as she looked out at the water. He'd never seen her before, but something about her was familiar—the gentle slope of her shoulders, the way her back swayed down into a perfect rounded butt. A lot like Robbie. And yet, very different from Robbie. This girl seemed vulnerable, as though she didn't quite know what she was doing here. Jeremy was tempted to rush to her side and rescue her, but he resisted the impulse. He'd learned his lesson last year about going after needy, wounded girls when he'd gotten involved with his father's graduate assistant. And look how that had ended.

A boat went by, kicking up a large wake and making lots of noise. The blonde girl tensed like a cornered cat. She looked like she was either going to run away or jump over the rail into the water.

Screw past lessons, he thought, crossing the pool deck toward her.

"It's just Marine Patrol," he said, when he was beside her.

"Huh?"

"The boat that went by," Jeremy said. "Sometimes they like to exercise the engines."

"Oh." The girl stood slightly pigeon-toed, as though in a trance. She had straight, shoulder-length, white-blonde hair with long bangs that covered the tops of her oversized sunglasses. Her lips were so full they seemed about to burst.

"I'm Jeremy," he said.

She turned back to the water. There was a tattoo he couldn't quite make out near the base of her spine. She might have been blowing him off, but he didn't think so. Her jaw quivered. She couldn't be cold; was she going to cry? He realized how young she was. Probably his sister's age—Elise was almost eighteen. She'd be graduating soon, then going off to college. When was the last time he'd visited her and their grandfather? A couple of weeks? No. It had to be longer. It made him feel like a real shit. And this girl? What was her story? She looked awfully unhappy.

"Are you from around here?" he asked.

No answer. Her fingers tightened around the railing. No rings. No jewelry. Most of the girls around here wore something.

He took a cautious step closer like he might do with an injured, frightened animal. "Listen," he said, "if you want to get out of—"

"How ya doin,' Muscleman?" The female voice—deep and rich as fudge—came from behind them. Tyra was a regular at the club scene and Jeremy often saw her at BURN. Her wild bronze hair was tucked into an African-print scarf, gold hoop earrings dangling. She was tall and painfully skinny with her naked breasts the size of cantaloupes, and she gave off a spicy smell that made his throat contract. She was completely at ease as her large brown nipples taunted Jeremy. He guessed Tyra was in her thirties, though she played at being much younger. She put her long dark arm around the blonde. He never could figure out whether Tyra was deeply tanned or if that was the natural color of her skin. Tyra whispered something to the blonde, and the girl's body went slack.

Was the blonde a club girl too?

Tyra smiled at Jeremy, stained teeth that wouldn't be noticeable in the fake, glittering club lights. She reached over and ran her long fingers up and down his arm. "Mmmm, nice. I need you to personally train me sometime, Muscleman."

"My pleasure. Sixty an hour."

"Oooo, only sixty?" She fluttered her lashes over eyes too green to be natural. "Don't sell yourself so cheap, baby. If you've got something worth selling, you can name your price."

"Okay, for you a hundred."

She threw back her head and let out a low guttural laugh. The sunlight glinted off her hoop earrings.

The blonde girl remained motionless, as though in a daze.

Tyra stopped laughing. "So, Muscles, you comin' out to BURN tomorrow? Friday's always hot. "

"Probably. What about you and your friend?"

"Why don't you see for yourself?" Tyra tightened her arm around the blonde and guided her toward the lounge chairs. "Come on, angel, you need to get some sun. Your tan's just about faded."

"Hey," Jeremy called after the blonde, "what's your name?"

The blonde looked confused.

"This is my friend, Angel," Tyra said. "She'll be stayin' with me for a while."

"If you ever want to hang out," Jeremy said to Angel.

"She won't." Tyra said. "Angel's a busy girl."

"I'm in apartment eight twenty," he finished.

Tyra shook out a large white towel and spread it over the lounge. She reached over and unfastened the back of Angel's bikini top. The girl's breasts fell out, bouncy, white and conspicuously natural.

Angel's hands flew up to cover herself, but then she let them drop to her sides.

"You can come by anytime," Jeremy said, giving her a small smile that he hoped wouldn't scare her away. "Eight twenty."

Angel pushed her sunglasses up in her blonde hair and glanced back at Jeremy.

His smile fell off when he saw her eyes. They were the color of slate—deep and hard and empty.

Chapter 13

It was starting to feel like a conspiracy. Everything that could possibly go wrong, was.

Wednesday and Thursday nights were turning into a sleepless marathon for Robbie. One of the bartenders was sick and another had quit, leaving Leonard begging Robbie to cover their shifts, in addition to her own. She worked on Wednesday from eleven p.m. until four the next morning. Then today, she was assigned overlapping shifts starting at four in the afternoon that would run twelve hours straight through Friday morning.

The boater guy, Puck, had been in the bar Wednesday and was back again tonight. His Bud N' Mary cap shadowed his eyes and black-rimmed glasses as he sipped his beer. She was aware of Puck glancing at her from time to time, but his interest felt benign, almost like a father watching over his daughter.

Robbie served drinks in a zombielike daze, thinking about her sister, wondering what else she could do to find her. She was surprised to see Maddy come in wearing leather shorts, heels, and a tank top. Maddy slipped in behind the bar, waved to Robbie, and began taking drink orders. She looked at least ten years older than when Robbie had seen her at the beach with her young son. Maddy's blonde hair was pulled up in a messy ponytail and thick eye shadow and false eyelashes enlarged her hazel eyes.

"You first," Robbie said, as they both reached for a bottle of vodka.

"Thanks." Maddy poured sloppy shots into a couple of glasses, then handed the bottle to Robbie.

"This going to be your regular shift?" Robbie asked.

"Hope so," Maddy said.

"How's your little boy doing?"

"Good." Maddy topped off the drinks with grapefruit juice and returned to her customers.

Robbie wondered who was taking care of Maddy's son tonight.

She remembered when she and her mom first moved to Boston, occasionally one of her aunts would come into the city from the suburbs to watch Robbie if her mom was working late at the department store. But there were often arguments between Robbie's mom and her sisters. And the aunts stopped coming. Instead, young women from one of the colleges would babysit for Robbie. Rarely the same one twice. But once there was a babysitter who came week after week, and Robbie adored her. Her name was Lauren. She wore wire-rimmed glasses and her front teeth stuck out too far, but she was fun and loved to teach Robbie math games. Lauren was studying to be a CPA. Then in June, she brought Robbie a present. A calculator. Robbie thought it was the coolest gift ever, until she realized it was a going away present. Lauren graduated and Robbie never saw her again. After Lauren, Robbie never bothered learning the other babysitters' names. They rarely came back more than twice.

Robbie poured cranberry juice into the glass, then started on a martini. Maddy returned for the vodka. She was fast but imprecise as she mixed the drinks and a couple of times she got the ingredients wrong. Although it bothered Robbie, she forced herself to overlook it. Maddy needed this job.

"This woman who lives next to us watches him," Maddy said, as though she'd read Robbie's mind. "Eric likes her and she works for practically nothing."

"What's her name?" Robbie asked.

"Huh?"

"Nothing. Never mind." Robbie brought the drinks to her customers.

A large group came in and Robbie and Maddy worked side by side.

"The guy with the cap—he your boyfriend?" Maddy asked, as she put a drink down on the bar.

"What?" Robbie turned and realized Maddy was referring to Puck. He looked away when she caught his eye.

"No," Robbie said.

"Oh."

"Why?"

"I don't know. He's like been watching you the whole time."

"Really?"

"Not in a weird way, or anything, that's why I figured he was your boyfriend." Maddy overfilled a martini glass, ignoring the spillage on the bar. "He's kind of cute."

"Nope. Not a boyfriend. Just a customer."

But Robbie felt a little spooked. Maybe Puck's coming here every night wasn't all that benign. She went over to him. "Everything okay?"

"I wouldn't mind another Heineken." Puck smiled. Friendly, not crazy.

Robbie relaxed. "Sure."

She brought him the beer.

"I was watching you work," he said. "You're good."

"Thanks." The door opened and more people swarmed in. "Sorry," she said. "Excuse me."

Even with Maddy beside her, the pace became frenzied as the bar filled to capacity. Robbie focused on filling drink orders, but she could tell that Maddy was overwhelmed. Eventually Maddy let Robbie fix anything more complicated than a rum and coke or vodka and soda.

Maddy went home at two, but Robbie hardly missed her.

At a little before four, Robbie closed out her register, while the lumberjack-sized security guard went around telling the few remaining customers it was closing time. Puck sat alone at the bar finishing his Heineken.

"Well good night," Robbie said, waving to Puck.

"Night," he said.

Robbie stepped outside, taking deep breaths of the warm early morning air, clearing her lungs of stale cigarette smoke. She'd go straight home, take a quick shower, climb into bed, and sleep until the afternoon.

She noticed the homeless woman who always watched her bike was passed out on her bench, an empty bottle of vodka beside her. Poor Zelda. She'd been so proud of staying off alcohol and drugs. Maybe things had gotten too much for her.

Robbie went to unlock her bicycle, immediately noticing something was wrong. The tires were flat. Both of them. How was that possible? She bent over to see better. Slashed. She kicked the bicycle frame in rage. "Oooooo." She pulled at her hair. "Ooooo."

"What's happened?" Puck asked, hurrying toward her from the door of the bar.

She pointed at the bike.

Puck got down on his knees and examined the tires. "Looks like they were slashed with a knife."

"Why would someone do something so hurtful?" Robbie said. "I understand stealing a bike for profit, but vandalizing it? Who gains from such a thing?"

Puck shook his head. He looked miserable, as though it had happened to him. "Do you want to call the cops?"

"What can they do? I've already had two bicycles stolen. They'll probably tell me to be grateful that they left my bike this time."

Puck stood up slowly. He took his cap off, smoothed his hand over his bald pate as though he still had hair, then stuffed the cap into his back pocket. "May I give you a ride home?"

Robbie's antennae shot up. "I thought you didn't have a car."

"I decided to rent one."

Puck was probably a perfectly nice guy, but he was still a stranger. "Thanks, but I can call a cab."

Instead of getting insulted, he nodded. "Good. You shouldn't let men you meet at the bar know where you live."

"It's nothing personal."

"I understand. Really. I'd be more concerned if you accepted a ride from me." He ran the open palm of his hand over the handlebar. "But would you allow me to take your bike and get the tires fixed?"

"Thank you. That's very sweet, but I'll manage."

"How? Do you have any means of conveying it?"

"I, I don't know, but I'll figure out something." Robbie felt drained suddenly—a missing sister, three shifts of work and lack of sleep catching up with her. She just wanted to go home and not have to deal with any of this.

"Let me do this for you, Robbie. Please."

What harm? "Well, thank you, Puck." She unlocked both locks and disengaged them from the bike. "I don't know what to say. I really appreciate this."

"It's my pleasure." He smiled like a kid whose parents have agreed to let him stay up past his bedtime. "My car's just over there. I'll pull it over."

Robbie phoned for a taxi as she watched him run across the street and climb into a large black SUV. He backed the car up, got out, then hoisted the bike easily into the rear compartment. He was much stronger than he looked.

"I'll bring it to the lounge tomorrow after I get it fixed," he said, as he slammed the rear door shut. "Is that okay?"

"That's great. Thank you."

They stood in silence, waiting for the taxi. Occasionally, she heard the sound of car wheels on pavement swishing by in the distance. A couple of cars drove slowly down the street. Neither of them the taxi.

Puck had taken his cap out of his back pocket and was wringing it, reminding her of a teenager on a first date.

Why was he doing this for her? But Robbie was too tired to analyze. She just wanted to get into bed and let these last few days be over. The taxi arrived a few minutes later. Robbie said goodbye and climbed in.

Puck stepped into the street in his clumsy sweatshirt and baggy pants watching her go.

Robbie leaned against the backseat of the taxi, the bar lock and chain in her lap. Puck was just a nice guy, she decided. A genuinely nice guy.

How strange that seemed. But how reassuring to know that in a world where shitty things happened, there were still people who cared.

Chapter 14

On Friday, at one in the afternoon, annoying beeping sounds woke Robbie up. She reached for her phone. Text message from Leonard. *Someone brought your bike here. The lounge is not a goddamn storage facility.*

And there was a voice mail from Detective Lieber. Robbie held her breath as she listened. But Lieber was only calling to see if Robbie could meet her and Robbie's father at three p.m. at Monty's Raw Bar to discuss the medical examiner's report.

Robbie called Lieber back, left a message that she'd be there, then took a taxi over to the lounge to retrieve her bike.

Leonard had locked the bike in the office before he left for the afternoon. At first, Robbie thought it was someone else's. It had two new tires and someone had polished it so it looked like it came out of a showroom. She couldn't believe that Puck had gone to so much trouble for her.

She got to Monty's Raw Bar by the Miami Beach Marina a little before three. The Friday after-lunch crowd at the outdoor restaurant was thin—a few boaters, some locals in cutoffs and flip-flops, and a table of men in rolled-up shirtsleeves with ties loosened around their necks, as though they'd decided to make a day of this.

She sat down at a picnic-style table beneath the overhang. The downtown Miami skyline was in a haze on the other side of the broad bay. The view was not that different from the apartment she used to share with Jeremy. But of course, it would be about the same—the SOBE Grande was only a few blocks north of here. She wondered what Jeremy was doing. He hadn't called since they'd met near the pier on Monday, four days ago.

Four days. Well, he had made a life for himself—just like she'd asked him to—so what did she expect?

"Can I get you something?" asked a waitress in a T-shirt and shorts.

Robbie glanced back into the restaurant, then along the outside path beside the bay that ran from the parking garage. No sign of her father or Detective Lieber.

"A diet Coke with lemon, I guess," Robbie said. The waitress nodded and went to the table with the guys in ties.

Lieber had mentioned in the voice mail that it was Robbie's father's idea that Robbie join them. That surprised Robbie, especially after their awkward parting at her apartment two days ago. She'd seen him on the TV news making a plea to whoever knew the where-abouts of his daughter, Kaitlin, to please get in touch with the police or call him directly. He'd even given his cell phone number.

"Please send my daughter home to me safe and sound," he'd said, his drawn face grotesquely large on the TV that was perched on the dresser in Robbie's bedroom. "And Kaitlin, honey. Remember that I love you."

The waitress put the soda on the table with a straw and menu.

Robbie pulled the paper off the straw and took a sip of her drink. She squinted into the sun. A man in a billed cap was walking toward the marina carrying a bucket, probably with live bait. She remembered that this was where Puck had his boat docked. She strained to see if the man was Puck, but he was moving too quickly for her to tell.

Someone came up to the front of her table, blocking the sun and her view.

"Hello, Roberta," her father said. He must have come up from the path on the right. He was wearing a light blue polo shirt that was a size too large for him and had new-shirt creases. She guessed that he'd run out of clothes from home and had bought some new ones. "Mind if I sit down?"

"Of course not."

He slid onto the bench opposite her. She was still taken aback by his face, expecting something else. She tried to picture him holding her small hand in his large one, leaning across her bed to kiss her good night. But she no longer had a clear recollection of what he had looked like when she was a child.

The guys in ties were laughing too loudly.

"I saw you on the news," Robbie said.

Her father ran his tongue over his dry lips. "No response yet."

"I figured or you would have called me."

He picked up the paper from her straw and rolled it between his fingers.

"It was good what you did," Robbie said. "If Kate saw it, she'd be happy to know how much you love her."

He squeezed his eyes shut and covered them with his hand. Then, he took his hand away and gave her a small smile. "Thank you for saying that."

Lieber came up the outside steps, noticed them, and took a seat on the bench next to Robbie's father. She put her battered leather case down on the table. "Sorry to keep you waiting." She was wearing an outdated pantsuit with shoulder pads and a sheen to the fabric from too many dry cleanings.

The waitress left a pitcher of beer with the guys in ties, then came over to take their orders.

"Just coffee." Lieber's brown eyes seemed more recessed and shadowed than the other day. "Black."

The waitress looked at Robbie's dad and waited.

"Oh, I'm sorry." He glanced at Robbie's Coke. "I'll have one of those. Thank you."

"I appreciate you both meeting me." Lieber reached into the leather case and pulled out some papers. There was an unfamiliar formality in Lieber's manner that Robbie attributed to her father's presence. "As I mentioned on the phone, Dr. Brooks, I have a few questions for you. I also want to go over some things in the medical examiner's report. I've already discussed this with Joanne's parents. They know we're talking. They're willing to do anything that might shed light on what happened to their daughter."

Robbie's father sat a little straighter, his lips pressed together in a tight line.

"Apparently Joanne's father knows the right people," Lieber said. "He was able to persuade them to get us the results of the toxicology report in forty-eight hours. It can sometimes take several weeks."

"Several weeks while my daughter goes missing? That's outrageous and inept."

"Well, it's certainly frustrating when that happens. But since we were lucky enough to get the report on a timely basis, how about us reviewing the findings instead of making accusations?"

Robbie's father flushed and looked away from Lieber.

"There are several items of particular note in the ME's report that I want to share with you." Lieber flipped through the papers in front of her. "First, the medical examiner found water in Joanne's lungs."

"So she did drown," Robbie's father said.

"Yes, Dr. Brooks." Lieber folded her hands and brought them up to her chin. "Except there's one problem. The water in her lungs was not seawater. It was chlorinated. That suggests she drowned in a swimming pool and was later taken to Indian Creek."

"I don't understand," he said.

Robbie felt a rising nausea. She thought about the crowd gathered around the creek, the divers searching for a second body. "So it wasn't accidental," Robbie said. "Someone dumped her in the creek."

"Actually," Lieber said, "it's possible she drowned accidentally and someone panicked and brought her body to the creek."

"But this changes everything," Robbie said. "Someone is covering up something."

"If I may continue," Lieber said, "there are a few other things I would like to tell you about. The medical examiner also found indications of a physical struggle and sexual activity." Lieber lowered her eyes. "There's evidence that Joanne had been a virgin."

Robbie's father was squeezing his hands together and his fingertips were white. "She was raped?"

"It's a decided possibility."

Robbie thought about the photo of the smiling girl hugging her horse. And now, what did this mean for Kate?

Lieber was flipping through the report. She looked up. "The third item of note was that a powerful sedative was found in Joanne's body fluids. Flunitrazepam is usually sold as Rohypnol and known on the street as 'roofies.'"

"'Roofies' are a date rape drug." Robbie's mind rushed forward to the possibilities. She thought about the bars and the club scene, the naïve underage kids who dressed up to appear older. "But I don't get it," Robbie said. "Let's say Joanne had gone out partying and accepted a drink from the wrong person. I don't understand how she could have drowned in a swimming pool, or why she would have been dumped in the creek."

"That's what we're trying to figure out," Lieber said.

The waitress put the coffee and Coke down on the table. "Anything else?"

Robbie's father waved her off, focused on Lieber. "But what about Kaitlin? What about my daughter? What are you doing to find her? To make sure she's safe?"

"First of all," Lieber said, "we don't know for certain that the two girls were together."

"You don't know? Then where is she? Where's my daughter?"

"Please, Dr. Brooks. We're working on that. And if you could clear up a few details, that might help our investigation."

He squeezed the edge of the picnic table with both hands. Robbie sensed that he was having a tough time maintaining his composure.

"Joanne's parents said the girls drove down from Deland in Joanne's Volvo. Can you confirm that?"

He nodded. "Kaitlin's car was still in the driveway at home when I left to come down here Sunday morning."

Lieber wrote something in her small notebook. "Okay. At least we know there's only one car involved."

"Have you found it?" Robbie asked, surprised by how raw her own voice sounded. "Have you found Joanne's car?"

Lieber shook her head. "We've also checked credit card charges for both Joanne and Kaitlin, but haven't found anything since last Thursday when Joanne bought gas on Miami Beach with her credit card and Kaitlin bought some clothes at the South Beach Urban Outfitters on her card on Friday morning."

Urban Outfitters. There was something so personal about that. Robbie liked to shop there too. And once again, the connection hit her. Her sister, not some disembodied name, was missing. Her sister, Kate. And she had very likely been raped and—what?

"We've been interviewing people at all the clubs to see if anyone remembers Joanne or Kaitlin," Lieber said. "So far, we're coming up empty-handed."

"What do you think happened to Kate?" Robbie asked.

"Assuming she was with Joanne, there's a good chance that she may have gone through . . ." she hesitated, "through the same experience as Joanne."

"But it's been two days since Joanne was found," Robbie said. "Wouldn't Kate's b—" She glanced at her father and started over. "Wouldn't you have found Kate by now?"

"Not necessarily. The creek connects to the bay."

The unspoken implication hung over them. Robbie looked out toward the broad expanse of water. If Kate's body washed out to sea, she might never be found.

Robbie's father spoke finally. "You're talking like you've already written my daughter off."

"That's not true, Dr. Brooks."

"Why aren't the police doing more?"

"We're doing everything possible."

"Everything possible? My daughter may have been drugged and raped and is very likely now being held captive." He ran his fingers through his gray hair with a quick, nervous motion. "Why haven't you called in the FBI? Why aren't you going door-to-door to find her?"

"I know how upset you must be. But we're looking into every angle. House parties the girls may have attended. Other victims."

"Flunitrazepam is known to induce anterograde amnesia," her father said. "Kaitlin may have no recollection of an abduction or rape. She may be wandering about lost."

Lieber sighed, shaking her head ever so slightly. "The drug would probably only block her memory of that specific incident," Lieber said. "If she is out and about, why hasn't she contacted anyone?"

A shrill whistle came from the table with the men in ties. They were looking out toward the bay front path. An attractive woman in a bikini was rollerblading behind a stroller with an infant. She ignored the ogling men.

"Let me ask you something else, Dr. Brooks," Lieber said. "Did Kaitlin give you any indication that she had plans to leave her group of friends on South Beach?"

"I already told you when you asked me before. No."

"Other than Robbie, does Kaitlin have any friends or relatives in the area that she may have decided to visit?"

"I told you. No." He picked up the flattened straw wrapper and rolled it between his fingers.

"Has Kaitlin ever gone off somewhere without telling you?" Lieber said.

He shook his head, not looking up.

Hoots and banging came from the table with the guys in ties. The waitress went over to them with her pad.

"What if it wasn't rape?" Robbie's words came out haltingly, the idea only half formed. "Or what if it was, but the girls had somehow been complicit, maybe giving their abductor the wrong message. Like they were open to having some fun."

Her father's face turned red.

"What makes you think that?" Lieber said.

"You said Kate and Joanne told their friends they might be going off somewhere and not to worry or call their parents." She didn't look at her father, but she could hear him breathing harder.

"That's right," Lieber said.

"Kate wrote something odd to Joanne on Facebook about their trip to South Beach. 'We'll return broken, but fixed.'"

"I saw that," Lieber said. "Do you have some idea what she meant?"

"I've been thinking about it quite a bit. The girls are—were—

eighteen. They'd be going off to college in the fall. They may have viewed virginity as some kind of social stigma."

"Well, Kaitlin isn't like that," her father said. "She and I discussed it many times. She understood the risks and consequences."

"But she's only a teenager," Robbie said. "Teenagers have their own value systems. And what if part of their spring break plan had been to lose their virginity?"

Her father stood up. "Your sister is missing and probably in serious danger and all you can think of are ways to smear her reputation?"

"But don't you see?" Robbie said. "If I'm right, there's a good chance Kate is alive."

"So what are you saying?" The vein in his forehead pulsed. "That Kaitlin and her friend took drugs and got themselves laid? Then how did Joanne end up dead in the creek? And why hasn't Kaitlin come to me or the police?"

"I don't know," Robbie said. "Maybe she instigated the plan and feels responsible for what happened to Joanne. Or guilty. How the heck am I supposed to know what's going through her head? I've never met her. I just know how eighteen-year-old girls sometimes think. And believe it or not, they're not always rational."

"Well Kaitlin is rational. And she doesn't think like you. Thank God for that."

And then he was down the steps, down the path, and gone.

The men in ties started banging and cheering.

Chapter 15

After saying goodbye to Lieber at Monty's, Robbie biked home in a fury. How dare her father treat her like she was the enemy? First he asks for her help, then he attacks her.

His words stung. They stung a lot.

Well Kaitlin is rational. And she doesn't think like you. Thank God for that.

She wished she could just get on with her life and forget this man. But Robbie was determined to find Kate.

According to Lieber, it was likely that Joanne had been date-raped. If Robbie was right about the girls' plan to lose their virginity, where would they have gone? The best-known club on Miami Beach was BURN. Robbie could almost see how it would have played out. Kate and Joanne, a couple of naïve out-of-town teenagers, reading all about BURN and the club scene in magazines. Figuring out outfits to wear to make themselves look older. Maybe paying someone to make them fake IDs. She thought about the girls she'd seen in their party clothes, conked out at the police station.

When Robbie got back to her apartment, she called Brett. BURN was one of his favorite hangouts, but she'd always resisted going there. It didn't require much arm-twisting to persuade him to take her tonight.

Just before two a.m., they pulled up to the valet beneath the overhang at the elegant Côte d'Azur Hotel, one of the Miami Beach grand dames from the 1950s, which housed BURN.

Brett had insisted they arrive when things were already under-way, but after working the last few nights, Robbie yawned as they got out of Brett's BMW. Brett was wearing a black T-shirt, white blazer, and red suede shoes. The silver buckle on his belt was prominent against his tight black jeans. Robbie had concocted an outfit for herself, since she didn't have club clothes in her wardrobe. With her highest heels, she wore a sleeveless black, low-cut T-shirt, which actually worked as a dress. A very short dress. She accessorized it with a beaded belt and wore dangling earrings with beads and feathers. She knew that even with her connected boyfriend, it didn't hurt to look "hot" if they wanted to avoid standing in line for an hour or so.

They went past a ragged, disorganized line of young people that snaked through the hotel lobby, waiting to get into the club. The girls were a blur of long hair, big eyes, and lots of skin. Robbie slowed and looked into their faces. Beneath the heavy makeup, she guessed some were well under twenty-one and using fake IDs. Could Kate be in this crowd? Her father didn't believe so. In fact, he was adamant that his younger daughter was made of higher moral fiber than that. But Robbie wasn't so sure.

She pictured Kate growing up motherless in Deland, a back-water town, with her dad. What kind of father was he? Was he lov-ing? Caring? She imagined he was, but Robbie could also see him as overprotective and controlling. Maybe a little oblivious. After all, he didn't seem to fully grasp the pain he'd caused his firstborn; why then should he be aware of how his behavior could be affecting his younger daughter?

Robbie glanced around at the deco curves of the lobby, the ad-jacent bar with its blue fluorescent flooring, the wall of windows that overlooked the pool and ocean. Above the rounded sofas and '50's-style chairs hung massive chandeliers.

"Pretty cool, isn't it?" Brett said, as though he was personally responsible.

"They did a good job retaining its authenticity."

"They spent enough for it." It was widely known that investors had invested over half a billion dollars on the transformation of the Côte d'Azur into the ultimate luxury destination.

They continued to the right of the lobby. So many girls! Dozens and dozens. Robbie searched their faces, hoping to see someone who resembled Kate. They all did, and none of them did.

"Are you looking for someone?" Brett asked.

She still hadn't shared her sister's disappearance with Brett. Every time she thought about telling him, he was distracted by his BlackBerry. And now, she just didn't have the energy to get into the whole thing. "Nope. Just looking."

"These chicks have nothing on you." He gave her a wide grin like a six-year-old. "I can't believe you finally agreed to come here with me. You're going to love it."

"I'm sure," Robbie said, not sure at all.

The marble steps to the club were guarded by a pair of large, muscled men. They weren't allowing anyone who was standing in line to pass, but rather ushered in a couple of older men with several tall, stunning young women hanging on them.

Brett approached one of the bouncers, a guy with a shaved head and tattoos covering both of his arms. "Hey, man. What's up?" They pounded each other's fists. Brett led Robbie up the steps, nodded at a frazzled brunette with a clipboard, then greeted two more men who were checking IDs by the door.

Brett waved at them like they knew him, and held open the door for Robbie.

The smoky vestibule overlooked a huge multilevel room. Mutating purple and pink lights played against the domed ceiling and then rotated down, spotlighting hundreds of bodies pressed against the bars or gyrating on the dance floor. The noise was almost deafening.

The club was the antithesis of The Garage—it smacked of decadence, with rows of large booths on the upstairs level, white sofas arranged in groupings down below. Glittering people were everywhere, like glowing algae at the bottom of the sea. There was an elaborate soundstage on the dance floor and a DJ manipulating the electronics with the dexterity of a brain surgeon.

Robbie stayed close behind Brett as he pushed through a throng of people to a table near the back of the balcony, which overlooked the dance stage and downstairs bars. She recognized Brett's boss, Mike, in his white guayabera shirt, his thin orangey hair pulled back in a ponytail. Mike was ensconced on a sofa between two gorgeous women. A good-looking guy with dark hair, thick eyebrows, and a scarred upper lip stood behind the sofa. It looked like he'd had surgery for a cleft palate and the surgeon had done a lousy job. Robbie wondered if he was one of Brett's coworkers. He seemed detached from the scene, until his eyes met Robbie's. Then he scowled, his thick brows merging into one.

"Mister M," Brett shouted above the din. "Look who I brought."

Mike smiled up at Robbie, his tightly stretched skin straining at the effort. "What're you having, sweetie?" He held up a bottle of Grey Goose vodka.

"I got it." Brett took the bottle from Mike. He fixed two vodka and sodas and handed Robbie a glass. She almost objected—what made him assume she'd be drinking what he was having?—but she decided not to make a scene and gave him a thank-you nod.

Mike's booth was filled with older men and girls much younger than they. The men checked Robbie out, their eyes running up and down her skimpy dress and bare legs, making her feel uncomfortably exposed. One of them smiled at her with lots of teeth, reminding Robbie of the wolf in *Little Red Riding Hood*. She turned away.

Brett, Mike, and the good-looking guy with the messed-up lip were involved in conversation.

"I'm going to walk around," Robbie said into Brett's ear.

He gave her an okay signal with his fingers.

She decided to be methodical about her search, first walking the upper level. Then she'd go downstairs and check out the dance floor, the bars, and the people at the private tables. She pushed past people gesturing too broadly, and scrutinized the faces of girls who could have been Kate—the ones who were the right height, with blue eyes, or black hair, or heart-shaped faces. Some smiled back at her, others ignored her. None of them was Kate.

Robbie went down the stairs to the stage, which was guarded by more bouncers. It appeared that only certain people had dancing privileges—maybe the freaks, or the regulars, or perhaps they were hired by the hotel. She didn't care enough to ask Brett about it later. One girl was dressed only in underwear—white lace bra and panties, stockings held up by garters. She danced alone. Around her were small groups of mainly girls, their tongues flicking each other's like snakes. Robbie felt a little sickened by the public display. The idea that her sister could be here seemed less and less likely. Or was it that she was now thinking like her father and wanted to deny the possibility that her sister would be attracted to this scene?

The music pulsed around her, a deep bass rhythm that made her feel like she was experiencing a heart attack. Cigarette and cigar smoke clogged her lungs. Everywhere people were moving, a continuous merry-go-round. To the bar, to the tables, to the stairs, to the bar, to the stage. Her drink felt heavy and wet in her hand. Her too-high heels hurt her feet. She'd never find her sister here. She wanted to go home.

A jowly man in his mid-fifties with short black hair and deep wrinkles above his bushy eyebrows staggered by, held up by two women. He looked familiar to Robbie, as though he could be someone famous or important, but now was so drunk, he probably wouldn't have been able to say his own name. The tall woman was laughing, shaking her large gold hoop earrings, as though having the time of her life. She was painfully skinny with caramel-colored skin. The man's head rested against one of her large breasts like it was a pillow. The other woman was younger and moved like an automaton, seemingly indifferent to the man's hand squeezing her shoulder. She had platinum shoulder-length hair with bangs that partially covered her vacant gray eyes. There was something about her that made Robbie pause. But no—this girl clearly wasn't Kate. The three stumbled up the stairs.

Robbie glanced over at the balcony. Brett was talking to Mike's friends and laughed at something. He must have sensed her looking up at him. He smiled and waved, then went back to his conversation.

She needed to sit down. The sofas were crammed with strangers. No stools at the bar. She started toward the stairs, passing people clustered around tables set up with bottles and mixers.

And then she saw him. They were separated by dozens of people, but it felt like thousands. Jeremy, in a brown T-shirt and dark jeans, stood out like a sapling in a flower garden. He was at a table between the stage and the bar. Robbie recognized the forced smile on his face, the one that didn't reach his eyes. Girls were sitting on each other's laps on the sofas surrounding the table. Guys hovered nearby, smoking, drinking, laughing. She saw Ben and a few of Jeremy's other friends, but they either didn't see or didn't recognize her.

Robbie worked her way through the crowd until she was beside Jeremy. He glanced at her, then looked away. An instant later, he turned back. "Shit Robbie. What are you doing here?"

"I was looking for—" She couldn't hear her own voice above the din.

"One second." Jeremy put his drink on the table, then took Robbie's hand and led her away from the crowd to a secluded corner between the bar and one of the staircases. A side door opened and a janitor came out carrying a mop.

"It's a little quieter here," Jeremy said in an almost normal voice.

"Much better." She took a sip of her drink. It tasted like bitter ice water.

Jeremy was holding back a smile. "I honestly didn't recognize you. Is that makeup you're wearing?"

"Yes, it's makeup. I do wear makeup sometimes."

"Really? Because in the more than a year I've known you, I can't remember one time—"

"It's not that big a deal."

"And the cleavage—where'd that come from?"

"This is a club, Jeremy. I wasn't going to show up looking like some kind of freak in a T-shirt and flip-flops."

He held up his hands. "Hey. I'm not complaining. I'm just surprised. You look great, by the way."

"Thanks." She stirred her drink with her finger. It occurred to her that Jeremy thought she'd come to see him tonight and she got a sinking feeling about disappointing him. "I'm actually here on a mission."

"Oh yeah?" That half smile.

She was making it worse. "I'm looking for my sister."

He sobered. "She's here?"

"I don't know. I thought she might be."

He gestured toward the room. "Talk about searching for a needle in a haystack."

"I know. It was a stupid idea."

He took a step closer to her. She could smell his perspiration beneath cologne. He never used to wear cologne when it was just the two of them. "Did you get some new information about her?" he asked. "Does Lieber think she might be coming here?"

"Not exactly."

"I heard about her friend," he said. "I was going to call you." Flashes of purple and pink from the light show reflected in his dark brown eyes. "Should I have called you?"

She didn't know how to answer him, so she changed the subject. "My father thinks she's been kidnapped and held against her will."

"But you don't?"

She shook her head. Why was she having such a hard time talking to him?

"Is there something I can do?"

"I, I don't know."

"You don't have to go through this alone," he said.

They were so close she could feel the heat from his body. What was happening to her? Why was she drifting toward him?

He lowered his head. So close to her now.

She raised her chin. Their eyes locked.

"There you are." Brett's voice was behind her. Then she felt his fingers tighten on her shoulder.

Jeremy's face hardened.

"Mike was wondering where you went," Brett said to Robbie. She could smell liquor on his breath. "He was going to introduce you to someone."

Robbie wanted to toss his hand off her. She wasn't his territory. She wasn't anyone's territory.

Brett extended his free hand toward Jeremy. "Stroeb, my man. Been a while."

Jeremy shook the hand. He was a couple of inches shorter than Brett, but slightly broader.

"I keep hearing about the new you." Brett tugged on his ear.

"Big change from high school. Word is you're always hanging with the hottest girls."

"Man, I'm flattered." Jeremy looked Brett directly in the eye. And Robbie knew Jeremy was anything but flattered.

"I was just coming upstairs to find you, Brett," Robbie said. "I'm ready to go home."

"Are you kidding? Things are just starting to get good."

"I'll take a taxi. You don't need to drive me."

"Of course I'll drive you."

"Really, Brett. I'm fine."

"I don't know what you're used to." Brett looked Jeremy up and down. "But when I bring MY girl somewhere, I take her home."

Jeremy took a step toward him. "What the hell's that supposed to mean?"

"Take it easy, man," Brett said. "If you've got a problem—"

"Okay," Robbie said, fuming. "That's enough. It's late. I'm out of here. And I'm going by myself."

A couple of bouncers materialized on either side of Brett and Jeremy. How could they possibly have noticed a fight brewing?

"Listen," Brett said to Jeremy. "There's no reason—"

But Jeremy had pushed past the bouncers and was heading back into the crowd.

Robbie took a deep breath of smoky air to calm herself. Why did guys have to be that way? They all thought they owned you.

Brett got in step with her as she went up the stairs. "Sorry," he said. "I guess I had a little too much to drink."

Robbie didn't answer.

Brett glanced up at the table on the balcony. Mike was watching them.

Chapter 16

She opened her eyes and saw only white. Then things came into focus. White pillows. White comforter. A white light brightening the room, hurting her eyes. She remembered, now. Her name was Angel, so she must be in heaven, right?

Not right. She was the Angel of Death, they'd told her. She had killed her friend. They said they'd protect her and not tell anyone. But she had to be good and do what they said.

And so she had. She took the pills they gave her or sniffed up the white powder. And she really didn't mind that part. It filled her head and kept the bad stuff out. The bad stuff that kept trying to push its way in. Joanne clutching her bag. Begging Kate to leave.

Why hadn't she listened?

Joanne face down in the pool, her hair floating all around her head.

The truth made her sick. So sick she could hardly stand it. She'd killed her friend. Her best friend. It was all her fault. She couldn't remember how, but it didn't matter. She knew she was guilty and now this was her life.

She'd never, ever be able to go home again.

Tyra came into the room. Angel could smell her—some spicy perfume that made Angel's throat contract. Tyra pushed the sheer curtains aside, letting in the rest of the light. Angel squeezed her eyes shut. When she opened them, Tyra was sitting on the edge of the bed with a glass of lemon-colored liquid and a pill. Breakfast. Oprah should start telling people about this incredible diet on her show. *Lose as much as ten pounds a week, effortlessly.* Angel couldn't remember the last time she'd eaten food. She couldn't even remember how long she'd been here.

"Here you go, my little Angel," Tyra said. "Drink up."

Tyra's wild bronze hair was loose on her shoulders and she wore a waffled white spa towel that only barely covered her private parts. Her long arms and legs were so skinny, Angel could see the outline of bone and cords of muscle. "Sit up, Angel." Tyra's voice lost its slippery sweetness as she pressed the cold glass against Angel's face.

Angel raised herself up on one elbow and took the glass and pill from Tyra. She should swallow her pill so she wouldn't have to think about things.

Joanne floating. The disgusting men who hurt her and made her do dirty things. But she was in hell and this was her penance.

Tyra smiled. Her teeth were stained. "That's a good girl." In the bright light, she wasn't pretty at all. Her skin was splotched and her shocking green eyes were full of anger. But Tyra was Angel's new best friend. "Practically joined at the hip," Tyra had said when Angel had moved into her apartment.

Angel sipped the sweet drink, pretty sure there was more vodka in it than usual. Her mother used to drink. Sometimes, Kate would come home from school and her mother would be passed out on the sofa or with her head on her arms at the kitchen table. Kate would help her into bed. It made Kate's father very angry that her mother would drink, but he didn't stop her. And then one day she took the car and killed herself.

Angel put the pill in her mouth. Her mother was an alcoholic, her father had explained. She couldn't control herself. She needed help. *So why didn't you help her?* Kate had wanted to scream at him, but never did. What was the point of saying anything to him? Nothing would change. Her mother wasn't coming back. And her father hated Kate more than ever.

Angel pushed the pill under her tongue. If she swallowed it, she'd forget everything.

A bitter taste seeped into her mouth.

She had killed Joanne. Or had she? She couldn't remember because her brain was always fuzzy. And she was getting tired of being fuzzy.

Her mother was always fuzzy.

The pill hurt the soft area under her tongue.

But she wasn't like her mom. She didn't need her dad. She could help herself. First she'd get out of here, and then figure out what to do next.

Angel sipped the drink. She was careful not to swallow the pill, but made sure it looked to Tyra as though she had.

"I have to pee," Angel said, pushing the comforter away and getting out of bed. She glanced down at her nakedness and remembered last night. The ugly man with the jowls and dark bushy eyebrows. Tyra had called him "Tricky Dick." He'd laughed. "You haven't seen any of my tricks yet, honey," he'd said. They made Angel dress up like a little girl. Kneesocks and heels. Short skirt. White blouse, no underwear. "Lick my lollipop," he'd said and Angel had puked all over his disgusting black-haired legs.

The white marble was cold beneath her bare feet. She walked quickly before Tyra stopped her, and sat down on the toilet, holding her drink. Tyra couldn't see her for the moment. Angel poured the drink into the toilet and spit out the pill, flushing the whole mess out of sight.

"You were a bad girl last night," Tyra said, stepping into the bathroom.

Had she seen Angel flush the pill?

"Good thing the asshole was too drunk to know what the hell was going on."

Angel stood up, went to the sink and turned on the water. Tyra was close behind her, waffled spa towel on the floor, her giant boobs touching Angel's back. "Pretty girl," Tyra said.

Angel looked at her new face. The strange gray eyes, puffy lips, high cheekbones that she'd always wished for. One day she was Kate Brooks, cute, dark-haired, blue-eyed high school senior who thought her biggest problem was being a virgin. The next day, she was a murderess, half alive under a secret identity. The transformation had been easy. Contact lenses and collagen. And Tyra had cut and dyed her hair a white blonde. "Now you really look like an Angel," she'd said.

Tyra wrapped her arms around Angel's waist—cold tentacles.

Angel put toothpaste on her brush and began brushing her teeth. She jabbed Tyra in the ribs with her elbow.

"Bitch," Tyra said, releasing her. "What the fuck's going on with you?"

Angel could see Tyra watching her in the mirror. "Did you take your pill?" Tyra asked.

Angel's insides turned to slush.

"You didn't, did you?"

"What are you talking about?" Angel said. She tried to act confused, foggy. "Why wouldn't I?"

"I don't know, honey. I don't know why you wouldn't love it in la-la-land."

Angel forced a smile.

"But maybe you're getting used to it. Maybe you need more."

Angel felt panic. Run. Run. But where?

Tyra took Angel by the wrist and pulled her into the living room. Sofa cushions and pillows on the floor, glittery sandals, last night's skirt, kneesocks, white blouse. A wet spot on the rug where Angel had thrown up. Tyra pushed Angel down on the sofa and opened a drawer, just below the large-screen TV that they never let her watch except for DVDs.

"What's up?" Luis asked Tyra, coming into the room from the kitchen. He was in jeans and shirtless. Tattoos covered most of his chest, as well as his upper arms.

Angel was relieved to see him. There was something about Tyra that scared her.

Tyra stepped closer to him and said something Angel couldn't hear.

Luis rubbed his shiny bald head and narrowed his eyes as though considering something. Then he crossed the room and sat down beside Angel. "You doing okay?" he said, slipping his arm around her. He didn't seem to notice that both Angel and Tyra were naked.

Angel nodded.

"Everyone treating you good?"

She nodded again.

"Because you don't have to stay here, you know."

Angel felt bugs crawling around her insides.

"You can go anytime." He took a deep breath through clogged nostrils. "Of course, once you leave here, we can't promise any protection. You understand, don't you?"

Angel nodded.

"The cops are everywhere. Your picture is everywhere. Not you, Angel—the other you, with the blue eyes and black hair." He ran his finger over the arrowhead tattoo she'd gotten at the base of her spine where her dad would never see it. "So if you want to leave, just say the word. We'll fix your hair and face and put you back just the way you were when we found you—"

Angel was breathing in and out, too fast, like a train heading for a wreck.

"Just like you were when we found you after you killed your little friend."

White blurs flashed in front of her eyes. She was breathing too fast.

"Is that what you want?" Luis asked.

Angel shook her head.

"I didn't think so."

Tyra was kneeling in front of her holding out a white pill. "Here you go, Angel," she said. "Let me help you with this." She put the pill on the back of Angel's tongue and shoved it in farther.

Angel choked and coughed. She gulped down the drink Tyra handed her.

"That's a good girl," Tyra said.

Luis took Angel's face into his hands. He smiled at her, even white teeth against a dark tan. "But anytime you want to leave, just say the word."

Whiteness filled her head. Leave? Why would she want to leave?

Chapter 17

The ringing of her cell phone woke Robbie. Her father? Jeremy? Someone calling about Kate?

"UNKNOWN" flashed on the display.

Robbie picked up. "Hello?"

"Robbie?" The woman's melodious voice was uncertain.

"Yes."

"This is Gina Fieldstone. I hope I'm not disturbing you."

Gina Fieldstone? Robbie glanced at the clock on her nightstand. 11:42 a.m. It seemed like only a couple of hours since she'd gotten home from BURN. "No, not at all. How are you?" Robbie sat up in bed. What in the world did Gina Fieldstone want? And how did she have Robbie's phone number? Then she remembered. The "Missing" flyer. Her phone number was on the flyer. But that still didn't explain why Gina was calling.

"I was wondering about your sister," Gina said. "Hoping that you've found her?"

The way her intonation went up at the end made Gina sound very young.

"No," Robbie said. "No news on her, yet."

"I'm sorry." Gina paused. Robbie could hear her breathing through the phone. "I know how frustrating that must be for you. I'd like to help, if I can. Even if it's just to be a sounding board."

"That's so nice of you," Robbie said, touched once again by the kindness of another human being.

"Would you like to meet this afternoon? Perhaps for coffee?"

This afternoon? Robbie still wasn't thinking clearly. Didn't she have something to do? Her sister? Her father? Brett? Jeremy? But how nice it would be to have someone to sort through everything with.

Gina was still talking, suggesting a time and place. Robbie said she'd be there and disconnected from the call.

Robbie brought her feet over the side of the bed. The blinds were closed against the morning light, muting the tangerine-colored walls that Robbie had painted herself, the scratched oak dresser, chest of drawers, and rocking chair purchased at a secondhand store. Matilda was lying on the white comforter—a mound of vanilla ice cream in the snow. She picked up the cat and hugged her.

Gina Fieldstone wanted to meet for a cup of coffee.

How deeply Robbie missed her mother.

Robbie got to the Café at Books & Books a few minutes early, just before two. She found a table in the arcade near the entrance to the bookstore and sat down facing the strolling crowd on Lincoln Road so she could spot Gina Fieldstone.

She'd taken a couple of Motrin, but she couldn't get past the heaviness in her chest. Last night sucked. It really did. But she'd had it with Brett. Especially after his face-off with Jeremy. Brett used to be fun and easy. But that had changed recently and it just wasn't worth it to her to put up with his increasingly volatile moods.

It was time to tell Brett that things just weren't going to work out between them. And no—this wasn't about fear of commitment. It was about being her own person.

Umbrellas shaded the café tables, which overflowed from the arcade into the outdoor mall area. Most were taken. Robbie double-checked to make sure Gina wasn't at one of them waiting for her. She noticed a guy in sunglasses and a floppy hat sitting alone. He brought a magazine up in front of his face as though he'd been watching her and was embarrassed at being caught. He was probably just checking her out like guys often did. Robbie turned back to the crowd to watch for Gina.

The street mall was mobbed as usual—a mix of tourists and locals in shorts and sandals. A teenage girl with long black hair walked by. Robbie strained to see her. She caught a glimpse of her face as the girl turned to look in a shop window. Large nose, dark eyes. Not Kate.

Robbie thrummed her fingers against the tabletop. It was two o'clock. Where was Gina Fieldstone? She scanned the crowd again. No slender, elegant woman approaching the café.

Robbie leaned back on her chair. She was close enough to the magazine rack to see the headlines and photos on the magazines and newspapers.

The name *Fieldstone* caught her attention. Robbie leaned back further to see better. *Fieldstone Promises to——*

She took the paper off the rack and opened it on the table in front of her.

Stanford Fieldstone was balding with a shiny scalp, clean-shaven face, and dark, intelligent eyes. There was something familiar about him, but she couldn't quite place him.

"Hello, Robbie." The woman's voice coming from over Robbie's shoulder startled her. Robbie turned.

Gina Fieldstone was standing near the entrance to the bookstore. She stepped around to the front of the table. "I'm so sorry," she said. "I didn't mean to ambush you."

"That's okay. I wasn't expecting you to come from back there." Robbie extended her hand to shake Gina's, but Gina was adjusting the clasp on her cardigan and didn't seem to notice.

"I was just in the bookstore talking to the manager," Gina said.

"She asked me to sign a few of my books that she had in stock. I hope you weren't waiting long."

"Just a few minutes."

Gina set her handbag and a Books & Books shopping bag on an extra chair, then dabbed at her forehead with a white handkerchief as she sat down. A trace of peach-colored makeup remained on the handkerchief.

The waitress came by and Gina asked her to bring a couple of glasses of water.

"Coffee for you?" Gina asked.

Robbie nodded.

"And two coffees," Gina said to the waitress.

In the daylight, Robbie could see fine lines around Gina's eyes and mouth and realized Gina was older than she'd originally thought—perhaps early forties. Gina was again dressed oddly for South Beach—a pink gingham cotton blouse tucked into pressed white slacks and the white cardigan over her shoulders, despite the heat. Her ash brown hair was teased up in a half ponytail in a style Robbie remembered seeing in a high school photo of her mother.

"He's an amazing man," Gina said, glancing down at the photo of her husband. "Someone who has the ability to truly make this world a better place."

To make this world a better place. Hadn't someone else said that to Robbie recently?

Gina folded the newspaper and rested her arm over it so that her husband's photo was no longer visible. She was clutching her handkerchief, and Robbie could make out the initials GT next to the lace border. Gina Tyler. Robbie wondered why there was no "F" for Fieldstone.

"But it isn't easy to accomplish the things we aspire to," Gina continued. "There are always obstacles—people, circumstances, even acts of God, which seem to get in the way."

Robbie thought about her parents' divorce, the move to Boston, her mother's illness. She certainly understood what Gina was talking about.

The waitress set the water on the table, along with two cups of coffee and a creamer.

"And that's really why I wanted to meet with you today," Gina said. "I know how important it is for you to find your sister, and I thought I might be able to offer a little support and encouragement."

"I honestly don't know what to say," Robbie said. "I'm sure you're busy with your book tour."

"But Robbie, my book is about helping women find what's missing in their lives. If I didn't stop and try to help some of you, I'd be a fraud."

"Well, I'm very grateful."

Gina took a sip of water, leaving behind the pink imprint of her lipstick. "But maybe I'm being presumptuous. You must have plenty of support—family, friends, a boyfriend?"

"No. I don't really have anyone. My mom died a few years ago and my father's pretty much been out of my life since my parents divorced when I was a little girl. As for a boyfriend—" Robbie shook her head.

"So the young man you were with the other night isn't someone special?"

"No."

The word hung in the air like a staccato drumbeat.

Robbie added sugar and cream to her coffee. It was true. Brett wasn't anyone special. She hadn't even told him about her sister.

Gina was squeezing her handkerchief like it was a stress ball. "Well, why don't we talk about your missing sister? Tell me exactly what happened and what's been done so far."

A small group of teenage girls in cutoffs and flip-flops walked by laughing and swinging their hips.

"Kate and her friend Joanne disappeared a week ago Friday," Robbie said. "Then on Wednesday, Joanne's body was found in Indian Creek. "

"Oh, no." Gina brought her hand to her throat.

"The medical examiner believes Joanne was drugged and raped."

Gina looked pale. She fanned herself with the newspaper. "And your sister? What are the police doing to find her?"

"Flyers, talking to people at clubs, checking out parties. I guess what they usually do."

"In other words, not much."

"Well, I'm not sure what else they can do. To tell you the truth, I'm feeling very discouraged."

"Discouraged." Gina waved the word away. "And you? What have you been doing to find her?"

"I keep hoping that Kate's all right. I went looking for her last night at one of the clubs."

"What else?"

"I've distributed flyers, walked the beach."

"But just one club? Aren't there dozens on South Beach?"

"Yes, but I've been working."

"At night?"

"I tend bar at a lounge. I had to work Wednesday and Thursday nights."

"Had to?" Gina widened her eyes. They looked violet in the shade of the arcade.

"Well, yes. I had to."

"I see."

"I have a job. It's my responsibility to be there when the boss calls me."

"I'm sorry, Robbie. I didn't mean to make you feel like you're not doing your share. It's just, I know the longer someone remains missing, the less likely that the person will be found. Now's the time to step up your efforts, before they no longer matter."

She sounded like Robbie's mother lecturing her. Be strong. Do what you can. Tough love.

"After I gave up my daughter for adoption," Gina said. "I thought about her every day and it tore a hole in my heart. By the time I realized I needed to find her, too much time had passed. Records were lost, people retired. I should have acted sooner. Done more when my actions would have made a bigger difference." Gina leaned closer to Robbie. She smelled like overripe flowers. "That's why you need to find her now."

"It's true," Robbie said. "There's more I can be doing. There are lots of clubs where Kate might be." But what was the likelihood Kate would be at any one of them? Or for that matter, that Kate was anywhere Robbie could find her? But she had to try. "I'll go back out tonight to look for her."

"Good," Gina said. "Taking action really helps." She softened her voice. "You know, Robbie. It's not just about finding your sister. I sense that she's not the only one who's lost."

What was Gina implying? But Robbie understood at a fundamental level that what Gina said was true. When Robbie found Kate, she might find something of herself that had been missing.

Gina opened up the newspaper to her husband's photo. "There are also things I can do," she said. "I'll talk to Stanford. Ask him if his people could help."

"You'd do that?"

"Of course. Why wouldn't I?"

"Thank you," Robbie said. "Thank you so much."

Gina took another sip of water, ignoring the coffee. "Well, I'd better get going, but I'll stay in touch." Gina left money on the table and stood up to leave. She clasped her handkerchief against her chest and looked intently at Robbie. "If we do our parts, we'll succeed," she said.

Robbie could only nod.

Gina left the arcade, passing close to the table where the guy with sunglasses and hat that Robbie had noticed earlier still sat alone, his magazine open in front of him. Gina turned to Robbie, smiled, and then disappeared into the crowd.

Chapter 18

Pink and blue lights from outside brightened the dark walls like intermittent fireworks. Marylou Madison paced across the soft carpeting in her bare feet, a blanket around her shoulders. She had an uneasy feeling in the pit of her stomach, like when she was a child and she tried to be quiet as a mouse so he would forget she was there.

But sometimes he came into the closet where she slept, his breath too sweet. She'd try not to move, not to cry when he hurt her. She would look at the peeling paint, the cracks between the wood planks where she could see a tiny piece of black sky. Sometimes, if she really concentrated, she could see the sparkle of a star. And she'd make a wish. "Please, please God. Make him stop."

Then later, after he left, her mother would sit on her narrow bed and wash her with a warm rag.

She talked softly to Marylou, careful not to wake him. She would tell Marylou about the big city, the fine restaurants, and the wonderful clothes she used to wear. "I almost had it all," her mother said. Sometimes, she would take photos of herself out of a small leather box and show Marylou. How glamorous her mother was! But she had made a mistake and here she was. "In purgatory," her mother would say. "But you, my darling girl, you're my hope. You'll get my dreams back for me."

"Oh Mother," Marylou said now, surprised to hear herself

speaking aloud. "I'm so sorry." She sat down on the edge of the bed, pulling the blanket tighter around her shoulders. Marylou had tried everything—the slick men who promised her the world, then working as a hostess, a dancer, and even doing things that made her cringe at the memory. And now, even as she was getting closer to her goal, the seductive pull of Miami Beach was going to ruin it all for her. "I want to make you proud, Mother, but things keep getting in the way."

But Marylou knew she was cleverer than all the forces working against her. Whatever it took, she was prepared to do, to save him from himself, to save their dream.

Her mother's dream.

A noise came from the next room. Marylou held her breath. She hoped she hadn't awakened him. He needed his sleep. From outside, she could hear the sound of boisterous drunks out for a night on the town, but nothing more from her little boy. He must have fallen back asleep. Thank God.

Marylou let out a sigh. He was a trial to her, her son was. A colicky baby, an angry toddler, and now that he was older, he was even more difficult to control. But he was her son, and she would do anything for him. And he for her.

"Ma?" he called.

"Yes, my darling boy. I'm coming."

Chapter 19

Robbie went home and made a list of nightclubs that Kate was likely to go to. She thought about calling Jeremy. He'd probably be willing to help, but was it fair to turn to him only when she had a problem? She'd go to the clubs herself.

Brett had left numerous text messages to call him, but Robbie didn't need the distraction of a breakup while she was focused on finding her sister. She wrote back that she was busy and would talk to him later.

She found ten of the most popular clubs and plotted them out on a street map. She'd start at the far end of South Beach and work her way up. It didn't make sense to go out before midnight since only unknowing tourists went clubbing earlier, so she decided to take a short nap.

The phone rang just as she was getting into bed. It was Leonard calling to ask Robbie to come to work tonight.

"I'm sorry, but I can't," she said.

"Please, Robbie. It's Saturday, our busiest night, and I have no one. Two of the bartenders have the flu and sound like they're on their deathbeds. And that new girl I hired? You know, Maddy? I can't believe after begging me for extra shifts, she just up and quit. No notice. Didn't even have the courtesy to call me herself. Had some guy call me. So there's no one. I'll be working myself, but just me, a barback, and a couple of cocktail waitresses won't cut it."

Saturday night. It was also the most likely night that Kate would be out—assuming she was able to go out and wasn't being held captive, or worse. But being a runaway in the club scene was the only option that explained Kate's disappearance, in which Robbie could actually do something.

"I'm desperate, Robbie," Leonard said in her ear.

"Okay. I'll be there."

She felt like she was letting Gina down, and somehow that translated to letting her mother down. But Leonard's problem was real. And Robbie knew, that as much as she wanted to believe the opposite, the likelihood of Robbie finding her sister club-hopping was remote.

She got to The Garage around nine thirty, bracing herself for an unfamiliar crowd, but she found Ben sitting at the bar in a smoky haze. She looked around. No sign of Jeremy.

Leonard came in from the back and gave her a thumbs-up as he slipped in behind the bar. How strange that Maddy had quit without notice. Maybe she'd had enough of South Beach and gone back home with her son.

"Hey, little Robbie," Ben said, rubbing his clean-shaven head. "What's? You never come in on Saturdays."

"I missed you."

Ben gave her a big grin. "Yeah, I'll bet you did. Saw you at BURN last night. Almost didn't recognize you all dressed up."

"Thanks, I guess."

"So you and Jeremy are getting back together?"

"What makes you ask that?"

"Come on, Robbie. You guys disappeared into a dark corner, then I didn't see either of you for the rest of the night."

The music was a dull background thump. She picked up Ben's empty glass. "Want another?"

"Sure. So? What's going on with you two?"

"Nothing. Nothing's going on." She wondered where Jeremy had gone after she left. Probably home.

She put a fresh rum and coke down in front of Ben. Several new customers came in and she took their orders.

The crowd was still relatively light. About half the stools at the bar were taken and some people had congregated around the groupings of car benchseats. Leonard was filling orders for the cocktail waitress down at the other end of the bar. The door opened.

"Oh well," Ben said, "I guess the ball's still in play."

Robbie checked out the people who had just come in. Brett and his boss. What were they doing here? Brett was wearing a pressed pin-striped shirt and Mike was in his standard white guayabera. They looked out of place among this grungy crowd.

Mike wandered off in the direction of the restrooms while Brett approached the bar.

"Honestly, Robbie," Ben said in a low voice, "what do you see in him?"

Brett stepped up to the bar, glanced at Robbie, but looked away quickly and pounded his fist against Ben's. "Hey man. Saw you at BURN last night. Sorry I was too busy to say hi."

"Oh yeah?" Ben said in an exaggerated voice. "Sorry *I* was too busy to say hi."

Robbie sucked in her cheeks to keep from smiling. How she missed Jeremy's friends.

Ben finished his drink, put the glass down on the bar, and signed his credit card receipt. "Well, gotta go. I'm meeting the guys at Townhouse."

She wondered if that meant Jeremy, too. "Have fun," she said.

"Don't I always?" He waved and left.

Robbie wiped down the bar with a white cloth.

Brett was watching her, shifting from foot to foot, reminding her of a kid who needed to go to the bathroom. It was hard to stay mad at someone who behaved so much like an eight-year-old.

"I was hoping you'd be here," Brett said finally.

Robbie grabbed a couple of beers and handed them to a guy who'd ordered them.

"You hate me," Brett said.

"I don't hate you."

"How come you wouldn't talk to me?"

"I've been busy."

"I've been an asshole," he said. "I want to make it up to you."

"Don't worry about it."

Someone ordered a martini and she went to fix it.

Brett leaned against the bar. "Can we do something tomorrow? Maybe brunch?"

She took several more orders and worked on filling them. Brett stood there watching her. "I'm sorry, Brett, but I need to work."

He handed her a small wrapped package.

"What's this?"

"An apology gift."

"That's not necessary."

"Please, open it."

She ripped off the paper. It was a book about jewelry making that she'd admired in a bookstore shortly after they'd started dating. A surprisingly thoughtful gift.

Brett was pulling on one of his ears, the shadow of his spiked hair falling across his forehead. They used to have such fun together. Did she really want to end things with him?

"Thank you," she said. "This was very nice of you."

"It's okay? I was hoping you hadn't gotten it for yourself."

"It's great."

"So I'm forgiven?"

Such a little boy.

"Yes, Brett. You're forgiven."

Mike was approaching from the restroom, smoothing his thin orange hair into its rat tail.

"So what are we having, Mike?" Brett picked up a stack of coasters and shuffled them. "A couple of martinis?"

"Do you have Goose or just house brands?" Mister M asked Robbie as he sat down on one of the stools.

"This is The Garage, Mike," Brett said. "Not some shit hole."

Nice to see Brett stepping up to the plate.

She fixed two Grey Goose martinis while Brett left to say hello to some people he knew. His usual frenetic energy had returned.

Mike rested his elbow on the bar and picked up one of the flyers of Kate from the stack Robbie had left out the other night, as she had at the Fieldstone event. Mike probably thought she was blanketing all of South Beach with the flyers. And he'd be right.

"Still haven't found her?" he asked.

"Nope."

"How long's she been gone?"

"About a week." Robbie didn't know why, but she felt uneasy sharing anything about her sister with this man.

"That's too bad," Mike said. "My experience is if a kid doesn't come home after forty-eight hours, she's probably not coming back."

Robbie's face heated up. "Well, I'm not sure what you base your experience on, Mike, but in this case I believe you're wrong."

He smiled at her, his skin stretching in the wrong places. "Sorry. I didn't mean to upset you." Mike left cash on the bar and picked up the drinks. He called over to Brett, who was talking to some girls. "Let's shoot some pool."

At around eleven, Robbie noticed Puck coming into the bar. He adjusted his glasses, then rubbed the stubble on his cheek as he took in the room. He was wearing his customary oversized sweatshirt, clumsy jeans, and Bud N' Mary's billed cap. His eyes fell on Robbie. He smiled slightly, and then went directly to the seat Mike had vacated.

"Heineken?" Robbie asked, bringing over a beer.

He nodded. His face was transformed into almost handsome when he smiled.

"Thank you again for getting my bike fixed," she said. "That was really sweet of you."

"My pleasure." He put a twenty down.

"Tonight's my treat."

He looked at her curiously. "You don't have to do that."

"It's *my* pleasure."

"If you insist." He took the bill back.

There was a constant flow of customers who kept Robbie busy and didn't leave her time to talk to anyone. Brett had settled down with Mike and some people she didn't know across the dance floor.

After Puck finished his third beer, he switched to Scotch and left a twenty on the bar. "Thanks for the beers," he said, "but the rest are mine." He was definitely drinking more and faster than he had the other nights. "And please, let me buy you one."

"Thanks, Puck, but I don't like to drink when I'm working."

"I figured, but I had to ask." He drank down his Scotch and signaled for another.

Robbie brought it to him.

"I was afraid you wouldn't be in tonight," Puck said, picking up his glass. "You said you didn't work Saturdays."

"A couple of the regular bartenders are sick and another one quit."

He tapped on the side of his glass with his manicured fingernail. "I decided to stay in Miami a while longer than I was planning." Puck seemed to be talking to himself. "It's good to stop and smell the roses." He gave her a half smile. "If you'll excuse the cliché."

"You're right," she said. "It's easy to forget the roses."

"I wish my wife would understand that."

"Ah. So you're married."

His face flushed. "I wasn't trying to mislead you. Yes, I'm married, but it's a façade. We have nothing in common. We never did."

It was funny what men would talk about when they had too much to drink. "No need to explain," Robbie said.

"But I'd like to. You don't really know me and I sense that you're not judgmental." Puck took a sip of his Scotch. "I know this sounds like a copout, but I feel like she manipulated me into marrying her."

"You don't seem that naïve."

"Well. She was kind of a client."

Kind of a client? What did that mean?

"I shouldn't have gotten involved with her," he said. "Especially in my position. It compromised me. But she was extremely attractive. And then—I know this sounds stupid—but I was afraid if I didn't marry her, she'd use our affair to ruin me professionally."

"She blackmailed you?"

"Pretty much."

"I see."

"I'm not saying I couldn't have been stronger," Puck said. "I could have. But you know the expression about men's tendency to think with a part of their body that isn't their brain."

Robbie had certainly seen plenty to corroborate that.

"Anyway," Puck said, "bottom line, I married her because she was sexy and beautiful." He tapped his fingernail against his glass. "And it's funny. She seemed so vulnerable. Like she needed to be taken care of." He let out a short laugh. "Man did I get that wrong. I never dreamed she'd turn into an ambitious monster."

Right. It's always the woman's fault. "So if you're not happy with her, why don't you get divorced?"

He brought his head back in surprise. "That's a damn good question."

A large, rowdy group came into the bar.

"Sorry," Robbie said. "I need to take care of those guys."

"No problem. Thanks for listening."

Robbie turned her attention to getting drinks for her new customers. Out of the corner of her eye, she noticed Puck sliding off the bar stool. He waved at her and shouted over the din. "I'll be back. Bring me a fresh one, would you?"

She signaled okay.

Robbie handed out the drinks and cashed the group out. There was a momentary lull. She took a sip of water. She wasn't sure what to make of Puck's candor. It bothered her when people didn't take responsibility for their own actions. But why did she even care? He was obviously some rich guy playing at being a boater to get away from an unhappy marriage. But he had been so thoughtful and generous to her the other night, helping with her bike, that it saddened her to see this other side of him.

"Hey sexy," Brett said. He had left Mike sitting with the group of people she didn't know. "I didn't realize how hard you work."

"It's not usually this busy during the week."

"You know the guy who was sitting here? The one with the dumb cap that you've been talking to all night?"

"Not all night."

"Anyway, what's his deal?"

"He's been in a few times."

"Oh yeah? Do you know his name?"

"Puck. I don't know his last name."

"Puck?"

"It's a nickname, I guess."

"Can you do me a favor?" Brett asked. "Actually it's for Mike.

Mike would do it, but it's awkward for him to approach this guy directly. Can you invite him to BURN tomorrow night?"

"Invite Puck to BURN?"

"That's right.

"So you know him?"

"Mike sort of does. Would you do it? Invite him to BURN?"

"I don't think he's the type."

"It looks like he'd go if you were there."

"But I won't be there." Robbie picked up a shot glass and started polishing it.

"Can you tell him you might?"

"Why?"

"Mike wants to meet him there, to talk to him."

"Why doesn't he talk to him here?"

"This is a hangout kind of place," Brett said. "I don't think Puck came here to talk business."

"Well, he wouldn't be going to BURN to talk business either."

Brett put his elbow down on the bar and leaned closer. "Right, but at least Mike would be on his home turf. You know, where he has the advantage."

"Who is he?" Robbie put the glass down and picked up another. "Why does Mike want to talk to him?"

"I don't know. You know Mike. He always has something going on. Would you do this for me, Robbie? It's no big deal, really, is it? And it means a lot to my job."

"I don't like to misrepresent myself."

"Fine. Then I'll take you to BURN tomorrow night. So you won't be misrepresenting. It's the least I can do for you after last night's bust."

"Thanks. But I've had my fill of BURN."

Puck was coming toward them.

"Two more martinis," Brett said.

Puck sat down on the stool and picked up the glass of Scotch Robbie had left for him.

Robbie fixed Brett's drinks and put them down on the bar in front of him. If Brett knew she was annoyed, he gave no indication. He grinned broadly. "You're the best."

She watched him carry the drinks high in the air, swinging his hips, in a parody of a gay cocktail waiter. A few people laughed as he passed. He sat down next to Mike, who was leaning his chair back against the wall beneath an enlarged photo of a junkyard.

She hated being in this situation. When friends asked you for a favor, it wasn't cool to say no, especially something that was important to Brett for his job. And was what he wanted her to do such a big deal?

"Busy night for you," Puck said.

"Do you ever go out to the clubs?"

"Not my scene."

"I know what you mean."

He sipped his drink. "Why? Do you?"

"Sometimes."

He raised an eyebrow.

"I'm thinking of going to BURN tomorrow night." God, she hated doing this, especially after him telling her about his problems with his wife.

"Oh yeah?"

"They have a great DJ on Sundays and it's not as crazy as Friday or Saturday night." She didn't know this for a fact, but it sounded right.

"That sounds interesting." He looked pleased, as though she'd invited him out.

Damn. Why had she gone along with Brett? Now Puck would

show up and she wouldn't be there. She almost told him never mind, but that would only make things worse.

She felt Brett watching her from across the room. She turned and caught him leaning closer to Mike, saying something to him.

No. She wasn't going to do this. It wasn't right to mislead people. "I'm probably not going to be able to make it tomorrow," she said to Puck. "It was just an idea."

"Hey." He held up his hands. "Not a problem. I'm a big boy. If you're there, great. If not, I understand."

The door to the bar opened. Within minutes the place was crawling with people.

Robbie worked without a break. Occasionally, Puck would ask for another drink, but she didn't talk to him again the rest of the night. All of her attention was focused on fixing drinks and making sure she rang up all the charges properly. Leonard worked with frenzied concentration beside her.

Finally, closing time. Last call was announced and the security guard ushered the last few people out of the bar. Exhaustion hit Robbie like a dump truck. She leaned against the bar and took in the scene as the busboys cleaned up and Leonard settled up the tips. Cigarette butts and napkins littered the floor. One of the bucket seat chairs had broken loose from its base and was lying on its side. The tables were covered with overflowing ashtrays, beer bottles, empty pitchers, and glasses with cigarette butts floating in amber liquid.

Brett and Mike were long gone. Brett had said goodbye to her and whispered thanks, a couple of hours ago. She'd been too busy to tell him what a shitty thing he'd asked her to do.

The stool where Puck had been sitting was empty. His Bud N' Mary's cap was on the bar. Beneath it was more than enough money to cover his drinks and a paper napkin with something scribbled on it. A phone number. And next to it, a hand-drawn picture of a rose.

Chapter 20

Robbie had promised herself she wouldn't wake up until eleven at the earliest, figuring five hours of sleep wasn't too much to ask for, but her internal clock had her up at eight a.m. Jesus, it was unnatural—eight a.m. on a Sunday morning. She covered her head with a pillow and tried to fall back asleep, but it was hopeless. She was so angry with herself over last night. How could she have allowed Brett to manipulate her like that? Ooooooo. She shuddered in self-disgust. It wasn't just the fact she had lied to Puck. What infuriated her most was that she hadn't had the guts to tell Brett "no."

She finally got out of bed a little before nine and put on jogging shorts, a tank top, and sneakers to go for a run. She stuck a bottle of water and an energy bar into her waist pack with her cell phone, fed Matilda, and stepped outside.

The air was heavy with ocean water and the piquant smell of plants whose names she didn't know. In another hour, it would be too hot to run. She trotted down to the bottom of the stairs to stretch her legs. She pressed her sneakered foot straight up against the second step and leaned forward.

A movement came from the shrubs near the pool. A possum? A bird? She stretched out her other calf, and listened, her sleep-deprived body hypersensitive to her surroundings. A slight shuffling sound. Someone was watching her.

Robbie came to a standing position and began walking rapidly toward a street with car traffic. She could hear footsteps behind her. She broke into a run.

"Roberta," a familiar man's voice called. "Roberta, wait."

She stopped and let her father catch up. What did he want now?

His navy shorts and golf shirt looked recycled, and his penny loafers had lost their shine. She hadn't seen him since Friday afternoon when he'd left the raw bar in such a huff.

Her annoyance turned to apprehension. "Is everything okay?" she said. "Is there news about Kate?"

"No. No news." He was a little breathless and his lined face and his arms were covered with a film of perspiration. "The detective has some new information. Not much." He wiped the sweat on his forehead with a tissue. There was stubble on his cheeks, as though he'd missed a day of shaving. "I've been waiting at the pool. I didn't want to call and bother you."

Robbie felt herself soften. This had to be incredibly difficult for him. Yes—he'd acted stupidly at the marina, but it was now almost ten days since his younger daughter had disappeared.

"We can sit somewhere and talk if you'd like," she said.

"Are you sure? I don't want to interfere with your run."

"It's okay. I can go later. If you don't mind walking a little, there's a park not too far from here."

They stayed on the shaded side of the street, and she walked slower than usual so he could keep up.

"What did Lieber say?" she asked.

"They found Joanne's car. The white Volvo."

Robbie stopped. "On Miami Beach?"

He nodded.

She was afraid to ask, but if Kate's body or blood had been found, he would have been more upset. "Did they find anything suspicious?"

"Nothing obvious. They've towed the car off somewhere so the experts can check it out."

They continued past several old apartment complexes much like Robbie's. The trees were denser when they got to Meridian. Oaks and banyans lined both sides of the street. They crossed to the park and sat down on a shaded bench. Yellow and green leaves blanketed the dirt and thin grass. Robbie remembered reading about an infestation that was causing certain trees to lose their leaves. She glanced up at the ficus tree with its massive trunk growing in sinewy cords. A few small leaves drifted down. Something seemed familiar. Autumn leaves falling all around. Her mother. *Nothing is forever.*

Her father dabbed at his forehead with his wadded-up tissue. He was still sweating profusely.

She took out her water bottle and held it out for him. "Want some?"

"That's okay. You'll need it for your run."

She pressed it into his hand.

"Thank you." He gulped down the water.

A golden retriever charged past them after a Frisbee.

"How long were you waiting for me to come down?" Robbie asked.

"Maybe an hour. Not much else for me to do."

"Why don't you go back home? Lieber will call you if she has any news."

"I can't do that. What if Kaitlin needs me? I can't be five hours away."

"I understand." She took out the energy bar, broke it down the middle and gave a half to her father.

He hesitated. "Thank you," he said, taking it. He seemed to be studying it. "I want to apologize about the other day. I behaved like an angry child stomping off like that."

"You're under a lot of stress."

"That's no excuse." He turned the energy bar over in his hand. "Here you were nice enough to meet with me and the detective.

You'd even done some research about Kaitlin on your own. And instead of being grateful, I attacked you and your theories because I didn't want to hear anything negative about Kaitlin."

A German shepherd joined the retriever and the two dogs trotted after each other kicking up leaves.

"I hardly know anything about her," Robbie said. Her voice came out small.

Her father shifted closer to her on the bench. How she wanted him to put his arm around her. Several yellow and green leaves drifted down.

"When she was younger, Kaitlin reminded me of you as a little girl."

He remembered what Robbie was like?

"She was curious about everything. My medical instruments, microscope, giving injections."

Robbie remembered the plastic skeleton he'd kept in a corner of his office. How it had fascinated her.

"And she loved physical activities; still does—rollerblading, biking, swimming, running. She's on the track team at school."

Track? Like Robbie. She wondered if Kate had been running from something, too.

"She used to be quite the gymnast," he said. "But then she had a little accident and never wanted to get back up on the bars. And that was the end of gymnastics."

"An accident?"

"She slipped and fell during a competition. Was more scared than injured, but wasn't interested in competing after that. I guess she was embarrassed or her pride was hurt."

Robbie was turning her emerald ring around and around on her finger. She slid her hand under her thigh. "What do the two of you do together?"

"Ordinary stuff. Food shopping on Saturdays. Home Depot.

Maybe a movie. Kaitlin's often busy with her friends, but we usually have dinner together during the week. After her mother died, Kaitlin started cooking. Nothing fancy. A hamburger. Tuna salad. Sometimes we go out to a restaurant."

"Where?"

"Where?" He frowned, his eyes a dark blue from the shade of the towering ficus.

"Where do you go for dinner?" This was what life with her father would have been like had their family remained a family.

"Kaitlin likes this little place on the river. They have great fried shrimp and hush puppies."

She could almost imagine being there with them. "What do you talk about?"

"School, her classes, her friends. What it's going to be like at college next year." He looked at the energy bar he was still holding and put it down on the bench next to him. "How much I'm going to miss her."

Robbie touched his shoulder. "We'll find her."

Tears ran down his unshaven cheeks. He brought his arms around Robbie and pulled her close. Robbie wasn't sure what to do. His smell was so damn familiar. She relaxed into his arms as he cried silently against her, an occasional shudder passing through him.

She remembered again the day he said goodbye. He'd been crying then, too.

He took a deep, uneven breath and pulled away. "What a mess I've made of things." He reached into his pocket for a tissue and blew his nose.

"What do you mean?" Was he talking about Kate? About Robbie?

"I don't know what your mother told you, but I hope you'll let me tell you my side."

His side? Did she want to hear this? She thought about her childhood fantasy where he'd been held in a dungeon against his will, unable to reach out to her.

The retriever and German shepherd lay down in the shade, panting. A plump young woman set down a large bowl filled with water, and the dogs lapped at it.

"My mom didn't say anything. And I was afraid to ask. Afraid it would upset her. I thought——" Robbie's throat tightened. "I thought you didn't want us anymore."

He closed his eyes as though in pain, then opened them. "I always wanted you."

"Then why didn't you call or come see me?"

"Your mother was very angry. She wanted to punish me for the divorce. She took you to Boston and told me never to get in touch with you."

No. Her mother wouldn't have done that. Or was it possible? She pictured her mother pressing her lips against Robbie's forehead as though to suck out all her pain. *We have each other, baby. We don't need anyone else.*

Just like Maddy the bartender with her son.

"I shouldn't have listened to her," her father said. "But I told myself I'd done enough harm to the two of you. The least I could do was respect your mother's request to leave you alone."

"And you honestly believed that was best for me? To grow up without a father? To grow up thinking you hated me? That I'd done something so terribly wrong that you couldn't bear the sight of me?"

His eyes widened. "Oh, Roberta, not a day went by that I didn't think about you. Worry about you."

He touched her hair. A bolt shot from her scalp to her heart. Was it true? Had he always been thinking about her?

"You know your mother's cousin Peter?" he asked.

Robbie nodded. Peter used to live in Boston and would have dinner with Robbie and her mom almost every week. He was a ballet dancer who never made it to a professional company, but he loved teaching Robbie what he knew. Robbie adored him and was brokenhearted when he died a few years before.

"He was the only one in your mother's family who didn't shut me out," her father said. "I used to call him once a week and he'd tell me what you were doing. When you gave up ballet for track. Then every track competition you won. Your grades on your exams. All the colleges you were accepted to."

He knew all about her? She felt a surge of anger. "But then you would have known about my mom. How sick she was. How much we needed you. Why didn't you do anything?"

He looked at his hands, folded in his lap against the creased navy shorts. "I tried to."

"You tried to?"

"I called and spoke to her when I heard she was ill. I said I wanted to see her. To see both of you. She told me not to come."

She'd told him not to come?

"And then, when she died, I tried one more time. At your mother's funeral."

"What are you talking about?"

He didn't lift his head. "Peter had called to tell me of her passing. I didn't even think about it. I caught a flight to Boston to be there for her funeral. To see you."

He'd been there? Impossible.

"Peter had been sending me photos, but it was the first time I'd seen you in person since you were a little girl. You were wearing a black dress that was too big for you, but I couldn't believe how lovely you were."

The dress. He had been there. Robbie hadn't had anything appropriate to wear and had borrowed the black dress from a girl in her dorm.

"You had flown in from New Orleans. You were in your freshman year at Tulane."

He knew every detail.

"I stayed in the background," he said. "I didn't want one of your mother's relatives to see me and create a scene. But you walked past me on the way to giving your eulogy for your mother. You dropped your notes."

Robbie remembered the words she had written on the plane ride to Boston. Her memories of her mother. The paper had fallen from her trembling fingers as she made her way to the front of the room. A man had swooped down and handed it to her. A man in a suit with a beard and blue eyes. She had said thank you, and he said something to her. She remembered thinking he looked familiar, but didn't pursue it. She had her mother on her mind.

"And I picked up your notes and gave them to you," her father said.

She stared at him.

"And I said we would talk later."

That was what he'd said. *Later. We'll talk later*. "But we didn't," Robbie said. "I didn't see you again."

"There was no recognition in your eyes," he said. "And then, when I heard you speak about your mother, I realized I was more dead to you than she was."

"So you left without saying anything else to me? Because at a time of terrible grief, I didn't recognize a man I hadn't seen in over ten years, who had grown a beard?"

"It wasn't that." He shook his head. "I thought I'd made a mistake coming. You had grown up without me. I didn't want to intrude on the memories you'd built with your mother. I decided to honor her wishes and leave you be."

Her father had come to her.

Leaves drifted down from the tree. Green, yellow. They fell in her hair, on her shoulders.

Robbie remembered a beautiful day. She was seven years old and she and her mom had just moved north. The air was cold, the sky so blue it hurt her eyes. And the trees so many colors. *Yellow, gold, russet, crimson, burgundy, magenta*, her mother had said.

And then a gust of wind, and all around them, the leaves began to fall thick as a blizzard.

And Robbie had begun to cry.

Nothing is forever, her mother had said.

"She was wrong to turn me against you," Robbie said to her father.

"I didn't mean to make you angry with your mother. She was lashing out the only way she knew how."

"She should have let me see you."

He touched the emerald ring on Robbie's finger. "Did she give that to you?"

Robbie shook her head. "I found it in her jewelry box. After she died. I was surprised I'd never seen her wear it."

"I gave your mother that ring. It was for our engagement." He moistened his lips with his tongue. "I hurt your mother, Roberta. I hurt her deeply. She believed we would be together always and for- ever. And when I told her I was leaving her for someone else—a woman who was pregnant with my child—I think I destroyed some- thing very fundamental in her. Her trust and faith in others."

Nothing is forever, her mother had said. Of course she would have felt that way after her husband's abandonment. But her mother had done a terrible thing keeping Robbie from her father.

Robbie put her other hand over the emerald ring. Her mother was gone. She had had such an unhappy life those last few years— deserted, unloved, dealing with the pain of cancer and the knowl- edge that she would soon be leaving her daughter behind. Yes, she had made a mistake with Robbie, but she was just a woman. A mother who was trying to do what she believed best for her child.

So what did that make her father? He had cheated on his wife, left her for another woman and a new child. But he hadn't meant to hurt anyone.

Neither had meant to hurt Robbie. But they had. Deeply.

Her father took a yellow leaf out of her hair. "I'm so, so sorry, Roberta."

Tears rolled down her cheeks. She reached out toward him and he pulled her close. He held her, then. He held her tight. People came and went. Dogs barked. When finally they pulled apart, his eyes were red.

The retriever came by sniffing, picked up the energy bar on the bench, and dashed off.

Her father looked after the dog. "If I could give you one piece of advice," he said, "it's this. Don't let anyone ever force you to be anything but the person you want to be." He touched her chin with his forefinger. "Okay, Pocahontas?"

Several leaves drifted down around them.

"Okay, Daddy."

Chapter 21

Robbie was barely conscious of where she was going as her feet pounded the pavement. She had said goodbye to her father at the park, but her emotions were still in turmoil. In finding her father, she felt like she had lost something of her mother.

Robbie had seen her mom as a victim who had suffered the desertion of her husband and a devastating illness. But her mother always put on a front of strength and taught Robbie independence and self-sufficiency. Robbie had never imagined these lessons had been the result of vindictiveness born of pain.

But now that Robbie was a woman herself, she was beginning to understand the depth and complexity of her mother's feelings. How much she must have suffered raising Robbie alone, worrying whether she was doing the right thing for her daughter.

No—Robbie hadn't lost anything of her mother. If anything, she had gained a greater understanding of the woman her mother had been, and this new perspective made Robbie love and appreciate her mother all the more.

And then there was her father—the person she associated with her cold, lonely childhood. But he was back in her life now, along with the knowledge that he had always wanted her. That he had made a mistake allowing Robbie's mother to keep him from seeing his older daughter.

Well, Robbie was going to take his advice. She wasn't going to let anyone keep her from doing what she believed was right.

She reached the path that wound around the bay side of Miami Beach. A breeze came off the water like a cool embrace. Her jogging shorts and top were soaked through. She squeezed out the dripping sweat from her hair. She had made a mistake last night and she was going to fix it.

She went toward the marina. Yachts and smaller vessels overwhelmed the narrow concrete docks, which extended out into the water like tentacles. She examined the smaller cabin cruisers hoping to spot *Aimless*—Puck's boat.

People strolled past her, walking their dogs. They probably lived in the apartment buildings that lined the promenade. Robbie found *Aimless* at the end of the last dock. It was a little before eleven in the morning. There was no sign of anyone on the boat.

Now that she was here, Robbie was having second thoughts. What was she going to do? Get on the boat and tell Puck she had lied to him about going to BURN tonight? That she was trying to do a friend a favor? The whole explanation sounded lame. And worse than that, what would Puck make of her coming to his boat? He might think she really was interested in him.

Telling him the truth would cause more problems than just leaving things alone. And big deal—what if he went to the club tonight and she wasn't there? She'd already told him she probably wouldn't be going.

Robbie backed away from the dock, bumping into a big guy wearing a Hawaiian-print shirt, mirrored sunglasses, and a floppy hat. "Sorry," she said, but he hurried away without acknowledging her.

Puck wasn't the real problem, she knew. She left the marina and reached into her waist pack for her cell phone. Brett answered on the fifth ring.

"Yeah." His voice was sleepy.

"It's me," she said. "Can you meet me for coffee?"

"Shit. What time is it?"

"Eleven."

He moaned. "I'm sleeping."

"Sorry. Didn't mean to wake you. Never mind."

"No, wait, wait. Where do you want to meet?"

"Starbucks on West Avenue?"

"Okay, let me just wake up for a minute. I'll be there soon."

Robbie arrived before Brett, so she ordered a couple of lattes and went back outside. After seeing that all the umbrella tables were occupied, she sat down at one in direct sunlight. Her hair and jogging clothes had already dried out from the late morning heat. She knew she looked disheveled, but surprisingly, she felt more composed on the inside than she had in a long time.

She checked out the people at the surrounding tables—a young couple with their bulldog, a heavyset guy talking on his phone in a loud voice, several middle-aged people reading newspapers. No "Kate" candidates. Well tonight Robbie didn't have to work, so she'd go back to the plan she'd talked to Gina Fieldstone about and hit some clubs that Kate might be at. Definitely not BURN. Robbie wasn't going back there and risk running into Puck. And she certainly didn't want to see Brett and Mister M. She'd had enough of that scene.

Robbie noticed a black BMW pull into a No Parking zone. Brett got out of the car. He was dressed in pressed khaki shorts and a white shirt with rolled-up sleeves. Sunglasses hid his eyes, and his blond hair stuck out in gelled spikes. "Hey," he said, leaning over to give her a kiss.

She turned so he connected with her cheek, not lips.

"Oh man. I see it's going to be one of 'those' talks." He sat down, took the cover off one of the lattes, and took a sip. "So what's up?"

"Sorry to drag you out, but I didn't sleep all night. This has really been eating at me."

"What?" He looked genuinely baffled.

"I didn't like the way you made me feel last night."

"What are you talking about?"

Amazing. He had no idea.

"What did I do?"

"You asked me to lie to that man at the bar."

"What man?" He pulled on his earlobe. "Oh. You mean the guy in the hat you were talking to? I just asked you to invite him to BURN."

"You asked me to lie."

"A small favor and it wasn't even for me. It was for Mike and for my job. I don't know why you're making such a big deal about this."

"Because to me it is a big deal." She was turning her emerald ring around her finger. The ring her father had given her mother. "I don't see our relationship going anywhere, Brett."

"Oh, come on. I didn't know it would bother you or I never would have asked you. Let's just forget about it. I promise I won't do it again."

"It's not just about last night."

"You're making too much of this, Robbie."

"I'm not myself when I'm around you and I don't like that feeling."

"You're tired. You said you didn't sleep last night. Let's talk about it later."

"Don't do this, Brett. It's over. Let it go."

He slammed his hand against the table, causing his latte to spill over the side of the cup. "No. I'm not letting it go. You're the first girl I ever really liked. I'm not letting you go over something so dumb."

"Brett, I'm sorry but—"

His cell phone rang. He glanced at it. "Give me a minute." He leaned back in his chair. "Yeah?"

Robbie gathered up her napkin and cup. No—she wasn't going to sit here while he took his call.

"Oh shit," Brett said to the phone. It seemed his face had turned pale, but it could have been the angle of the sun. "Now what?"

Robbie got up and threw the trash in the garbage. When she turned back to the table, Brett was gone. She looked around. He was getting into his car, his phone still against his ear.

She watched in disbelief as he pulled out and drove away.

"It was nice knowing you, too," she said.

Chapter 22

Robbie returned to her apartment and, without consciously deciding to, began scouring the bathroom floor. It was a familiar ritual—Robbie always cleaned when there was disorder or a major change in her life. Like each time before her mother came home from the hospital, Robbie would try to eradicate the evil germs or vibes that might be lurking in the bedding, under the sofa. On some level, Robbie had believed the process would help her mother recover.

But Robbie had also cleaned the house after her mother had died. She had scrubbed and vacuumed until she had finally collapsed exhausted on the sofa, clutching her mother's pillow.

Now, she wondered what was behind the latest cleaning frenzy. A desire to clear away the remnants of anger she'd felt toward her father up until this morning? To wipe out any remaining molecules Brett had left behind? Or was she driven by frustration over her sister's disappearance?

Fumes of cleanser filled the tiny bathroom, but Robbie continued scrubbing until the sink and bathtub sparkled. Then Robbie attacked the rest of the house. She vacuumed cat hair from the sofa, shook out the comforter and pillows, washed the sheets and towels, mopped the wood floors. It was almost six o'clock when she finished and realized that she hadn't eaten all day. She started a pot boiling with water for pasta, then opened her computer on the kitchen table.

She scanned the new entries on the Facebook page that Joanne's friends had created for her. There were declarations of love, of grief, and also the sweet, private memories. *Remember the time*— But there was nothing from Kate. At least nothing Robbie recognized as coming from Kate and her arrowhead icon. How frustrating that she didn't have access to Kate's Facebook page.

Robbie left Facebook and Googled the latest entries on Joanne Sparks and Kaitlin Brooks. It had been four days since Joanne's body was found and still no news about Kate. Was that good? Bad? Did it mean Kate was still alive?

She got up and put ziti into the boiling water, stirring while she looked out the window. Palm fronds shifted against a whitish-gray sky. She wondered if Gina had spoken to her husband about having some of his people check into Kate's disappearance. Robbie had a feeling that even though Gina had been enthusiastic about her husband putting together a special task force, it wasn't likely that someone as important as Stanford Fieldstone would have the time or interest to get involved with some missing high school kid.

Even if a lot of well-intentioned people were trying to find Kate, Robbie knew better than to rely on them. Her mother's lessons on self-sufficiency ran too deep.

She drained the ziti, added tomato sauce, then took the bowl back over to the kitchen table. Lying beside her computer was the street map she'd made yesterday with the ten most popular South Beach clubs plotted on it.

Gina Fieldstone was right; Robbie needed to do something before it was too late. So tonight, she would make the rounds at these clubs and see if her sister was at one of them.

Robbie's cell phone rang. The caller ID read RESTRICTED. Gina? But Gina's last call had registered as UNKNOWN.

She opened her phone. "Hello?"

"Hi Robbie. It's Judy Lieber. Are you home?"

Robbie's heart started pounding. "You've found Kate?"

"No. Nothing like that. But I'd like to talk to you. May I come up to your apartment? I'm just down the street."

Lieber arrived a few minutes later carrying her battered leather case. She was wearing black pants and a short-sleeved white shirt, yellowed with age. It was probably still very hot outside if she'd ditched her jacket.

Lieber glanced at Robbie's shorts and sweaty tank top splotched with white scouring powder. There were shadows under Lieber's eyes. "Am I interrupting something?"

"I was just having an early dinner. Would you like some pasta?"

"No thanks. Water would be great, though. And please, go ahead and eat."

They went into the kitchen, Matilda twining herself around Lieber's legs. Lieber put the briefcase down and picked her up. "Same cat?"

Robbie was confused. She held the bottle of water she'd taken from the refrigerator against her chest. Then she remembered. Lieber had been to Robbie's townhouse in Coconut Grove a year before. "Yes. Same cat. Her name's Matilda. She stayed with Jeremy's grandfather while we traveled."

Lieber scratched the cat's neck, then released her. "Mr. Weiss. Such a nice man. How's he doing?"

"I guess okay. I haven't seen him in a while. I feel kind of badly."

"I'm sure he understands. You're busy with your own life."

"Still." Robbie handed Lieber the bottle.

"Thanks." Lieber sat down at the table, glancing at the open laptop screen and street map.

"So you said you're not here about Kate," Robbie said as she sat back down in her chair.

"You ever hear of Richard Griswold?" Lieber asked, taking a sip of water.

"The congressman?"

"That's right. He's been in Miami Beach at a health care summit."

"And?"

"This morning, he took a header off the balcony of his room at the Regency Hotel."

"He jumped?"

"Probably. It appears to be a suicide, but for the time being, we're classifying it as a suspicious death."

"Suspicious? Why?"

"I've talked to Griswold's family and colleagues. There was no reason for him to kill himself. His career was really taking off. There was even talk that he was in line for Speaker of the House. No health issues. Good family life. Two kids—both out of college and doing well."

Robbie picked at the ziti with her fork. "But why are you here? Do you think his death is connected to Kate?"

"I'm here because Griswold was at BURN Friday night."

BURN again. Puck was probably going to be there tonight hoping to see Robbie. But that couldn't have anything to do with Griswold. BURN was the kind of place that out-of-towners gravitated to.

"Griswold left with two women," Lieber was saying. "I'm trying to find out who they were and whether there's any connection to his death."

"And you happen to know I was at BURN on Friday?"

"I met with Jeremy a little while ago, since I know he sometimes frequents BURN. As it happens, he was there Friday and he gave me the names of everyone he remembered seeing."

"So he saw Griswold leaving with the two women?"

Lieber shook her head. "No. He doesn't remember seeing Griswold at all. A couple of other people did. But no one can identify the two women with him. Or if they can, they're not willing to tell me who they are. I was hoping you may have seen something."

Lieber reached into her case and pushed several photos across the table toward Robbie. There were the standard, posed photos of Richard Griswold she recognized from the newspaper. Mid-fifties, short black hair. But there were also a couple of candid shots. Robbie held up one of the congressman laughing, deep wrinkles above his bushy eyebrows, jowly cheeks.

"You saw him at the club?" Lieber must have picked up on something in Robbie's face.

"Yeah. I'm pretty sure I did. I thought he looked familiar at the time." Robbie tried to recreate the moment from her memory of Friday night. "He was very drunk. Almost out of it. Two women were hanging onto his arms. No. That's not quite right. It was more like they were holding him up."

"Did you know the women?"

Robbie shook her head. "Never saw them before. But that was also the first time I've been to BURN. I'm not exactly into the club scene."

"I know. That's why I'm hoping you'll be able to give me a more objective take on what you saw than some of the other people I've spoken to."

"You think they'd cover if they knew the women?"

"Frankly, yes. South Beach is a small town. No one likes to be known as someone who rats out friends or even acquaintances."

Robbie wondered how the people whose names Jeremy had given Lieber would react if they knew what Jeremy had done.

"What can you tell me about the two women?" Lieber had her little notebook out with a pen.

"One was very tall and skinny. Dark tan, but it could have been the natural color of her skin. Really big breasts."

"South Beach. What else is new?"

"She was laughing. Having a great time." Robbie thought for a minute. "The other woman—actually she was more of a girl. Anyway, she had straight light blonde hair with bangs. She was out of it. Not having fun like her friend."

"Do you remember anything else?"

Robbie shook her head.

"Would you recognize them from photos?"

"I'm not sure. They went by in a blur." Robbie took a sip of water. "Why do you think there's a connection between his death and the women?"

"I spoke to the concierge at the Regency. He happened to be on duty Friday and Saturday and saw Griswold when he left the hotel, then when he returned. He said Griswold was in high spirits Friday night. His aide had left unexpectedly and Griswold was acting like a kid without a chaperone. Griswold told the concierge he was going to check out BURN. Then, other people confirmed seeing Griswold leave BURN with two women a little after two a.m. When Griswold returned to the hotel around eleven a.m. on Saturday, he was still wearing what he'd had on the night before, but was disheveled and appeared drunk or stoned. The next time he was seen was this morning, splattered on the oceanfront dining terrace."

Robbie shook her head.

"Anyway, it seems Griswold spent much of Saturday night and early this morning drinking, according to the room service tabs and the state of his minibar. Something may have happened after Friday night that changed his state of mind."

"Did he have any calls or visitors?"

"No visitors. A few calls, one that we're unable to trace."

"Did he leave a suicide note?"

"No. But he called his wife very early this morning, and she said he was uncharacteristically upset."

"So it points to a suicide."

"Maybe. But if so, why? This is a story of national interest and the media are about to have a heyday with it. You know, South Beach—hotbed of vice. I want to be sure there's nothing to that." Lieber gathered up the photos, then pushed out her chair and stood. "Thanks for your help and for the water."

"You're welcome." Robbie looked at her laptop on the kitchen table. Earlier she'd been looking for Facebook messages from Kate. "Does this mean searching for Kate and figuring out what happened to Joanne is being put on a back burner?"

Lieber hesitated, then she sat back down. It was a moment before she spoke. "Actually, I'm not officially investigating the congressman's death. The FBI's taken the lead. I just like to know what's going on in my own backyard. Many times, when there's a spike of negative activity, I find there are connections. I'm processing my findings here with the information I have about Kate and Joanne."

"My father told me you found Joanne's car."

"That's right."

"Anything about the car that's helpful?"

Lieber tapped her fingers against the edge of the table.

"You found something?"

"Actually, we did," Lieber said.

"What?"

"A crumpled receipt. It was under the seat. Probably missed by whoever cleaned out the car."

"And?"

"It was from a Circle K. For two bottles of water. It was dated the Friday the girls disappeared."

"A Circle K where?"

"Key Largo."

"Key Largo? But I thought the car was found on Miami Beach."

"It was. That's why the receipt's probably a dead end. Even if the girls drove down to Key Largo, it appears they returned to Miami Beach."

"But maybe they went to a party down there and that's where Joanne drowned."

"Then how'd the car get back to Miami?"

"I don't know. Could someone have driven the car back so the girls wouldn't be associated with Key Largo?"

"It's possible. I have a couple of people down in the Keys checking things out. But all we know is that their car was most likely in Key Largo. We don't know for sure whether the girls were with it."

Robbie stood up and went to the window. It was quiet outside. The sky had turned a darker gray, and the palm fronds were perfectly still, like in a painting. Two bottles of water purchased in Key Largo the day the girls disappeared. There had to be a connection.

"Robbie?"

"Mmm-hmm."

"I told you, it's being investigated. And it's very likely a dead end."

Robbie turned back to Lieber, her arms folded across her chest. She was feeling strangely chilled. "You already said that."

Chapter 23

Lights. Throbbing. Pink. Purple. Green. Blue. Like icicles. Melting icicles. Melting into thump-a, thump-a, thump-a. Her heart? The music? It was all the same. Thump-a, thump-a, thump-a.

Angel stretched her arms up and moved with the beat. Her satiny dress cool and slinky against her.

Tyra gave her a smile. "You're startin' to like this shit, aren't you, baby?"

Angel didn't answer. No need to talk. No one listened, anyway.

BURN again tonight. Smoke melted the icicle lights. Red, orange, yellow. Not icicles, flames. They were in hell. Burn, baby, burn.

Hell. What was Angel doing in hell?

A big black bouncer with dreadlocks passed close to Tyra. "Everything cool?" he said in a deep baritone.

"I guess." Tyra kept her eyes on the room, without even a glance at the bouncer.

"Heard there was some trouble. The Man said to keep our eyes open. Make sure no one's messing with the game."

"Don't know why we don't just lay low for a few weeks," Tyra said. "But no one wants my opinion."

"Hey, babe. You need to trust The Man. He says this fucker's too big to let go."

"The Man's not the one with his tits hanging out while the cops sniff around."

"Don't you worry, sister. I'm watching. You girls got no worries." He squeezed Tyra's nipple, then slinked through the crowd.

Tyra muttered under her breath. "The Man don't know shit, just thinks he's smarter than everyone else. Thinks he's untouchable."

Angel wondered what was going on. Tyra had been acting weird since the phone call she got this morning. But none of this concerned Angel. She had her own problems.

Abruptly, Tyra stood alert, shoulders back, like a cat ready to pounce. "There he is," Tyra said. "Almost didn't recognize him with the Clark Kent glasses and stubble. Angel, pay attention."

Angel focused. Tyra had lightened up on the drugs tonight, explaining that Angel might need to help out in case the target didn't want to cooperate. And if Angel was good, Tyra had promised, they'd ease up on her a bit. But if she was bad—Angel didn't want to think about that.

"See the bald guy at the bar?" Tyra asked. "Wearin' a suit, no tie? He's checking his watch."

Angel kept moving her hips with the music, playing her part. She glanced at the man in the suit. Just an ordinary guy. But once he was naked, he'd be like the others. The thought made Angel almost retch. She took a few deep breaths and stared at her feet, not at the guy, not at the lights. Maybe if she made believe she really was Angel, she wouldn't get so sick that she puked.

Tyra's breath was close to Angel's ear. "I think you're more his type than I am, but I'll be watching you. You know I'm always watching you."

No choice. Do what Tyra says. You're Angel tonight. And just remember—Angel isn't you.

She looked again at the guy at the bar. Younger than her dad, but like him. Nervous, awkward. Didn't belong here. The other targets didn't either. Too dorky. But they had lots of money—that's what Tyra said. And a lot to lose.

The guy was checking out the room, like he was getting ready to leave.

"Come on." Tyra had Angel by the arm. "And when we get back to the apartment, don't be making a fuss like you did the other night. Or puking on his dick."

The guy was coming toward them.

Tyra held Angel tighter and blocked his path. "Hey honey." Big smile. "Buy me and my friend a drink?"

He didn't even look at them. "Some other time." He tried getting around Tyra.

She pinched Angel's arm and gave her a look that meant she had better do something or else. But Angel had pretty much forgotten how to flirt.

"Hi," she said to the man.

He stopped trying to escape and took Angel in with brown eyes magnified behind his black-framed glasses. He had a nice face. Soft lips, a few day's beard growth, his eyebrows almost touching in a concerned kind of way.

"Are you all right?" he asked.

Angel glanced at Tyra, who was giving her a warning look.

"Yeah. I'm good. Can you buy me and my friend a drink?"

"Are you old enough to drink?"

"Sure. I'm here, aren't I?"

"Tell you what," said the man, "why don't you and I sit for a few minutes and talk?"

Tyra gave her a little nod. Angel was doing a good job.

The man pulled out a stool and Angel sat down. He stood beside her, his arm resting on the bar. Lights were swimming over the room. Pink. Purple. Thump-a, thump-a, thump-a. Angel ignored the guy and moved to the beat. Maybe he'd just leave.

She looked around for Tyra. Gone. She was gone. Angel's heart sped up. No one was watching her. She could escape, just run right out of here if she wanted to. But where would she go? What would she do?

The man said something to her.

If she ran away, they would find her. Tell the police what she'd done.

The man was looking at her like he expected an answer.

"Huh?"

"I said, what's your name?"

Her name. "K——" she started to say. "Angel."

"Angel." He shook his head like he didn't believe her.

"What's yours?" she asked.

He seemed taken aback by her question, then he laughed. "Puck. You can call me Puck."

"Puck?"

"It's as good a name as Angel."

He was almost handsome when he smiled. And there was this light in his eyes, like mischief. Then, he got serious. "What are you doing here, Angel? Are you in some kind of trouble?"

She shook her head hard.

"Here you go." Tyra handed Angel a drink with a leaf floating in it.

Where'd she come from?

"Good thing I know the bartender. Got you one, too," Tyra said to Puck. "My friend makes the best mojitos in town."

"No thanks," he said, but she pushed it into his hand.

"Come on. Have a little taste." Tyra inched closer to him. "Maybe I didn't spend my own money on it, but I did carry it over here and now my hand's all cold." She dropped her arm between her hips and the man's groin and pressed closer. "So cold."

Puck's eyes widened. He brought the drink to his mouth and took a sip.

"Good, ain't it?" Tyra said in a voice like hot fudge. "Like I said, best ones in town."

He took another swallow.

Tyra smiled, pressing Puck against the bar. "So, you from around here?"

Puck shook his head, but not in answer to her question. He looked really annoyed with himself. He put the drink on the bar and shoved Tyra away.

Tyra held up her hands in mock surrender. "Okay, okay. So I'm not your type. No need to get all huffy."

She backed away and gave Angel a look that Puck couldn't see. Angel understood. It meant take it from here, or else.

Angel reached for Puck's drink. "Please," she said, handing it to him. "Can you just make believe?"

Tyra had evaporated.

"What do you mean, make believe?"

"That you're having fun with me. So I don't get in trouble."

"What's going on? Who's that woman?"

"Please," Angel said. "Don't look mad. Just drink your drink and make like you're having a good time."

Puck frowned, but he brought the glass up to his mouth and drank.

Angel started moving to the beat, holding her arms up in the air while he watched and sipped his drink. He didn't seem turned on by her little show—more like he was thinking about something, ana-lyzing the situation—but at least he was drinking.

God, she hated this. But she knew Tyra was watching her and she'd better do her job.

"We can dance, if you want," Angel said.

"What I want is to find out what's going on here. Why are you so frightened?"

Angel glanced around. People everywhere. Dancing, drinking. Where was Tyra?

"Because I can help you," Puck said. "I'll take you out of here and we can call your parents, or anyone you'd like."

Red, orange, yellow, green, blue, purple, pink.

He wanted to help her. Maybe he could.

He touched her shoulder, his fingers cold from the drink, but so gentle. Daddy, she thought. Help me.

Something was burning her eyes. Tears. They were running down her cheeks. Oh God. What to do?

"Let's go outside," he said.

His arm was around her and he was leading her through the crowd. Past the bar area, the dance floor, and tables and couches. They were almost by the stairs. Just a little farther, then up the stairs and through the lobby and she'd be free. Or would she?

"It's okay," he said in her ear, like he knew she was frightened. "We'll figure it out."

Hurry, she wanted to scream. We have to hurry.

And then something bumped into her, hard.

"Going somewhere?" Tyra blocked them.

"What are you doing here with this girl?" Puck said. "Who are you?"

"What do you mean?" Tyra asked. "Angel's my friend."

"I doubt that."

Tyra dug her nails into Angel's arm. "What's wrong, baby? Did this man make you cry?"

Puck touched his head. He was blinking his eyes. "Shit. What did you put in my drink?"

"In your drink?" Tyra asked. "What are you talking about?"

"I'm calling the cops."

"You don't want to do that, honey. Not after you made this poor sweet child cry. You brought her here and made her cry. And I'll bet she isn't more than fifteen or sixteen years old."

"Hooow daaaare yoooo."

Tyra slipped her arm through Puck's. He tried to push her away.

"Why don't we all go outside to talk?" she said, clinging to him. "I'm sure we can work it out."

The big black bouncer with dreadlocks came over. "Problem?"

"Sheeeee—" Puck couldn't get the words out. His head and arms swayed like one of those inflatable figures at a car wash.

"He's drunk," Tyra said. "Can you help him outside? We'll get him home."

"Sure thing." The bouncer held Puck around the waist as easily as a mom with a toddler, and dragged him toward the stairs.

Tyra followed with Angel, pinching her arm as they went. "You little whore," Tyra said under her breath. "What the fuck were you thinking?"

"Nothing," Angel said.

The room was on fire—red, orange, yellow. Burn, baby burn.

"Well you better be sweet with him when we get back to the apartment. You got that?"

Angel didn't answer. She was never getting out of hell.

Chapter 24

Angel drifted in and out of darkness. Sleep. She just wanted to sleep. Her head ached and she smelled cigarette smoke on the cushion. Bad taste in her mouth. She sank deeper against the sofa. Too tired to go to her room. Something warm and soft pressed against her back. She tensed. Someone beside her.

She tried to remember. The man from BURN. Swinging his arms in rage as they pushed him into the car, then collapsing. Back at the apartment. Tyra stripping the man, holding him up. Making Angel get naked. But the man was out, not cooperating.

Tyra yelling, "Fuck. It's no good."

Luis talking to Tyra. Telling her not to worry. Then quiet.

Sleep. Angel just wanted to sleep.

A weak light came in through the sliding doors. Almost morning. Angel shifted on the sofa, careful not to disturb the man. Why was he still here? Luis always got the men out when they were finished.

The man's arm slid around her waist, his breath was in her hair.

He was still drugged. He couldn't know what he was doing.

His hand cupped her breast. She felt him harden against her butt.

No, she thought. Please, no. She dared not move. She'd just lie here and let him finish. She'd squeeze her eyes shut and think about something else. Not the pain, the roughness, the dirtiness. Sex was awful. Who ever said it would be great?

Something else. Think about something else.

Holding her parents' hands. She was little; they were big. One, two, three, up, they all sang. One, two, three, up. And Kate would throw her head back and laugh as they swung her through the air.

The man's hand slid up and down her leg. Different from the others. Gentle, like silk and satin. His breath warm. He stroked the inside of her thigh. Higher, higher, his fingers danced. She relaxed against him.

He turned her toward him and nuzzled against her neck. His light beard tickled her. He held her face between his hands and kissed her. His lips firm. She opened her mouth. His tongue tasted sweet. Nice.

One, two, three, up. They swung her through the air.

He slipped inside her, easy. So easy. She held him there, tight. Don't let go.

Don't let go.

One, two, three, up.

Tighter, tighter. Good, so good. One, two, three, up.

One, two, three, up.

One, two, three, up, up, up.

She melted into him. She saw his face. The man from BURN. The nice man who wanted to help her.

Puck.

His eyes were closed, his breathing even.

She kissed his eyelids.

"Thank you," she whispered.

"Thank *you*, Angel," said a sandpapery voice just beside her.

Luis blocked Puck's mouth with a chloroformed rag, then carried him over his shoulder like a dead man.

Chapter 25

"Ten more," Jeremy said, as he hovered near the weight bench.

His client groaned. She was a gorgeous woman who looked about thirty-five, but had to be close to sixty based on the age of her oldest child. Her white ribbed tank top was soaked in sweat, but she balanced forward for ten more reverse triceps curls with a fifteen-pound weight in each hand. Her large breasts barely moved.

Ba-boom, ba-boom. The bass track of the music was as constant as a heartthrob.

The gym resembled an upscale club more than a place for working out. It wasn't really Jeremy's thing. He preferred Gold's where the harsh light bounced off dull linoleum tiles, well-used equipment, small, threadbare towels. Here at David Barton's, the towels were lush and large and so were the hourly fees for his personal training services.

"Eight, nine," Jeremy counted. "Five more."

"Nooo, you piece of shit."

"Come on. Do you want the skin on your arms to hang like a turkey's wattle?"

"Very graphic," she said, but kept going, even after the extra five curls.

"Okay. Good job. Let's stretch."

She checked her watch. "Don't have time. Nail appointment."

"You've got to stretch or you'll undo all of your hard work."

"Bullshit," she said, kissing his cheek and pressing a wad of bills into his hand. "See you tomorrow at eleven."

"I'll be here."

He put the money in his pocket. Sixty bucks an hour. Not bad. And it sure beat being an accountant.

The woman disappeared through the dark corridor into the locker room. It was around eleven and Jeremy's next client wasn't until one. Plenty of time to get in his own workout. He headed toward the more serious section of the gym. Mondays in the middle of the day were pretty quiet. A few people came in during their lunch hour. And then there were the bodybuilder freaks who seemed to be here 24/7. Jeremy recognized a couple of them. Bouncers at BURN. He wondered if they knew he'd mentioned them to the detective yesterday. Probably not. Lieber wouldn't have given out his name.

He went to the machines to warm up. The throbbing ba-boom numbed his brain and he went through his routine hardly thinking about what he was doing.

How weird it was talking to Lieber yesterday afternoon. His pulse had gone berserk when he noticed her coming into the gym. Not that he didn't like her. He had always liked Lieber. But the sight of her triggered memories, one worse than the next. So many deaths, so much pain. And the first thought that came to mind was of his sister.

"Is Elise okay?" he'd asked.

And Lieber's face had fallen. "Geez. I'm sure she's fine. I'm sorry, Jeremy. I should have called. I didn't realize you'd associate me with—"

And he'd interrupted her and made like it was no big deal. That it was good to see her. And they'd gone out for a cup of coffee, where she told him about the congressman who tried to fly like Superman, but couldn't.

He'd given her the names of everyone he could remember who had been at BURN on Friday night. She glanced up when he mentioned Robbie, but she hadn't commented. Just took down everything he told her.

And when she left, he had felt like going after her. Begging her to stay for a while longer. Because as much as he hated the bad memories, there was something about Lieber that brought his parents back to him.

He lay down on the bench and lifted the barbell slowly over his chest. A hundred and sixty pounds. All the way up, then slowly down.

When he was alone, with time to think, the memories would come at him in a rush. His mother making breakfast, sipping coffee. His father bent over his computer in his office, Mozart playing in the background. Robbie sticking her tongue out at him. But wait, that came later. He always thought of Robbie with his parents. It was as though she was a bridge to them. An easy, accessible bridge. And without her, the connection to them was so much more painful.

Sweat soaked through his T-shirt. He lifted the barbell all the way up, then slowly down.

He wished he had the balls to call her. Seeing Robbie at BURN the other night was like being offered a candy bar, then having it pulled right out of your mouth. But he wasn't going to call her. Let Robbie make the move when she was ready. If she was ever ready.

He raised the barbell straight up, then lowered it. Slowly up, then slowly down. His arms trembled under the strain. Slowly up, then slowly down.

There was a change in the air behind him. Someone standing nearby. Jeremy could feel eyes on him. A tense energy.

The barbell shook. Jeremy almost lost his grip. He brought it down cautiously, sat up, and turned. Brett was just behind the bench.

"Brett," Jeremy said. "What's up, man?"

"I want to know who the hell you think you are."

Jeremy remembered Friday night at BURN. How pissed Brett had been that Jeremy and Robbie were talking.

Jeremy stood. Brett's hands were in fists. He was a couple of inches taller than Jeremy, but Jeremy felt he had the advantage in muscle bulk.

The other guys who were working out slowed their movements and watched them.

Even in the darkened room, Jeremy could tell Brett's face was red. A vein was throbbing in his forehead in time to the music.

Ba-boom. Ba-boom.

Brett spoke first. "Why are you talking to fucking detectives?"

So that's what this was about. Jeremy felt a moment's annoyance. Had Lieber mentioned Jeremy's name or had Brett figured out that Jeremy had told her? "Chill, man," Jeremy said. "She just asked who was at BURN Friday night. Everyone saw you there. It's not like I was giving away any big secrets."

"I don't like my name thrown around."

Jeremy started to reach for his barbell, but Brett grabbed Jeremy's arm, his fingers digging in. "I said I don't like my name thrown around."

Jeremy pulled out of his grip. "Get your damn hands off me."

"I want to know that you'll keep out of my business."

"Are you serious? What's your problem?"

"Say it, Stroeb. 'I promise to keep out of Brett Chandler's business.'"

"You're an asshole, Brett. I can't believe Robbie's wasting her time with you."

Jeremy saw the punch coming and blocked it before Brett's fist connected with his face. "Hey, man. This isn't the place."

"It's your fucking fault," Brett said. "What did you tell her about me?"

"I didn't tell Lieber shit."

"Not the detective. Robbie. What did you tell Robbie? She talks to you and the next thing I know she's done with me."

Robbie dumped Brett? Jeremy felt a warm sensation ooze through his veins. "Robbie's a smart girl," Jeremy said. "She can figure things out herself."

Brett pounced on Jeremy, catching him in the chest and knocking the breath out of him.

Jeremy recovered and lunged toward Brett, but a couple of the bodybuilders grabbed his arms. Two others were holding Brett back.

"That's enough, dudes," someone said. "Go somewhere else if you want to beat each other's brains out."

Brett shrugged off the guys hanging onto his arms. He ran his fingers angrily through his spiked blond hair. "This isn't the end, Stroeb. You're getting in my face and I don't like it."

The two guys who were holding Jeremy released him. Jeremy picked up the barbell and walked away, the cool darkness all around him.

Robbie had broken up with the asshole.

Ba-boom, ba-boom.

Ba-boom.

Chapter 26

At a little after eleven on Monday morning, feeling as though she had nothing else to lose, Robbie got on her bicycle and pedaled. East. Toward the gym. To Jeremy.

Was she crazy? Or was this the sanest thing she'd done in months?

Yesterday, after Lieber left Robbie's apartment, Robbie had studied the street map she'd marked up with South Beach clubs. But doubts about her plan to spend Sunday night looking for Kate at any of them grew. Was that really the most likely place to find her sister? The bottled water receipt Lieber had found in Joanne's car had been from a Circle K in Key Largo.

Not South Beach.

Robbie wasn't sure why, but she had this nagging feeling that's where her sister was.

She biked down a side street, swerving to avoid a construction truck that was backing up. What if Jeremy wasn't at work? Or what if he was and didn't want to help her?

She turned onto Collins Avenue and slowed. Jeremy's gym was up a couple of blocks, but the entire street was obstructed by equipment and men in hardhats who were digging up the road and sidewalk.

Robbie got off her bike and walked it. A temporary chain-link fence cut off all traffic.

She had to get to Jeremy.

She told herself it was because she needed his help. But was that the real reason? So much had happened over the last few days that she felt tangibly altered. As though she wasn't the same person who had tried to distance herself from Jeremy these past months.

She maneuvered her bike around the fence, ignoring the shouts from the construction workers. The sound of a jackhammer started up and white dust rose all around her, settling on her hair, arms, T-shirt, and jeans. She kept walking, pushing her bike along.

But what about Jeremy? How would he feel about her showing up, especially after the scene with Brett on Friday night?

She stopped, only barely aware of the hammering. The ground vibrated beneath her, making her feel woozy.

Maybe she should have called him. But this wasn't something she wanted to do over the phone. She wanted Jeremy to see her. So he would understand how much—

"Robbie." The shout came from just ahead, beyond the construction. Through the cloud of dust. Jeremy's voice.

She went quickly toward it, pushing her bike forward over broken cement.

And then she felt someone take hold of the bike and drag it beyond the torn-up street. The hammering stopped. The dust cleared.

"Jesus," Jeremy said, still holding the handlebars. "Are you crazy? You're in the middle of a construction site. You could get hit by flying debris or something."

"I needed to see you."

He was scowling, but at her words the frown lifted. "That's interesting. Because I was on my way to see you."

"You were?"

His lips twitched like he was holding back a smile. He reached over and removed a small piece of chalky debris from her hair.

"Why?" she asked.

The hammering started up again. Jeremy signaled for her to follow him. He locked her bike against a post, then took her hand and led her down a side street toward the ocean. They reached the oceanfront path where Robbie liked to run. The wide buildings screened the construction sounds; they were surrounded by the rush of the waves breaking, the screeching of birds.

"So you were saying something about needing to see me?" Jeremy asked, ignoring her question. His black T-shirt was soaked through as though he'd just finished a workout.

Now wasn't the time for an emotional watershed. She was here because of her sister. Whatever else was going on inside her had to wait. "I need to go to Key Largo."

He tilted his head, waiting for her to continue.

A group of joggers ran by on the path, forcing Jeremy and Robbie to move aside. Robbie glanced over the barrier of sea oats at the wide expanse of beach. She turned back to Jeremy. "I think my sister may be there."

"Oh yeah?" He raised an eyebrow.

"Lieber told me there was a receipt for two bottles of water in Joanne's car. It was from a Circle K in Key Largo, and it was dated the Friday the girls disappeared."

"But Joanne's body was found here in Indian Creek."

"I know. But I need to figure out what the girls were doing in Key Largo."

"So you came to say goodbye?"

"Actually." Robbie pushed her hair behind her ear. "I was wondering if you'd mind driving me. Sixty miles is a bit far to go by bike."

He glanced up the street to where they'd left her bicycle just beyond the construction. "Yeah, I can definitely see where that would be a problem."

Chapter 27

Robbie watched Jeremy. He was holding the steering wheel, his too-long brown hair blowing helter-skelter by the breeze through the windows of his father's old red Corvair.

Jeremy had showered, changed into faded jeans and a white T-shirt, and cancelled his appointments before picking her up from her apartment. Robbie had also cleared her schedule with Leonard and asked for the next couple of days off.

As they drove, Robbie told Jeremy about her reconciliation with her father and what she had been doing to find her sister. They were soon out of Miami, heading south on the turnpike, windows open to compensate for the broken A/C. The conversation dwindled. Robbie looked out at tract-housing communities and car dealerships, then at groves of palm trees—unnatural, perfect rows of cabbage palms, royals, and silvery Bismarck palms.

Jeremy seemed to be waiting her out. She almost asked again why he had been on his way to see her, but didn't want to press him.

The turnpike ended at U.S. 1 and they slowed as they passed a giant outlet mall, then an ugly stretch of fast-food restaurants, gas stations, billboards, and motels.

"Last chance," Jeremy said.

"Last chance for what?" She felt herself blush.

He pointed to a sign on their right. "Last Chance Saloon. No booze until we get to Key Largo. Think you can make it?"

She grinned back at him.

The billboards fell away with the traffic lights. They picked up speed as they left Florida City behind. Robbie could smell a change in the air—warmer and saltier. Her feathered earrings fluttered in the breeze.

Jeremy slid a cassette into the tape player. Mozart's *Requiem*. The music sent shivers through her. It was what they had listened to the last time they'd left Miami together. When it was just the two of them, and anything was possible.

"So," Jeremy said, "do you have a plan?"

Robbie pulled herself back from the Mozart. "Of course."

"And?"

"First, I thought we'd stop at the Circle K and see if anyone remembers seeing Kate or Joanne. I brought the flyers with their pictures. Maybe the girls said something to the store clerk about where they were going."

Jeremy nodded. "Then?"

"Well. I tried to think like an eighteen-year-old. Why would they have gone down there, except probably to party? So I Googled bars and clubs from Key Largo to Islamorada and printed them out."

"Good."

"We can take the flyers around and see if anyone recognizes them. Then I think we should check out motels where the girls may have spent the night. Lieber said she had someone doing that, but, well, you know."

"I do know." There was a laugh in his voice. "You're still such a control freak."

She knew he meant it with admiration, but it rankled Robbie. She wasn't that much of a control freak.

"But I agree," he said. "It's not likely Lieber's people spoke to every single person who may have seen your sister. Besides, I think the locals are more likely to talk to you than to cops."

They continued down the straight, two-lane highway that followed the abandoned Florida East Coast Railway right-of-way. Signs warned them to drive slowly. The scenery had become monotonous—flat, brown swampland with occasional stands of Australian pines and little islands of jungly trees. Powerline posts zipped by at even intervals.

Robbie realized with heightened awareness this was the route her sister would have taken. Was Kate still down here? And if so, how did Joanne's Volvo get back to Miami, and why?

"Brett came by to see me," Jeremy said, jarring Robbie back to the moment.

"He did? When?"

"This morning. At the gym." Jeremy kept his eyes on the road. There were construction barricades on the shoulders.

"What did he want?"

"To beat the shit out of me."

"Seriously?"

"It sure looked that way."

"Why?"

"He said it was because I told Lieber he was at BURN Friday night, but he seemed more upset about something else."

White egrets were perched on the branches of dead trees, and dense, tangled mangroves rose out of the dark, swampy water.

"I ended things with him."

"That's what I picked up."

"He blamed you?"

"Let's just say he thinks I was a motivating factor." Jeremy slowed as a car passed on their left in the oncoming traffic lane. "Idiot," he said. "Can't he see this is a no passing zone?"

"I should have done it sooner," Robbie said. "I didn't realize how different his and my values are."

"I guess he didn't like being told it was about him, so he's looking for someone to lay it on."

"Did he make a scene?"

"He had to. The guy's got a big ego."

Robbie rested her arm on the window frame and watched a thicket of trees go by. She hadn't noticed that side of Brett until recently. The early days of their relationship had been all about having fun.

"So now that Brett's out of the picture," Jeremy said, "I was wondering—Shit!" He slammed on the brakes and tightened his grip on the steering wheel. A black car with tinted windows, passing on their left, cut in front of them suddenly to avoid an oncoming car.

"Jesus, what an asshole." Jeremy pushed down on the horn and held it for a few seconds.

An arm popped out of the driver's window of the black car, giving them the finger. Then the car pulled back into the oncoming traffic lane and disappeared ahead of them.

"Why do people have to be such jerks?" Jeremy said.

Why indeed? Robbie thought.

They continued in silence, the harsh sound of the Corvair's engine competing with the wind through the open windows. Jeremy didn't finish his thought about Brett being out of the picture. Robbie wondered if he was waiting for her to say something.

Rivulets of cobalt water appeared in the brown sawgrass, spreading into wider blue-green canals that wound their way through the mangroves. In the next moment, Robbie caught her breath as the turquoise, crystalline waters of Card Sound appeared on their left, the bay on their right. They climbed a bridge. Masts of small boats bobbed in a cove, the sky a perfect cloudless blue.

Robbie had been to the Keys once before, but what about Kate? Had this been her first time? Would her sister have also been awed by the startling beauty? Would she have felt a sense of freedom as she crossed into paradise?

Beyond the bridge, was Key Largo and civilization.

The Circle K was the first thing they saw. They pulled into the parking lot and went inside. It was a large, modern store with a dozen people milling about. Two women in matching red shirts were working behind the checkout counter. When Robbie showed them the flyers, the women looked at each other and laughed. "Do you know how many people come through here every day?" the chubby one said. "There's no way we'd remember them."

Robbie and Jeremy went back to the car.

"It's just our first stop," he said. "Someone will remember them."

"Yes," Robbie said, trying to sound more certain than she felt. "Someone will remember them."

They went south on U.S. 1, passing low pastel-painted buildings and strip malls, RV parks, sandal outlets, and dive centers. Jeremy drove slowly, stopping at each bar so they could talk to the bartenders and customers. Most of the bars were dark and seedy and seemed to cater to a local crowd. At many of them, they were told someone had already been in with flyers of the girls, but no one recognized either of them.

"At least Lieber's guys are doing their job," Jeremy said, back in the car.

Robbie nodded, but wondered how much good that was if no one remembered seeing Kate.

They continued toward Islamorada past roadside pottery stands, bougainvillea nurseries, and then through stretches of undeveloped land. On either side of the causeway, there were turnoffs leading to the bay and ocean. Robbie caught glimpses of expensive houses where the shoreline jutted out into the bay.

Jeremy pulled off the road into a parking lot next to an outdoor tiki hut bar. "This place looks promising," he said.

They walked on packed sand. There was a dance floor made of wood planks, and a steel band in one of the tiki huts was playing reggae. The crowd was light. Tourists were recognizable by their red arms and faces, the white outline of bathing suit straps on the shoulders of women in halter tops and sundresses. The regulars had skin like brown rawhide, and wore faded print shirts or T-shirts. The smell of fish was particularly strong from the nearby docks, where charter fishing boats had returned with buckets of fish to clean.

They talked to the young guy who was tending bar and showed him the flyers.

"Sorry," he said. "Can't help you."

"Damn," Jeremy said when they got back to the car. "I was sure that was the place."

Robbie nodded and bit down on her lip. Was it possible they wouldn't find a single person who had seen her sister?

Jeremy turned south on the highway. The cars ahead of them were going about five miles an hour. Without air-conditioning and the flow of wind through the open windows, it had gotten uncomfortably hot. Robbie rested her elbow on the window frame and watched the signs go slowly by: key lime pie, T-shirts, gifts, shells, souvenirs. Bud N' Mary's Marina.

She did a double take. That was where Puck's billed cap was from. The marina was five miles ahead.

"Traffic's pretty heavy," Jeremy said. "Any point to keep going?"

She thought about Bud N' Mary's, but it wasn't likely the girls would have gone to a marina. "I guess not. Let's head back and ask at motels."

"Okay." He made a U-turn at the next intersection and drove back up toward Key Largo.

The northbound traffic was flowing, and a breeze cooled the inside of the car. Robbie started feeling more optimistic, certain that the next person they asked would recognize her sister's photo.

The roadside motels were mostly mom-and-pop establishments, hidden behind palms and banana plants. They smelled old and musty, like they'd been around for fifty years, which Robbie supposed they had.

They stopped at each one and showed the flyers. No one remembered seeing Kate or Joanne.

Just before they reached the north end of Key Largo, Jeremy pulled into an overgrown driveway on the bay side that led to a motel. There were several freshly painted cottages and flowering plants shaded by live oaks and palm trees. Beyond, they could see the bay lapping up against a small semicircular beach with lounge chairs and umbrellas in the sand.

"I don't know about your sister and her friend," Jeremy said, "but this is the kind of place I'd stay at."

Was it her imagination or was there a hint of suggestiveness in his voice? But Jeremy said nothing more, just continued to the office.

A tall, gray-haired woman in a flowing white muumuu was arranging exotic-looking flowers on a table in the corner of the clean, cheerful room. Robbie explained why they were there and showed her the flyers.

"Sorry. No. I'd remember if they'd checked in." She handed the flyers back, and cocked her head. "But I have a nice room available for tonight if you two are interested."

"No thanks," Robbie said, without meeting Jeremy's eyes. "We're just down here for the day."

They returned to the car. Jeremy sat without turning on the engine. He puffed up his cheeks, then blew out an explosive breath. "What now? There's nothing farther up ahead."

This couldn't be the end of it. There had to be something they were missing. And then it hit her. "It's only seven o'clock," Robbie said. "The girls probably would have gone out later. Do you mind if we go back to one of the bars and hang around until there's a shift change?"

"Sounds like you have some place in mind."

"Yeah. The tiki bar. It definitely felt like the kind of place a couple of out-of-town teenage girls would go."

"Even if it isn't, I'm about ready for a beer."

Jeremy started up the car.

The parking lot adjacent to the tiki bar had filled with cars since they'd been there two hours earlier. They went to sit on wooden stools at the bar. The young bartender was still working, but told them his shift was almost over. They both ordered beers and Robbie left him a generous tip.

They drank their beers straight from the bottles. The steel drum music was soft and easy and the breeze felt like a baby's breath on her cheeks. The tension of the last few hours seeped out of her. They were on the ocean side of the highway, not the bay, and couldn't see the sun setting on the water, but the sky had turned deep orange with purple streaks. A parasailer floated through the air and it looked as though the sky was on fire behind him. Jeremy stared out toward the water at the rocking boats. There were permanent frown lines in his tanned forehead that she didn't remember from a year ago. Otherwise, he looked pretty mellow. There was a time when Jeremy had reminded her of a shaken soda bottle on the verge of exploding. A time when finding his parents' murderer had hardened him.

He gave Robbie an uncertain smile. "What?"

"It's nice being here with you."

"Yes, it is."

She rolled her cold beer bottle between her hands.

"You doing okay?" he asked.

It was what she was about to ask him. She nodded.

He took a pull of his beer. "It's good you and your dad had a chance to talk things over."

"Yeah."

"But?"

"It's just, sometimes I feel like I'm starting over." She watched the parasailer float down and land in the water. "Like all those years I thought I was growing up were nothing. Just running in place."

"My mom used to say every experience—good or bad—makes you a stronger person."

"You believe that?"

"Yeah. But that doesn't mean I'm happy about the things I went through that made me stronger. I'd sooner have my parents and still be an irresponsible jerk."

Robbie placed her hand over his.

He winced and she started to pull away, but he took her hand in his own. "Cold," he said with a smile. "From your beer."

"Oh." Her heart was racing.

"I'm thinking it may not be a great idea to drive back to Miami tonight," he said. "I don't want to have to deal with that road and Miami crazos like the guy this afternoon."

"We shouldn't drive back," she said.

The music was louder. Or maybe it was her imagination. She could feel the bass pounding in her chest.

What was she doing? What were they doing? The sky had turned pomegranate red. There was a tension between them, like she remembered as a teenager on a first date.

"Another beer?" a woman's voice asked.

The female bartender was new, and Robbie was brought back to the reason they'd come back here. "Sure," Robbie said.

"Me, too," Jeremy said.

The bartender set two more Coronas on the counter.

"Thanks," Robbie said. "Do you mind if I ask you something?" She held out the two flyers. "Do you recognize either of these girls? They were in here a week ago Friday." She didn't know that for sure, but figured saying it couldn't hurt.

The bartender, a tired-looking woman, studied the flyers. "Last Friday? My shift, but I don't recognize them. They look awfully young."

"They were probably wearing a lot of makeup."

The bartender shook her head. "Sorry. Friday's a busy night." She put the flyers down and went to fix someone else's drink.

"Who are they?" asked an older man on the stool next to Robbie's. He looked and smelled like he'd come off one of the fishing boats—stained khaki shorts, faded floral shirt open over an undershirt, graying wind-swept hair surrounding dark, tough skin.

"Why?" Robbie asked. "Do you recognize them?"

"Depends."

Sure, Robbie thought. A local wasn't likely to give out information to strangers.

"This girl's my sister," she said.

He looked from Kate's photo to Robbie, then back again. He took a sip of his drink. She could smell the Scotch. "I saw them."

Jeremy's hand tightened over hers.

Robbie took a deep breath. "Do you remember anything? Who they were with? Where they went?"

"This one," he pointed at Joanne, "she looked like a scared little puppy dog. She sat here holding this pocketbook that was almost as big as she was. Holding it like a giant shield, or something." He took another sip. "The other girl—your sister—first I thought she was older. Real pretty girl. I got the impression she was the one who wanted to be here."

"Were they alone?" Robbie could hardly hear her own voice against the music and rising din.

"At first. Then a couple of punks joined them."

"Do you know them?"

"I've seen them here before, but they're not locals. Too full of themselves. Probably from the mainland. I haven't seen them since that night, though."

"Can you describe them?"

"Not really. They looked like punks. One had a shaved head, the other had brown hair and thick eyebrows." He shrugged. "I've seen guys that look like them a million times."

Jeremy rested his hand on Robbie's shoulder and leaned around her toward the man. "Did the girls leave with them?"

The man took Jeremy in, seemed to decide he was okay. "I wasn't paying all that much attention, but yeah, I saw the four of them leave. The girls looked pretty drunk." He glanced at Robbie, then lowered his eyes. "I don't imagine they were much used to drinking." He took another sip from his glass.

"Any idea where they may have gone?" Jeremy asked.

"Beats me. A party, maybe. On weekends, you get a lot of the rich mainlanders coming down to their big, fancy houses. A lot of them live over by the bay. They think they own the place, driving around in their black limos and little sports cars." He signaled to the bartender for another drink.

Jeremy left some money on the bar and gave Robbie a tug. "Thanks for your help," he said to the man.

"Yes. Thanks so much," Robbie said. "I wonder, would you mind giving me your name and number?"

"I'd rather not." The man looked down at his drink.

"I understand, but here's mine." Robbie handed the man a flyer with her phone number. "If you happen to see those guys, would you give me a call?"

"Sure."

Jeremy was walking toward the parking lot. She wondered why he was in such a hurry to leave.

Robbie slid off the stool.

"I have a daughter," the man said, looking down at the flyer. There was an edge of melancholy in his voice. "I hope you find your sister."

Chapter 28

Headlights on the cars coming from Miami brightened the interior of the Corvair every few seconds. Robbie watched Jeremy hunch forward over the steering wheel, his head turning to follow each one.

They were parked outside a deserted strip mall a ways north of the tiki bar. Turquoise awnings announced local gifts, souvenirs, shells. It was dark and quiet with no pedestrians and only the constant stream of cars filing by.

"Are you going to tell me what we're doing here?" Robbie asked.

"I'm looking for black cars," Jeremy said.

A car whished by.

"Well, you just missed one."

"That was an old Corolla. Totally wrong. It needs to be something fancier—like a Town Car or sports car. Tinted windows would help."

Robbie thought for a second. "You're looking for cars from the mainland heading to a house party? But the guy at the bar said the parties were on weekends, not Monday night."

"Maybe we'll get lucky. Remember the asshole who passed us on U.S. 1? Black car, tinted windows?"

"Yeah, but honestly, isn't that a bit of a long shot?"

"All we have right now are long shots."

Robbie felt tired suddenly, the beers getting to her. Jeremy was right. Sure, they'd found someone who'd seen her sister, but the old guy at the bar hadn't given them much useful information. A couple of punks? They could be anyone or anywhere.

She looked at Jeremy clenching the wheel. The scar extended over the back of his hand like a starburst.

They didn't need to be chasing after shadows. The last time they did, they'd almost gotten killed. The smart thing was to tell Lieber about the man who saw Kate. Tomorrow. Not tonight. Tonight, all she wanted was to curl up next to Jeremy on a big soft bed and let him hold her. Just like he used to.

Another car sped by. The lights played on Jeremy's face—his prominent forehead, several-day-old beard covering his cheeks and cleft chin.

Hadn't he told her at the bar that he didn't want to drive back to Miami tonight? What was she waiting for?

"Jeremy." She put her hand over his scarred one.

He turned toward her. His eyes were a deep rich brown. She saw them for an instant in the light of a passing car. And then, his lips were on hers. She tasted him, melted against him. They clung to each other, kissing, touching. His skin so warm. His muscles so hard. "Jeremy," she whispered.

They pulled apart to study each other. He took a lock of hair out of her eye.

A car sped by, too fast. They both looked. Black sedan, tinted windows.

"Forget about it," he said, pulling her close. "It was a stupid idea."

"No." Robbie straightened up. "Go. Follow it."

He hesitated for barely a second. Then he pulled onto the road, hand on the gearshift. First, second, third—hurrying to catch up with the car. Hurrying away from the moment they almost had.

Later, Robbie told herself. They still had later.

They got lucky. The sedan was stopped by a red light and they pulled up behind it. The light turned green. The sedan screeched forward, turning right at the next street, which led toward the bay. Jeremy followed, holding back so they wouldn't be obvious to the sedan. The street wove around a neighborhood of two-story houses with Bermuda shutters that looked like they'd been built in the 1950s and '60s. As they continued down the road, the shrubs and trees thickened. The houses became larger, newer, and more widely spaced apart. Just like the neighborhood the man at the tiki bar had described as where the mainlanders lived and had their parties. The sedan turned onto what appeared to be a private driveway.

Jeremy stayed back, killed the lights, and slowly approached the opening where the car had turned in. A garage door opened at the end of the driveway; the sedan slid inside the garage with the door closing behind it. There were no other cars. No evidence of a party.

"Looks like I was wrong," Jeremy said.

Robbie was surprised by how relieved she felt.

"Of course, we still have Plan B." He leaned over and kissed her.

"Plan B sounds good. Very good."

Jeremy turned on the headlights. He drove down the winding road to where it dead-ended at the bay, then started turning the car around. A car driving too fast pulled into a driveway just to their right. A black car with tinted windows.

Not now, Robbie thought.

"It's probably nothing," Jeremy said, but he slowed where the car had pulled in.

Oak, ficus, and palm trees formed thickets on either side of the road. Cars were parked haphazardly on the grass and in the circular driveway. Expensive shiny sedans and coupes, Porsches, Ferraris, other sports cars she didn't recognize. Mainly black, some red, a yellow one. They all had tinted windows.

"We don't have to stop," he said.

There wasn't necessarily any connection between this party and her sister, but what if there was?

"We're here," Robbie said. "We should at least check it out."

Jeremy turned into the narrow road, then pulled the Corvair off to the side in a darkened copse of trees and bushes so it wasn't conspicuous.

"How are we going to handle this?" Robbie whispered as they got out of the car.

"Just act like we belong."

"We're not exactly dressed for a party."

"Sure we are."

Small white pebbles covered the circular driveway that led to the house. There had to have been hundreds, maybe even thousands of them. Robbie and Jeremy stayed on the grass, near the shrubs and trees.

At the end of the driveway, a white rectangular house elevated on stilts backed up to the bay. There was a red metal sculpture of a jumping or flying dragon in the courtyard.

The front door was tall, wide, windowless, and white. Jeremy took hold of the doorknob.

"You're not going to knock?" Robbie whispered.

"Nope. We just walk in like we belong."

He pulled the door open, but a large black man with dreadlocks was on the other side blocking their entrance. "Name?" he said, looking down at his clipboard.

"Shit," Jeremy said. "I forgot something."

He led Robbie back to the bushes.

"Now what?" she said.

"We wait and see what happens."

Several people walked along the driveway, their shoes scattering the pebbles. They must have been in the black car that Robbie and Jeremy had followed in. The bouncer let them inside.

"So we stand here all night?" Robbie asked.

"Not all night. We'll give it another few minutes, then we're out of here. I'm thinking of that sweet motel on the bay. Didn't the woman in the office say she had a room for us?"

Robbie again heard the sound of crunching pebbles. A slender woman in a Jackie Onassis-style dress and jacket was walking gracefully toward the house. Her hair was parted on the side so that it covered her forehead at an angle and was then brought back into an upsweep.

"It's Gina Fieldstone," Robbie whispered. "What's she doing here?"

"You know her?"

"Yeah. Her husband's an up-and-coming politician. Gina said they'd try to help find Kate."

"Go." Jeremy gave her a little push.

Robbie shook her head.

"Go," he said a little louder.

The clicking sound stopped. The woman turned toward Jeremy's voice.

"Gina," Robbie called, waving as she stepped from the bushes.

Gina drew herself up like a cornered cat, then she relaxed. "Robbie. You surprised me." Her champagne-colored suit was illuminated by the floodlights positioned atop the house. "I hadn't realized you'd be here. What a relief. I was afraid I wouldn't know a soul."

So Robbie's presence here, wherever here was, wasn't that extraordinary. "I'm glad to see you, too." Robbie hoped to get a handle on whose party this was. "Is your husband with you?"

"My husband?" Gina looked momentarily flummoxed. And then she let out a few notes of her lingering xylophone laugh. "No. Certainly not. Stanford keeps away from these events like the plague." She took in Robbie's jeans and T-shirt. "Oh well. I'm inappropriately dressed, as usual."

"Anything goes at these parties."

"Well that's good." Gina glanced down the pebbled driveway. "If I'd known it was such a long drive from Miami, I never would have come. My publisher is clueless about distances when he sets something up for me. He assumes everything in Florida is a half hour away."

Robbie wondered how Gina had gotten down here. Had she come herself or had her escort from the other night driven her?

Gina seemed to be studying Jeremy, as though not sure what to make of this handsome guy with his scraggly beard.

"This is Jeremy Stroeb," Robbie said.

Gina fondled a rhinestone button on her suit jacket. "Nice to meet you."

"You, too."

Gina took in a deep breath and let it out slowly. "Well, I suppose we should go inside."

"Sounds good." Jeremy held the front door open.

"Gina Tyler Fieldstone," Gina said to the dreadlocked bouncer. Robbie and Jeremy followed her into a foyer with a staircase leading up to the main part of the house. Music was coming from above and a smell of something sweet—perfume? Incense? Marijuana? And there was something else familiar, that didn't seem to belong. Chlorine.

They climbed the staircase. The upstairs vestibule opened onto a huge area with an indoor swimming pool.

Robbie felt a quickening. Lieber had said that Joanne had very likely died in a swimming pool. But lots of houses had swimming pools; what were the odds it would have been this one?

Robbie looked up. The dark, starless sky was visible through a roof made of see-through panels.

People surrounded the glowing blue rectangle. They were dressed like an upscale South Beach crowd—short black dresses on the women, black T-shirts or sport jackets on the men. No one was quite as casual as Robbie and Jeremy. Robbie's hand went to one of her feathered earrings. She was feeling extremely conspicuous.

There were bars at either end of the pool and women in bikinis and stilettos were walking around offering trays of hors d'oeuvres to the guests.

"Hmmm," Gina said. "You're certainly not in Kansas City, Dorothy."

Robbie did a double take. The servers were wearing transparent bikinis, making the young women virtually naked.

"What are you drinking?" Jeremy asked.

"I guess a beer," Robbie said.

He looked at Gina, waiting.

"Nothing for me just yet," she said. "Thank you."

Jeremy walked toward one of the bars, shoulders back, arms swinging, like he totally belonged.

Gina watched him, frowning slightly. Robbie remembered telling her that she didn't have a boyfriend and, in less than a week, Gina had seen Robbie with both Brett and Jeremy. Robbie hated giving Gina the impression that she was loose.

"Jeremy's an old friend," Robbie said. "He's helping me find my sister."

Gina tilted her head. "Here?"

"Maybe. There's a good chance that Kate and Joanne were in Key Largo the Friday they disappeared."

"Sounds like the police are getting closer."

"I hope so. I worry about what you said the other day. That the longer Kate's missing, the less likely she'll be found."

Gina nodded solemnly and rolled the rhinestone button between her fingers. "I've spoken to Stanford about the case and he has a few people checking into it as well."

"Really?"

"Why are you so surprised?"

"I know you offered—and I thought that was amazing of you—but honestly, I didn't think your husband would have time to do anything."

"You sound jaded, Robbie. As though you don't have faith that people want to help each other."

"Most people don't. But I'm truly grateful to you for all you've done."

Gina looked away, as though embarrassed. "I'd better find our host."

Before Robbie had a chance to ask who their host was, Gina slipped into the throng of guests, conjuring up for Robbie the image of a white swan amidst a flock of dark ducklings.

Jeremy returned and handed Robbie a beer. "Where's your new friend?"

Robbie gestured toward the crowd with her head. "She just told me her husband has some people trying to find Kate."

"No kidding," Jeremy said. "He must be pretty connected."

"I guess. He's with the Department of Justice."

"But isn't that federal? How would he get his people to check on something local?"

"I don't know, but she said he'd managed it somehow."

A dark-haired server sashayed by. Her sheer organza bikini shimmered. Robbie had a flash of something unpleasant. Kate? But there was no way her sister would be here, parading around almost nude knowing her best friend was dead.

"We should go," Robbie said. "Before someone realizes we don't belong."

"Let's just walk around for a minute," Jeremy said.

"But it's a waste of time. This isn't the kind of place Kate and her friend would have gone to. These people are older and have money; they're not a bunch of wild partiers where a couple of teenage girls might have gotten in trouble."

A server with a perfect hourglass figure held out a tray of hors d'oeuvres. "Raw tuna with wasabi dumplings," she said to Jeremy. "Want one?" It wasn't clear whether she was offering something from her tray or her personal menu.

"Thanks." Jeremy took a dumpling and popped it into his mouth.

The server walked away. She had an amazing butt.

"Pretty good," Jeremy said, taking a pull from his beer bottle. "What? You're not enjoying this?"

"We're not here to enjoy. We came to see if this might be where those guys brought my sister and it obviously isn't."

"Come on. One walk through." He licked his fingers. "It's ridiculous to me that some people live like this. And this is probably just a vacation house. It had to have cost five or ten million."

Reluctantly, Robbie followed Jeremy past windowed rooms. She could see the reflections of a couple of party crashers in jeans and T-shirts holding bottles of beer. She put her face against the glass to look inside. Bed, dresser, flat-screen TV, a painting of something flying. A dragon? The far wall was a window through which Robbie could see the bay, a black horizon against a moonless sky.

She and Jeremy continued down the hallway. Curtains were drawn in some of the rooms and Robbie wondered who was in there and what they were doing.

A very large long-haired cat appeared from out of nowhere, reminding Robbie of the Cheshire cat. Robbie watched it slip through flaps covering a kitty door that led outside, probably to a porch or balcony.

"That cat has the right idea," Robbie said to Jeremy. "Can we leave now?"

"I guess."

They squeezed past people holding cocktails and champagne glasses. Giant canvases covered the white walls. Each painting depicting a monochrome dragon—red, green, blue. The dragons had large, distorted penises.

"Someone has an interesting fixation," Jeremy said. "I wonder who the dragons mate with."

"Let's go," Robbie said. She put her beer bottle down on a table with other discarded drinks. "This place is starting to creep me out."

Jeremy slid his arm around her and guided her through the crowded pool area. "Okay, little Miss Wholesome. We'll head back to that nice motel on the bay where there are no scary drag—"

"Shit," Robbie said.

"What?"

"Keep walking," Robbie said in a low voice. "I don't want her to see me."

"Who?"

"This girl Maddy, who used to work at The Garage. She's the server standing by the bar. The one with blonde hair and a mermaid tattoo on her arm." Robbie figured she didn't need to specify the large breasts and dimpled butt in the sheer bikini.

"So?" Jeremy said. "What's the big deal if she sees you?"

"It's just embarrassing. She quit without notice. Really inconsiderate."

Just then, Maddy turned toward them holding a tray of drinks. Her eyes met Robbie's. Maddy looked confused, but then she noticed Jeremy and smiled.

"Hey," Maddy said, as she got closer. "I was worried for a minute."

"About?" Robbie said.

"That you were still dating Brett." She puffed out her chest when she got near Jeremy.

"You know Brett?" Robbie said.

"Yeah. He got me this job. Wasn't that sweet? Said he had an anonymous client that wanted to make sure I was taken care of. And this pays way better than The Garage so I don't have to be away from my son so much."

Was Brett somehow connected to this party?

Maddy raked her fingers through her wild blonde hair, balancing the drink tray in the crook of her other arm. "And like, I heard you and Brett weren't a thing anymore."

"We're not."

"So as long as my boyfriend doesn't find out—" Her voice faded off. Robbie followed her eyes.

Brett's head, with its spiked hair, stuck out above the crowd. He was on the other side of the pool, facing a couple of men. His body was stiff like he was primed to hit someone. And then Robbie noticed the orange ponytail and taut face of Brett's boss, Mister M. Could this be Mike's house? Mike's party? It made sense that Gina would be here; she was a client of their public relations firm.

Mike appeared to be saying something to calm Brett down. Robbie recognized the other guy from BURN Friday night—good-looking, with brown hair and a messed-up lip. He put his hand on Brett's shoulder. Brett shrugged him off, then pushed through the crowd with the jittery motions of a prizefighter between rounds.

"Jesus," Maddy said. "What's everyone so angry about?"

Brett's eyes connected with Jeremy's. Then he took in Robbie.

"We should leave," Robbie said to Jeremy in a low voice. "We don't need a confrontation."

But Brett was heading toward them, breathing hard. He didn't look right—eyes bloodshot, unfocused. Robbie wondered if he'd been taking drugs.

"I'm out of here," Maddy said, and slithered into the crowd.

Jeremy's face was tight. He stood with his legs apart and leaned forward like a football player defending his territory.

"What the fuck are you doing here?" Brett sniffled and wiped his nose with the back of his hand with a quick motion.

"We happen to have been invited," Jeremy said.

"No fucking way Mike invited you."

"We came with Gina Fieldstone," Robbie said, hoping to defuse the situation. "But we're leaving." She tugged on Jeremy's arm.

"I told you not to fuck with me," Brett said, poking Jeremy in the ribs with his finger.

"Hey man," Jeremy said. He put his beer down on a table. "What's your problem? We're guests here."

Robbie became aware of someone beside her. Mike was twirling his ponytail around his finger and scowling as he studied Robbie.

"Hi, Mike," she said. "Great house."

He tilted his head, not buying.

"We're here with Gina Fieldstone," Robbie said.

"I see. Gina Fieldstone." Mike gave his ponytail a tug and turned to Brett. "I thought you were leaving."

"I was." Brett's face was red, an odd contrast to his spiked blond hair. It seemed to be an effort for him to speak. "But my friend wants to see the grounds."

"Fine with me," Jeremy said, his eyes not moving from Brett's.

"Jeremy, no." Robbie grabbed his hand, determined not to let him go.

But Jeremy pulled his hand away. "I'll be back in a minute."

Robbie felt pressure on her shoulder. Mike was leading her away. "I saw Gina over by the buffet table." Mike waved backward over his head. "You boys watch out for alligators."

She couldn't let Jeremy leave with Brett—not with Brett in that angry state. She turned back, but Jeremy and Brett were almost at the stairs. Mike squeezed tighter. Was he trying to keep Robbie from following them?

The crowd had swelled. She'd never be able to get to them. Her hand still smarted from the sensation of Jeremy pulling out of her grasp. She had lost her mother's hand, too.

Jeremy, she almost called out, but he was out of sight.

"Ah, here she is," Mike said.

Gina had her back against a column as she watched the party. She had something up against her ear.

"Mrs. Fieldstone," Mike said.

Gina turned to Mike's voice, said something into the phone, then slipped it into her clutch.

Mike extended one hand while keeping his other firmly on Robbie's shoulder. "I'm so glad you could make it, Mrs. Fieldstone."

Gina smiled, but ignored the hand. A muscle in her neck twitched.

Mike brought his unshaken hand back and twirled his ratty ponytail. "Your little friend was looking for you."

"Such a big house and so many people," Gina said, nodding at Robbie. "It's easy to lose someone. Thanks for reuniting us."

Mike's grip on Robbie relaxed, apparently satisfied that Robbie hadn't crashed his party. But Robbie had to get out of here and find Jeremy before he and Brett went at each other.

"You'll have to excuse me." Robbie began backing away.

"What's your hurry?" Mike asked.

"Bathroom." She turned and threw herself into the crowd before Mike could stop her.

People were everywhere and Robbie felt like she was in a game where her opponents linked arms and wouldn't let her escape. It took several minutes for her to pass through the crowd and get to the stairs.

She maneuvered around people sitting on the steps with their food and drinks, then past the dreadlocked bouncer, and finally was out onto the pebbled path.

The house was surrounded by dense bushes and trees, but lights played only on the front of the house and the red dragon. The mini-forest was dark. Robbie ran through it to the back of the house, calling Jeremy's name. Dark, silent. The only sound came from the house behind her—music, barely contained by the boxlike walls.

She followed a landscaped path down to the water. The bay was the color of used motor oil and lapped against the man-made beach, a semicircle of dirty sand.

"Jeremy?"

Perhaps he was waiting for her in the car.

Something slinked against her leg and Robbie covered her mouth to contain a scream. But when she looked down, she saw two small glittery lights. Then she heard an annoyed meow. The long-haired cat. It raced through the bushes, then climbed the stairs that led to a deserted side balcony.

Robbie walked back toward the house, then along the bushes beside the pebbled driveway. There were many more cars than when they'd arrived almost an hour ago.

Something in the undergrowth caught her attention. White, shiny. A piece of paper? She bent down and picked it up. A woman's sandal with a clear Lucite heel. It was unlikely that it had anything to do with Kate, but just in case, Robbie put it in her canvas satchel, then continued through the shrubs.

The Corvair was where they'd left it, hidden in a darkened copse of trees. At first, it looked like Jeremy hadn't returned. But when Robbie got closer, she realized he was slumped down in the driver's seat.

She pulled on the door. "Jeremy?"

He opened his eyes. One was swollen and there was blood on his face and white T-shirt.

"My God. Are you okay?"

He nodded.

She got into the car. "What happened?"

"Got things settled." He turned on the engine and backed the car up.

He drove slowly out the winding roads onto U.S. 1, then headed north.

He didn't ask if Robbie wanted to spend the night in Key Largo, just continued on through, back to Miami.

Chapter 29

Robbie stood in front of her apartment building and watched Jeremy drive away. He hadn't said a word during the long ride back from Key Largo, even though she'd pressed him repeatedly to tell her what had happened. It had been nerve-racking and even worrisome as she'd glanced over at his bruised face, his bloody shirt. What had gone on in the time he'd been alone with Brett? Had Brett told him lies about Robbie and their relationship? She couldn't imagine what else could have caused Jeremy to become so remote.

She took the steps up to her apartment slowly. The sky was a tawny black, as though smudged with dirt, and palm fronds hung limp in the still air. There was a tight pain inside Robbie's chest. A lot like the one she'd felt after her mother had died, when breathing had become a forced effort.

At her door, she got out her house keys. A cat meowed. Robbie turned in its direction. A white cat that looked a lot like Matilda was scurrying toward her along the walkway.

The cat wove around Robbie's legs. Robbie picked it up.

Dear God, it was Matilda. Outside? Robbie was certain she'd left the cat in the apartment when she went to meet Jeremy earlier this afternoon. How could Matilda have gotten out?

Robbie's heart started pumping hard. She looked at the kitchen window over the catwalk. It was unbroken and closed. She examined the door. There were no marks near the lock that suggested some-one had broken in.

Still holding Matilda, she tested the doorknob, ready to run if it opened. But the door was secure.

She stuck her key in the lock. The key turned easily, as though she hadn't double locked it.

Robbie thought back to when she'd left the apartment. She had been wound up about driving down to Key Largo with Jeremy. She had pictured the two of them riding in his old car, as though they'd never been apart. The fantasy had been so strong in Robbie's head, it was possible she had forgotten to lock the door and hadn't noticed Matilda slipping out of the apartment.

But what if someone had broken into her apartment while she was gone? Should she call Jeremy? The police?

She went to the kitchen window. Through the sheer curtains, she could make out her laptop on the kitchen table. If an intruder had broken in, wouldn't he have taken her computer?

She returned to the front door, opened it, then reached over to flip on the light switch while still standing outside.

The living room appeared exactly as she'd left it. Beads, feathers and half-completed jewelry on the tables, an afghan flung over the sofa, books in the bookcases. No sign of forced entry or an intruder.

She must have left the door unlocked. It was out of character for her, but there'd been so much upheaval in Robbie's life the last ten days, she knew she wasn't being herself.

She stepped inside and sniffed the air. Cleanser and lemon pol-ish from her cleaning spree the day before. No unusual or unfamil-iar smells. She released Matilda and the cat slinked into the kitchen. Robbie could hear her lapping at her water bowl.

She was spooking herself, she decided. After Mike's house, everything felt off.

At the bedroom door, she turned on the light. The bed was

made, the pillows exactly as she'd left them. Robbie went into the bedroom, checked the closets, the bathroom. Nothing. Just her imagination.

She took a couple of Motrin from the bathroom cabinet and got ready for bed. She slid under the comforter, too tired to remove the throw pillows. She felt strained and weak. The tears came quickly.

Robbie cried and cried. Was it over Jeremy, who had just come so close to getting back in her life? Over the sister she'd never known and might not ever? Or over her lost childhood with a sick mother and a father who had been unwilling to reclaim her until recently?

She didn't remember falling asleep. When she woke up the next morning, she felt sore all over. She went into the kitchen and pressed a couple of ice cubes against her puffy eyelids while the coffee brewed. The outside light was too bright, too happy. Robbie brought a mug of coffee back into her bedroom. She left the shades drawn and got under the covers, propping up the pillows behind her. Her cell phone was on the nightstand. Should she call Jeremy? Find out how he was doing? Maybe apologize? But for what? What could Brett have said to him?

The phone rang as she reached for it. Eagerly, she checked the caller ID. Not Jeremy. It said RESTRICTED. Lieber?

Had the detective found out that Robbie and Jeremy had gone to Key Largo, and was calling to reprimand her? Reluctantly, Robbie opened her phone. "Hello?"

"Hello, Robbie," Lieber said. "I need for you to come down to the station."

Coffee sloshed over the top of Robbie's mug, wetting her hand, and spilling on the sheets. "What is it? What's wrong?"

"We'll discuss it when you get here."

"Is it about Kate? Have you found her?"

"It's not about Kate." Lieber's voice softened. "Please, Robbie. We'll talk at the station."

Lieber hung up before Robbie could say anything else.

She dressed quickly, made sure that Matilda stayed behind in the apartment, then double locked the door.

Gabriele was just arriving home, carrying a pair of very high heels and padding across the catwalk in his bare feet. His ebony skin gleamed in the sunlight and his platinum wig was at an unnatural angle on his head.

Robbie remembered walking into her mother's bedroom, surprising her as she stood in front of her dresser mirror adjusting her wig. Her mother had turned to Robbie, the wig still off center, and had given Robbie a big smile. Her mother's eyes were bright with tears. And she knew at that moment her mother would soon be gone. That Robbie would be all alone.

"Good morning." Gabriele covered a yawn with his hand.

"Morning." Robbie waved and started down the stairs.

"Someone staying with you?"

Robbie came to a short stop. "What?" She turned back.

"I was wondering if you have a guest."

"No. Why do you ask?"

"I saw someone by your front door yesterday. I thought maybe he was staying with you."

Robbie went back up the steps to Gabriele. He drooped over her like a giraffe.

"What did he look like?" she asked.

"I'm sorry, Robbie. I didn't get a good look. And now I've alarmed you. Is something wrong?"

"I—I don't know. Was the guy young? Old?"

"I don't know. I should have checked him out, but I was hurrying off to meet Oscar." His eyes widened. One of his false eyelashes was dangling. "Did something happen?"

Robbie shook her head. "What time? Do you remember what time you saw him?"

"Let me think. A little before five. I was meeting Oscar at five." He touched Robbie's shoulder. "What's wrong? Tell me what I can do to help."

"It's nothing," Robbie said. And it probably wasn't. She gave Gabriele a small smile. "Everything's fine. Really."

"Okay, Robbie. But I promise I'll keep a better watch."

"Thanks." She went back down the steps. She didn't have time to be chasing after imaginary intruders. Lieber was waiting for her.

She got her bike, then pedaled almost recklessly down Washington Avenue, thoughts of who may have been outside her door yesterday afternoon pushed to the back of her mind by more immediate concerns. Why had Lieber asked her to come to the police station? She'd never done that before.

Robbie checked in at the main lobby, and a young uniformed cop escorted Robbie upstairs. He brought her into a small room with a long narrow table and a couple of chairs. An interview room? Interrogation room? What was going on here?

"Detective Lieber will be right with you," the cop said, closing her into the room.

Robbie started pacing in the small space between the door and the table. There was a mirror in the wall, just like in the movies. This was the kind of place they brought criminals, not something that was in Robbie's personal frame of reference.

Robbie felt like she was suffocating. What could have happened?

The door opened. Lieber came in carrying a Styrofoam cup of coffee, a laptop, and some other items tucked under her arm. She took a quick inventory of Robbie's puffy face, T-shirt, and jeans. Robbie realized she was still wearing the feathered earrings she'd had on last night.

"Cream and sugar," Lieber said, handing Robbie the coffee.

"Thank you." Robbie put the cup on the table.

Lieber remained standing. Robbie's eyes fell to Lieber's black sneaker-like shoes. The hem on one of her trouser cuffs was coming undone.

"So are you the good cop or bad cop?" Robbie asked.

"What do you mean?" Lieber asked.

"Isn't that how it works? First one, then the other?"

"Sit down, Robbie," Lieber said, pulling out a chair and sitting down herself. She put the laptop, her notebook, and a small rectangular device on the table.

"I'd like to know what this is about," Robbie said, not moving. "I don't like the feel of it. Do I need a lawyer?"

"Have you done something that you'd need a lawyer for?"

Robbie shook her head and sat down.

Lieber tapped on the keyboard, then looked up at Robbie. "I'd like to ask you a few questions." She touched the rectangular device. "Do you mind if I tape our conversation?"

"Please tell me what's happened. I don't know what to think. Is Jeremy okay? My dad? You said this isn't about Kate."

Lieber hesitated, then said, "Jeremy and your dad are fine as far as I know."

If they were okay, how bad could things be?

Lieber touched the recorder and waited.

"Can't we talk without that?"

"Okay, Robbie." Lieber took her hand off the recorder. "Let's just talk. Where were you yesterday?"

The transition was so abrupt that Robbie was momentarily nonplussed. "We, I—" How much did Lieber know? Probably enough. Robbie started again. "Jeremy and I drove down to Key Largo."

"And did what?" There was no reprimanding, no judgment in Lieber's voice.

Robbie recounted their afternoon and evening going to bars and motels asking about Kate and Joanne. Then she told her about the man at the tiki bar who recognized the girls from the flyers. That got Lieber's attention.

"What do you mean he recognized them?" Lieber asked.

"He said he saw them at the bar a week ago Friday. That two guys bought them drinks—he called them punks—and the girls left with them."

Lieber scribbled something in her notebook. "Did he know the two guys? Could he describe them?"

"One had a shaved head, the other had brown hair and thick eyebrows. He said he'd seen them around before, but not since the night they left with the girls."

"And what about the man? Did you get his name?"

Robbie looked down at her untouched coffee. "I asked, but he wouldn't tell me. I guess I should have tried harder."

"That's okay," Lieber said, a hint of empathy slipping into her voice.

"But I think he works on one of the charter boats and I'd be able to recognize him if I saw him again."

She told Lieber what she remembered about the man and how he believed the two guys had taken Kate and Joanne to a party. "So that's why we ended up at Mike's house."

Lieber didn't look surprised by this information. "You knew Mike was having a party?"

"No. We followed a black car with tinted windows, figuring it would lead us to a house party. It didn't, but as we were turning around, we saw a bunch of cars parked by another house. We had no idea it was Mike's house until we went inside."

"So Brett hadn't told you about the party?"

Robbie shook her head. Something was wrong here. It seemed it was the party that interested Lieber, not Kate and Joanne's disappearance.

"But you occasionally go with Brett to his company's events," Lieber said. "Was there some reason he wouldn't have mentioned this one?"

"We—I—Brett and I aren't dating anymore."

"Really? Since when?"

"Since Sunday."

"Who broke up with whom?"

"Why are you asking me this? Why does it matter?"

"Did Jeremy know about the party?"

"No. I already told you, we followed a car and found a house with a lot of cars parked outside. We thought there was a remote chance that if we found a party house, it would be the one Kate went to."

"Remote's a good word for it. Do you know how many houses there are in Key Largo?"

Robbie felt blood rush to her head. Why was Lieber putting her on the defensive? "But most people don't throw big parties. And the ones that do usually throw them all the time."

Lieber didn't seem to hear her. She was tapping on her laptop. "So tell me what happened when you saw Brett at the party."

"We were surprised. So was he." Robbie stopped. How did Lieber know they'd seen Brett there?

"Was Brett angry to see you with Jeremy?"

Brett. Jeremy. Angry. Robbie had a sick feeling in the pit of her stomach. She answered slowly. "I guess."

"I see. Then what happened?"

There was a brown sticky streak on the Formica tabletop. Spilled coffee? Dried blood?

"Robbie?"

"They left."

"What do you mean?"

"Brett and Jeremy went outside."

"Just the two of them?"

Robbie nodded.

"And what about you?"

"I was with Gina Fieldstone and Mike. I went to look for the guys a few minutes later."

"Where'd you look?"

"Out back, by the bay."

"And did you see them?"

Robbie shook her head.

"Then what did you do?"

"I went to the car to see if Jeremy was waiting for me there."

"The car? His dad's Corvair?"

"Yeah."

"And?"

"He was."

"Was what?"

"Waiting for me."

"Did he say anything about Brett?"

Robbie shook her head.

"Did you notice anything unusual?"

Robbie thought about the blood on Jeremy's T-shirt, his bruised face. His remote behavior on the drive back to Miami. But Jeremy and Brett had had a fight, that was all.

"Robbie? Was there anything unusual about Jeremy?"

She felt tears starting up. Not now, she willed herself. Not now. "Detective Lieber," Robbie said, trying to control the trembling in her voice. "Would you please tell me what this is all about?"

Lieber closed her notebook and stood up. "Brett's dead, Robbie. And the last person he was seen alive with was Jeremy."

Chapter 30

As soon as Robbie left the police station, she pressed the speed dial button for Jeremy.

His cell phone rang once, twice. *Jeremy, please answer.*

He picked up just before it would have gone to voice mail. "Yeah."

"Jeremy. Where are you?"

"Home."

"Are you okay? Has Lieber—"

"Yeah. I've already been to the station."

"But you're home, so they don't think—"

"Maybe you'd better come over."

She biked to the SOBE Grande, remembering how this had once been her routine, her home. Now it felt so alien. Jeremy still lived there but he was more a stranger to her than ever. Could he possibly have known about Mike's party? Had he planned to see Brett there? But no—that was impossible. She knew Jeremy better than that, and she would have picked something up in his behavior. Bumping into Brett last night had been an accident. An unfortunate accident.

And then it hit her.

Brett was dead.

Her bike swerved, nearly hitting a parked car. She pulled to the side, got off her bike, and leaned against the trunk of a palm tree for support. Rays of sunlight broke through the shifting palm fronds, stabbing her eyes with painful brightness.

Brett was dead.

She could see his goofy smile, oversized ears, spiked Dennis-the-Menace hair. He used to make her laugh, picking her up and swinging her around like a rag doll. Then something changed. A tension, a darkness, that hadn't been there when she'd first met him. What? What had happened? And why was this once-happy young man now dead?

She wanted to cry for him. For the weeks of fun they'd had together. But the tears wouldn't come. It felt like glue had seeped through her veins and tear ducts, stopping up the flow of blood and tears, almost paralyzing her. Brett was dead. And Jeremy was the last person he'd been seen alive with.

She got up to Jeremy's apartment on the eighth floor. She knocked. No answer. Jeremy often left the front door unlocked and it used to infuriate Robbie when they lived together. After what happened to his parents, how could he not be worried about the wrong person coming in?

She tried the door. It was open. She stepped inside and looked around the studio apartment. Almost nothing had changed since she'd lived here. Facing the wall of sliding windows was a cordovan-colored sofa that opened into the bed she'd once shared with Jeremy. Only one bike, his, leaned against the wall beneath the arrangement of mirrors she had made when they'd first moved in. The Oriental rug that had belonged to his mother covered the area between the window and the sofa. Jeremy was lying on it, his head resting on a pillow. Asleep?

She sat down on the rug near him, folding her legs beneath her.

"So here we go again," he said, without picking his head up. "Wherever Jeremy Stroeb goes, dead bodies are sure to follow."

"Don't give me that self-pity bullshit. This isn't just about you. I want you to tell me what happened with Brett last night. And why aren't you under arrest?"

Jeremy rolled onto his side. One eye was swollen shut. He took a moment to answer. Was he trying to make up something that sounded good? Finally, he sat up. He moved stiffly, as though he was in pain. "I'm sorry." He took her hand. His knuckles were raw. "I was so angry, I wasn't thinking. Brett was someone you cared about. I'm really, really sorry."

She nodded thanks as she pulled her hand out of Jeremy's. "So tell me what happened."

His chest sagged beneath his wrinkled T-shirt. "I've just been through this with Lieber. She brought me down to the station first thing this morning. Apparently, the party cleanup crew found Brett's body in the bushes near the bay. When Mike was questioned, he told the police about you and me showing up at the party."

"You and Brett were seen leaving together. And you were both very angry."

"I know. But I didn't kill him."

"Are you sure?"

"Jesus. What's that supposed to mean?"

"By accident. Could you have hit him and maybe he fell and banged his head or something?"

Jeremy shook his head. "We took a few swings at each other, but he wasn't badly hurt. I got his nose and there was some blood, but he was standing and screaming at me when I walked away."

"So you walked away?"

"What are you, double-teaming with Lieber?"

"This is serious, Jeremy. After you spoke to Lieber, she called me in for questioning. That means even if she let you go, you're still a suspect."

"I know. I know."

"What happened when you left? Did he follow you?"

Jeremy brought his hands up to his unshaven cheeks and rubbed them. There were traces of ink on his fingers. "It was weird," he said. "First, Brett came after me, shouting to stay the fuck out of his life. Then—it was really strange—he just sank down in the grass and started to cry."

"Cry?"

"Yeah. These really pitiful sobs like he felt his life was coming apart."

"And did you go back to him?"

"Shit. Are you kidding? I took that as a sign of defeat and got the hell away."

Robbie ran her finger over the kaleidoscope pattern in the Oriental rug—turquoise, emerald green, magenta. She thought about other colors. *Yellow, gold, russet, crimson, burgundy, magenta. Nothing is forever,* her mother had said.

"Why didn't you say something on the ride home last night?"

"I was too upset."

"About?"

"The fight. It seemed pointless to me. It wasn't like I hated him or anything. And I don't think he hated me. It was more like he was just so angry he needed someone to take it out on. And I guess I felt sorry for him."

"But why didn't you talk to me about it? I kept asking you and you wouldn't even look at me."

"Jesus, Robbie. I was pissed at myself. I should have walked away, but I let my animal instincts take over." He looked down at the raw knuckles on his scarred hand. "I was hoping I'd gotten past that."

The sound of muffled voices raised in anger came through the wall of the adjacent apartment. *Get the hell out of here,* a woman shouted. *Just get the hell out.*

"What happened with Lieber?" Robbie asked.

"I think this is very tough for her."

"What do you mean?"

"She doesn't want to believe I did it, but a lot of things point to me. I'm guessing if Lieber hadn't known me personally, she would have locked me up."

The neighbor woman's voice broke through the silence. *How could you?* She sounded like she was crying. Then a door slammed.

"But Lieber's not the only one involved in this," Jeremy continued. "Once the DA has enough evidence, she'll have no choice but to arrest me."

"Then we have to figure out who killed Brett and why."

"Sure. Detectives from Miami Beach and the Keys are all over this, but a bartender and a personal trainer should have no trouble cracking the case."

Robbie waved him off. A fresh thought had occurred to her. "Did Lieber say how Brett died?"

"Well, she asked me if I owned a knife."

A knife. Robbie felt chilled. Was that how Brett had died?

"I'm guessing they haven't found the murder weapon," Jeremy said. "Or if they did, it doesn't have my prints on it, or they would have already locked me up." He glanced at the trace of ink on his fingers.

A knife. Robbie tried not to think about it. "Well, there were a lot of people there. A lot of cars."

"But a knife is associated with crimes of passion. And lots of people had seen me and Brett fighting."

"Right. But we know you didn't kill him."

Robbie looked at the arrangement of mirrors on the wall. "Don't you get the feeling there's more going on here?"

"What do you mean?"

"Kate and Joanne are down in Key Largo, Mike has a big party at his house, Brett dies. It's got to be more than a coincidence."

"And what about the congressman who committed suicide? The one who was at BURN Friday night? That's like Mike's major hang-out."

"I don't know about the congressman, but if we could connect Kate to Mike or his house, I think we'd be onto something." And then Robbie remembered. She reached for her satchel.

"What?" Jeremy said.

"This." Robbie pulled out the white sandal. "I found it in the bushes near Mike's house."

"So? It could belong to anyone."

"It could, but most people leave with both their shoes," she said. "Unless they're not able to for some reason."

They stared at the shiny white sandal with its clear Lucite heel. "Also," Robbie said, "Look at the label. Lela Rose for Payless."

"And that means what exactly?"

"The women who were at the party don't shop at Payless. This is the kind of sandal a teenager would wear. Especially one from a small town like Deland."

Jeremy picked up the sandal and studied it. "It doesn't look like it's from last night. There's soil and water spots on it, like it was sprayed by a water sprinkler. But it doesn't look very weathered either. I don't think it's been outside for more than a week or so." He frowned. "Do you think your father would know if it's Kate's?"

"I don't know." Or was she afraid of taking her father along on some wild-goose chase?

"What about her friends?"

"They're all back in Deland. Besides, I don't know their names or how to contact them without going through Lieber or my dad."

Jeremy turned the sandal around in his hand. "Cinderella's slipper. Looks like it would fit you."

"Wait a minute." She dug through her satchel for her cell phone, then took the shoe from Jeremy. She placed it on the rug and snapped a picture. "I'm going to post this on Facebook. Joanne's friends set up a group to celebrate Joanne's life. Maybe someone will recognize it. If we can show that Kate was very likely at Mike's house last Friday, that means—shit. What does it mean? That Mike is somehow connected to Joanne's and Brett's deaths and Kate's disappearance?"

Jeremy had gone over to the breakfast bar and gotten his laptop. He set it down on the carpet and logged on. "Just post it. If someone recognizes the shoe as Kate's, it gives us a lot more to go on."

Robbie uploaded the photo to her Facebook account, sent it to the "Remember Joanne Group," then wrote a message.

> Hi. I'm Kate's sister. Please let me know if you think this
> sandal belonged to Kate or Joanne. It may help us find Kate
> and figure out what happened to Joanne.

"Wait," Jeremy said. "Don't say sister. They don't know Kate has a sister. Just say you're a relative and you're helping her dad find Kate."

"Good idea." Robbie made the change and sent it, then clicked through the other comments sent to Joanne. Since she'd looked the day before, there were dozens and dozens of new entries. She scrolled through them, saddened by the anguish Joanne's friends expressed over her death.

And then she saw an entry and her breath caught.

"What's wrong?" Jeremy said.

She could only point. "She, she's—"

"What?"

"She's alive."

"Who? Joanne?"

"No. Look." She touched the picture on the screen. The picture of an arrowhead tattoo. "My sister. She's alive."

Jeremy leaned over and read the entry aloud.

> It's my fault you're in heaven. But remember, Joanne. You
> were always better than an angel.

Chapter 31

"Shit," Jeremy said. "So Kate was involved with Joanne's death?"

"It doesn't make sense," Robbie said. "If she was, why would she announce it here, so publicly? And why would she write this and not come out of hiding?"

Jeremy leaned back on the rug, resting on his elbows. His brows were knit, the gaze from his uninjured eye so intense it made up for the closed, swollen one. "We don't know for sure Kate wrote that."

"It had to be, unless someone got into her Facebook account using her password."

"Which means any one of her friends could have written it," Jeremy said. "Kids all know each other's passwords."

"But why would a friend do something so damaging to Kate?"

Jeremy reread the entry. "Someone could have forced the password out of Kate, then posted this to make it look like Kate had something to do with Joanne's death." He sat forward and massaged the back of his neck. "Or to make it look like Kate's still alive."

"She is alive," Robbie said.

"Oh yeah?"

"There's something about the message that doesn't sound like someone else wrote it. It's too . . . too specific. *You were always better than an angel.* It's like some secret the two of them shared. And we know that Kate's into cryptic messages. Like her last one to Joanne about leaving broken and returning fixed."

"All right, so assuming Kate wrote it, what's the next step? Calling Lieber? Your father?"

"First, I'm going to send Kate a message. And this time I'm not going to be evasive."

Jeremy looked over Robbie's shoulder as she typed.

> *Dear Kate:*
>
> *I wrote to you a few days ago, but I didn't tell you the whole story. I'm your half sister—Robbie Ivy. My mom and I moved away from Deland when I was seven. I'm twenty-five and I live on South Beach. I didn't know you existed either until our father came here looking for you. We're both very worried. I saw your picture. I looked a lot like you when I was your age. Please get in touch with me. I want so much to know you.*
>
> *Love,*
> *Robbie*

"It's good," Jeremy said.

She sent the message.

Jeremy's fingers were folded over his bruised knuckles. "I think you should tell Lieber."

Robbie got up and stood by the sliding window. The bay was choppy. She could see the whitecaps of waves, clouds coalescing above the Miami skyline. On the balcony, the small wicker table and two chairs where she and Jeremy used to sit most evenings were covered with a layer of grit, as though no one went there anymore.

"Robbie. I said you should tell Lieber."

"Tell her what? That my sister may have admitted to killing her best friend?"

"We don't know that's what she meant."

"But that was our first interpretation. What do you think Lieber will make of it? That not only are you a possible murderer, but so's my sister. I'd rather wait to hear from Kate. Find out what she meant. Where she is."

"I don't agree, Robbie. This may help the investigation."

"I'll think about it."

"And your father? Are you going to tell him?"

Robbie didn't answer. The clouds had darkened and a gauzy curtain of rain blurred the buildings of the downtown skyline. But on either side the sky was a brilliant blue. "My father," Robbie said. "I guess I'd better."

Robbie waited for her father at a bench overlooking Government Cut. The rain clouds had drifted south, but had left a residual coolness. Behind her was the newly constructed South Pointe Park with a man-made hill that attracted skateboarders of every age. The sound of wheels rolling over concrete competed with the squawking of seagulls that hovered over the wide inlet that opened to the ocean.

There'd been a park a few blocks away from the high-rise where Robbie grew up. Sometimes she sat there and watched the other kids play. The skateboarders would set up jumps for themselves and go flying into the air. Robbie always wanted to try it herself. One day, one of the kids offered her the skateboard to try. She thought about her mom back in their apartment vomiting from the chemo, said no, and left. She never went back to the park.

She slumped down against the bench. Her head ached and she felt an uncomfortable fullness in her stomach, although she hadn't eaten or drunk anything all day. Not even the coffee Lieber had offered her at the station this morning.

She reached into her bag and took a mint out of a small tin box, just like one her mom had when Robbie was a little girl. Sometimes peppermints made her feel better.

She thought about Brett with sadness. Someone had killed him. But it hadn't been Jeremy. She was certain of that. Then who? And could his murder tie to her sister's disappearance?

She rolled back the last few days she'd been with Brett. When had he started acting strangely? There was last Friday night at BURN when Brett had the confrontation with Jeremy. That was also the night the congressman was seen leaving with two women, who Lieber thought may have had some connection to the congressman's suicide. Then, Brett had been so angry with Jeremy for telling Lieber he'd been at BURN Friday night that he went to Jeremy's gym and got into a fight with him. Two fights between Jeremy and Brett in Miami, then the one at Mike's house made three. Robbie had assumed they were about her. But Brett was also upset that Jeremy had connected Brett with BURN and the congressman. And something else?

There was the phone call Brett got late Sunday morning while Robbie was breaking up with him. If their relationship was so important, what could the call have been about to make Brett just get up and leave in the middle?

All those phone calls and plan cancellations. Things hadn't been that way when Robbie and Brett first started dating. And in retrospect, she realized how sketchy things had become. Something at the PR firm where Brett worked must have been affecting him. And his job was connected to Mike, who owned the house in Key Largo, the town where Kate and Joanne's car had been. Where Brett had been killed.

So who killed him? Obviously someone at the party Monday night. One of Mike's PR clients? Someone else working for Mike? Someone who hated Mike? Could it have been drug-related?

And had whoever killed Brett also killed Joanne and done something to Kate? But that was too far-fetched. Robbie only knew that Kate and Joanne had most likely gone to a party in Key Largo, but she had no way of knowing if they actually had and if there was any connection to Mike's house. And besides, why would the same person who killed Brett have an interest in a couple of high school girls?

And then there was Kate's post on Joanne's group's page, which made absolutely no sense.

Too many pieces were missing. Maybe Lieber had some of them. Was Jeremy right? Should Robbie tell her about Kate's message and take the chance of implicating her sister?

"You look tired, Roberta." Her father stood beside the bench. He was in wrinkled shorts and a golf shirt he'd worn a few days ago. He had shaved, but the breeze blew his gray hair in all directions. It had been only two days since she'd seen him, but it felt like much longer.

"I'm okay." She got up and gave him a hug. There were puffy bags under his eyes. She wondered how he spent his time. Wandering the streets looking for Kate? "How are you doing?" she asked.

He gave her a weak smile. "I'm okay, too." They sat down on the bench and he took her hand. He wore his wedding band. She wore the emerald ring he'd given her mother.

"I've been thinking about you a lot since we talked on Sunday," he said. "I'm very angry that I caused you so much pain." He shook his head. "How could I not have realized it?"

"Well, we're back in each other's lives and that's what matters."

"I'm glad you called today. I wanted to see you again, but I didn't want to rush you."

Behind them came the loud scraping thud of a skateboarder hitting the concrete after a jump.

"I need to talk to you about something I found," Robbie said.

"About Kaitlin?" The tension transferred from his hand to hers.

"Yes. About Kaitlin." How could she phrase this without alarming him? "Remember how I showed you that people send each other messages on Facebook?"

He was squeezing her hand so hard, her mother's ring dug painfully inside her fingers, but she doubted he was aware of it.

"Someone posted one to Joanne using Kate's Facebook account. I think it's from Kate, but I can't be absolutely certain. Someone who knew her password could have logged in as her. But I think—"

"What…what did she write?"

This was the tough part. "Well, she sort of apologized to Joanne, then she wrote something about Joanne being an angel."

"What did she write, Roberta? What were her exact words?"

Someone yelled over the scraping sound of the skateboards.

"She wrote, 'It's my fault you're in heaven. But remember, Joanne. You were always better than an angel.' "

He pulled back and blinked several times. "It's my fault you're in heaven?" He released Robbie's hand. "She said it was her fault?"

"Yes, but that could mean anything. She could just be feeling guilty about the whole trip. Maybe it had been her idea."

"So you're starting on that again? That Kaitlin deliberately set up herself and her friend to get into trouble?"

"Please, Dad. I'm just telling you this so you know that Kate is very likely alive. That she probably sent the message."

"Impossible." He slammed the bench with his open hand. "Impossible. She would never have written such a thing."

"Well, that's something Detective Lieber will have to try to figure out."

"You've told the detective about this?"

It had become clear to Robbie that she had to tell Lieber. "Not yet, but I'm planning to."

"So that she should think Kaitlin is a murderer?"

"No, Dad. So that she can try to find Kate. Maybe there's some technology that can trace the message. Or maybe Lieber can fit this piece of information with other things she knows. I don't think it does Kate any good to keep her message hidden from the police."

"And you believe this will help them? That they'll do something with it? What have they done so far? Nothing. Absolutely nothing."

"That's not true."

"Then where is she? Why haven't they found her?"

"I don't know."

"It's been twelve days. Twelve days since she's disappeared. They've done nothing to find my little girl." He covered his face with his hands and his shoulders shuddered.

She understood how overwrought he must be. She wanted to touch him, to comfort him, but he gave off a vibe—as though choosing to remain closed to her. Behind them, skateboard wheels scraped against concrete going up the hill, then down. Up the hill, then down.

When her father raised his head, his cheeks were wet. "So you're going to tell the police that you think Kaitlin murdered her friend. And you believe this will help them? Sure it will. It will give them a tidy explanation for everything. Joanne's death, Kaitlin's disappearance. They'll have their case all wrapped up nice and neatly thanks to you."

"They won't do that."

He stood up. "I thought you cared about her. That you wanted to help her."

"Of course I do."

"I never imagined you'd be this hateful toward your only sister." He began walking away.

Anger flared up inside her. "Wait a minute. Stop."

He turned to look at her, his face almost unrecognizable in its flatness.

"I'm not being hateful. You're the one who's twisting things. You just don't want to admit that whatever happened to Kate may have something to do with you."

"How dare you?"

"No. How dare you? I'm finally starting to understand you. Why everything is always someone else's screwup, never yours."

His face turned red, his jaw twisting. "My screwup?" Spittle formed on his lip.

"You're the one who walked out on my mother after cheating on her. You could have fought for joint custody or at least visited me, especially when my mom was sick, so why didn't you? And then there's Kate's mom. You're a doctor, for God's sake. Couldn't you see she was an alcoholic and needed help? Couldn't you have intervened? And . . . and then there's Kate." Robbie paused to catch her breath, enraged. "Kaitlin, you still call her. That's not her name. She calls herself Kate. How well can you possibly understand her if you don't even acknowledge the name she uses?"

He stared at his scuffed penny loafers. His lips moved. "Kate," she thought he said.

"That's right. Kate. Did it ever occur to you that maybe she ran off because of something you did or didn't do? That all this is your fault?"

He slumped like a broken old man, the wind blowing his hair.

Robbie's anger dissolved. But in its place was emptiness. She had her father back, but he was anything but the misunderstood victim she had believed he was two days ago.

She turned from him and walked toward the hill. The sound of wheels scraped the concrete paths, getting louder and louder. Up the hill, then down. Up the hill, then down.

Chapter 32

Jeremy leaned against the balcony railing outside his apartment. The rainstorm over downtown had passed and there was a coolness in the air. But it wouldn't be long before the heat burned through. Directly below him was the pool. It was almost noon, but only a few people were out. A middle-aged man and woman reading newspapers, a man in a loud print shirt and floppy hat covering his face. Not the usual crowd.

How long had it been since the last time he'd come out on his balcony? Weeks? Months? It had been his and Robbie's favorite place to hang out. They'd share a bottle of wine and watch the downtown lights, the bay rippling in the moonlight. But after she left, he couldn't stand being out here without her.

How close they'd come to getting back together. The drive to the Keys in his dad's Corvair. Like old times. The way she kissed him, looked at him. They'd been so close. So damn close.

He breathed in the smell of bay water. His eye throbbed from where Brett had punched him. He'd punched Brett, too. He knew his blood and Brett's had mingled, that forensics would confirm they'd fought. But Jeremy had readily admitted it. The question was, who had gotten to Brett after Jeremy had left? And why?

He remembered his efforts to find his own parents' murderer. How Marina, his father's graduate assistant, had helped him put together lists of suspects and motives. It had been over a year, but he still felt a stab when he thought about her—her wild copper-colored hair, her small round mouth.

But Marina was gone. And now it was Robbie trying to solve the puzzle of what happened to her sister and sister's friend. She was with her father now. Would she talk to Lieber about her sister's message? Jeremy wanted her to, but not, as he'd told Robbie, because he thought it would help Lieber's investigation. His purpose had been more self-preserving. He was hoping this clue from Kate would direct Lieber's attention away from him. Because if Lieber was chasing after Kate—well, she couldn't be in two places at one time, could she? And that would buy Jeremy some time to clear himself from suspicion in Brett's murder.

Jeremy thought back to the scene at Mike's house. Lots of money had been poured into that place. Did a guy who owned a PR firm make that kind of money? Maybe. But there was something sketchy about Mike—the crowd he hung out with at BURN, all those cars with tinted windows, the waterfront house. To Jeremy, it smelled like drugs. Maybe that's what this was all about. Maybe Brett had gotten sucked into it and wasn't playing along. He sure looked like he was coming unglued at BURN last Friday, then at the gym on Monday. Maybe Mike felt like Brett couldn't be trusted any more. Or maybe someone was pissed at Mike and was making an example of Brett.

But how could Jeremy get on the inside of that? He didn't associate with the drug crowd.

Metal scraped against concrete. Jeremy looked back down at the pool. Sunbathing time. The club girls set up their lounges close to the bay and pulled off their bathing suit tops. Even from this distance, Jeremy could see Tyra's boobs bouncing like a couple of volleyballs.

Tyra might know what was going on with Mike and his crowd. She was a regular at BURN and probably mingled with its darker side, too. The question was, would she be willing to talk to Jeremy?

Jeremy took the stairs down the eight flights, feeling like he could use the exercise after the intensity of this morning with the detective. He put on his sunglasses so his swollen eye wouldn't be conspicuous, and approached the lounging area near the swimming pool. In his sneakers he didn't make much noise.

Tyra was lying on her back. Her breasts shone like a pair of greased-up piglets, ready for the spit. On the lounge beside her, close enough for Tyra to touch, was the blonde girl called Angel. She was lying on her chest, face turned to the side, eyes closed as though asleep. Her full lips and makeup-less face reminded Jeremy of a child's.

Tyra cupped her hand over her eyes and squinted up at Jeremy. Her hair was wrapped in a scarf and her gold hoop earrings pulled her earlobes down. "You're blocking my sun, Muscleman."

"Sorry." Jeremy moved aside and dragged a lounge chair around to the other side of her. The couple he'd seen earlier reading newspapers had gone into the pool and were splashing each other playfully. They looked like visitors—the woman in a one-piece bathing suit, the man with swimming trunks pulled up to his waist. The other man wearing the loud shirt was still lying on a lounge chair. He had his face covered with a floppy hat, his head resting on his beach bag.

"So," Jeremy said, not sure how to get into this, "how's it going?"

Tyra sat up on her chair and scowled. Her green eyes reminded him of fake jewels in a cheap doll. "Goin' good. Why do you care?"

"I don't know. We're neighbors. I see you at BURN all the time. I'm just being friendly."

"Friendly?" She angled her head, clearly not buying.

"Okay. I want to ask you something. There are some people at BURN. I don't know them very well, but I was hoping you could tell me about them."

"Why would I tell you anything?"

"I don't know. Because you know I'm a good guy. And I think these other people are into some bad shit."

"Like what?"

"Drugs, maybe."

"So you think I'm into bad shit?"

"No, no. Nothing like that. It's just, I always see you there. And you're a smart lady. I'm guessing you pick up on things. That you know who's trouble and who to stay away from."

"You sayin' I like to watch my ass?"

"Well, who doesn't?"

"You got that right, Muscles."

"So what about this guy Brett Chandler? You know him?"

"Maybe."

"You heard someone killed him?"

She shrugged. "What if someone did?"

"Just that Brett wasn't the kind of guy who gets killed. Good family. College boy. Well-connected."

"I see. So he was a friend of yours?"

"I knew him years ago. In high school."

"So what do you want from me?"

"I'm trying to figure out who may have had a reason to kill him."

"You're talking to the wrong person. I'm no detective."

"Please, Tyra. Help me out here. What's the deal with Brett's boss, Mike—Mister M?"

Tyra lay back down on the lounge. "Go away, Muscles. You're eating into my tanning time."

"Is he into drugs?"

Tyra didn't answer. Her chest muscles tightened under the fake boobs.

"Just tell me who I should talk to. Does Mike have enemies? Someone who was getting to him by making an example of Brett?"

"Go away," she said without opening her eyes.

"Come on, Tyra. I know you know stuff."

She sat up. There was rage in her eyes. "I said get the fuck away from me."

The couple in the pool stopped laughing and splashing. The man on the lounge was peering out beneath his floppy hat.

"I just want to find out what's going on before someone else gets hurt."

"Get away from me," Tyra screamed. "Get the fuck away."

Jeremy stood up. "Okay. Fine. Calm down."

"Away," Tyra said. "Stay away from us. You hear me, mother-fucker?"

Jeremy glanced back at Angel. She was watching him, head slightly raised. Her full lips moved, ever so slightly. But he was pretty sure he could read them.

"Help me," she mouthed. "Help me."

Chapter 33

Robbie biked up Washington Avenue so fast that her leg muscles hurt. She was furious with her father.

What she'd said to him was true. She knew it. He knew it. He was a weak-willed, self-righteous bastard who never took the blame for anything. He was the reason Kate was gone. And now, it was like destiny playing a big joke on him. He'd given up one daughter willingly, and his other daughter had left him in turn.

She slowed her pedaling and came to a stop at a red traffic light. The early afternoon sun beat down on her while a crowd of jostling teenage girls and boys crossed in front of her bike.

But was her dad really a horrible person or just an ordinary man with human failings? And how perfect was Robbie in her own relationships that she should criticize him?

The light turned green. Cars moved around her. Someone honked. She stepped on the pedal and pushed off. Would she have reacted much differently if her own child had been missing for twelve days? Would she have blamed herself? Probably. Maybe her father did, too. Perhaps his anger and denial were just a reflection of how ineffectual he felt.

But even if that were the case, it didn't stop the hurt. The truth was that her whole life Robbie had secretly believed if she did everything right, everything she possibly could to be a good girl, her father would realize he made a mistake and return to her with all the love she had missed out on.

The police station was to her left. Robbie waited until the oncoming traffic cleared, then turned onto Eleventh Street. She pushed her bike into the stand and locked it. She thought about her meeting with Lieber this morning. How focused the detective was on Jeremy's connection to Brett's death. Was Robbie, as her father believed, making a mistake coming to talk to the detective now? Would Robbie's information just give the detective an easy out in wrapping up the case of who killed Joanne and why Kate had disappeared?

Her gut told her it was the right thing to do, so why did she feel so unsettled?

Robbie went to the check-in window, asked for Detective Lieber, and was told to wait. The sunlight coming in through the windows created a pattern of rectangles on the floor. A few minutes later, the same uniformed cop who had escorted her earlier brought her back upstairs. This time he led her through an open area with dozens of workstations. He continued to the back, stopping in front of a large windowed room with a door.

Robbie guessed this was where the more serious crimes were investigated. There were several desks in rows, occupied by people looking at their computers or engaged in conversation with each other. Well, at least it wasn't the interrogation room.

Lieber was sitting behind a corner desk covered with files and a computer monitor. Behind her were whiteboards filled with writing in different colors. Her face was drawn and strands of hair escaped from her hairclip. "What's wrong?" Lieber asked.

Did the detective think Robbie had returned to tell her that Jeremy had, in fact, killed Brett? And Robbie realized Lieber was probably working as hard as Robbie to clear Jeremy of suspicion.

"I have some new information about my sister."

Lieber's face relaxed. "Please, sit down." She touched the chair that was catty-corner to the desk.

There was a coffee stain on Lieber's white blouse that hadn't been there this morning, and Robbie noticed the cover of a folder on the corner of the desk was dark and damp, probably from spilled coffee.

"So tell me," the detective said.

"I think Kate posted a new message on Joanne's Facebook page."

"Damn. How could I have missed that?" Lieber tapped on a few keys, going directly to the group page set up for Joanne. "I've been checking back for messages from time to time." She scrolled down, stopping at the arrowhead photo. "Well, look at this."

She read it and shook her head.

> It's my fault you're in heaven. But remember, Joanne. You
> were always better than an angel.

Lieber tapped her fingers against her desk. There were age spots on the backs of her hands. Around them was the buzz of voices, phones ringing. "I don't know, Robbie. Anyone could have posted it."

"But I think it was Kate. That she's still alive."

"And announcing to the world that she may have been complicit in Joanne's death? That doesn't make sense."

"But isn't there some way you can trace the message? Figure out where it was sent from? Then maybe you'll be able to find her."

"We can try that, but even if we find the computer that this was sent from, that doesn't mean Kate will still be near it. She could have used one at an Internet café, or hotel business center. Or more likely, it wasn't even sent by Kate in the first place." She typed something into her computer. An e-mail. Then she pressed "send." "Okay, I've asked one of our techie guys to trace this."

"But look at the message itself. It feels like Kate was giving us a clue here."

"Maybe." Lieber scrolled up to the recent messages.

Robbie saw the one she'd posted with the picture of the sandal. There was no reply.

Lieber leaned in closer. "What's this? You found a sandal?" She read aloud:

> *Hi. I'm a relative of Kate's. Please let me know if you think this sandal belonged to Kate or Joanne. It may help us find Kate and figure out what happened to Joanne.*

"Where did you find a sandal?"

"At Mike's house in Key Largo. In the bushes."

"Where is it now?"

Where was it? At Jeremy's apartment? No. She'd put it back in her satchel. "Here," Robbie said. Jeremy had sealed it in a plastic baggie to preserve the soil and water spots.

Lieber took it from Robbie. "What made you pick it up?"

"I guess I wondered why someone would leave a shoe behind."

Lieber studied it. "It's from Payless. There must be hundreds of girls and women who could own this shoe."

"Right. But don't you see? The women at Mike's house aren't the types who shop at Payless. A teenager from Deland might."

Lieber shook her head.

"It's too much of a coincidence," Robbie said. "A water bottle receipt from Key Largo was in Joanne's Volvo, someone saw the girls at the tiki bar, then this sandal is lying in the bushes. How can there not be a connection?"

"I'm not saying there isn't."

"Then Kate's disappearance and Joanne's death are connected to Mike. It has to be."

"It's a possibility."

"No. It's more than a possibility."

"Calm down, Robbie. This is a good lead. And we'll be following up on it. But we're also juggling lots of other things right now. Things that point to who may have killed Brett Chandler."

A heaviness settled in Robbie's chest. "Like what?"

Lieber leaned closer to Robbie. "You must know Jeremy's in a bad situation."

Robbie looked down at the damp folder on the corner of Lieber's desk.

"He was seen arguing with Brett at BURN, then at the gym on Monday morning. In fact, a couple of guys had to hold them back from each other. Then several people saw them angry and leaving Mike's house together. Jeremy's admitted that they got into a physical fight."

"But Jeremy didn't kill Brett. You know that."

"What I believe is irrelevant. When the DA has enough evidence—"

"But then you'll stop looking for the real killer. And that's very likely someone who's connected to Kate's disappearance and Joanne's death."

Lieber put the sandal, still in the plastic bag, down hard on her desk. "I'm doing everything I can, Robbie."

The light caught the Lucite heel of the delicate shoe.

And Robbie thought about her sister wearing it. How pretty it would have looked on her foot.

Chapter 34

Something was wrong. Very wrong. And Angel was scared. More scared than usual. Even the fuzz in her head couldn't block the needles. The needles that flew out of Tyra like a runaway sewing machine—jabbing, jabbing, jabbing.

"What the fuck's he thinking?" Tyra said under her breath. She was watching that guy go back into the building. The sad-looking one named Jeremy. Angel liked him. Had liked him the first time she'd seen him and he told her to come by if she ever needed something. But she hadn't dared. What could he possibly do to help her, anyway?

"Trouble," Tyra muttered. "That's all we need now. More fucking trouble." She sat up and fastened her bikini top. "Come on, girl," she said to Angel. "Get dressed. I need to get upstairs and make some calls."

Angel tied the back of her top while Tyra gathered up their towels. The sun burned through her back. Burned through the blur in Angel's head. Tyra was distracted. Not watching Angel like she usually did. For an instant, Angel's heart raced. She could bolt. Run across the pool area out to the lobby. Tell the concierge to call the police.

But then what? Then she'd be back with the same old problem. They'd ask about Joanne, and they'd lock her up for good.

Tyra walked ahead, expecting Angel to follow. Angel lingered, adjusting her sandal. What was she thinking? Was she crazy? Like early this morning when everyone was arguing in the living room. Someone had left a laptop opened on the kitchen table and Angel had gone and sent Joanne a message. Almost like she wanted to get caught.

Tyra stopped and turned around. "Get a move on, Angel."

Angel followed Tyra into the lobby—white marble floors, backless black leather sofas. And cold. Angel shivered in her sheer cover-up as they waited for the elevator. Two of the four were out of commission. Tyra tapped her foot and muttered obscenities. Her toenails were long and painted orange with tiny, sparkly diamonds.

Something was going on. Why had that old, weird-looking man yelled at Tyra and Luis this morning? He'd been talking about fuck-ups, some client jumping off his balcony. Angel thought he meant the creep from Friday. The one she vomited on.

Tyra had acted all tough with the old guy until he said that someone got killed last night. And that freaked out Tyra. Like suddenly she was scared for herself.

The elevator door opened. Tyra tugged Angel's arm and pulled her in. But just before the door closed completely, some guy stuck his hand into the elevator and the door opened back up. He kept his mirrored sunglasses on, even though he was inside.

Angel recognized him from the pool. He was wearing this dumb shirt, a floppy hat, and carrying a beach bag. He glanced at the lit floor button and didn't press any others.

Tyra slipped her arm through Angel's and pulled her closer.

The elevator opened on fifteen, and Tyra and Angel got out. The guy followed. Tyra held Angel tighter and Angel had the sense that she was being used as a shield. Tyra slowed down as they got to their apartment. The guy kept walking past.

"Fucker," Tyra said under her breath. She relaxed her grip on Angel, reached into her bag for the key and unlocked the door. Angel stepped inside the apartment, but as she did, Tyra screamed.

The guy with the floppy hat had barged in, slamming the door behind him. He had his arm around Tyra, a knife at her throat. "Where are they?" he asked.

Angel froze.

The man poked the tip of the knife into flesh and squeezed Tyra tighter. A spot of red appeared. It began to drip down Tyra's neck. "Where are the fucking videos?" he asked. His voice was rough and squishy, like he was trying to disguise it. "Talk fast, or I'll fucking kill you."

Angel darted into the bedroom. No lock on the door. Angel already knew that after trying to lock herself in. None in the bathroom, either. The closet was shallow, under the bed too obvious. There was nowhere to hide. She ran out to the balcony. Fifteen stories up. She never came out here, afraid to look down. Afraid of heights since she'd fallen from the uneven bars in gymnastics five years ago.

The balcony continued the length of the apartment with no barriers. But on either side was a concrete wall separating it from the adjacent balconies. The walls extended the height of the room and the width of the balcony. How the hell was she going to climb around to get to one of the other apartments? But she had no choice.

She sat up on the railing and kicked off her sandals. Then she stood on the narrow metal edge, holding onto the concrete wall. The blurriness in her head cleared, replaced with the sound of her breathing. Like someone had put a mike up to her mouth and turned the volume too high. She clutched the wall, feeling her entire body trembling. The rough concrete scraped her fingers. The bar felt familiar beneath her curled feet.

Don't look down, she told herself. Don't look down. Somewhere in the distance she heard Tyra scream.

Go, she told herself. Do it.

She reached around the concrete wall with her other foot, until she was suspended between the two balconies, holding onto the jutting divider with both hands.

One more step. Do it. One more step.

She brought her other foot around. When it touched the rail, she propelled herself forward onto the balcony. She landed hard on the neighbor's Astroturf. She got up, rubbing her shoulder, and ran to the sliding door. Locked. She could see inside. Unmade bed, dead plant, a pile of clothes. She banged on the door. No answer.

She ran to the next room—the living room—and tried the door. Locked. Shit. Shit. Shit. Then she tried the next door, which led to the dining room. Also locked.

She wrapped her arms around herself, trembling uncontrollably. What to do? What to do? Would the man come after her when he was finished with Tyra? He'd know for sure that she'd climbed over to one of the adjacent apartments. There was nowhere else she could have gone.

She couldn't take a chance. She had to get to the next apartment before the man came looking for her.

She went to the end of the balcony and climbed up on the railing. You've already done it once, she told herself. It's no big deal. She grabbed the concrete wall, reached around with one foot.

Don't look down. Don't look down.

Someone was shouting from below. Her eyes turned to the sound.

Oh my God. Little people like ants. Trees below her. Water. A big blue rectangle. Oh my God. She swooned, her feet clenching the bar. Falling. She was falling. She threw her body forward to counterbalance herself and landed with a thud on tile, knocking over a planter. Smell of damp soil all around her. She started to cry. She was shaking. So scared. Daddy, she thought. Please come help me.

But she knew he wouldn't. He probably thought she was dead.

Somewhere below came the sound of a honking horn.

She couldn't stay here. What if the man came after her?

She looked in through the sliding glass doors. The layout of the apartment was reversed. She tried the door that led to the dining room. Locked. Nooooo.

She went to the living room door. Locked.

She doubled over, crying hysterically as she pulled on the bedroom door. It slid open. She stepped inside, locking it behind her, and sank to the floor.

She wasn't sure how long she sat with her legs pulled up to her chest. Just sat there and cried. Five minutes? Ten?

She looked around the bedroom. Bed made up with dozens of pillows. All different. She wanted to climb between the pillows and just hide there. Hide forever.

But what happened when the people who lived here came home? They'd call the police. Of course they would. Breaking and entering. Not that it was a big deal after murder.

And what about the man? Would he come looking for her? Could he smash the glass door when he found her? Would he kill her?

She had to get out of here. But where could she go?

And then she remembered. The sad guy who said he'd help her. *You can come by anytime*, he'd said. *Apartment 820*.

Anytime, he'd said.

Chapter 35

Jeremy paced across the Oriental rug in front of the sliding doors that led to his balcony. Back and forth. Back and forth. There was nothing else to do. Nowhere to go. He pounded his fist into the palm of his other hand. It was sore from punching Brett. Brett, who was dead.

How long before the cops came to arrest him? And here he was with no idea how to get out of this mess.

There was a knock on his door. He froze. But the cops wouldn't knock so lightly. He let out a relieved breath. It was probably Robbie back from talking to her father. He wondered if she'd also gone to tell Lieber about the message Kate sent Joanne on Facebook.

The knock again, more urgent.

The door was unlocked; why didn't Robbie just come in like she always did?

Jeremy crossed the room and opened the door.

Not Robbie. A sexy chick wearing a see-through shirt over a bikini. On second glance, he recognized the blonde girl from the pool. She was hugging herself, her face wet with tears, her nose red. Jeremy just stood there caught off guard. The girl came inside without asking, looking behind her as though afraid someone was following her. Jeremy closed the door after her. He hesitated for a second, then locked it.

The girl was barefoot.

Angel. That's what Tyra called her. Damn, she looked young, despite the sexy body. Young and scared shitless.

"Hey," he said softly. "What's wrong?" His impulse was to give her a hug, but he didn't dare touch her. She looked like she might scream or something if he did.

She began to cry harder. "You, you said I could come here. Remember? You, you said."

Just like Elise. He couldn't help himself. He slipped his arm around her and held her like he would his sister. She didn't resist, just cried against his chest. "It's okay," he said. "It's okay."

He led her to the sofa and she sat down. She wiped her face with the back of her hand. "I didn't know where else to go."

"Here is good," he said. "Do you want water or something?"

She shook her head. Her face was puffy. Her red-rimmed eyes were a dark gray. So dark he couldn't read them. She let out a shuddering sigh.

He sat down beside her on the sofa. "Tell me what's wrong."

"Tyra. Someone with a knife. I ran away." She spoke in gasps. "Climbed around the balcony. I'm afraid. Afraid he'll come after me."

Tyra? Maybe a half hour ago, Tyra had been screaming at Jeremy at the pool. What was going on here? "Who'll come after you?" Jeremy said. "Start at the beginning."

"After you left the pool. Tyra was angry. We went upstairs. Someone followed us into the elevator."

"Who?"

"He'd been at the pool—wearing a floppy hat and a stupid shirt."

Jeremy remembered the man lying on one of the lounge chairs using his beach bag for a pillow. "Did you see his face?"

"Not really. He was wearing sunglasses."

"So he got into the elevator. Then what?"

"We got out on our floor. So did he, but he kept walking. When

Tyra opened the door, he like jumped out of nowhere. He grabbed her and held a knife to her throat." Angel hugged herself. "He, he cut her. He said he'd kill her."

Jesus. "And you ran away?"

She nodded.

"Did you see anything else? Hear anything?"

Angel slid her feet under her. She was trembling hard.

Jeremy got up and took a pale blue blanket from the closet. He wrapped it around her.

"Thank you." The tears started up again. "Thank you for being so nice."

He waited for her to calm down. "Tyra might be hurt," he said. "I should call the police."

"No. No." She pressed herself against the corner of the sofa. "Not the police. Please no."

"Okay, no police. I won't call the police."

She blinked her dark eyes rapidly. Wrapped in the blanket, she looked like a swaddled injured bird.

"Talk to me."

She shook her head.

"You said you're afraid the man will come after you. Why? Why would he come after you?"

"The DVDs. He was yelling at Tyra. Asking where the videos were."

"What videos?"

"I don't know. Maybe he was in one of them."

Tyra, Angel, videos? "Did you and Tyra make videos with men?"

"I guess." She pulled the blanket up and gripped it beneath her chin. Only her face was visible. A small, frightened face.

"I know you don't belong with Tyra," he said. "Was she keeping you against your will?"

Angel stared down at the Oriental rug.

"Please. Talk to me. I'm not going to do anything that would hurt you."

"I don't know what to do."

"Let me help you."

She sank into the sofa. "I'm tired. I'm really tired."

"Okay. Sleep a while."

She rested her head on the arm of the sofa and closed her eyes.

Within seconds, her breathing became soft and even. Her brow relaxed. A child's sleeping face.

What the hell was she doing in this mess?

Chapter 36

Robbie's world was coming undone. And it had all started with her father showing up at her door. Why hadn't he stayed away? Her life had been perfectly fine until he appeared and announced she had a sister. A sister who had gone missing. And since then, terrible things had been happening. Kate's friend's unexplained death, Brett's murder, and now Jeremy was under suspicion as his killer.

She wished—oh, how she wished—her father had never come back.

She locked her bicycle to a post near Jeremy's building. It was early afternoon and very few people were about. A girl walking her dog, a UPS man, a young couple pushing a shopping cart with groceries. Robbie went inside to the large, open lobby area.

She shivered as she waited for the elevator. Why did they keep the air-conditioning so damn cold in here? A middle-aged man and woman in long terry-cloth robes were at the concierge's desk. The concierge's arms were folded across his chest. Robbie took the couple to be visitors, since most of the people who lived here were young. The woman's voice was shrill. Her husband was trying to calm her down.

The elevator door opened.

"Just lying in the hallway," the woman said to the concierge. "It's a mess. A bloody mess."

Someone had probably left garbage out in the hall, but the

woman was clearly overreacting. Robbie stepped into the elevator and pressed eight. The elevator took forever. What next, she wondered? Would the police pursue the lead of Kate's sandal at Mike's house? Would they change the focus of their investigation away from Jeremy and to someone connected with Mike? Was there even a link between Joanne's and Kate's and Brett's deaths?

The elevator opened.

What should she and Jeremy do next? Waiting here for the cops definitely didn't seem to be the smartest option.

She went down the hallway to Jeremy's apartment. She tried the knob. It didn't turn. That was odd.

If the door was locked, he probably wasn't home. Where would he have gone? Should she wait for him here? She still had the key to the apartment. Jeremy knew that. When she'd tried to give it back to him after she moved out, he told her to hold on to it. *In case of an emergency.*

She unlocked the door and pushed it open. She was surprised to see Jeremy standing in front of the sliding glass door, staring at the sofa. His eye was still swollen, his hair mussed, his beard like smudged charcoal covering his cheeks and chin. He seemed to be thinking about something and didn't notice her. His expression was wistful. She remembered a time when he used to look at her like that.

How she wished they could go back to the way it had been. Just yesterday, it had seemed like they almost had. She started toward him. "Hey."

He looked startled, then brought his finger to his lips, signaling for her to be quiet.

She didn't understand. Was someone else here? She stepped around the sofa.

A girl—a woman. Young, but not so young. Blonde, with the face of a child and a body that any female on South Beach would envy. She appeared to be asleep, wrapped in a pale blue blanket—one that was all too familiar to Robbie. The top of the blanket had fallen away from the girl, revealing a bikini-clad body and a sheer cover-up that did anything but.

Robbie wanted to scream. How could you? How could you, Jeremy? That's our blanket. Ours!

Jeremy seemed to read Robbie's face. He took her hand and pulled her toward the sliding door. "Shhh," he whispered. "Outside."

She was too stunned to speak. He closed the door behind them and they stood on the balcony, the air thick.

"I don't want to wake her," he said. "She's been through a lot."

"A lot?" Robbie found her voice. "I'm sorry. She's been through a lot? Who the hell is she?"

Jeremy looked surprised. "She lives in the building. She came by a little while ago, all scared and shook up. This woman she lives with—one of the club girls named Tyra—was attacked at knifepoint. Angel came here. She didn't have anywhere else to go."

"Angel?"

"That's her name."

"Why did she come here?"

"I once told her she could."

"I see."

"It's not like that."

"No, stop. It's not important. We don't have any claims on each other."

"But we do. We have major claims on each other." He rested his hands on her shoulders and pulled her toward him.

"Please, Jeremy. Not now." She was overloaded with emotion.

"Okay. Not now, but later." He kissed her forehead. "Right now, we need to figure out what the hell's going on here."

"You mean with this girl?"

"With this girl. With Tyra."

"The one who was attacked?"

"Yeah. Tyra's a regular at BURN. I always figured her for being a high-end hooker, or something. But then, I saw her at the pool a couple of times with Angel. And it bothered me. Angel definitely doesn't belong in this scene. Then she comes by here a little while ago, banging on my door, and tells me someone attacked Tyra, saying he wanted the videos."

"What videos?"

"I'm not sure. But the way I'm putting it together is that Tyra and Angel brought guys back to their apartment and made videos with them."

"But why would the man threaten Tyra and ask for the videos?" Robbie thought for a moment. "Unless the videos were made without the men's knowledge."

"And then were used to blackmail them," Jeremy said.

Robbie remembered something. "What does Tyra look like?"

"Tall, skinny, gigantic breasts. A lot of copper-colored hair."

"Darkish skin?"

"Yeah. You know her?"

"Maybe," Robbie said. "Last Friday at BURN, I saw the congressman who killed himself on Sunday. He was very drunk, or maybe even drugged. He was with two women. One looked like you describe Tyra." Robbie glanced through the sliding door at the sleeping girl on the sofa. "The other one looked like her."

Jeremy pressed his back against the balcony railing. Beyond, the bay was almost perfectly still. A couple of girls were sunning themselves near the pool.

"So let's say Tyra and Angel brought him back to their apartment and made a video of their evening together," Jeremy said. "Then, either Tyra or someone she's working with could have blackmailed the congressman the next day. If the video became public, he'd have a huge amount to lose."

"Maybe even enough to explain why he committed suicide."

Jeremy rubbed the back of his neck. "But then, who's the guy who attacked Tyra? Another blackmail victim?"

"Sounds like it."

A shrill voice came from the pool area. Robbie looked over. The middle-aged couple in terry-cloth robes who had been arguing with the concierge were talking to a man in a sports jacket. Two cops were standing nearby.

"Tell me again what happened with Angel," Robbie said. "You said she came here because someone was attacking Tyra at knife-point?"

"That's right. Followed them to their apartment."

"Their apartment in this building?"

He nodded.

Robbie had a nagging feeling, like there was something she was supposed to know, but it just wasn't connecting. "Does Angel know what happened to Tyra? If the man hurt her?"

Jeremy shook his head. "She ran away."

The shrill voice rang out again. The woman was pointing to a lounge chair, then gestured toward the building.

Just lying in the hallway, the woman had said. *It's a bloody mess.*

The woman hadn't been talking about someone's garbage.

"Tyra's dead," Robbie said.

"What? How do you know?"

"The woman at the pool. She saw something. That's why the cops are here."

"Shit," Jeremy said.

"What's wrong?"

"She and that man were at the pool when Tyra started scream-ing at me."

"What are you talking about?"

"I went down earlier to ask Tyra about some people at BURN.

Whether they could be connected to Brett's death. And she started screaming at me to get the fuck away from her."

"And that man and woman saw you?"

Jeremy nodded.

Several more cops had arrived at the pool.

"Jesus, Jeremy." Robbie grabbed his arm and pulled him back into the apartment. "The cops are going to think you did it. We need to get away from here." She slammed the sliding door shut after them.

The girl shifted on the sofa and the blue blanket fell to the floor. Her shoulders were slender, and the arch of her back swooped down into a perfect rounded butt.

"Come on, Jeremy," Robbie said. "Wake up your friend and let's go." She started to turn away from the girl, but something caught her eye.

At the base of her spine, just above the edge of her bikini was a bluish mark.

Robbie bent closer. It took her a second to process what she saw.

An arrowhead tattoo.

Chapter 37

The girl opened her eyes. She looked startled at the sight of Robbie.

Not possible, Robbie thought. Not possible. Even though the arrowhead tattoo was the same as Kate's Facebook picture, this girl had blonde hair, eyes the color of slate, full lips and high cheekbones. Nothing like Kate's high school photo. But then Robbie remembered what Kate had written to Joanne. *You were always better than an angel.*

This girl's name was Angel, which could explain—

"Who are you?" the girl asked, pulling up the blanket and covering herself.

"Robbie. Robbie Ivy."

The girl's mouth was open, eyes wide, as though Robbie were a ghost.

"Robbie's a friend of mine," Jeremy said.

Robbie stared back. Right age, right size. Even the girl's heart-shaped face was the same as in Kate's photo.

"Robbie," Jeremy said. "We need to go."

"And who are you?" Robbie asked the girl.

The girl hesitated. "My name's Angel."

"Your real name."

"I, I don't know what you mean."

If she was Kate, why wouldn't she say so?

Robbie spoke gently. "Are you sure it isn't Kate Brooks?"

"Jesus," Jeremy said.

The girl gasped. "Oh my God. Who are you? Are you the police?"

"No," Robbie said. "We're not cops." She sat down on the edge of the sofa. Was it possible? Could this really be her sister? Contact lenses, hair dye, and collagen injections would explain the changes. She took the girl's hand. Cold and trembling. The fingers were long and slender and the nails covered the nail bed with almost no white. Just like Robbie's. Just like their father's.

"You are, aren't you?" Robbie said. "You are Kate Brooks."

The girl began to cry, her shoulders convulsing. "Please—please don't call the police."

Was she somehow responsible for her friend's death like she wrote in the Facebook message? Robbie doubted it, but then why was she so terrified? "We're not going to let anyone hurt you. I'm—"

The sound of sirens pierced through the glass door.

Kate jumped, clutching the blanket. "Oh, no."

Jeremy went to the sliding door and looked down. "Cops are swarming this place. I'll bet that man and woman described me to the cops and they're going to come looking for me. We need to get out of here."

No time now. They'd talk later. Robbie glanced at Jeremy—several days' beard growth, long hair, swollen eye, jeans, and T-shirt. "Is that what you were wearing when the couple saw you with Tyra?"

"Yeah. But I had sunglasses on."

"Change," Robbie said. "I'll find something for Kate to wear."

"Good idea." Jeremy rummaged through the closet, pulled something out, and went into the bathroom.

Robbie opened a drawer where she used to keep her clothes. Shoved in the back, she found a pair of worn jeans, a crumpled tank top, and a baseball cap, all splattered with paint. Work clothes from when she and Jeremy had first moved into the apartment. Had she left them behind deliberately? She handed the clothes to Kate. "Try these."

Kate slipped on the jeans over her bathing suit. Their bodies were so similar Robbie could have been looking at herself in the mirror. Her sister. She found her sister. She wanted to rush across the room to hug her, but the police could be coming for Jeremy at any moment.

Robbie found a pair of her old sneakers in the back of the closet.

A buzzing sound came from the bathroom.

Kate put on the sneakers and pushed her hair up into the baseball cap Robbie had given her. "Thank you. Thank you for helping me."

The door to the bathroom opened. Jeremy had shaved his face and trimmed his hair. He was dressed in a suit and open shirt. It took her back over a year ago when they'd both worked together at the CPA firm.

"I don't think they'll be looking for someone in business clothes." Jeremy checked out Kate. "Good. That's good. " He held out his sunglasses. "Should I wear them?"

"Yeah," Robbie said. "You're more conspicuous with the swollen eye."

He pushed them on. "Okay. Let's go."

"Is it safe to take your car?" Robbie asked.

He paused at the door. "Probably not. The police are very likely setting up a perimeter around the building and the garage."

"But how would they know the guy arguing with Tyra at the pool was you?"

"They wouldn't. Not by name. But they'll definitely be checking everyone who leaves the garage or goes through the front and back entrances of the building."

"So how are we going to get out of here?" Robbie asked.

"You'll see," Jeremy said.

They left the apartment and followed Jeremy to one of the stairwells.

Kate pulled down on the bill of the paint-splattered baseball cap, shadowing her eyes. She wrapped her arms around herself as she walked.

Her sister. Robbie had found her sister.

On the second floor, Jeremy pushed open the exit door, took a quick glance into the hallway. "Okay. All clear."

He led them down the empty hallway.

"I see what you're doing," Robbie said.

SOBE Grande consisted of three buildings. To an outsider, they appeared to be separate, but they were actually connected by a corridor that led from one building to the next, so people could get to and from the parking garage without getting wet if it rained. Jeremy lived in the north tower.

They continued down the hallway until they reached the center building. This corridor had windows on both sides and was visible from the outside. Jeremy put his arms around Robbie and Kate and the three of them walked through. When they reached the south tower, they hurried down the hallway to the stairwell that led to the back of the building and the loading dock.

They ran down the steps to the first floor. Robbie pushed open the exit door and stuck her head out. The outside door was propped open. A couple of men were moving furniture into the elevator. They got the last piece in, and the elevator closed behind them.

Robbie, Jeremy, and Kate stepped into the vestibule. Jeremy rubbed his clean-shaven cheek. The skin was pale compared to the dark tan around the bridge of his nose and on his forehead. "Let's hope they haven't extended the perimeter around all three buildings," he said.

"I'll check." Robbie walked out of the building and scanned the loading area. There was a trail of furniture leading from the moving truck, a few parked cars, a couple of shopping carts. A security guard was leaning against a column near the loading dock eating a candy bar, his gun conspicuous against his dark pants.

Robbie stepped back into the vestibule and spoke to Jeremy and Kate in a low voice. "There's a guard, but I don't think he's been alerted to anything. Let's just walk like nothing's wrong."

The three of them left the loading area. Robbie smiled at the security guard without stopping.

He waved.

They kept walking, heads up, arms hanging loose. In the background, sirens screamed. Almost to the gate. Just a little farther and they'd be clear. They picked up their pace.

The sound of a staticky voice came over a walkie-talkie.

"Hey," the security guard called after them.

The three of them froze. Robbie and Jeremy exchanged a look. Kate was biting her lip. Run or stay?

Jeremy turned back to the guard. "What's up?"

"Have you seen anyone that doesn't belong here? A guy with a beard, long hair, jeans, T-shirt?"

Jeremy shook his head. "Why? What happened?"

Robbie wanted to kick him. Let's go, she said telepathically. Stop making goddamn conversation.

"Not sure," said the guard.

More static on the walkie-talkie. The guard held it up to his ear.

Kate slipped her arm through Jeremy's. "Come on," she said softly.

The three of them started walking away.

"What's that?" the guard said into the walkie-talkie. "Huh? No. Ain't seen no one here."

Robbie, Jeremy, and Kate went through the narrow swinging

door in the gate, then continued walking south at a brisk pace, away from the noise of sirens.

"Don't look back," Kate said, taking Robbie's hand. "It's Sodom."

And Robbie remembered the story of Lot and his wife led away from the city of Sodom by angels. And how Lot's wife didn't listen to the angels. She had glanced back to look at the home she was leaving and became a pillar of salt.

"Don't worry. We won't look back." Robbie squeezed Kate's hand tighter as they walked. This girl who had called herself Angel. What kind of hell had her sister been living in these last twelve days?

Jeremy stepped into the street and signaled a taxi. It stopped and the three of them climbed into the back.

"Where to?" the driver asked.

Jeremy took off his sunglasses and glanced at Robbie. "Coconut Grove?"

Robbie nodded.

Kate leaned back against the seat looking scared. "What's in Coconut Grove?"

"Sanctuary," Jeremy said.

Chapter 38

No one spoke during the taxi ride to Jeremy's grandfather's house in Coconut Grove. Kate stared out the window, chewing on her finger.

Her sister. But Robbie sensed that now wasn't the right time to tell Kate. The girl seemed too close to a breaking point. And although Robbie knew she should call her father, it was clear that Kate wasn't ready to make her presence known to anyone. Robbie would wait until she understood what had happened to Kate and why she was so afraid.

The taxi got off the highway and took a route through dense shrubs and trees that overgrew the sidewalks and shadowed the narrow streets.

"Turn left here," Jeremy said to the driver. "Second house on the left."

The taxi stopped in front of a small one-story house that was barely visible behind blooming bougainvillea bushes and drooping palm trees. Robbie remembered the first time she'd come here with Jeremy. How comfortable his grandfather had made her feel, despite his sorrow over his daughter's recent death.

Jeremy paid the driver and they got out. There were no cars in the driveway. "Looks like no one's home, but we can go inside. My grandfather won't mind." He went to the front steps, reached into a planter and pulled something out. He used the key to unlock the front door.

Kate was standing so close to Robbie that their shoulders touched. She tugged on a strand of blonde hair that had escaped from her baseball cap.

"Let's go inside," Robbie said.

Kate hesitated, then followed Robbie up the front steps, through the screened-in porch, and into the house.

Sunlight poured through the windows, falling across hanging baskets of philodendron, the worn sofa, club chairs, ottoman, bookcases, and coffee table covered with family photos. There was a vague smell of dog and Robbie wondered if old Geezer was still alive. In the corner of the room was an upright piano with an old-fashioned clock on the wall above it. The house was happier and better cared for than the first time Robbie had been here. Probably Jeremy's sister's touch.

Kate stood in the middle of the living room, feet slightly pigeon-toed, a finger in her mouth.

Jeremy came back from the kitchen with three small bottles of water. He handed one to Robbie, another to Kate. "Would you rather have a Coke or something?" he asked.

Kate seemed surprised by the bottle of water in her hand. "Oh. No, this is fine. Thanks."

He patted the sofa. "You can sit down."

She did, on the edge.

Robbie sat next to her. Jeremy continued standing, resting his elbows on the back of one of the club chairs. He had thrown the suit jacket on the piano bench and rolled up his shirtsleeves.

Kate stared at the unopened bottle of water in her hands.

"We need to talk about what happened to you, Kate," Robbie said.

Kate took off the baseball cap. Her blonde hair cascaded to her shoulders. She didn't speak.

"Okay," Robbie said finally. "How about this? We'll tell you what we know and you can fill in the missing pieces."

When Kate didn't respond, Robbie continued. "You and Joanne disappeared a week ago Friday. Your dad came down to Miami to find you."

Kate widened her eyes. How fake the dark gray looked.

"He's still in Miami," Robbie said. "Do you want me to call him?"

Kate shook her head—an emphatic no.

"He's very worried," Robbie said.

Kate sucked in her lower lip and looked back down at the water bottle.

"All right then," Robbie said. "You tell us when you're ready for him to know."

Kate mumbled something. It sounded like thank you.

Robbie wanted to tell her to take the gray contact lenses out, but it was clear to her that she'd better not rush things with Kate. She continued in a soft voice. "I imagine you know Joanne's dead."

A tear dripped onto Kate's worn jeans, creating a dark blue spot.

Again, Robbie wondered if Kate was somehow complicit in her friend's death.

"Her body was found in a canal on Miami Beach last Wednesday."

"In, in a canal?"

"Yes," Robbie said. "But the medical examiner said that she'd probably drowned in a swimming pool. Do you know anything about that?"

Another tear stained Kate's jeans, then another.

Robbie continued talking while Kate stared at her lap. Robbie explained how the receipt in Joanne's car led her and Jeremy down to Key Largo, and how someone at the tiki bar recalled Kate and Joanne and saw them leaving with two guys. She left out the part about Joanne very likely being raped.

"Can you tell us where those guys took you and what happened?" Robbie asked.

Kate wiped her eyes and put the water bottle down on the coffee table. She picked up one of the photos. It was of Jeremy and his mom, dad, and sister. Kate glanced up at Jeremy, then back at the photo. "So you are cops."

"No, Kate," Robbie said. "I told you before. We're not cops."

"Then why do you care about this so much?"

Jeremy was massaging his bruised knuckles. He gave Robbie a slight nod.

"When your father came to see me right after you disappeared, there was something else he told me." It was clear to Robbie that Kate hadn't seen the Facebook message Robbie had sent her explaining their relationship. "Something I never knew."

Kate's body stiffened.

"You and I are half sisters."

"What are you talking about?"

"Our dad was married to my mother before he married yours."

Kate shook her head. She hadn't known.

"I lived in Deland until I was seven. Then my mom and I moved to Boston after the divorce. I never saw Dad again until he came looking for you. That was the first time I learned about you."

"You're my sister?"

"Yes, Kate."

"But he never told me. Never said a thing about you."

"I know."

"How could he not—" Kate's voice drifted off.

Her expression went from anger to hurt to doubt. She seemed to be taking Robbie in all over again. "Our eyes," Kate said. "Your eyes are just like mine. And we're the same size, and—she looked Robbie up and down. "Oh, my God. Oh, my God. You are. You really are my sister."

Robbie reached over then and hugged her. Kate smelled like suntan oil, but there was also a vague, familiar scent coming from her hair. How many times as a child had Robbie looked in the mirror and played with her imaginary sister, braiding her hair, painting her nails?

Oh, Kate, she thought. *I've finally found you.*

When they pulled apart, Robbie noticed that Jeremy hadn't moved from the club chair. He was staring in the direction of the window and his cheeks were wet, as though he'd been crying.

He caught Robbie's eyes on him, wiped his face, then walked toward the kitchen. "Anyone want more water or something?"

Robbie shook her head.

Kate was studying Robbie's hand. "He should have told me."

"Yes. He should have. But right now, Jeremy's in a lot of trouble. The police think he killed someone. Anything you could tell us about what happened to you would be a big help."

Kate looked over at the club chair where Jeremy had been standing. "Is he your boyfriend?"

"Not exactly. Maybe. He was. It's a long story."

"That's okay," Kate said. "He's a really nice guy."

Jeremy came back in the room, put a platter of cookies on the coffee table, then sat down on the ottoman. "My grandfather. He always keeps cookies in the house."

Kate leaned back on the sofa and pushed her hair behind her ear. "Okay." She folded her fingers together and squeezed them. "Those guys at the tiki bar? Well, I think they drugged us, or something."

A wave of heat passed over Robbie. So here it came.

"They drove us somewhere. I don't remember much. Just that everything felt wrong and strange. And then, I remember walking around the house looking for Joanne."

She stopped talking. The room filled with the sound of white noise, the hum of the air conditioner, the clock ticking over the piano.

"She . . . she was in the pool. And I called her, but she didn't answer. She . . . she just floated. And I knew. I knew she was—"

Robbie slipped her arm around her. "It's okay. It wasn't your fault."

Kate pulled away. "But it was. They told me I killed her. And they, they said they would tell the police if I didn't do what they said."

So that was it.

"But you didn't kill her, Kate," Robbie said. "Those men drugged her. And then, she probably drowned accidently. But it wasn't your fault. It was absolutely not your fault."

Kate got up and went to the window that overlooked the back-yard.

"What did they tell you to do?" Jeremy asked.

"They gave me a lot of drugs." She continued facing the window. Robbie had to strain to hear her. "Then I went to live with Tyra. And they said to do what she said or they'd change me back to the way I was and the police would find me."

"Change you back?" Jeremy asked.

"My face and hair. They said they changed me to protect me. So no one would recognize me."

"And you believed them?" Jeremy asked.

Kate turned to them. "I don't know. I was so scared. And Joanne. Poor Joanne. If I hadn't made her come with me, none of this would have happened. She'd still be alive."

"They drugged you, Kate," Robbie said. "They took advantage of you."

Kate returned to the sofa and folded her hands over her lap.

"So when you moved in with Tyra, what happened?" Jeremy leaned forward on the ottoman, elbows on his knees. "What did she tell you to do?"

"Mostly she gave me pills and I slept a lot. Then at night, we'd go to the club. And we'd bring men home with us." She looked at her hands. Her knuckles were white. "I'd rather not talk about that."

"What about during the day?" Jeremy said. "Did any people come by to see Tyra? Was anyone angry?"

"Everyone was always angry."

"Who's everyone?"

"Well, mainly Tyra and Luis. And then, this morning, this old guy came by."

"Luis and an old guy?" Jeremy asked. "Who are they?"

"Luis was one of the guys who brought me and Joanne to the house."

"What does Luis look like?"

"He's like really built. He shaves his head and has a lot of tattoos."

"And the old guy?" Jeremy asked.

"He was really creepy looking. You know, like Michael Jackson?"

"How like Michael Jackson?"

"Skinny and his face was fake, like he'd had a lot of work done on it."

Creepy, like Michael Jackson. Something was gnawing at Robbie.

"And you said they were angry?" Jeremy asked.

"Well, mainly the man was angry. He was yelling at Luis and Tyra. Something about the DVDs. And Tyra got all pissed at him. She said, 'You don't tell me what to do, mister. You don't own me.' And then the man said, 'I made you, I own you. And I can just as easily unmake you.' And Tyra said, 'You got that backward, mister. I can unmake you.'"

Jeremy's face was alive. "What do you remember about the house in Key Largo?"

"Huh?"

"Sorry," he said. "I'm jumping around here. The house they took you to after the tiki bar. What do you remember about it?"

"Not much. I slept a lot."

"Anything," Jeremy said. "Any little detail."

Kate scrunched up her forehead. "Lots of windows, like mirrors. A swimming pool inside. Pictures on the wall. Red, blue, green."

"What was in the pictures?"

"Don't remember." She shook her head. "Oh. But there were pebbles. Like millions of pebbles."

Pebbles, Robbie thought. An indoor swimming pool.

"Anything else?" Jeremy asked.

"It's really blurry."

"Do you remember what shoes you wore to the tiki bar that night?" Robbie asked.

"My Cinderella slippers."

Robbie's heart lurched. "Can you describe them?"

"White," Kate said. "White sandals with see-through heels. I remember I lost one of them. Just like Cinderella."

"Lost it where?"

"In the pebbles. In the pebbles by the jumping red dragon."

Chapter 39

"What is it?" Jeremy asked her.

Robbie realized she was taking short, quick breaths. "Mike," she said.

"I know. There's obviously a connection."

Robbie shook her head. "I think he believes I'm involved."

"Involved? What are you talking about?"

"The flyer. The one with Kate's picture."

Her sister was looking at her, frightened.

"The flyer had my phone number. And I wrote 'Call Robbie' on it."

"So?" Jeremy rubbed the back of his neck.

"Mike saw the flyer on the bar at the Fieldstone event. He said something about it being my name and number. He knows I'm connected to Kate."

"Okay. Let's say he does."

"I think he broke into my apartment."

"What? When?"

"Yesterday afternoon. My cat got out and my neighbor saw someone outside my door."

Kate had brought her knees up to her chest and hugged them tightly.

"So if Mike was involved with killing Brett and believes you're somehow able to connect him to Kate—" Jeremy turned toward the sound of the front door opening.

His grandfather stepped into the living room, wisps of white hair floating around his shiny scalp like cotton candy. Beside him, tail wagging, was Geezer, a low, brown shadow.

"Jeremy," he said, "you gave me a scare. I didn't see your car in the driveway."

"Sorry, Grandpa." Jeremy went to hug his grandfather. He towered over the frail old man.

Robbie could tell by the strain in Jeremy's face that he was trying hard not to alarm his grandfather. She tried to calm herself, to not think about Mike lurking in her apartment yesterday. What had he planned to do if she'd arrived home while he was still there?

"We took a taxi, and let ourselves in," Jeremy said. "I didn't mean to frighten you."

"Taxi?" Mr. Weiss pulled back, surveying Jeremy. "Your eye. Have you been in a fight?"

"Nothing serious." Jeremy bent over to scratch the dog behind his floppy ears. "Hey, buddy. How ya doin'?"

His grandfather pushed his thick glasses up on his nose. His scowl lifted. "Robbie, dear." He extended his arms. "It's been too long."

"Yes it has." Robbie stepped around the coffee table and club chairs to hug him. "Way too long."

"And this young lady is?" The old man smiled at Kate, who hadn't gotten up from the sofa.

"This is Kate. My sister." Robbie got a shiver saying it. My sister.

Mr. Weiss raised an eyebrow, but made no comment. He hadn't known Robbie had a sister, but Mr. Weiss, an old-time accountant himself, was always scrupulously discreet. "So nice to meet you, Kate."

"You, too." Kate's voice was barely audible as she tugged on her straight blonde hair. Geezer went over to sniff her, but Kate seemed uncertain what to do.

Robbie wondered if they'd done the right thing bringing her here.

"I have a granddaughter about your age," Mr. Weiss said. "Elise should be home from school any time now."

"This is her in the photo, right?" Kate pointed at the family portrait.

"That's right."

"She's very pretty."

"Just like you."

"Thank you, but—" Kate looked down at the dog.

Mr. Weiss cleared his throat. "Well, I think I'll go make some nice hot chocolate for everyone."

"We're good, Grandpa," Jeremy said. "Why don't you sit down and we'll fill you in."

"That's not necessary."

"Actually, it is," Jeremy said. "We need to borrow your car."

"I see. This should be interesting." Mr. Weiss arranged himself on a club chair and Jeremy sat down facing him on the ottoman.

His grandfather's car. Robbie's abdomen contracted as she sat back down next to Kate. What was Jeremy planning?

"Grandpa, did you read about the two high school girls who disappeared on Miami Beach during spring break?"

"Yes, of course," Mr. Weiss said. "One of them—oh dear."

"That was Kate's friend Joanne they found in the creek," Jeremy said.

"I'm so sorry," Mr. Weiss said to Kate. "What a tragedy to lose someone close to you."

Kate nodded, but was unable to look him in the eye.

"And the other girl?" Mr. Weiss asked. "Was she also a friend? Have they found her? I'm not always able to keep up with the news."

"Kate's the other girl," Robbie said.

He blinked several times behind his thick lenses. "But you're safe now." He took in Kate's lowered head, trembling shoulders, withdrawn manner, then he leaned forward on his chair and spoke softly. "I'm sure you've had a terrible time of it."

"Kate was kidnapped," Jeremy said. "They changed her hair and face so she wouldn't be recognized. She managed to escape, but we're still sorting out what happened and who's behind everything."

"I understand," Mr. Weiss said. "But I'm sure the police will pick up the pieces and take care of whoever did this terrible thing to Kate and her friend." He looked from Robbie to Jeremy, then shook his head. "Please don't tell me the police don't know Kate's here."

"It's a long story," Jeremy said.

Mr. Weiss's face reddened. "I don't know what's going on here, Jeremy, but I sense that you and Robbie have decided to take matters into your own hands." He inhaled deeply. "Please. Don't try to play the hero again. Call the police. Talk to that nice detective Lieber. This poor child shouldn't be left in limbo like this. She needs to go home, to be with her family."

"No," Kate said, so abruptly that Robbie jumped.

Geezer sat up, alert.

"No police. Please, no police." Kate began to cry.

Mr. Weiss looked distraught. He cocked his head toward Jeremy.

"It's complicated, Grandpa."

"It's always complicated."

Jeremy picked up one of the photos from the coffee table. Would he tell his grandfather about Brett's murder? Tyra's? How the police were probably looking for him? That Mike might be after Robbie?

"Please, Mr. Weiss," Kate said, "don't be angry with Jeremy. I asked them not to call the police or my father."

"But why not, dear?" Mr. Weiss's voice was gentle.

"I'm afraid the police will think it was my fault. That Joanne died because of me."

"I'm sure the police—"

"We need to check something out before we go to the police." Jeremy put the photo back down on the coffee table. Robbie could now see it was his mother's picture. His grandfather could see it, too. "Please, Grandpa. We have to borrow your car so we can show the police who's behind all this."

Mr. Weiss had his eye on the photo. "I've always had a sense that your mother never left us. That she's watching over you, Jeremy." He took his glasses off and rubbed his eyes. Then he put his glasses back on and sighed. "I pray to God I'm right."

"So we can have the car?"

His grandfather nodded, barely perceptibly. "But I ask you one thing. Let Kate stay here with me and Elise. She's been through enough."

"Of course," Jeremy said.

"Please, Mr. Weiss," Kate said, "I must go with them."

"Must go where?" said a familiar voice. Elise came into the room and flew into her brother's arms. She was small and delicate despite her ungainly school uniform—a navy polo shirt and knee-length khaki shorts. She looked more like her mother than ever with her green eyes and shiny dark hair pulled into a high ponytail.

"And why do you only come here at moments of grand drama?" Elise drew her head back and studied her brother. Her iridescent skin glowed beneath a dusting of freckles across the bridge of her upturned nose. "Damn, Jeremy. Your face is a mess."

"One of my clients missed the punching bag," he lied.

Robbie wondered how long Elise had been standing in the hallway, how much she had overheard.

"Here we thought you'd stay out of trouble as a personal

trainer." Elise gave Jeremy another squeeze, then crossed the room to embrace Robbie. "Hey, girl," Elise said, "I've missed you."

"I've missed you, too," Robbie said. She sensed Kate fidgeting on the sofa.

Elise smiled at Kate. How much more confident Elise had become in the last year. "I'm Elise, Jeremy's sister."

"I'm Kate. I'm—" She hesitated as though not sure.

"Kate's my sister," Robbie said. "We just found out about each other."

"I can sort of see a resemblance."

"My hair." Kate ran her fingers through her white blonde hair. "My eyes. This isn't what I look like."

"I overheard you talking," Elise said. "I can change you back, if you'd like."

Kate was still holding a strand of pale hair, looking at it. They called me Angel," she said. "Me. An angel."

She let the hair fall and began to cry. Geezer licked her hand.

"Change me back," Kate said. "Please change me back. I don't want to be an angel anymore."

Chapter 40

The old Honda smelled like heat, tired upholstery, and faded memories. Robbie leaned back against the passenger seat of Jeremy's grandfather's car, thrumming her fingers against the dashboard. She was feeling an odd energy. So many competing emotions.

Kate, her sister. So real, and yet the connection reminded Robbie of a thread of fresh glue—still fluid and delicate. The sisters hardly had had time to speak to each other over the last few hours, let alone get to know each other. They'd hugged goodbye at Jeremy's grandfather's. "We'll talk later," Robbie had said.

But Kate had just nodded, the corners of her mouth tugging downward. A child left behind on her first day of school, not quite certain her mother was really coming back for her. Robbie certainly knew that feeling.

And then there was Jeremy. He was driving, eyes on the bumper-to-bumper traffic heading south on U.S. 1. Shaved now, hair short, jaw set. So different from their ride down to Key Largo in the Corvair. She had an image from then of Jeremy's hair blowing in the wind through the open windows. Together once again on a mission.

When was that? Just yesterday?

"Rush hour," Jeremy said. "We probably won't get down to Key Largo before dark."

A mission. How tired Robbie was becoming of missions. "I suppose it's better for us if it's dark."

"You know we don't really have a choice," Jeremy said.

Robbie looked out at the gas stations and fast-food restaurants that went slowly by.

"I want to know exactly where that bastard is and what he's planning next." Jeremy shook his head. "I can't believe it. Breaking into your apartment, waiting to do God knows what."

"We don't know for sure it was he at my apartment."

"Jesus, Robbie. We still have enough to tie Mike to everything that's gone down. Kate's shoe on the pebbles near a jumping red dragon? For chrissake—how many houses have jumping red dragons in their front yard? Then, Brett's body being found there. And when Kate talked about the creepy old guy that reminded her of Michael Jackson, that had to be Mike."

"But I don't see how he could have pulled off the murders," Robbie said. "He was still in the house when you went outside with Brett. And even if he sneaked out later, I just don't see Mike over-powering Brett."

A large truck was stopped in front of them, making it impossible to see what was going on up ahead. "That's a good point," Jeremy said.

The truck began to move and they ground forward. "And if Mike was the one who'd attacked Tyra," Robbie said, "Tyra and Kate would have recognized him in the elevator."

"That's true," Jeremy said. "I saw the guy with the floppy hat lying on a lounge chair. It wasn't Mike. "

"You saw his face?"

"No. It was covered with the hat. But he wasn't old and skinny—I could tell that much."

"Then Mike probably has someone doing his dirty work." Robbie thought for a minute. "Remember at the party when Brett was angry with Mike? There was this other guy—brown hair, nice-looking, messed-up lip."

"I remember."

"Well, after you and Brett left the party, I noticed he was missing. I wonder if he followed you, then killed Brett after you left."

Jeremy was tapping on the steering wheel with his thumbs.

"Do you think he could have been the guy in the floppy hat that killed Tyra?" Robbie asked.

"It's possible."

"I'd seen him before," Robbie said. "He was at BURN Friday night, hovering over Mike like his watchman or something."

Robbie remembered the way the guy had looked at her that night. Almost like he recognized her—probably because of her resemblance to Kate before they had altered her appearance. So very likely he was the one who'd broken into Robbie's house yesterday afternoon. She wondered if he had also slashed her bike tires, perhaps as a warning. That had happened a couple of days after Mike had seen Robbie's number on Kate's flyer.

"Okay," Jeremy said, "so assuming he's Mike's personal goon and he killed Brett and Tyra, once we get to Mike's house, what are we looking for? And the place could still be crawling with cops. Brett's body was only just found early this morning. "

Early this morning? It seemed to Robbie a lot more time had gone by with all that had happened. Jeremy under suspicion for Brett's murder, Robbie's fight with her father, Tyra getting killed, Kate's escape. And, of course, Kate's and Robbie's discovery that they were sisters.

"We don't really have a choice," Robbie said. "We need something tangible to connect Mike with the two murders or you're the primary suspect."

"And Mike might still be figuring out how to shut you up."

They stopped at a traffic light. Cars were streaming into a strip mall with a store selling lottery tickets, a florist, a liquor store, a video rental.

"We need to find the DVDs," Robbie said.

But what would DVDs prove?" Jeremy asked. "Just that Mike's in the blackmailing business."

"But think about the stuff going on at BURN, which happens to be Mike's favorite hangout," Robbie said. "That's where the congressman went last Friday, then left with Tyra and Kate. What if after the congressman killed himself, the cops and FBI turned up the heat? And then, what if the people who worked for Mike started double-crossing him? Or if Mike was afraid they would? We both saw that Brett was losing it. And according to Kate, Tyra threatened to expose him. If Mike believed those two might topple his blackmailing operation, that's a pretty good motive for him to want Brett and Tyra dead."

"And you, if he believes you're onto him."

Robbie ignored Jeremy's remark. It was easier to think clearly if she wasn't worried about herself being a target. "So," she continued, "if we find blackmail DVDs at Mike's house then there's a logical link between Mike and the murders."

"Right," Jeremy said. "The house. Even if the cops aren't there, how the hell are we going to get in?"

"I think there's a way."

"Really?" Jeremy glanced over at her.

The truck had stopped again, blocking the road ahead. "Maybe."

"And what if Mike or his henchman is home? Or what if there's a caretaker?"

"Then we have a problem."

Even after the rush hour congestion should have subsided, it was still slow going as they continued down U.S. 1. "I don't get how there can be so much traffic on a Tuesday night," Jeremy said.

Just south of Florida City, the sound of a siren grew behind them. "Shit," Jeremy said. "They couldn't be chasing us." He glanced in the rearview mirror. "They don't know my grandfather's car. Unless Lieber figured out where we went."

Robbie turned and looked at the traffic clogging the road. Could the police back at the SOBE Grande have connected Tyra's murder to Jeremy? Or maybe the DA had finally put together enough evidence to arrest Jeremy for Brett's death.

The siren got louder. Cars were pulling over to the shoulder. An ambulance drove through.

"Not the police." Jeremy let out a breath of relief.

"It looks like there's an accident ahead," Robbie said.

There were flashing lights as they approached the dangerous section of U.S. 1 they'd driven through the day before. The north-bound lane on the two-lane highway was closed and a cop was directing traffic. A couple of cars looking like crushed soda cans were off to the side of the road, surrounded by fire rescue, an ambulance, and several police cars.

Jeremy strained to see. "This doesn't surprise me. Remember how that asshole cut us off and almost caused an accident yesterday?"

Traffic eased up beyond the collision. Robbie gazed at the mangroves reflected in the dark, swampy water. The possibility that the police were looking for them was very real. It was just a matter of time. If she and Jeremy were unable to find a connection between Mike and the murders, Jeremy would very likely be arrested. But going to Mike's house presented risks, too. Someone might see them, figure out what they were doing, and try to stop them.

Either scenario potentially ended with an outcome that terrified Robbie—losing Jeremy.

They reached Key Largo at a little after eight, but the sky was still light. Jeremy pulled the car into a McDonald's drive-through.

"What are you doing?"

"Getting something to eat. I haven't had anything all day. And by the time we're done, it should be dark."

Robbie didn't argue. Any delay was welcome.

They ordered Big Macs and fries and ate in the car with the windows down. The fishy ocean air mingled with the smell of cooking oil as cars streamed by on the two-lane highway. Jeremy ate like he was ravenous, but Robbie felt her stomach convulse each time she tried to swallow.

"My grandparents used to take me and Elise to McDonald's when we were kids," Jeremy said, his mouth full. "In this car, as a matter of fact. It's amazing this clunker still runs."

Did he not realize what was at stake?

"Jeremy," Robbie said, "there's something I want to talk to you about."

"Sounds serious."

"I don't know how to say this. Everything's been so messed up the last couple of weeks. I thought I knew what I wanted, but now I'm not so sure."

He looked at her. His dark, serious eyes, beautiful mouth, cleft chin raw and exposed without the beard. "Talk to me."

Robbie ran her thumb and forefinger up and down her feather earring. "When I said I didn't think we should live together, I twisted things and made it seem like you were the one with the problem. That you were restless for fun and other girls. But that wasn't it at all."

He put his half-eaten hamburger down on the wrapper on the console.

"I had the problem," Robbie said. "I was afraid if we stayed together, eventually you'd leave me."

"Like your father did."

"That's right." Was what she was discovering about herself so obvious to him?

"And you're not afraid anymore?"

"I'm still afraid. But it isn't fear of you leaving me by choice. I'm worried about losing you because of other people—police, bad guys."

He reached for her hand. "Nothing's going to happen to me."

"Oh Jeremy. You've always believed you were invincible. But you aren't."

"I told you, nothing's going to happen to me."

"I want you to know how I feel about you. How even when we're apart, you're the one I'm always thinking about."

"Stop it, Robbie. You sound like the police are going to lock me up, or worse."

"I just don't want it to go unsaid."

He brought her hand to his lips and kissed it. "And you're the one I'm always thinking about."

Cars went by on the roadway, whirring wheels the only sound. The half-eaten burgers and fries sat on their wrappers on the console between them. So much to say, but she didn't have the words. She reached into her handbag for a tin of mints. She offered it to Jeremy and took one for herself. The sky was darkening. Jeremy reached for another mint.

"Keep it," she said.

He slipped the tin into his pocket, then got out of the car and threw their trash away. When he got back, he leaned across the console and kissed Robbie hard on the mouth.

She wondered if someday the taste of peppermint would bring back painful memories.

Chapter 41

It was dark. Only their headlights illuminated the narrow, tree-lined road. They drove slowly. The brightness increased. A car behind them. Robbie held her breath. The car passed and continued on.

"There are other people who live on this street, you know," Jeremy said.

"I just wasn't expecting to see anyone."

Jeremy stopped the car at the edge of Mike's property. No sign of people or cars. The entrance to the long pebbled driveway was wide open. Beyond the trees and hedges, the house was barely visible, a rectangular outline with no interior lights on.

"Looks like the crime-scene crew is gone," Robbie said.

"It's strange that the floodlights aren't on," Jeremy said.

He drove a little farther and pulled into an adjacent property with a "For Sale" sign. The house looked deserted, with uncut grass and no cars.

"I'll leave the car here," Jeremy said. "We can walk down to the bay to get to Mike's house."

Insane, she told herself. This was totally insane.

Clouds blocked the stars and moon, but Robbie's eyes adjusted to the darkness. This house was another McMansion with a barrel-tiled roof and giant windows. There were cracks in the stucco and a pile of broken roof tiles near the side of the house. She noticed a couple of crumpled candy wrappers in the heap of tiles, but they were probably from workmen. It looked as though no one had ever lived here.

As they neared the bay, the foliage became denser. Jeremy held a low-hanging branch aside so Robbie could pass. Although she was in jeans and sneakers, Jeremy was still wearing the suit pants and leather shoes he had put on at his apartment to avoid the attention of the police. Not the best clothes for breaking and entering.

The hedge between the McMansion and Mike's property extended practically to the water. The ground was soggy and water seeped into Robbie's sneakers. "Shit," she said under her breath.

They stepped over onto Mike's property. The shrubs were just as dense, but in a pattern that suggested a professional landscaper. Night sounds were all around them—croaking, buzzing, soft plops from surfacing fish in the bay water. A damp, earthy smell hung in the air.

"It looks like we have the place to ourselves," Jeremy whispered. "I'm dying to see how you're going to get us into the house."

"Yeah. Me, too."

Crime-scene tape extended around the perimeter of the property, including the bay side.

"I wonder why they're keeping this section blocked off," Robbie said. "Could they still be looking for the murder weapon?"

"At least they're not checking things out tonight."

A detached three-car garage stood at the far side of the property. Jeremy went over and looked in through the windows. Robbie joined him, but she wasn't tall enough to reach the windows.

"There's a car in there," Jeremy said. "I'm guessing Mister M likes to keep a spare."

Something rubbed against Robbie's ankle and she let out a gasp.

"What?" Jeremy turned to her. "What's wrong?" He bent over. "Well look who's here."

The large, long-haired cat they'd seen the night of the party meowed up at them.

"I wonder who feeds her if no one's home," Robbie said.

"Maybe she fends for herself—birds, fish, wild berries."

Robbie shook her head. "I don't think so. This cat's well tended. Look at her fur." Robbie put her hand on Jeremy's arm and lowered her voice. "There must be a caretaker who lives here."

"But no lights are on."

"Maybe he's coming back."

"Then we should hurry."

She glanced at the entrance to the house. In the darkness, the flying dragon sculpture looked particularly menacing, as though it might come to life if anyone tried to cross the threshold.

The cat meowed again, then took off toward the back of the house. Robbie went after her.

"Where are you going?" Jeremy asked. "We were just back there."

"You'll see."

The cat climbed the open wooden staircase leading to a rear balcony, then disappeared.

Robbie followed her up the steps.

"We're going in through a sliding glass door?" Jeremy asked. "What makes you think it's unlocked? And even if it isn't locked, opening the door would set off an alarm."

"That's not how we're getting in."

They reached the wide balcony with its unobstructed view of the bay. There were two lounge chairs and a small table between them. On the table were a couple of bottles of beer, still with liquid in them.

Jeremy pointed at the beer.

Robbie nodded. Was someone home? Not likely with all the lights out. Maybe the beer was from last night's party.

She stepped closer to the sliding glass doors. The interior drapes were drawn, making it impossible to look inside the room. From the desirable location, Robbie guessed this was the master bedroom. The sliding doors extended most of the length of the balcony, but there was a small section of outside stuccoed wall. And in the wall was something Robbie remembered from the night of the party. A kitty door.

She bent down and pushed the flaps aside. Meowing came from inside.

"You're going in through the cat door?" Jeremy asked. "You'll never fit."

"I think I will. The opening's pretty big."

Robbie got down on her hands and knees and manipulated her body through the rectangle, pulling herself up on the other side. It was dark, but she recognized the hallway from which she had seen the cat slip outside through the flapped opening last night.

Jeremy put his head between the thick plastic flaps and tried to squeeze his shoulders through. "I don't think I can make it."

"I'll check if the alarm's on." Robbie opened the door to the room with the balcony. Too dark to see anything. She took out her cell phone and flipped it open, using it like a flashlight to look around. It was, as she'd expected, the master bedroom. At the side of the door was an alarm panel. It said "Enter code to arm system."

Strange that it wasn't armed, but she wasn't going to argue with luck. She went to the sliding doors, unlocked one, and pulled it open. Jeremy stepped inside.

"Pretty cool," he said. "You should become a cat burglar."

"Very funny."

"I wonder why Mike wouldn't have turned on the alarm," Jeremy said.

"Maybe the police were the last ones here and didn't know the code."

Jeremy opened the drapes. A dull light leaked in, casting the room in black and white, like an old movie.

Jeremy held out his open cell phone. The weak light fell upon a platform bed, mirrored wall and ceiling, flat-screen TV over a built-in black laminated cabinet. Opposite the mirrored wall was another grotesque dragon painting. This dragon had breasts.

"Nice taste in artwork," Jeremy said.

A white rug covered much of the marble tiles.

"Damn," Robbie said.

"What?"

She pointed at the floor. Their muddy shoes had left footprints on the tiles and rug.

"Shit."

"Should we clean up?" Robbie asked.

"There are probably muddy prints everywhere outside and on the stairs and balcony. Fingerprints, too. We'd better just hope we find what we came here for."

Robbie went over to the cabinet and opened a drawer. "He very likely kept the videos in his bedroom."

"I'll check the bathroom," Jeremy said.

Robbie sorted through the drawer—handcuffs, whips, chains. In another drawer was an assortment of sexually provocative outfits. Other drawers had underwear, clothes, more sex toys. She pulled open the drawer beneath the TV. It was filled with carousels of DVDs. She used the light from her cell phone to go through them.

Jeremy came back into the room. "It's interesting," he said, "the medicine cabinets are empty. I'm guessing Mister M cleaned out the illegal stuff in case the cops decided to have a look around."

"Look at these," Robbie said. "There must be hundreds of DVDs."

Jeremy examined one. "These are commercially labelled. I don't think he'd stash his blackmailing videos in with these."

"But there are a few that have strange labels with nothing on them but handwritten numbers." She held one out for Jeremy.

"Could be something."

Robbie went quickly through the rest of the videos. She found only a few with the numbered labels and put those in her satchel.

"Let's check out his office," Jeremy said. "That's also a likely place for him to keep DVDs."

"I think we should go. What if the caretaker comes back?"

"Come on, Robbie. We're here."

Unhappily, Robbie followed Jeremy down the hallway, past the dragon paintings. A faint gray light came in through the transparent roof above the pool. Jeremy opened one door after another. All bedrooms.

The cat was back, meowing with some urgency.

"She must be hungry," Robbie said.

They walked around the pool to a section of the house they hadn't been in last night. There was a large den with a billiard table and built-in bar. The cat meowed.

"I'm sorry," Robbie said to the cat. "I don't know where your food is."

The next room had double doors. Jeremy pushed them open. The cat rushed in ahead of them.

The drapes were drawn so it was difficult to see, but it appeared to be an office. The light from her cell phone was dimmer, as though the battery was weakening, but Robbie could make out a large black desk protruding from a wall of built-in cabinetry, a sofa against the far wall, a strange shaped table in front of it. She heard the cat lapping water under the desk.

Something was wrong. Drawers and cabinet doors were open. Papers and books littered the desktop and marble floor.

Jeremy was bending over the strange table in front of the sofa. She followed the light from his cell phone.

Not a table. Someone was lying stretched out on the floor, stomach down, arms extended as though reaching, face turned toward Robbie. She took a step closer. The eyes were open and bulging, tongue protruding from a mouth puckered like a fish gasping for air. And then she saw the thin white scar cutting across his distorted lip up to his nose.

Dead. Mike's henchman was dead.

"Looks like he was strangled," Jeremy said. "But it doesn't make sense. Who would want to kill him?"

Robbie felt dizzy. With all the death she'd come so close to, she had never actually seen a dead body. She tried to keep herself from falling, from throwing up.

The cat wove around Robbie's legs, leaving muddy paw prints on the white tile. Had the cat stepped into mud, too?

Robbie leaned over and touched the cat's paw. Her finger came away sticky. It had a metallic smell.

Blood? But there was no blood here.

The light from Jeremy's cell phone swept over the marble tiles brightening the area behind the desk.

First, Robbie made out two silver cat bowls. The food bowl was empty.

Then she processed the shape next to the bowls.

Mike was crumpled up on the floor like a discarded mannequin, his thin ponytail pasted to his cheek. His mouth and pale eyes were open, as though in a permanent scream. The blood from his slashed throat pooled on the white marble floor. In the dimness, it looked black.

The cat nosed its food bowl and let out a pitiful meow.

Chapter 42

Robbie and Jeremy raced out of the office, down the stairs, and through the dense shrubs at the property line. Branches and thorns cut into her arms, but she ignored the stinging pain. She heard something fall through the bushes, and then hit the ground. It sounded like a small rock, but they didn't have time to stop and check it out. They had to get away from here.

When they reached the old Honda, they were both breathing hard. They climbed into the car and Jeremy pulled out of the driveway. He sped along the dark, winding road coming to a stop at the two-lane highway.

"Wait," Robbie said. "We need to go back and call the police."

"Are you crazy?"

"No. Jeremy, listen. Our footprints and fingerprints are everywhere. They're going to think we killed Mike and the other guy."

"And you honestly believe if we call the police, we're clear? How are we going to explain what we were doing at his house?"

Robbie leaned back against her seat, holding her satchel against her chest. There were bloody scratches on her arms and her toes felt cold and nasty in her soggy sneakers. "Let's at least talk this through before we drive away."

"We can talk while we're driving." He turned into the flow of traffic.

Robbie was vaguely aware that a car had come out of the road behind them and also made the left turn.

"I know you don't like leaving," Jeremy said, "but think about what happens if we stay and call the police. They'll bring us down to the station to question us. They already believe I killed Brett. Do you really think just because we call them, they won't consider us suspects in these new murders? We'll be top on their list."

"But when we explain everything to them—"

"Now you're just being naïve."

Robbie was silent. The northbound traffic was moving quickly. They were getting farther and farther away from Mike's house. And the farther they went, the more pointless it would be to turn back. "So what are you thinking?" she said finally.

"Hopefully, the bodies won't be discovered until tomorrow. That gives us time to figure out what's going on before the cops connect us to them."

"It's not going to look good for you."

"But you and I know I didn't kill anyone. So who did?"

They drove past the strip shopping mall with the turquoise awnings where they had stopped last night. They had kissed and were about to go to a motel for the night when Jeremy had noticed a black car with tinted windows.

Later, Robbie had told herself. *We still have later.*

But if they didn't figure out who the killer was, there would never be a later for the two of them.

"We assumed Mike was behind everything," Robbie said. "If it's not Mike, then who killed Brett and Tyra, and why?"

The streetlights illuminated Jeremy's bruised eye and cleft chin. He was looking straight ahead. "Let's do this logically. What's the connection between Mike and Brett and Tyra?"

"We think they were all in on the blackmailing business. If we stay with that assumption, then who would have a reason to kill them?"

"Did Mike have a partner?" Jeremy asked. "Someone who would have had a lot to lose if the blackmailing operation was exposed?"

"I don't think so. Brett never mentioned anyone." Robbie realized she was clutching her satchel. In it were the numbered DVDs she had taken from Mike's bedroom. "Wait. What if we're looking on the wrong side? What if it wasn't someone involved in the blackmail scam, but a victim?"

"A victim?"

"Yeah. Let's say it works like this. The blackmail victim is told there's a DVD showing him in a compromising situation. He's told to pay up or else."

"Like the congressman," Jeremy said. "Except he chose a third option and killed himself."

"But there's another alternative that the blackmailers probably hadn't considered. And that's the victim turning on the blackmailer."

"How do you mean?"

"What if the victim doesn't want to be held up for the rest of his life and can't afford to be exposed?" Robbie asked. "Then he might try to eliminate all connections to whoever made the video and is trying to blackmail him."

"So he'd kill Brett because he thought Brett had set him up. Mike for being behind it, and Mike's henchman for obvious reasons."

"And he'd try to find and destroy the videos. That's why Mike's office was ransacked."

"And why the man attacked Tyra," Jeremy said. "Kate said he was looking for the videos."

Kate. Something was forming in Robbie's brain.

"But if the victim killed Tyra trying to eliminate the connection to the video," Jeremy said, "what if Kate was also in the DVD?"

They glanced at each other quickly. "Then Kate would be a target."

Jeremy's fingers tightened on the steering wheel. The needle on the speedometer moved toward the right. The old car, not in condition for high speeds, shuddered.

"She'll be okay," Robbie said. "No one knows Kate's at your grandfather's."

"I know," Jeremy said. "But someone's on my tail."

Robbie turned around. A black car with tinted windows was almost on the bumper of Jeremy's grandfather's car. She tried to make out who was driving, but it was impossible.

They were coming up to the dangerous stretch of U.S. 1 where they'd seen the accident earlier. Mangroves and swamps were on either side of the two-lane highway.

Jeremy was pressing down on the accelerator. Robbie read the speedometer. Eighty. Eighty-five. Ninety. The car was shaking hard. The black car was still on their tail. The road signs read "No Passing."

A slow car was just ahead. Jeremy swerved into the oncoming traffic lane to pass. The black car stayed behind them. The lights of a southbound car were getting brighter.

Jeremy swerved back in front of the northbound car. The black car made it in behind them, just as the southbound car zipped by.

"Jeremy, you can't outrun him in this car."

"What choice do I have?"

"Pull over. Stop."

"He won't let me. He'll run us off the road."

Jeremy was gaining on another car in the northbound lane. Trees, water, trees, water—everything rushed by in a blur.

Jeremy accelerated and pulled into the southbound lane to pass, the black car pinned to his tail. There were several cars in the northbound lane, driving so close together it was impossible to get back in between them. The old Honda was shaking. It didn't have the power for this.

Another southbound car was approaching. Closer, closer. The lights brighter, brighter.

No opening between the cars in the northbound lane. Water and mangroves to the left. Crashing into the mangroves at this speed would likely kill them. Their only chance was to get in front of the first northbound car before they collided with the southbound car.

"Floor it," Robbie screamed.

Jeremy was pressed forward against the steering wheel. The lights from the southbound car were blinding. Robbie felt the car swerve. She squeezed her eyes shut, grabbed the edge of her seat, and waited.

Behind her came the sound of screeching, then a crash. Then just the whirr of their car's wheels against pavement.

Jeremy was slowing down.

Robbie opened her eyes and turned around. She could see a pile up of cars, but couldn't tell how bad the accident was.

The black car was no longer on their tail.

The headlights from a southbound car brightened Jeremy's face. It was wet with sweat.

In the distance, Robbie heard the sound of a siren. It got louder and louder, then went past them on their left.

She slumped back against her seat.

The siren got softer and softer.

Chapter 43

Robbie watched Jeremy's grandfather as he paced between the club chair and the draped window, hands clasped behind his back. The floorboards creaked as he went back and forth, back and forth. Otherwise the room was quiet, except for the ticking of the old clock above the piano. It was a little after eleven p.m.

Robbie and Jeremy sat beside each other on the sofa, their knees touching. Every once in a while Mr. Weiss would glance down the hallway. Then he'd shake his head and return to his pacing.

Elise and Kate were busy with something in the back of the house and still hadn't come out, even though Robbie and Jeremy had arrived almost a half hour earlier.

Robbie's wet sneakers were on the front porch and her feet were wrapped in a towel. Mr. Weiss had made them hot tea with honey, which Robbie and Jeremy drank while they filled him in on what had happened over the last day and a half. They realized with all that was going on, they could no longer keep Jeremy's grandfather in the dark.

Mr. Weiss stopped pacing and pushed his glasses up on his nose. "You must call Detective Lieber."

Jeremy shook his head. The bruise around his eye had turned black-and-blue. "She'll arrest me. She'll have no other choice."

"But someone tried to kill you on the highway. If you tell her what happened, she can be looking for that person."

"We can't prove the black car was trying to run us off the road," Robbie said. She took another sip of hot tea, but nothing helped. She was chilled through and through. "It will look as though we were running from the scene of the crime and caused the accident."

"This is terrible," Mr. Weiss said. "I don't see a way out."

"We have to figure out who else Mike was blackmailing," Robbie said. "Until we do, and stop him, Kate's at risk."

"Wait," Jeremy said, getting up from the sofa. "Maybe he's no longer a threat."

"Who?" his grandfather said, but Jeremy was already out of the room.

"The guy who was trying to run us off the road," Robbie said, remembering the screech and pileup of cars behind them. "The murderer may have died or been seriously injured in the crash."

Jeremy returned with a laptop and sat back down on the sofa next to Robbie. He logged on, the tapping of his fingers on the keyboard competing with the ticking clock.

"Okay. Good," Jeremy said. "Here's a report of the accident."

Robbie leaned closer, trying to read.

"Five-car accident just north of Key Largo on Highway 1 at approximately ten p.m.," Jeremy read aloud. He paused and let out a slow breath. "No fatalities and no one seriously injured."

"So he's still out there," Robbie said. "And we have no idea who he is."

A door opened at the other end of the house, followed by the sound of voices, then footsteps and the click of dog claws against the wood floor.

Elise came into the living room first like a mischievous elf. The old jeans and T-shirt she'd changed into were splattered with something black and her dark ponytail swung behind her.

"Okay, everyone. I'd like to present the real Kate Brooks." Elise stood aside and made a flourish with her hands.

The frightened, nervous girl with platinum blonde hair and slate gray eyes was gone. The young woman who stepped into the room had shiny black hair, blue eyes, and a heart-shaped face. Her lips tugged up at the corners, accentuating her dimples.

Robbie's throat constricted.

Kate was still wearing Robbie's old jeans and T-shirt, but like Elise's, they were splattered with hair dye. She looked at Robbie and her mouth drooped. "Is something wrong?"

"Oh, Kate," Robbie said finally. She crossed the room and hugged her sister. For the first time in her life, Robbie was responsible for another human being. And the idea was humbling.

"My lips are still fat from the collagen injections they gave me," Kate said, "but they'll probably go back to normal over time."

Collagen injections. And again Robbie was reminded of what Kate had suffered for almost two weeks. *Dad*, Robbie almost said. *We need to call Dad and tell him you're all right.*

She thought about the last meeting with her father at South Pointe Park, about the accusations they threw at each other. And then, a few hours ago, Kate's reluctance to have Robbie call him.

"You definitely look like sisters," Elise said. "Almost like older and younger versions of identical twins." She glanced from her brother to her grandfather. A crease appeared between Elise's brows. "What's wrong? Something else happened?"

"There are some complications," Jeremy said.

Later, Robbie thought. *She'd call their dad later.*

"The people who kidnapped Kate were running a blackmailing ring," Jeremy said.

"I know," Elise said. "Kate explained everything. We figured you went down to the house where she was kidnapped to look for the videos. Did you find any?"

"A few."

"But we also found a couple of dead bodies," Jeremy said. "And unfortunately, the police will think we killed them."

"Oh no, Jeremy." The smattering of freckles on the bridge of Elise's nose became more pronounced as her face grew paler. "Not again. Please, not again."

Jeremy's grandfather looked away.

The ticking clock was the only sound. *Not again.*

"We want Kate to see the DVDs," Robbie said. "To see what she remembers."

Kate sat down on the corner of the sofa. She slipped off the sneakers, brought her knees up to her chest, then rested her head on her knees, making herself into a tight ball.

Elise glanced over at Kate, then back to Robbie. "Does she really have to watch them?"

"One of them may have the murderer on it," Jeremy said.

"It's okay." Kate's voice was muffled by her knees.

Robbie rummaged through her satchel and took out the DVDs. She'd only found five with the strange numbered labels on them.

Elise brought them over to the DVD player. "You're sure the killer's on one of these?"

"No," Robbie said. "These were the only ones we found, but there could be others."

Elise popped one into the DVD player, then sat on the floor next to Geezer. She brought the end of her ponytail around to her mouth.

Mr. Weiss glanced at Kate still huddled on the sofa, then left the room.

Background music came on, a pulsing South Beach beat, and the sound of a woman's laughter. But the screen was white. Robbie realized it was a white sofa. And then something caramel-colored appeared. A back. A woman's back. Then wild copper hair. The laugh again. The woman moved out of the way. The man was visible now.

A bald, older man with a double paunch, powerful calf muscles, and hairless limbs. He was completely naked, a glass in one hand, his eyes out of focus. The woman climbed onto his semi-flaccid penis.

"That's right, baby," she said. "Give it to me nice and slow."

Robbie had sat down beside Kate. Kate glanced up at the screen, then put her head back down.

"I know him," Jeremy said from his seat on the club chair.

"You know him?" Robbie asked.

"I mean I recognize him. He's the CEO of some big corporation. He was one of the speakers at a motivational forum they had at the Convention Center a few weeks ago." Jeremy's eyes were fixed on the caramel-colored back bouncing up and down.

"Oooooo, baby. That's sooooo good, baby."

The man grunted.

Robbie turned away. Kate brought her hands up to her eyes.

"You can stop it now, Elise," Robbie said.

She heard the click of the DVD player.

"What a perfect setup for Mike." Jeremy leaned back against the club chair. "With his public relations business, he'd know who was in town and who to target. Whose career would be ruined if the video got out."

"So the CEO may be the killer?" Elise took her ponytail out of her mouth and twirled it around her fingers.

"It's possible," Jeremy said. "But he was in town weeks ago. I think the blackmail victim would have reacted quickly to shut down the blackmailers. That's why we should look for videos that Kate was in."

Kate raised her head from her knees.

"We believe the blackmail victim is targeting everyone who knows about him," Robbie said. "Trying to eliminate the video and anyone who might out it."

"So Kate's a target?" Elise asked.

"Kate was a target," Robbie said. "But the victim would be looking for a blonde, gray-eyed girl named Angel, not Kate. Kate's off the killer's radar."

"So we don't have to worry about the killer going after anyone in this room, right?" Elise asked.

Jeremy looked at Robbie. She knew he was thinking about Robbie's apartment.

"I don't know that anyone actually broke into my apartment," she said to him. "My neighbor saw someone outside and the cat was out, but nothing inside was touched. I think I let my imagination go when we thought Mike was involved. But Mike's dead, and a blackmail victim has no reason to connect me with the videos."

Jeremy nodded. "We're all off the killer's radar, Elise."

"But we still need to find who's behind the murders," Robbie said. "Because right now, the police think Jeremy is."

Jeremy got up and started walking back and forth between the club chair and the windows, where his grandfather had paced earlier. "Put in the next one."

Elise popped the DVD out and put another in.

The next video played. More of the same. This one featured Tyra and another girl, but not Kate.

They hit pay dirt on the third one.

Jeremy leaned closer to the TV. "The congressman. So we were right that he was a blackmail victim."

The bushy eyebrows and jowly face of Richard Griswold loomed in front of the camera. He was grotesquely shaped with a tank-like torso resting on skinny hairy legs. In the background, on a white sofa, sat Kate, Angel as she was known at the time. She was dressed like a little girl with pigtails and kneesocks.

Kate tightened back into a ball and turned her head away.

"No reason to watch this." Elise popped the DVD out. "He's already dead."

She tried the fourth and fifth DVDs, but Kate wasn't in either and the victims weren't familiar to any of them.

"That's it." Elise turned off the TV and leaned against the ottoman. "Does this mean you're out of leads?"

"Maybe."

"But then the police will still think you're involved," Elise said.

Jeremy massaged the back of his neck. Like Robbie, he had scratches on his arms from the hedges around Mike's house. "Could someone related to the congressman be getting even for his death?"

"That seems like a stretch," Robbie said. "His whole family's up north. I don't see how they could have put such a bloodbath together from a distance."

"Kate," Jeremy asked, "do you know how many videos you were in?"

She lifted her head, shook it, then rested it back on her knees. No one spoke.

"Maybe there's something in the paper," Elise said, finally.

"What do you mean?" Jeremy asked.

"Well, if it's someone like the congressman or the CEO, then he's probably in the news. Maybe Kate would recognize the man if she saw his picture."

"Kate?" Jeremy asked.

She didn't lift her head.

"Kate, can you help us here?"

She sat up slowly, releasing her knees.

"Okay, good," Jeremy said. "We know the congressman was with you Friday; what about Saturday night? Did anyone come back with you then?"

Kate shook her head.

"Sunday?" Jeremy asked.

Kate nodded, almost imperceptibly. Was she afraid of something that happened Sunday?

"Good. What do you remember about him?"

She looked down at her bare feet.

"Kate?" Robbie said. "I know it's hard for you to do this. But he may be the killer."

Kate shook her head. "He isn't. He was a nice guy. He wanted to help me."

"He may have been a nice guy whose career was about to be ruined," Jeremy said. "Maybe the video pushed him over the edge."

Mr. Weiss came into the room carrying a stack of newspapers. So he'd been listening in, after all.

"Do you want to look through these, dear?"

Everyone waited for Kate to answer. What was bothering her? Finally, she held out her hands.

Mr. Weiss moved the cups of tea out of the way and put the newspapers down on the coffee table in front of Kate.

The newspapers went back several days. Kate went through the front page of every section first, examining the photos of men.

Robbie was conscious of the clock ticking over the piano, Geezer lying on his side by the club chair panting in his sleep.

If Kate could identify the blackmail victim, they would very likely have the answer to who was behind the murders. Jeremy would be free.

Kate reached for the next section. There was a photo of a man on the front page. She stared and sucked in her lower lip.

Robbie looked at the familiar photo.

Jeremy leaned over the paper. "Stanford Fieldstone? Was that the man?"

Gina's husband? Not possible.

Kate tugged on a strand of silky black hair.

"Do you recognize him, Kate?" Jeremy asked again.

"I don't know. Maybe. I don't think so." She tugged at her hair like she wanted to pull it out.

"But something about him is familiar to you?" Jeremy said.

"I don't know," Kate said. "The man at BURN was wearing big black glasses and he needed a shave."

Robbie looked more closely at the photo. She imagined the face with eyeglasses, with the shadow of a beard.

"But it might be?" Jeremy asked. "It might be the same man?"

"Yes. No." Kate sucked in her lip. "I don't know what to do."

"Please, Kate." Elise came over and sat down next to Kate. Her face was pale, her freckles like a spray of fine dirt across the bridge of her nose. "If you think you know who was with you that night, tell us." She glanced at Jeremy, then turned back to Kate. "Please. I don't want to lose my brother, too."

The clock ticked, Geezer panted.

"I'm not positive," Kate said. "Stanford Fieldstone wasn't his name. It was something else."

"What?" Jeremy asked.

Kate pushed the newspaper away from her. Her eyes watered. "He was a nice guy. He wanted to help me."

"And what did he say his name was?" Jeremy asked.

Kate said it so softly that it took a moment for the name to register, to match what Robbie was hearing in her own head.

Robbie closed her eyes and pictured him sitting across the bar at The Garage. The glimmer of charisma she could see when he smiled, the manicured fingernails that were out of place for a boatman, the cocktail napkin he'd left beneath his cap with a sketch of a rose and a phone number.

Stanford Fieldstone was Puck.

And Puck was a murderer.

Chapter 44

Robbie felt clammy all over. "I need to go outside for a minute."

She noted the strange looks everyone gave her as she left the living room, then went through the old-fashioned kitchen and out the back door into a small hedged-in backyard.

She walked down the three steps and sat on the bottom one, her bare feet in the soft, freshly mowed grass. The bushes were so high the neighbors' properties weren't visible. In the corner of the yard, someone had planted flowers and rose bushes. Probably Elise.

Clouds shifted, blocking the moon and stars. Frogs chirped in the dark, muggy air. She was reminded of Mike's house and wrapped her arms more tightly around herself.

Puck. Was it possible?

How had he done it?

Could he have been in the bushes the night of Mike's party, jumping out and surprising Brett after Jeremy left? She thought about the candy wrappers at the deserted house next door. He could have hidden there.

And then, was he the man in the floppy hat waiting at the pool for an opportunity to attack Tyra and Kate? The murderer was a busy man. He would have had to jump in his car and drive back down to Key Largo, sneak into the house, and kill Mike and the other guy.

It was doable. Jeremy had been in all of those places at roughly the same times.

But Puck? Puck a murderer?

Robbie didn't see it. But then, she never would've imagined the wistful man at the bar was really Stanford Fieldstone traveling incognito.

She remembered back to the night that Puck confided in Robbie about his marriage. He'd said his wife manipulated him into marrying her and called her an ambitious monster. The wife he was talking about was Gina. But Robbie knew Gina didn't care about those things, so Puck had been lying about that, as well.

A liar and a murderer. Well, of course. They went hand in hand.

But if Puck was the murderer, then he was also the person in the black car who followed Jeremy and Robbie away from Mike's house and tried to run them off the road.

According to the news report, there had been no fatalities. So where was Puck now and what was he planning?

The back door opened behind her, then gently closed. She saw Jeremy's leather shoes and suit pants, both splattered with mud. He sat down beside her and handed her a beer.

"Thought you could use this."

"Thanks." She took a swig from the bottle.

The croaking got louder, the air heavier.

"They used to fill up a plastic pool for us." Jeremy's voice seemed to come from a different dimension.

"Huh?"

"My grandparents. When Elise and I were little and we'd stay with them. You know, weekends or if my parents were both out of town. They had this blow-up pool. My grandfather would fill it with water."

"That's nice."

"I have a lot of happy memories of this place."

Robbie rested her hand on his knee. His strong, sturdy knee.

She knew who the murderer was. They were one step closer to Jeremy being safe. "Stanford Fieldstone is Puck," she said.

"Yeah. That's what Kate said. So he used a fake name. What's the big deal?"

"Puck's a guy who's been coming to The Garage lately."

"Shit. You know him?"

Robbie nodded.

"And you didn't know he was Fieldstone?"

"No. He dressed like a boater—or at least a weekend boater. But he never let on who he really was."

"Damn—you knew him. I thought you were upset that the murderer was Gina Fieldstone's husband."

"That, too. It's a lot to absorb. Stanford Fieldstone. Puck." She shook her head.

"But it makes sense," Jeremy said. "Fieldstone's career is taking off. I guess the blackmailing was too much for him to handle."

"But—" Robbie pulled out a weed that was growing in a crack of the concrete step.

"But what?"

"He seemed so nice." Kate had said that, too. "And I liked him. But he was putting me on the whole time. I feel so, so—" She searched for the right word. "Deceived."

Robbie took another swig of beer. There was a vibration in her pocket. Her cell phone. She had turned it to vibrate and left it in her pocket when they were at Mike's.

She showed the display to Jeremy. Lieber.

"Don't answer it."

"I have to."

"No, Robbie. We don't have this figured out yet. It'll just make things worse."

"We have to trust someone."

He cradled his beer bottle as Robbie took the call.

"Where are you?" Lieber's voice was clipped.

Where was she? What should she say? Maybe Jeremy was right about making things worse. "Getting ready for work," Robbie said. "I'm on the late shift tonight."

"Really? Because I'm at your apartment and there's no sign of you."

Robbie looked at Jeremy for help. He shook his head and mouthed, "I told you so."

"And where's Jeremy? Is he with you? His car's at the SOBE, but he isn't."

"What's wrong? Why are you looking for us?"

"Jesus, Robbie. Why are you playing games with me? Haven't you figured out I'm on your side? That I'm probably the only one out here who's trying to help you?"

"We're in Coconut Grove," Robbie said. "At Jeremy's grandfather's."

Jeremy hit his head with his fist.

"Put Jeremy on," Lieber said. "I need to speak to him."

Robbie held out the phone. "She wants to speak to you."

Jeremy shook his head no. Robbie kept holding the phone out for him. Finally, he took it.

"Hey," he said. "What's up?"

Robbie couldn't hear Lieber's side of the conversation.

"Sorry," Jeremy said. He glared at Robbie. "I turned it off. I guess I forgot to turn it back on."

Lieber was talking for a long while. A dog barked somewhere in the distance.

"I understand," Jeremy said to the phone. "Okay. I promise."

He closed the phone and handed it back to Robbie.

"What did she say?"

"She told me about Tyra being found dead and a couple of people describing someone who looked like me getting into an argument with Tyra. She said she was worried about us. My car's in the garage and your bicycle was found chained outside the building. She thought something had happened to us."

"So she didn't assume you killed Tyra and ran away?"

"She didn't, but that doesn't mean the other investigators aren't thinking that way."

"And you agreed to stay here until she comes?"

He nodded.

"Aren't you afraid she'll arrest you?"

Jeremy sipped his beer. "She said she just wants to talk to me."

"And you believe her?"

"You're the one who said we have to trust someone."

"Does she know about Mike and the other guy?"

"She didn't say anything about Key Largo."

"What about the accident on U.S. 1?"

"Didn't mention it."

A light breeze carried the scent of roses. Puck. Where was he now and what was his next move? An idea was forming in her head. Robbie started to stand up.

"What are you doing?" Jeremy asked.

"I need to get out of here with Kate."

"What do you mean? You can't just leave."

"Please, Jeremy. I hate to subject Kate to going back over everything with Lieber."

"So you're laying it all on me?"

Robbie sat back down. What had she been thinking? She couldn't leave Jeremy now. Her plan would have to wait. It probably wasn't viable, anyway. "I'm sorry. That was selfish of me. We'll talk to Lieber together. Kate will be fine."

Jeremy stared across the dark lawn as though he was looking at the blow-up swimming pool from his childhood. "Go," he said finally. "You need to protect Kate."

"We can protect her together."

Jeremy pulled her head toward him and kissed her hair. "It's fine," he said. "I've got my grandfather and Elise. And you and Kate will be safe at your apartment. If Fieldstone is looking for her, he'll be after a blonde girl with gray eyes." He tensed. "Is there any reason to think he knows where you live?"

Robbie thought for a moment. "No," she said. "I never tell any of the customers at The Garage where I live."

Jeremy lifted her chin. He seemed to be memorizing her face.

Robbie was torn. Leave? Stay? "What about Lieber?" she asked.

"I'll tell her about Fieldstone."

"But we don't have proof. Just Kate thinking he's the guy she and Tyra brought back Sunday night. And that's not enough to tie him to the murder spree. Everything still points to you."

"Well, hopefully Lieber will believe me."

"But if she doesn't?"

"Then she doesn't. There's nothing more we can do."

Robbie could smell the roses, stronger now. "Don't say anything about Fieldstone, yet. I have an idea how to trap him."

Jeremy put his beer down hard on the step. "No way, Robbie. We're not doing this ourselves anymore."

"I wasn't planning to. I'm not that crazy. Just tell Lieber the basics. Nothing that might connect you to Key Largo. When I'm ready, I'll call you. Then you and the police can meet me and you can tell Lieber about Fieldstone on the way."

"Ready? Ready for what? What are you planning?"

"I don't have all the details worked out, but I promise I'll call you before I do anything dangerous."

Chapter 45

They sat inches apart from each other in Jeremy's grandfather's car. Two sisters, separated by eighteen years of memories that they weren't given the opportunity to share.

Robbie drove through the labyrinthine neighborhood of Coconut Grove, avoiding dead-end streets, maneuvering toward the main road that would lead them back to her apartment on Miami Beach.

It was around midnight, and the traffic was light. Robbie occasionally glanced over at Kate, who was sitting with her head resting against the passenger-side window, as though she was watching the overhanging trees and houses go by.

Was Kate thinking how strange it was to be here with her sister? A sister she hadn't even known existed a few hours ago?

Kate must have sensed Robbie looking at her. She tried to smile. Her facial muscles were tense and her blue eyes rimmed in red.

"You okay?" Robbie asked.

"Yeah. I'm good."

"This whole nightmare will be over soon."

"I guess." Kate chewed on her finger.

Robbie stopped at a red light. "I need to call Dad and tell him you're okay."

"Please. Not yet."

The light turned green. They drove past the walled, gated estate of Vizcaya. Wild bougainvillea cascaded over the stuccoed walls. "I know you don't know me yet, but I wish you'd talk to me, Kate. Why are you so afraid of calling Dad? He needs to know you're safe."

In the uneven light of the passing streetlamps, Robbie could see Kate had covered her face. Beneath the thin, stained T-shirt, her shoulders were trembling, as though she was crying.

Robbie wanted to kick herself. She was rushing things. Kate wasn't ready. And how could she blame her? Kate had just been held in captivity and abused for almost two weeks, believing she had killed her friend. After a trauma like that, how could she possibly be ready to open up?

"I'm sorry," Robbie said. "I didn't mean to—"

"He hates me."

A chill ran down Robbie's back. "What are you talking about? Who hates you?"

"Dad does."

"No, Kate. You're wrong. He loves you. He's worried sick about you. He's been here in South Beach the whole time looking for you."

"He hates me."

"Why do you say that?"

"He blames me for everything."

"Everything?"

Kate just stared out the car window.

Robbie turned onto a side street that wound down to the bay. She pulled up along the bayfront walk, towering condos across the road. A man and woman strolled with their dog down a street lined with palm trees. The bay rippled, undulating black moguls in the intermittent moonlight. Beyond, the lights of the Rickenbacker Causeway leading to Key Biscayne glittered like a tiara.

Robbie left the engine running and turned to face Kate. Old-car smells enveloped them.

"Talk to me. Please."

"I've never told anyone."

"I'm your sister."

Kate's entwined fingers rested on the faded, paint-splattered jeans Robbie had given her.

"Please, Kate. Start at the beginning, if that's easier."

Kate squeezed her hands tighter. "When I was a little girl, he didn't talk to me much. Sometimes, he'd tell me bedtime stories, but that was about all. I didn't think anything was wrong with that. I had my mom. And she always said he was busy. He had important work and I shouldn't bother him."

Robbie looked out toward the bay. She remembered her childhood house on the St. Johns River, Spanish moss hanging from towering oak trees. Her dad returning home from the hospital after a late night emergency call, standing on the flagstone patio that smelled like magnolias, staring at nothing. Then later that night, how Robbie had overheard him talking to her mother. *There's nothing I can do*, he told her. *Absolutely nothing*.

Had he been talking about his patient as she'd always believed, or his dying relationship with Robbie's mother?

"But when I got older," Kate said. "I realized something was messed up. I'd see my friends' parents and they were always doing stuff together."

"But not your mom and dad?"

"Dad was always busy. He'd stay in his office late, or go to the hospital. And my mom. She drank a lot. And I knew she had a problem, but I didn't know what to do."

Robbie ached for her sister. She'd had no one to turn to. Neither had Robbie.

"Then one day, my mom had a bad episode," Kate said. "I came home from school and found her lying in the shower. First, I thought she was dead. I called my dad and he came home and we got her into bed. And I knew my mom was sick. That she needed help. I screamed at my father and I told him to do something. And he got very angry at me."

"Angry? What did he do?"

"He didn't yell or anything. He just gave me this really cold look. Like he didn't want to have anything more to do with me."

Just like the look he'd given Robbie the other day when he disagreed with what she was saying. "Then what happened?"

Kate wiped her eyes. "A few days later, my mom died in a car accident. I was twelve. Dad never talked to me again."

"He never talked to you again?" Robbie asked. "I don't understand. He told me you two did lots of things together. That you made him dinner and you'd go shopping. Sometimes you even ate out at restaurants. And he told me you talked about things. School, and—"

"Not that kind of talking. Don't you understand? We spoke, but he never talked to me."

"I'm not following."

"He lectured. But not like he was my dad. More like he was a doctor instructing one of his patients. What I could and couldn't do. Never drink or I'd end up an alcoholic, never have sex until I was married or I'd end up with a terrible disease or worse."

"But he couldn't have been that protective," Robbie said. "He let you go away for spring break."

"Oh, my God. Do you know what I had to do to get him to say yes? Joanne's father practically had to get down on his knees and beg Dad to let me go." She bit down on her lip. "Don't you see, how can I ever face him again? He'll blame me for everything. If I had listened to him, none of this would have happened." She began sobbing hard. "And he's right. If I'd listened to him, Joanne would still be alive."

"Oh, Kate." Robbie reached across the console to hold her. "You can't do this to yourself."

"He's right to hate me. It was my fault."

"It wasn't your fault and he doesn't hate you." Robbie slid her fingers through Kate's hair. The texture so like her own. "He loves you."

Kate pulled back. Tears clung to her long dark lashes. "How can you say that? If he loved me, why didn't he show me?"

Why didn't he try to find me?

"Maybe he doesn't know how," Robbie said. "Or maybe he's so filled with guilt over the things he messed up that he doesn't know how to make them right."

"What do you mean?"

"He should have helped your mother," Robbie said. "Or maybe he tried and failed and couldn't acknowledge his failure. But that's his weakness. Our dad has a hard time taking responsibility for things."

Had her father's guilt over cheating on Robbie's mother kept him from a relationship with Robbie?

"But why would he act like he hated me?" Kate asked.

"Maybe he felt he didn't deserve you."

And suddenly Robbie got it. All those years that he'd stayed away from her. He was punishing himself.

Kate's head was tilted as though she was weighing what Robbie had said. Her straight black hair formed a perfect razor's edge against her shoulder. "Punishing himself for letting my mother die?"

"That's right."

"So he doesn't hate me?"

"No, Kate. He loves you."

"He loves me," Kate repeated, as though not fully convinced. She touched one of Robbie's feathered earrings. "You know, when I was a little girl, he would tell me stories about an Indian princess who wore beads and feathers."

Robbie got goose bumps up and down her arms.

"I loved those stories so much," Kate said. "In one of them, the princess found an arrowhead. I guess that's why I got a tattoo of an arrowhead. I always hoped Dad would love me again, like when I was a little girl and he called me his Indian princess. "

You're my little Pocahontas, he used to say.

"Is it okay if I call him now?" Robbie asked.

Kate nodded.

Chapter 46

Her father's phone rang once and went to voice mail, as though he'd turned it off or the battery was dead. "It's Robbie," she said to the tape. "Kate's okay. She's with me. Call me."

Kate's face fell. "He's not answering?"

Robbie shook her head. "But at least when he checks his voice mail, he'll know you're okay. But now I've got to do something to help Jeremy."

Kate nodded.

Robbie left her phone on the console as she drove. Kate's hand hovered near it, as though to grab it when it rang. But it didn't.

Their father. Where was he? And why hadn't he answered his phone?

When they got to her apartment, Robbie went straight into the kitchen, leaving Kate standing in the living room. But Robbie didn't have time to help her sister get settled in. Where had she put that napkin?

She opened a kitchen drawer and rummaged through bills to be paid, pencils, rubber bands. She found it between two take-out food menus. A square cocktail napkin with a picture of a rose and a phone number.

"What's that?" Kate asked from the doorway. She was holding Matilda in her arms. The cat purred loudly.

"The phone number of the man you were with Sunday night. Stanford Fieldstone."

Kate's eyes widened. "You have his phone number?"

"He used to come into the bar where I work."

"So you knew him, too."

There was something in Kate's voice that Robbie couldn't make out. It almost sounded defensive. But Robbie didn't have time to analyze. She studied her sister. The resemblance was uncanny. And with a wig, makeup and— "Do you still have the gray contact lenses?" Robbie asked.

Kate nodded slowly. "I was going to throw them away, but Elise thought the police might want them for something. Why?"

"I'll explain in a minute." Robbie brushed past Kate on the way to the front door. There was a static shock as they briefly touched. "I'll be right back."

Darkness had settled over the courtyard and pool, and palm fronds from the tall royals hung motionless in the thick night air. It was a little after midnight. She hoped he was still home.

She knocked on the door to Gabriele's apartment.

"Just a minute," called a singsong voice.

The door opened. Gabriele was wigless and bald, and for an instant, Robbie flashed on her mom looking at herself in the mirror while she was going through chemo. The fear in her eyes.

"Why it's Robbie!" Gabriele said. He was in full makeup and wearing a sequined bustier and ballet skirt. His dark smooth skin glowed in the dim light. The vision of her mother faded.

Gabriele kissed her cheeks. "Sorry for my surprise. I was expecting Oscar. We're terribly late for an event at LIV." He frowned. "Everything's all right, isn't it?"

"I need to borrow something."

"Of course." He fluttered his long fake lashes. "I always have a cup of sugar for my dear Robbie."

"Your platinum blonde wig. The one with bangs, shoulder-length straight hair. And I'm in a hurry. I'll explain tomorrow."

Gabriele straightened up and lost the cutesy. "I'll be right back."

He returned in less than a minute and handed it to her. "Don't worry about returning it. Oscar prefers me as a redhead." He gave Robbie a peck on the cheek.

"And can I borrow your cell for a minute? I don't want my name to come up on caller ID."

Gabriele pursed his lips. "What mischief are you up to?"

"Please?"

He reached into his bustier and handed her his thin phone.

It was warm and smelled like floral perfume. "Thanks. I'll bring it right back."

Gabriele leaned against his open door, long, muscular arms folded across his chest. He shook his head as she hurried along the catwalk back to her apartment.

Robbie found Kate in the living room examining one of Robbie's half-finished necklaces. Kate looked up. "Did he call?"

Kate was waiting for their father. "No. Not yet," Robbie said. "I need you to do something."

Kate scowled at the wig Robbie was holding.

"I'm going to dial Fieldstone's number, but I want you to talk to him. I'm hoping he recognizes your voice."

"I don't understand."

"I want you to arrange a meeting with him."

Kate glanced at the phone, then went to stand at the living room window. "I don't think I can do that."

"Please, Kate. I won't do anything dangerous or stupid."

Kate continued looking outside as she pulled on a strand of hair. What was upsetting her?

"You're setting him up for the police," Kate said.

"That's right."

"And they'll arrest him."

"Yes."

Robbie couldn't see Kate's face.

"But what if he isn't the murderer?" Kate said.

Robbie went over to the window and stood next to her sister. She spoke softly. "What if he is?"

Kate released her hair and let her hand drop to her side. "What do you want me to tell him?"

"Thank you," Robbie said. She told Kate what to say and punched the number Puck had written on the napkin into the cell phone.

A sleepy voice answered. "Yeah?"

Robbie held out the phone to Kate.

Kate hesitated for a moment, then took it. "Hi," Kate said, her voice trembling. "I'm not sure you remember me, but I'm the girl who was at BURN on Sunday night."

Robbie watched Kate's face, unable to hear Puck's side of the conversation. Kate sucked in her lower lip. She looked like she was going to cry. "I'm fine," she said. "That's not why I'm calling." She took a deep breath. "I have the DVD. The one you want. If I give it to you, do you promise not to hurt me?"

Puck didn't appear to answer. Kate pointed at the phone and shook her head. Then Robbie heard a voice coming through.

"I can bring it to your boat," Kate said, like Robbie had told her to.

There was another moment of silence, then Puck said something.

Kate held the phone to her mouth, as though she wanted to say something else. Then either Puck hung up, or Kate changed her mind. She closed the phone and handed it back to Robbie.

"Thank you, Kate. You did great."

Kate bit down on her lip.

"I'm just going to give the phone back to Gabriele, then I'll be right back."

When Robbie returned, Kate was holding the blonde wig behind her back. She reminded Robbie of a child who hides her mother's shoes, hoping that will keep her from leaving.

"Don't go," Kate said.

"Don't worry. I'm not going to be alone with him. The cops will be surrounding the boat. I've set it up with Jeremy." Robbie held out her hand for the wig.

"I wish you wouldn't do this." Kate's eyes filled with tears.

"Silly Kate. You're acting like I'm not coming back. I'll be fine. And once Fieldstone's arrested, we'll have plenty of time to get to know each other."

Robbie dressed quickly in a short black dress and heels, then put on the blonde wig and gray contacts that Kate gave her. She applied a lot of makeup and lip liner to make her mouth look fuller. The image in the mirror was startling. It was the girl Robbie had seen at BURN last Friday night. How empty the eyes looked. Empty and hopeless. Robbie had come so close to finding her sister that night. Friday. Before the murders.

She could see Kate watching her in the mirror, but Kate didn't say a word. She was tugging at a long strand of beads.

Robbie found an unlabeled DVD among her collection. She wrote some numbers on it, then slipped it into her satchel.

Kate followed her through the living room. Matilda took a few running steps after them, stopped, and meowed.

"Okay," Robbie said at the door. "I'll call you to let you know what's happening."

"I don't have a phone."

"That's right." Robbie took in a deep breath. "Well, I'll be back as soon as I can."

Kate's mouth sagged. She seemed unwilling to look Robbie in the eye.

"I thought she was gone," Kate said without raising her head. "I thought Angel was gone forever."

"She is, Kate. Angel is gone forever."

Robbie climbed into Jeremy's grandfather's car and sat in front of her apartment building without starting the engine. She could still get out of this. She hadn't admitted to Kate how scared she was. She remembered a year ago, going off to the deserted file room by herself. She had almost died that night.

But if she didn't set up Puck like this, would the cops have enough proof to connect him to the murders? They'd have Kate's testimony, but Robbie knew what a good lawyer could do with that. "Hadn't you been under the influence of drugs and alcohol, Ms. Brooks? How can you be sure this was the man you saw that night?" And even if they tied Puck to the blackmailers, would they also be able to prove that he had murdered in an attempt to eliminate evidence of his involvement? Especially when the murders pointed so convincingly to Jeremy?

Puck was a far more complex and calculating person than Robbie had imagined. She had no doubt now that he would be able to put off the police with his charisma and golden tongue. He was, after all, Stanford Fieldstone—the great crusader. And who was Jeremy Stroeb? A twenty-something kid scarred by the murders of his own parents, easily brought to anger. A loose cannon.

Loose cannon or great crusader? Whom would the DA prefer to prosecute?

Robbie took her cell phone from her satchel and dialed Jeremy's number. It rang and rang and rang. Robbie was so sure he'd answer that when the voice mail came on she was tongue-tied and didn't leave a message.

He must be in the middle of something with Lieber, Robbie reasoned. He knows I'm calling, so he'll be checking for voice mails.

She redialed his number and once again it went to voice mail. This time she left a message.

"I'm going to Puck's boat. It's in the Miami Beach Marina." She gave the location of the boat. "It's a twenty-six-foot cabin cruiser called *Aimless*. Tell Lieber everything and meet me there."

Chapter 47

Jeremy wanted a cigarette. He really, really wanted a cigarette. But he hadn't smoked since—well, he hadn't smoked since Marina. And after all that had happened with her, he'd sworn off smoking. But now, it was like déjà vu. And not a good kind of déjà vu.

He went over to the screened-in porch window. Outside, the street was quiet. What was Robbie up to? Why hadn't she called yet? He touched his pocket. His phone was in there, but he didn't want Lieber to see him checking it. He had turned it to vibrate at Mike's house, but he'd definitely feel it when Robbie called him.

He walked back across the porch. Damn, he wanted a cigarette.

"So?" Lieber said. "Are you going to stop pacing like an expectant father and tell me what's going on?"

Lieber sat on a floral-print chair, her hands gripping the wicker armrests.

She sure wasn't acting too cool herself. She had arrived at his grandfather's house a short while ago, and she and Jeremy had decided to stay on the front porch so they could talk out of the earshot of Jeremy's grandfather and Elise. But it was weird being out here with the rattan carts of plants and the slow-spinning ceiling fan. This wasn't a place for detectives. This was where Jeremy used to sit on his grandmother's lap playing with the rhinestone eyeglasses she always wore on a chain around her neck.

"Jeremy. I don't have all night."

"Okay." Jeremy sat down on the sofa, catty-corner from Lieber. He realized he was massaging his injured right fist with his left hand, and stopped. "Here's the *Cliff's Notes* version. First, I think you know this, but I need to say it up front. I didn't kill anyone."

Her face remained unreadable.

How much should he tell her? Too much and she'd overreact. Maybe even arrest him. And he couldn't let that happen. He needed to be able to go with Lieber to help Robbie.

"I had an argument with this club girl named Tyra down at the pool this afternoon."

Lieber tensed.

"Then a little while later, someone knocks on my door. It's this young blonde, who's always hanging out with Tyra. The girl tells me that someone attacked Tyra and she ran away because she was afraid for her own life."

Lieber hadn't moved. Jeremy's fingers were twitching. Where was Robbie? Damn, he wished he had a cigarette. "Then," he continued, "Robbie comes by and we figure out that this blonde girl, Angel, is really Kate."

"What?" Lieber leaned forward in her chair. "You found Kate Brooks? She's safe?" She started to stand. "Where is she? I must talk to her."

He needed to stall her. "Kate's fine. She's with Robbie. Please, let me finish and then you can go do your thing."

Lieber sat back down, remaining on the edge of the cushioned seat.

"Anyway, we realized that the cops might assume I had something to do with the attack on Tyra, so we left the SOBE. We took a taxi here."

"I'm not even going to ask how you managed to get around the police lockdown."

Jeremy shrugged. "We came here and Kate's safe, and that's pretty much it."

"That's pretty much it?" Lieber said.

How much more should Jeremy tell her? If he brought up the blackmailing ring, that would lead to him and Robbie going down to Key Largo, and then he'd have to explain about the two dead bodies. He wished Robbie would call, so he could tell Lieber what was going on. Why the hell did he let Robbie take off by herself and not tell him exactly what she was up to?

"Okay," Lieber said. "You said Robbie went home. Where's Kate now?"

"With Robbie. They wanted some sister time alone."

She shook her head. "You both know better than that. If Kate was a witness to the attack on Tyra, I need to talk to her. Why the hell would Robbie leave here with her? That was irresponsible and evasive." She reached into the pocket of her white blouse and took out her cell phone. "I'm furious with the two of you. Absolutely furious."

Jeremy looked down at the woven straw area rug. He hated being yelled at. Lieber made him feel like he was ten years old.

Lieber was about to punch something into her phone, when it rang. She looked annoyed, but answered it.

The expression on the detective's face changed to confusion, to disbelief, to anger. She listened for a long time. Finally, she said, "Okay. I've got that covered."

She closed the phone and looked at Jeremy, her lips so tight together, they practically disappeared. "After you and Robbie came back here with Kate, where did you go?"

Jeremy felt his body heat up and sweat break out all over him. "Nowhere," he said, looking her straight in the eye. "We stayed here. We've been here the whole time."

"Oh, Jeremy."

He could swear she was going to cry. Her grayish brown hair hung limply around her sagging cheeks. She was in her fifties—maybe a little older than Jeremy's mother would have been—why the heck was she putting herself through all this crap by being a detective?

"That phone call was from a detective with the Monroe county sheriff's department down in Key Largo," Lieber said.

Jeremy began to shake. He tried with all his might to control it, but it just made him sweat more. He could feel it running down his face.

"Where's your cell phone, Jeremy?"

He reached into his pocket and pulled it out. He stared at the object in his hand in disbelief. A tin of mints. He blanked for a moment, then it came back to him. Robbie had given him the mints in the car. But where the hell was his phone? He felt his other pockets. Empty. His phone was gone. Impossible. Robbie was supposed to call him. And then, he remembered hearing a sound in the undergrowth when they were running away from Mike's house. A sound like a small stone falling. He'd been in too big a hurry to check it out.

"The detective down in the Keys just found a phone, Jeremy. Your phone. In some bushes near Mike's house. He said they never would have seen it, but it started making a vibrating noise."

Robbie. That was all he could think about. Robbie was trying to reach him. She wouldn't be stupid enough to go forward with her plan without speaking to him first, would she?

"Why is your phone in the bushes near Mike's house?"

Cover or tell the truth? Robbie would wait to speak with him before she confronted Fieldstone; he was sure she'd wait.

"So that's where my phone is," Jeremy said. "I lost it Monday night."

Lieber shook her head. "The detective also told me there was a big accident on U.S. 1. No one was seriously injured, but eyewitnesses said an old, gold Honda was speeding and driving recklessly. It caused the accident."

A cigarette. He needed a cigarette.

Lieber was looking at his leather shoes, splattered with mud. "Where's your grandfather's car, Jeremy?"

"Robbie has it."

"I'm going to ask you again. Were you in Key Largo this evening?"

Robbie. She wouldn't wait. She'd leave a voice mail, since she knew he was expecting her call.

Jeremy needed to tell Lieber about Robbie. What Robbie was doing. That she had been trying to call him. That she was in danger. But where? Where had Robbie gone? Why hadn't he made her tell him?

"Two bodies were found at Mike's house," Lieber said. "They appear to have been murdered a few hours ago. Someone trailed mud into the house. There are footprints everywhere."

Lieber stood up and reached for something on her belt. Jeremy's grandfather was opening the glass door that led from the house to the porch, Geezer close at his heels. His grandfather pushed his glasses up on his nose, looking perplexed.

"Wait," Jeremy said to Lieber. "Please, listen to me. Robbie's in danger. You've got to send backup to help her."

"I'm sorry, Jeremy." Lieber took in a deep breath and tightened the handcuffs around his wrists. "Jeremy Stroeb, you have the right to remain silent—"

Chapter 48

Robbie stood near the apartment buildings on one side of the promenade. A short distance away, the *Aimless* was bobbing in the water, tethered to the dock by a couple of thick ropes. Lights were on inside the boat, but curtains blocked Robbie's view of the interior. Was Puck looking out, watching her?

The moon was struggling to push out from behind the dense clouds and there were intermittent flashes of light in the otherwise tarry sky. A group of young men holding beer bottles walked by, giving Robbie the creeps. She stepped away from them, closer to the buildings, wondering if anyone directly above could see her if there was trouble down here.

One of the men made a rapid kissing sound, but the group continued on.

She took a deep breath. The blonde wig felt hot and conspicuous on her head. The blank DVD was in her satchel, which she held against her chest. She was sure she felt it throbbing, like the telltale heart in Edgar Allan Poe's story. But she knew it was her own heart that was pounding.

What in heaven's name was she doing? There was no sign of Jeremy or the cops. What if he hadn't gotten her message? If she confronted Puck without any backup, she was as good as dead. And while Robbie knew herself to be reckless at times, she wasn't a complete idiot.

She started walking away from the boat, back past Monty's Raw Bar. It was after one in the morning and the restaurant was closed, though she could make out some people inside cleaning up for the night. She continued on toward the parking garage, where she'd left Jeremy's grandfather's car, and sat down on a gear locker that overlooked the bay. She took out her cell phone and dialed Jeremy's number. It went to voice mail.

Damn.

"Hi. I'm here," she said to the phone. It beeped. Shit. Low battery. "Please call me back so I know you got my message."

"I got your message," said a man's voice behind her.

Her breath caught in her chest. Oh my God. He must have been hiding in the garage, watching her.

Puck sat down next to her.

Stay cool, she told herself. He's not going to do anything out in the open.

She ventured a look at him. He was clean-shaven and dressed in a sweatshirt and loose jeans. No cap covered his bald scalp. He was wearing his heavy glasses, and stared out toward the bay, not at her. Now she could see the resemblance plainly. Stanford Fieldstone. The great crusader.

How many people had he killed? Brett, Tyra, Mike, and the guy with the scarred lip. And who knew how many more?

He reached for something in his pocket.

Robbie's fingers clutched the edge of the gear locker. Scream, she told herself. But what good was screaming? Even if someone heard her, by then it would be too late. She'd already be dead.

He shifted closer to her. She felt like passing out.

"Take this," he said softly.

He was trying to push something under her hand. It felt firm, but springy. She kept clutching the gear locker, but he was insistent. She glanced down. A wad of fifty dollar bills.

"I know you're not one of them," he said. "You're a good girl. A beautiful, lovely girl. Go home. Back to your parents, your family. But get away from here."

What was he saying? He didn't want to kill Angel?

"Go," he said. "Save yourself."

From him? Why was he giving her a chance to escape? But if she left now, how could Robbie prove he was behind the other murders?

She reached into her satchel and held out the DVD for him to see.

"I don't want it," he said. "Let them air it on CNN for all I care. I'm finished with all that."

"You are? You're going to turn yourself in?"

He was looking at her funny. Something was wrong. She said something she shouldn't have.

He reached over to touch her hair.

Shit. Her voice. He knew the voice was wrong.

He tugged and the hair came off in his hand. He looked from Robbie to the wig, then back again. "Damn." He squeezed his eyes shut as though in pain. "It's you. My rose girl." He opened his eyes, but his mouth drooped.

Why was she feeling sorry for him? The man was a murderer.

"And the missing girl in the flyer was the blonde girl—Angel. You're sisters, aren't you?"

She hesitated, but it was obvious. "Yes."

"You were behind it." His voice was tight. "What made you do such a thing?"

What was he talking about?

"But it doesn't matter now," he said. "I told you this wasn't the life I wanted for myself. I never wanted any of it. The fame, the power, the money." He looked at the blonde wig in his hands. "What's the worst they can do to me? Disbar me? Maybe I'll have to do some time, but then I'm getting out of here. Me and *Aimless*. Just the two of us. You were right about that, Robbie. I don't know why I was so afraid to let go of her."

Let go of her? Who? He wasn't making any sense. And he certainly wasn't acting like a murderer. He sounded and acted like Puck.

And so she spoke to him like he was Puck. "But if you didn't care about the videos, why did you do what you did?"

"What are you talking about?"

"Four people are dead."

"Dead? And you think——" He gave a nervous laugh. "Jesus. I didn't kill anyone."

How could he say it with such a straight face? If anything, he looked confused, not guilty. And then his expression darkened. "Four people?"

Was it possible he wasn't the murderer? That he didn't know what was happening?

"Tell me," he said. "Who's dead?"

"You really don't know?"

"Tell me."

"Brett, Tyra, Mike, some guy who works for Mike."

"Who are these people?"

She stared back at his baffled face.

"Tell me," he said again. "Who are these people?"

"The blackmailers. The ones who made the video."

"And they're dead? You say they're dead?"

He didn't know. He couldn't be faking the panic in his face, the rapid breathing. "But Angel—is she okay?"

"Yes."

"Dear God." He held his hand against his head. "I should have seen it coming. It was all there, right from the beginning."

"What was? What are you talking about?"

"They're all dead, you say? The blackmailers?"

"That's right."

"My sweet rose girl. You need to run and hide. You and your angel sister. Quickly. Where they can't find you."

"Who? Do you know who the murderer is?"

"Oh, God," he said. The moon broke through the clouds, brightening his face with a greenish hue. "I must go. I must go."

And he started to run, tripping over his own feet, then picking up speed.

"Wait," Robbie called after him. "Tell me who it is."

But he was already racing along the walkway, faster, faster.

The clouds massed over the moon, sucking up the light like quicksand.

Chapter 49

Robbie could no longer see him, or anyone else. She sat back down on the gear locker, the blonde wig and the DVD lying beside her with the wad of money Puck had given her. Her eyes hurt, a throbbing that came from the back of her head. She popped out the gray contacts and blinked in the fresh moist air, but the pain didn't go away.

If Puck wasn't the murderer, who was? And why had he run off like that?

Run and hide, he'd said. *Where they can't find you.*

They sounded like the ravings of a crazed man.

But who was she running from? No one had a reason to kill Robbie.

It's you. My rose girl. You were behind it. What made you do such a thing?

What did Puck mean by that? And then her breath snagged. Puck thought she had set him up to go to BURN Sunday night. He believed she was one of the blackmailers. That's why he told her to run. Because whoever was targeting the blackmailers would also try to kill Robbie. And Puck seemed to know who it was.

An engine started up somewhere in the distance. A boat slid across the black surface of the bay, sending out hundreds of ripples across the water. The ripples grew larger and larger.

Then I'm getting out of here. Me and Aimless. *Just the two of us.*

You were right about that, Robbie. I don't know why I was so afraid to let go of her.

There was a crushing weight in her chest as recognition hit.

Puck had told Robbie he had been trapped in a marriage he regretted. That his wife was holding something over him. It made sense now. Gina Fieldstone was the force behind Stanford's career. An ambitious monster, he'd called her. So he wasn't lying. Gina was the one who wanted him to succeed. The one who cared about her future being destroyed if those videos came out.

Gina Fieldstone.

Once again, Robbie had misread someone she had trusted. She tried to push aside her feelings of anger and deception as she reviewed the telltale signs that had always been there. Gina and Aidan had a black car with tinted windows. Gina must have told Aidan to watch Robbie from the first day that Puck walked into The Garage. Puck had shown an interest in Robbie, and that made her a threat to Stanford Fieldstone's political future. Had the slashed bicycle tires been a warning from Gina? When Gina met Robbie for coffee and encouraged her to go around to clubs looking for Kate, it was probably to keep Robbie from working at The Garage while Puck was in town. Then Gina's promises of help and getting her husband involved in finding Kate had all been fake, a way of getting Robbie to trust her.

Shit, shit, shit. Where was Gina now? Had she followed Robbie here thinking she was Angel? Robbie picked up the wig in a panic. Put it on, she was Angel. Leave it off, she was Robbie. Either way, she was a target.

But where the heck was Gina Fieldstone?

Robbie got up and walked quickly to her car in the parking garage. Shadows shifted all around her. Her high heels resounded from the concrete ceiling and walls like a cap gun. She was remembering a black car with tinted windows riding behind her bicycle one night when she left The Garage. Had Aidan or Gina been following her? Then Gina would know where Robbie lived. And the man Gabriele saw standing outside Robbie's apartment could have been Aidan. Had he been in Robbie's apartment waiting to kill her after Puck had been blackmailed?

Quicker, Robbie thought. Quicker. Get to the car.

It was just beyond the column. She ran the last few feet, slid into the driver's seat, locked the door and turned on the engine. She tried to catch her breath.

She had to call Kate and tell her what was happening.

But Kate didn't have a phone.

And Kate was at Robbie's apartment.

And Kate looked a lot like Robbie.

Where was Gina Fieldstone?

Oh, God. Oh, dear God.

Kate!

Chapter 50

Marylou Madison left the bayfront apartment she had rented a couple of weeks ago. It had been a perfect place from which to observe him coming and going, though her view was limited once he was off the boat. But then, it had simply been a matter of following him.

She glanced in the rearview mirror. She could see the distant pink and blue lights from the balcony beneath her apartment as her car sped forward.

His boat was long gone by now. She wasn't really surprised. He was scared and maybe a little overwhelmed—afraid of being caught in the spotlight.

After he'd told her about the message from the blackmailers, he had remained on his boat, not taking her calls, sulking like a little boy. But he would get over it. He always did. He understood that she knew what was best for them.

And then a short while ago, he had left the boat. She wondered where he was going. It couldn't be to that bar. They both knew Robbie wasn't there tonight.

But then, Marylou saw him racing back along the dock as though chased by a pack of dogs. He had jumped back on the boat. She heard the engine start up and the boat pulled out of its slip.

But he would be back. He always came back to her.

She flicked on the little light over the mirror. She could see herself clearly. The sheer silk scarf that covered her head and was flung casually over her shoulders had been her mother's. This was how her mother had worn it in a photo, smiling and waving from a convertible car.

It was all Marylou had of her mother—the scarf, the cardigan, and the little lace handkerchief. The photos were all in her head, but Marylou could see them as though they were right in front of her. A beautiful young woman who had given up a life of glamour and fame to become the wife of a drunken pervert in the middle of nowhere.

Marylou had taken the scarf, cardigan, and handkerchief the night her mother had beaten her and thrown her out.

She was only fifteen, but she felt so ashamed. And Marylou had never gone back.

Why should she? She had everything she needed—her mother's things and her mother's dreams.

She realized she was squeezing the lace handkerchief. Her mother was dead. Marylou had spent most of her life trying to make it up to her. She had so longed to see her mother's face one more time, to hear her say how proud she was of her daughter. Her daughter who had become everything she had always dreamed of herself.

Marylou gave the handkerchief a gentle shake and studied the hand-embroidered initials—GT. For her mother's maiden name. Gina Tyler—now her own.

"I'm proud of you," she said to the mirror.

And her mother smiled back.

Chapter 51

The plastic handcuffs resembled electrical cable ties and cut into his wrists. Beyond the screened porch, a car drove by, lighting up the street.

"Listen to me," Jeremy said. "Robbie's in trouble."

Jeremy's grandfather rested his wrinkled hand on Lieber's arm. He didn't speak, just met her eyes with his and held them for a few seconds. Geezer whimpered softly in the corner of the porch.

"Okay," Lieber said, looking away. "Go ahead, Jeremy. Talk. But talk quickly."

"You have to call the detective in Key Largo. Have him listen to the message on my cell phone. It's from Robbie. She's expecting us to be there."

"Where? Key Largo?"

"I don't know where. Please. Just listen to the message."

Lieber seemed about to protest, then she closed her mouth and hit some buttons on her phone. "It's Lieber," she said. "Can you listen to the voice mail on Stroeb's phone?" She turned to Jeremy. "What's your password?"

A lump formed in his throat. "Momdad."

"What?" Lieber said.

"mmdd—6633."

She nodded and repeated it into her phone. Her eyes grew wider, her mouth tighter as she listened. "Got it," she said. "Thanks."

She closed her phone. "It was from Robbie. She said to meet her at the Miami Beach Marina. Someone named Puck has a boat there called *Aimless*. What's going on, Jeremy? Who's Puck?"

Jeremy tried to pull off the handcuffs. They cut deeper into his wrists. "Did Robbie say anything else?"

"Yes. She said to tell me to go there with you."

"Please. Let's go. You have to call for backup. Robbie's going to confront him herself. She doesn't know I didn't get the message. She'll assume we're there, backing her up, watching her."

"Confront who? Who's Puck?"

"Dammit. Please. We have to go. Now. Puck is Stanford Fieldstone."

"Stanford Fieldstone? What are you talking about?"

"Fieldstone's the killer."

Chapter 52

Kate sank down into the sofa pillows. The cat curled up against her.

"Pretty kitty," she said. "I don't even know your name."

She massaged the cat's head. The cat closed her eyes and purred.

That's what Kate wanted to do. But she was too edgy. So many days hiding, frightened, making believe she was someone else. Not sure what to do. Run away? Stay? And here she was. She still couldn't believe it. She imagined at any minute one of them would burst through the door and drag her back. Back to hell.

The cat purred. But she wasn't in hell. She was safe here. Safe in the womb of her sister's apartment.

Her sister was probably with Puck now. Robbie was certain he was the murderer, but Kate couldn't match that up with the man who had been so kind to her. So gentle. He had made love to her and it had been good and sweet. The way she had thought it was going to be before all the dirtiness started. How could that same man be a murderer? She didn't believe it.

But then, her father had once been good and sweet, hadn't he? And he had turned into someone she hardly knew.

She looked at one of the necklaces Robbie was making. Just like an Indian princess in her father's stories would wear.

Did he really love her like Robbie said?

She felt the softness of a feather. She was remembering. A necklace with beads and feathers. *For my Indian princess*, he'd said, putting it around Kate's neck. There was sadness in his voice. And Kate had hugged him. *You're my Indian princess, now,* he had said. *You'll always be my princess.*

He'd been thinking about Robbie. It had always been there. She had taken his frown for coldness, but that wasn't it at all. It was loss. Loss and love.

Kate laid the necklace against her neck.

Her sister had made it. Her sister Robbie. Kate had a sister.

And Kate's head swam as she looked around the room. At the mismatched bookcases overflowing with books, the tables covered with beads and feathers. Her sister's things.

Why had Kate let Robbie go off by herself? What if Puck really was a murderer? She should have stopped her.

If only Kate had a phone.

She chewed on her finger. She wished her father was here. Had he gotten Robbie's message? Had he returned Robbie's call?

There was a knock on her door.

Thank God. She's back. Kate got up and hurried across the hardwood floor to open it.

But when she got to the door, she stopped.

Robbie would use her key, wouldn't she?

Chapter 53

Jeremy sat with his hands in his lap. He could see the red outline from where the handcuffs had cut into his wrists before Lieber had clipped them off.

She was driving very quickly through the near-empty streets.

After Jeremy had explained about the blackmail scheme, Kate identifying Fieldstone, and Robbie's plan to entrap him, Lieber had radioed the station. She told them to get down to Fieldstone's boat and arrest him.

Where was Robbie? She wouldn't have done something stupid, would she?

They crossed the Julia Tuttle Causeway. The bridge rose before them and for a moment, all he could see ahead was pitch black sky. Then the car crested, and against the darkness, the Miami Beach skyline came into view. Thousands of tiny lights, like fireflies on a summer night.

Lieber's phone rang. "Lieber," she said. A pause. "What?" Silence, except for her deep breathing. "Well, call the Coast Guard, damn it."

Jeremy tensed against the passenger seat. What the heck was going on? Coast Guard? Had Fieldstone taken his boat out?

"Jesus," Lieber said.

"What's wrong?"

"Fieldstone's gone. His boat's gone."

"What about Robbie? Is she on the dock? Is she waiting for us?"

Lieber gave him a quick glance. "Robbie?"

"Yes. Robbie. She was going to wait for us before she approached Fieldstone. Where is she?"

"Damn," Lieber said. She redialed her phone. "Is there a white female named Robbie Ivy there? You sure?"

Jeremy watched the lights of Miami Beach grow larger, the sky lighting up as though it was on fire.

"I see," Lieber said. She put her phone down.

"What?" Jeremy said.

"Robbie's not there."

Chapter 54

It was only a few more blocks. Robbie fumbled with her cell phone and punched in Jeremy's number again.

It went to voice mail.

She felt like banging the small black box against the dashboard. Jeremy, why aren't you answering?

She dialed Lieber's number. Pick up. Please pick up.

"Lieber," the voice said.

"Thank God. It's Robbie."

Robbie's phone beeped.

"Robbie. Where are you? What's going on?"

"This is urgent. I'm on my way to my apartment. I think Gina Fieldstone is heading over there. She may try to kill my sister."

She waited for Lieber to say something.

"Hello?" Robbie said. "Did you hear me?"

No response.

"Hello?" Robbie shouted.

She glanced at her phone. The screen was blank.

She wondered if Lieber had heard her before the battery had gone dead.

Chapter 55

The knock came again.

"Who's there?" Kate said.

"It's just me, Robbie," a pleasant woman's voice said.

Probably the neighbor Robbie borrowed the wig from.

Kate unlocked the door and opened it.

Chapter 56

Robbie pulled the car up to the sidewalk with a screech. The lights in her apartment were on. Was that good? Bad? Had Robbie gotten here in time?

She ran up the stairs to her apartment, kicking off her heels to make better speed.

She tried the doorknob. Locked. If Gina was here, the door would be unlocked, right? No. Not necessarily.

Think. Quickly. What should she do? Wait, hoping Lieber had heard her before the phone went dead? Knock on Gabriele's door? But he had been on his way out earlier, so he probably wasn't home.

Should she try to find a phone and call the police again? But what if Gina hadn't arrived yet? Then Robbie needed to get Kate out of here.

She couldn't wait.

She pushed her key into the lock and quietly opened the door. She stuck her head in.

The living room was as she'd left it. No sign of violence or a forced entry. But there hadn't been last time, either.

Robbie tiptoed into the room. Her bare feet were soundless on the wood floors.

Matilda jumped from one of the bookcases and took a few running steps toward her.

Where was Kate?

The door to the bedroom was closed. Could Kate have gone to sleep? Then Robbie needed to get her up and out of here. And quickly.

But what if Gina had already arrived and was in there with Kate?

What should she do? She didn't even have a weapon.

She went into the kitchen, took her sharpest knife from the butcher block, then stood outside the closed bedroom door. She pressed her ear against the door and listened. Absolutely quiet.

Sleeping. Please let Kate be asleep in there.

Robbie opened the door as quietly as she could. She stuck her head into the dark bedroom, the knife in front of her, just in case.

She tried to make out Kate's form on the shadowy bed as she stepped closer.

A heavy smell like overripe flowers hung in the air.

Oh, God, was Robbie too late? Where was Kate?

She felt a painful chop across her wrist. The kitchen knife clattered against the floor.

Something clamped hard over Robbie's mouth, jerking her head back.

No. STOP. HELP.

Arms tightened around her.

She couldn't scream. She couldn't breathe.

She kicked against legs as hard as stone pillars, but her bare feet were ineffectual.

Robbie felt herself being lifted, as though she was no more than a doll.

Light from the outside streetlamps cast the room in sepia.

Someone was sitting in the rocking chair beyond the bed in the corner of the room. A slender woman, a cardigan over her shoulders and a sheer scarf wrapped around her head. Gina Fieldstone. She was rocking slowly, back and forth.

Then the man holding Robbie was probably Aidan.

She tried to turn her head, but Aidan held her firmly. Kate. Where was Kate?

Gina was looking down at something in the narrow space between the bed and the wall. Robbie blinked, trying to make sense of the shape at Gina's feet.

A moaning sound came from the figure on the floor.

Dear God. Kate. Her arms were tied behind her back and something was stuffed in her mouth.

Robbie tried to bite the fleshy skin blocking her own mouth and nose, but it was pressed too tightly against her. Breathe. She needed to breathe.

The rocking chair creaked against the floorboards. "Bring her closer, Aidan," Gina said. "I want her to watch this."

Watch what? What was Gina planning to do?

Aidan dragged Robbie between the foot of the bed and the chest of drawers, stopping short of her sister.

Kate whimpered.

No. NO. This was her sister. Robbie couldn't let anything happen to her sister. She kicked and twisted, trying to break Aidan's hold.

He tightened his grip around her arms and mouth. Robbie strained against him, but she was weakening. Breathe. BREATHE.

Gina rocked back and forth. In the weak light, her high cheekbones, straight nose, and broad forehead appeared to have been carved from grayish wax. She was only a few feet away, on the other side of Kate.

"Well, I see you found your sister." Gina's voice, too high, too tight, sent shivers through Robbie. "Your journey's over."

Robbie grunted through the hand covering her mouth. Please, please don't hurt Kate, she tried to say.

"How does it feel?" Gina continued in the strange voice. "Your long-lost sister. Your dream fulfilled."

Robbie squirmed and kicked.

"Let her go, Aidan," Gina said. "She can't do anything."

Aidan's grip relaxed. Robbie dropped to the floor, choking as she sucked in the air. She covered her sister's body with her own and looked back at Aidan. One fist was balled up; in his other hand, he clutched a knife.

Robbie could feel Kate trembling beneath her. "It will be all right," Robbie whispered.

"All right?" Gina's features twisted into a distorted grimace, as though her face had partially melted, making the woman Robbie knew as Gina Fieldstone barely recognizable.

The transformation was chilling.

Gina unwound the silk scarf from around her head, then jerked it tight with both hands, like a garrote. She stared straight at Robbie. "How can anything ever be all right again after what you've done, Marylou?"

Marylou? Who was Marylou?

Gina got up abruptly. The rocking chair swung wildly back and forth. She was wearing the champagne-colored suit she'd had on at Mike's house, but there were splatters of blood on it. "My dreams," she said in a voice that made the hair on Robbie's arms stand up. "You tried to take my dreams from us." Gina's violet eyes bulged and a muscle in her throat twitched.

Robbie held her sister tighter, feeling the rise and fall of Kate's back as she breathed.

"I honestly believed you and I were alike." Gina's voice returned to normal, the rage gone from her face. "You with your unfortunate family, me with mine." She pushed a strand of hair behind her ear, exposing a pearl earring. "I even forgave you for bewitching him." She laughed her xylophone laugh, but now it sounded almost hysterical. "I actually saw myself in you. And I tried to keep you away from Stanford. But you ignored me. You couldn't leave your little game alone."

Keep her talking, Robbie thought. Maybe Lieber would get here in time. She was conscious of Aidan just behind her, the knife in his hand.

"But it wasn't my game," Robbie said. "I had no idea about Mike's blackmailing operation. I was just doing Brett a favor."

"And I realized, we're nothing alike, you and I." Gina seemed not to have heard Robbie. "Your wounds, your losses; they're nothing. A dead mother? An absent father? A lost sister? Nothing compared to what I suffered."

"I wasn't trying to compete. I trusted you. I believed you wanted to help me."

"Help you? Like anyone cared about helping me? Did anyone give a shit about me?" Gina inhaled and her nostrils flared. "Tell me again about your scars. Did your mother beat you and lock you in the cellar? Did she throw you out of the house when she found out you were pregnant with your father's child?"

Had that been Gina's life? Beaten? Abused? Pregnant with her father's child?

"I was fifteen years old. I had no one. Nothing. So tell me about how terrible your family was."

Gina came closer, her overripe smell filling Robbie's lungs. Robbie refocused. Whatever tragedy had shaped Gina, she was still capable of murder. Robbie needed to do something.

"She called me a slut and I hated her for it." Gina's voice was flat.

Robbie could grab Gina's leg and perhaps flip her, but Aidan was within striking distance with a knife.

"Hated that she let my father do what he wanted to me and then discarded me." Gina took a step back and adjusted her cardigan. She was just beyond Robbie's reach.

"But then I realized my mother had been right. And I decided to get them back for her. Her dreams." Gina ran the silk scarf through her fingers. "So she would love me."

The kitchen knife was on the floor behind Robbie, near the chest of drawers. Something tickled her cheek. Gina's scarf.

"I want you to know how it feels to lose what you love," Gina said, pulling the scarf back from Robbie's face. "To lose your dreams."

With no wasted movement, Gina slid the scarf around Kate's neck, tied a knot, and pulled. Kate let out a strangled cry.

"NO!" Robbie shouted. Not her sister. Robbie feinted toward Gina, then lunged in the other direction, toward the kitchen knife.

She sensed Aidan momentarily off balance. Her fingers grasped the knife handle. Got it. Then something heavy pounded down on her hand. Robbie saw a flash of white.

The pressure eased off her hand, though the pain was excruciating. Robbie thought she might throw up. Aidan was lifting his foot, to stomp on her again.

She jerked her hand away and rolled.

And then, Aidan cried out, his arms groping the air as though struck from behind. "Ma!"

Ma? Who was Aidan calling Ma?

His eyes bulged and he held his throat, gasping.

"Aidan, what's wrong?" Gina got to her feet.

Aidan toppled over Robbie, knocking the breath out of her. Something pierced her back. A loud thump shook the floor.

"Aidan," Gina shrieked.

Aidan was sprawled out in the narrow space next to the bed, eyes wide open, a ragged, ugly wheeze emanating from his gaping mouth, as though he was unable to breathe.

A man stood in the doorway, something clenched in his hand. A syringe. A hypodermic syringe.

Her father.

"Aidan." Gina threw herself across his prostrate body.

Aidan's face was frozen as the harsh rasping sound continued like a distant foghorn, and then faded off into silence.

"Breathe, Aidan. Please breathe." Gina buried her head against Aidan's chest. "Oh God. What have you done to my son?"

He was her son? So Gina had never given up her child? There was no lost daughter? But Robbie wasn't thinking clearly. She felt a warm pulsing in her lower back, then a drawing pain. Had Aidan stabbed her? My God. He had. She'd been stabbed. And blood was welling out of her.

"My darling boy," Gina cried. "Don't leave me."

Kate was lying still. Robbie needed to get to her and loosen the garrote, but she couldn't move. Everything spun around her, a whirlwind of light.

Her father pressed something against Robbie's back. "The bleeding's letting up," he said. "You'll be okay, princess."

"PRINCESS?" Gina said, in that strange, distorted voice. "SHE'S NO PRINCESS. MARYLOU'S A SLUT."

Marylou? What was she talking about? But before Robbie could process what was happening, Gina had slid off Aidan and seized something from the floor. And then she was straddling Kate, poised to plunge the knife into Kate's chest.

Everything was blurry. Robbie could hear her father breathing hard against her neck.

Two daughters, Robbie thought. Her father had two daughters. Two chances. If he chose Robbie, Kate would die. If he chose Kate, then Robbie would die.

In slow motion, Robbie saw Gina lift the knife above her head, then bring it down toward Kate, just as her father lunged across the room and sent Gina sprawling.

Gina kicked and flailed beneath him, and then lay still.

Her father got up.

Gina's eyes were terrified, her mouth open gasping for air. The hypodermic protruded from Gina's neck like a twig.

Everything went dark, then brightened.

Sirens and lights from the street filled the room.

Her father was beside her, pressing her lower back, once again.

She could hear her sister sobbing.

"Robbie, Kate," her father said.

He'd called them Robbie and Kate.

And then he said something else. Robbie struggled to hold onto the words, to hold onto the light.

His arms tightened around her. She saw a necklace with beads and feathers and heard his voice like a lullaby.

You're my Pocahontas, he said when he tucked her into bed. *You're my little Pocahontas.*

Chapter 57

Robbie sat next to her sister at a picnic table beside the St. Johns River eating fried shrimp and hush puppies from a ramshackle waterfront bar. Their father was across from them, the bench seat all to himself. Giant oak trees festooned with Spanish moss stood on both banks of the river and she smelled a sweet bloom in the air that reminded her of the magnolia blossoms of her childhood.

Robbie had taken the train up from Miami, and Kate was down from college for the weekend. The University of Florida was in Gainesville, only a couple of hours from Deland, so Kate was able to drive home whenever she was overcome by the panic attacks she still occasionally experienced.

This afternoon, Kate showed no sign of being anything but a happy, well-adjusted college freshman. She was laughing as she told them stories about her classes, the dorm, her new friends.

Their father leaned across the scarred wood table toward them. There was an expression on his face—intense and focused—a bit like marvel.

Kate reached for another shrimp and took a bite. She was wearing a beaded necklace and feather earrings that Robbie had made for her.

"So," Kate said, chewing slowly, "what do you think about Gina taking a plea of insanity?"

Robbie and her father exchanged a quick glance. The air around them seemed to change from mellow to electric.

"Come on, guys," Kate said. "It's okay to talk about it."

"You're sure?" their father said.

"It's not like I've been living under a rock. I get the news, you know."

So her sister hadn't been completely immersed in a cocoon these last six months. Robbie put her beer bottle down on the table, conscious of the stiffness in her hand from the healing fractures. Aidan's knife had missed her kidney and major arteries or she might have ended up another of his victims.

"Detective Lieber believes Gina's plea will probably hold," Robbie said.

"And her son?" Kate asked. "Is he also going for an insanity plea?"

"His lawyers are trying," their father said, "but the DA's confident of getting him on multiple first-degree murders."

Kate pushed her shiny black hair behind her ear. It was long again, below her shoulders, and she almost resembled her high school photo, except that her face was now sharper than it had been. The innocent girl was gone.

"There's something else I've been wondering about, Dad," Kate said. "How did you know to come rescue us at Robbie's apartment that night?"

He moistened his lips with his tongue. His eyes darted over to the screened-in section of the bar where other customers were eating and drinking. He finally spoke. "I'd been keeping an eye on Robbie, but I lost track of her. I decided to wait outside her apartment, figuring she'd return sooner or later. I was there for hours, not knowing where to go, what to do. Then, when two of you showed up and I realized you were safe, Kate, I was so relieved. I almost ran upstairs, but I didn't." He pushed his fingers through his gray hair. "Maybe I should have. That's been my problem all along. I watched, but I never took action."

"You saved our lives," Robbie said.

"After almost losing you both." He shook his head. "You know, Robbie. You're the one who taught me watching isn't enough."

Robbie's hand went to her emerald ring. The ring her father had given her mother. All those years, her father had been watching Robbie, but now he was here, part of her life.

A small plane appeared above the dark green trees and crossed the blue sky. They watched as it got smaller and smaller, the hum of its engine fading away.

"Robbie left a message on your cell," Kate said. "Why didn't you call back?"

"My cell?" Their father turned to her, momentarily startled. "I had turned it off. I hadn't expected Robbie to call, and I didn't want to take a chance it would ring while I was hiding in the bushes."

"So you knew about Gina and Aidan?" Kate asked.

He shook his head. "At that point, I didn't understand what was happening. Shortly after you girls returned to the apartment, I saw someone with blonde hair leave and get into the old Honda. I realized it was Robbie. I followed her to the marina in my car, then back to her apartment. She looked panicked and I was afraid that while I'd been following her, someone might have gotten to you, Kate. I had a bag with medical supplies in my car. I prepared the hypodermics before I went upstairs."

"I was sure you'd killed them that night," Kate said.

Their father's face lost its color. "Are you sorry I didn't?"

Kate sucked in her lower lip and looked down at the table. "What did you inject them with?"

"Succinylcholine. I've used it for certain procedures at the clinic. It's a fast-acting anesthetic that paralyzes all the muscles in the body and impairs respiration for several minutes. Enough time to incapacitate them until the police got there. "

"I read about them finding another dead body covered with tattoos," Kate said. "That was Luis. He was one of the guys that kidnapped me and Joanne."

"All of the blackmailers have either been caught or are dead," their father said.

"But that won't bring Joanne back." Kate wiped the corner of her eye and rummaged through her pocketbook looking for something. Robbie handed her a paper napkin.

They sipped their beers and watched the egrets fly to the opposite bank.

Some hurts would take way longer than six months to heal, Robbie thought.

Kate blew her nose into the napkin. She looked more composed as she fingered one of the feather earrings. "I still don't get how a successful guy like Stanford Fieldstone could become involved with someone like Gina Fieldstone."

It was a question a number of people were asking.

"When Gina first met him," Robbie said, "he was working for the Department of Justice. Aidan was being held for second-degree murder. Gina managed to get Stanford to drop the charges and marry her. Stanford always knew he'd sold out, but Gina had a way of making him feel important. She was pretty irresistible."

Kate's eyes narrowed, like she was about to ask Robbie something. Did she know that Robbie had also been taken in by Gina? But instead, Kate looked down and picked on the scarred wood tabletop. "So what's happening with him, anyway?" Kate's voice was strangely upbeat, as though she was trying to sound nonchalant. "You know, it's weird, but I still think of him as Puck."

Puck. That's who he'd always be to Robbie, too.

"He was disbarred and kicked out of the Justice Department because of his involvement in getting the original charges against Aidan dropped," Robbie said. "I have a feeling he didn't care. Lieber told me he moved onto his boat and travels from place to place."

Kate gazed out toward the water. A small fishing boat drifted by. Kate seemed to be slipping back into a memory. "I hope he's happy," she said, finally.

No one spoke. Long-necked sandhill cranes called to each other.

Their father's blue eyes lighted on something behind Robbie and he smiled.

Robbie didn't need to turn around to know who was there.

"Looks like your ride's here," her father said.

Jeremy came to their table, hugged Kate, and shook Robbie's father's hand. His hair was short and the beard was gone, but he was wearing jeans and a loose button-down shirt for traveling.

Robbie kissed her father and sister goodbye with promises to see them soon.

She turned to look back when she reached the screened door of the bar. Kate had switched to the other side of the picnic table to sit beside her father and their heads were practically touching.

Her father. Her sister.

Her family. She had a family.

Robbie and Jeremy took their time driving the scenic route in the old red Corvair, stopping at hiking trails and cozy B&Bs along the way. The leaves became more colorful the farther north they went.

Just outside Boston, Jeremy pulled off the highway and followed Robbie's directions. The narrow road wound through gentle hills covered with woods in full autumn splendor.

Seasons. How beautiful. Robbie had avoided them since her mother died.

Jeremy pulled the car into a small parking area just beyond the wrought iron gates.

The air was cold and Robbie slipped her hands into the pockets of her jacket. It was a good cold and it made Robbie feel alive.

They walked up a paved brick road. Oak trees shaded the rows and rows of rectangular stones, bouquets of flowers, hovering angels.

Robbie walked more quickly now. Almost there. A few more feet. The trees were denser here—maples, elms, and oaks. She stopped at the foot of the familiar white marble stone and touched the grooves of the letters. *Beloved Mother.*

The sky was so blue it hurt her eyes.

She remembered another day, the trees in many colors.

Yellow, gold, russet, crimson, burgundy, magenta, her mother had said.

A gust of wind stung Robbie's face. Jeremy put his arm around her and held her close.

Just like that other day, the leaves began to fall. They came down fast and thick, sticking to her hair, blanketing the grass, the graves.

Nothing is forever, her mother had said.

Robbie began to cry.

Jeremy kissed her.

Leaves continued to fall all around them. Soon the trees would be bare, the snow would come, then spring, then summer. Then the leaves would turn colors all over again. A never-ending cycle.

Yellow, gold, russet, crimson, burgundy, magenta.

Nothing is forever, her mother had said.

She wanted to call out to her mother, to let her know she had gotten it wrong.

Some things are forever, Mommy.

Robbie kissed the tips of her fingers, then touched the white marble.

Beloved Mother.

"Ready?" Jeremy asked. He took Robbie's hand as they left the cemetery, the leaves swishing beneath their feet.

He held her hand tightly. She knew he wouldn't let go.